THREE

TALES

from

VIENNA

THREE TALES *from* VIENNA

Ray Kingfisher

Cover Design by JD Smith Design

THREE
TALES
from
VIENNA

PROLOGUE
Leopoldstadt, Vienna, Austria-Hungary, 1917.

Greta Rosenthal could hear the footsteps outside her apartment door even above the noise of her children playing.

She dismissed all other sounds and tuned into the dull click of heels on concrete, willing the footsteps to continue past her front door. But they didn't, and three sharp knocks on the door echoed down the cold stairwell.

Was this the moment every married woman dreaded?

She rushed to the door and threw a hand up to the latch, then hesitated as if it might be red-hot. But no, there was no point ignoring the knocks; if the worst thing possible had happened, she wouldn't be able to change it.

She opened the door to find a man in a dark suit, still stroking his hair down flat and apparently mumbling to himself. Greta knew what he was doing: making himself presentable and rehearsing his lines. And the sudden weakness in her heart told her that his behavior could only mean one thing.

The man swallowed stiffly and drew a sharp gasp.

"Frau Rosenthal?" he said.

He seemed to be catching his breath even as he spoke. It might have been the four flights of steps he'd just climbed. It might have been nerves.

A few irrelevancies raced through Greta's mind: the neatness of the man's suit, his matching dark tie, his sympathetic eyes, the contrast of his appearance with hers. She knew she looked slightly unkempt: her hands were still wet and dirty from wiping the table, her apron was stained and crooked, her hair tumbled across her face on one side almost covering an eye.

Those thoughts faded, and she realized her mouth was agape in shock. The man looked as though he was accustomed to that reaction, which only made her feel worse. It was as if his eyes were telling her that a storm was imminent and unavoidable.

"Does Greta Rosenthal, wife of Albert, live here?" he said, his heavy forehead now projecting as much sympathy as his eyes.

"Yes, I'm Frau Rosenthal," she managed to say, her voice light and staccato, her throat arid.

Only now did she break eye contact with him, stepping aside to let him enter the living room, which was sparsely furnished but clean and neatly arranged. At least it made up for her disheveled appearance, she thought, immediately scolding herself for considering her pride at such a time. At this moment, and until she knew the truth, nothing in this room mattered.

The man introduced himself, but his name and position were merely noises that didn't register in her mind.

She shut the door with the gentlest of motions and turned to the three children sitting on the floor in the corner of the living room. "Hugo, Alicia, go into the kitchen and shut the door behind you."

"Why?" replied the boy, who was much larger than the girl.

"Please, Hugo. Just do as you're told, and look after Alicia."

"But what about Giselle?" he said, looking at the smallest child, who was preoccupied passing a wooden spoon from one hand to the other.

"Just go," Greta said sternly.

Once the two children had left the room, she nodded toward Giselle, now alone on the floor, and said, "This one's too young to understand. Please take a seat."

As the suited man did so, Greta hurriedly ripped off her apron and used her fingers as a comb to push her hair back so it fell behind her head, away from her face. Then she sat, forcing the tears to stay back, but knowing her twitching lips and blinking eyes were giving away her fears. Still, this man would be used to all that.

"The reason for my visit isn't what you think," he said.

She took two long breaths before replying, "Albert's not . . . dead?"

He shook his head firmly. "Let me assure you that your husband is alive, Frau Rosenthal."

She gasped, bowed her head, and could no longer stop herself weeping. The tears she'd kept inside were tears of sorrow, but the ones she now released were of gratitude and relief. The man handed her a handkerchief from his jacket pocket and waited for her to recover.

To their side, Giselle had become bored with her wooden spoon and was now on her feet, tottering toward the fire, which forced her mother to grab her and hold her in her lap.

"I'm sorry," she said to the man. "When I opened the door and saw you standing there, I thought the worst."

"Your husband is alive, Frau Rosenthal, but . . ." He paused as Giselle interrupted, although only a few unconnected words came from her mouth. "You need to know that he's a very courageous man. In fact, he's been commended for bravery."

"And can I buy food with that bravery?" She thought for a moment before adding, "I'm sorry. Albert's my husband and I'm proud of him, of course I am. Now, please tell me why you're here."

"You know he was fighting the Italians at a place called Isonzo, yes?"

She nodded, then held Giselle close and stilled herself to listen.

"He was involved in a particularly vicious battle. He caught some heavy gunfire."

"In what part of his body?"

"Only his legs. No vital organs."

"You don't consider his legs to be vital? Tell me, how did you get up to this apartment?"

"I'm sorry, Frau Rosenthal. I'm not suggesting it will be easy for him, but he'll be able to live a life of sorts. Some soldiers have suffered much worse injuries than his: head wounds, lung damage, burns over large parts of their bodies, terrible hidden damage from poisonous gases, even raging madness in some cases."

"Tell me more about his injuries. I want to know what happened and when he'll be coming home."

The man took a handful of letters from his inside jacket pocket, flicked through them, and handed one over. "Before I forget, this contains nothing I haven't already told you about, but it's official notification." He paused, collecting his thoughts. "Your husband was in a battlefield situation far from any medical teams when it happened. He suffered extremely bad injuries to both legs. He caught many, many bullets."

"And they couldn't . . .?"

He gave his head a brief, dismissive shake – clearly just enough to get the job done quickly and move on. "By the time your husband received medical assistance it was too late, gangrene had caught hold and they . . . they had to amputate both legs to save his life." He gave only a second for the words to sink in before adding, "You'll get help, of course, crutches to help him move around and so on."

Greta said nothing initially, at turns grimacing with fear and nodding with acceptance. "Thank you for telling me the truth," she eventually said.

"What did your husband do for a living before the war?"

"He was a railroad attendant."

"Oh, well, uh . . . I'm sure he'll be happy to meet his children again. I see you have three. Tell me, how old are they?"

"We have four. We have a very contented baby called Klara, asleep in the bedroom. Then there's this tricky little one, Giselle, who's two." She lifted the girl up and bounced her stubby feet on her thighs. "Not forgetting the two in the kitchen, Alicia is five and Hugo is seven. Alicia's a good girl. Hugo's the worst, as you've seen. He needs his papa. Oh, I'm sorry, I'm sorry. I'm just talking because I'm upset; I know it doesn't concern you."

"On the contrary. It . . . it helps me. I'm pleased your husband has something to look forward to when he returns." The man got to his feet. "And on behalf of the Emperor and the government, I wish you all well, but now I need to go."

"To tell the next poor woman her husband has been mutilated for no good reason?"

His face creased with discomfort, and for a second Greta thought he was about to cry.

"I'm sorry to be rude," she said. "I know it's not your fault. And for what it's worth, I hope his wife takes the news better than I did."

He showed her an awkward smile. "You took the news well, Frau Rosenthal. I'm pleased Private Rosenthal has a loving wife to come home to. On my next visit there is no wife."

"He isn't married?"

"He wasn't, no. He was only seventeen. It's his mother I need to talk to."

"Oh, that's terrible."

The man said no more words, just nodded politely and left.

For the rest of that day, Greta Rosenthal blotted out the noises of her children playing, instead thanking God her husband was still alive, but in the back of her mind also wondering how he would cope with the steps up to the apartment, how he would get around, and what he would do to support the family.

TALE ONE

Calm Waters, Ordinary Lives
1933 to March 1938

Austria has been free from German control for over a decade, but still struggles to escape the long shadow of its neighbor. In the Leopoldstadt area of the city of Vienna, the six members of an ordinary Jewish family go about their daily business as best they can.

Chapter One
1933

Alicia knew that neighbors considered the Rosenthals to be a broken family; she often heard the notion whispered behind her back around their home in Leopoldstadt. But there was no spite in the way people said it, only pity. And it was an understandable attitude when most people were unable to see beyond the fact that only the four women of the family were able-bodied.

Those remarks hurt Alicia more so than Giselle and Klara. After all, Alicia was the only one of the three sisters who remembered both Papa and their brother Hugo in good health; Giselle had been too young to appreciate the changes in them, and Klara had been little more than a baby.

Everybody knew what had happened to Papa because he would often say that the Great War changed his life forever, though rarely venturing near the horrific battlefield details. And he never complained about having to rely on wheelchairs, or balancing precariously on crutches, or tottering around on his hands and what was left of his legs. Equally, he never boasted of being one of the most skillful and reliable shoe and boot repairers in Leopoldstadt, even though everyone knew that was true.

Nobody spoke of Hugo's past, especially not Mama and Papa. Alicia was old enough to remember with some level of assuredness what Hugo had been like as a young boy, but not old enough to know what exactly had happened to him. The only thing she could be sure of was that his condition hadn't come about as a result of the war.

Hugo must have been less than ten years old when he'd changed, and it had happened very quickly as far as Alicia remembered. She grew up assuming that he'd suddenly contracted some sort of illness, but became less sure of that with each passing year, and would rather cut her own tongue out than ask Mama or Papa what had happened to him; she remembered the severe distress they'd suffered at the time and she never wanted to see them like that again.

Whenever the subject of Hugo's problems arose, the Rosenthals stuck to the story that he had palsy. They all knew that whenever that word was uttered no further explanation was required. But Hugo's life-changing event – whatever that was – had happened a long time ago, and it was only right that Alicia, who had taken on the mantle of the head child of the house, should keep to herself those memories of Hugo in better health, because anything else would upset Mama and Papa and confuse her two younger sisters.

But she knew that those memories of the old Hugo would never leave her. As a child he had a presence that only an older brother could. He seemed big and strong for his age, and was always protective of his three baby sisters, always willing to stand up to those who called them names in the streets. Now, of course, it was they who felt the need to protect the unfortunate creature he had become whenever insults were hurled at him.

Yes, it was probably for the best that Giselle and Klara would forever only know Hugo as he now was: just about able to walk with assistance, and unable to talk at all bar the hard-fought grunts and exasperated groans that fell from his mouth. Knowing he'd once been a healthy boy would only upset them, and Alicia was resolute that a white lie would forever be better than that.

Alicia knew that people thought she was boring, but her focus was always on keeping the whole family happy. That was why she occasionally scolded Giselle and Klara. It wasn't to upset or annoy them, but to bring them back into line, so to speak, because they both needed the help of their big sister now and then.

Giselle didn't seem to have a care in the world, and apparently didn't consider the future – hers or anyone else's. But she'd been like that since the age of fourteen, when she'd started to look at boys in a different way than before. Since then, Alicia had wasted a lifetime of hints and nudges telling her to stay away from certain types of boys.

But now, at eighteen, Giselle spoke as if she knew everything about men – and as if that meant she knew everything about life. Alicia was certain that those two things were very different. Yes, it was true that Giselle was the prettiest sister, and also that she'd known many more boys and men than Alicia had. But that wasn't something to be proud of – not at all.

And if Giselle's head was always in the clouds dreaming of the perfect life with the perfect man, then Klara was, in a sense, the opposite: her head was always in books and she didn't show any interest whatsoever in the less tangible but crucial issues of life such as religious observance or honoring her family. If she did have those dreams of marrying and having a family, she certainly didn't talk about them.

Alicia knew that sometimes books just filled a person's head with too much information, preventing them addressing the more spiritual requirements of life. It simply wasn't normal to study as much as Klara did. But Klara was only sixteen, giving her plenty of time to develop and change.

So Alicia simply accepted that because of Hugo's condition, it would forever be her duty as the oldest sister to protect the rest of her family. In particular, it would be up to her to guide the pretty Giselle and the clever Klara – to always keep them safe, together, and loyal to the family. Just as Hugo would have done in a better world.

§

Even a few years ago, Giselle felt she could have summed up each of her family members in a single word.

For Papa, the word would be that king of compliments: *heroic*. Despite his huge disadvantage in life, he was always cheerful and hardworking, repairing shoes most days from dawn to dusk and only taking a break when Mama insisted, bribing him with potato latkes still hot with goose fat or plum tart sharp as a rose thorn. Giselle knew that she would never in a million years be able to make herself work that hard or make those sacrifices; she simply couldn't see the point in working her fingers to the bone, especially as she possessed a face that her sister Alicia had once likened to Helen of Troy.

No, Giselle had loftier ambitions. It wasn't that she pitied Papa or looked down on him, just that she wished he wouldn't work so hard. Six days a week he would awaken at dawn, wheel himself to his workshop beneath a busy shoe shop just around the corner, and graft tirelessly all day. Only on the Sabbath would he rest, attending synagogue with the family, catching up on any news with friends and neighbors, studying the Talmud for an hour, then relaxing and reading the newspaper in the afternoon.

The word Giselle would use to describe Mama was *unbreakable*. She always worked tirelessly to keep her husband and four children fed and watered, to keep the apartment clean and homely. Like Papa, she had little or no time for herself and her own interests. And so, as with Papa, whenever Giselle took a long, hard look at her mama, she knew her own life was going to be a very different affair.

She was going to find a man who didn't have to work, who was already rich, who would let her indulge herself in a life of luxury and decadence. Well, wouldn't any attractive woman do that? Even at the age of eighteen she was very much looking for that man.

Choosing a word to describe her parents' first-born child was uncomfortable. Poor old Hugo cut such a sad figure, unable to speak and reliant on others to dress and feed him. But inside his prison cell of a mind there was, amazingly, a beam of happiness shining through the torture of everyday life.

Whenever she teased him – perhaps asked whether he had a girlfriend yet or how he would sum up the world's political situation – Alicia would scold her, but dear Hugo would simply grunt and twist his mouth into a smile, which Giselle took to be a laugh. And he probably knew she didn't really have a clue about politics, let alone what a summary of it would sound like.

Plenty of people would have chosen a word such as *helpless* to describe Hugo, but to Giselle he was *mischievous*, often contorting his face into an expression that only she understood to be a wry smile.

Klara, the baby of the family, was always either reading books or helping Papa mend shoes. And Giselle never gained any enjoyment whatsoever from either of those pastimes despite years of encouragement from her papa. He always told her there should be a purpose to whatever she did, but she preferred to believe that enjoyment was its own purpose, that reading books and helping mend shoes was hard work, and that there was no point in anyone working hard unless they absolutely had to.

As young children, Giselle and Klara would often play together on the floor of the living room or in the park at the end of the street. But as time went on and the older Giselle knew she should have been studying instead of playing, it was actually Klara who was making excuses to stop playing so she could immerse herself in various books. Inevitably, Klara excelled academically, whereas Giselle floundered.

And so it was easy for Giselle to choose a word to describe Klara: *bookworm*.

The word Giselle would use to describe Alicia, her oldest sister, was that simple word: *dull*. She loved Alicia, of course she did, but despite Alicia having helped feed and dress her all those years ago, and despite Alicia's almost constant protective presence, it was annoying that the prim oldest sister seemed obsessed with avoiding family arguments and intent on making Giselle, Hugo, and Klara obey their parents' every wish just as she herself did.

There was so little spirit or humor to Alicia's personality; it was as if she was preparing herself to be one of those boring politicians Papa was always talking about.

And that only left Giselle herself. What word would she use to describe her own personality? *Carefree*, not because she was, but because that was always what she was striving for, and how she saw herself in a few years' time, once she'd met that rich, handsome man.

§

Klara's earliest memory of her papa was watching him use his hands to clamber up onto a chunk of wood and then onto his seat at the dinner table. These days, she was just as likely to see him use the same trick to sit at his workbench, where he would seemingly spend days at a time repairing shoes for the people of Vienna.

Klara had been a baby when it had happened, and occasionally would wonder what Papa was like before the war – how tall he was, how he walked, whether he would sit cross-legged or knees apart whenever he occupied the armchair to read. She only had these images fleetingly, quickly telling herself to put such pointless thoughts away and to concentrate on the here and now.

It was the same with Hugo. She'd always assumed he'd been born that way, but it was never discussed, and his shortcomings didn't matter to Klara. In her teenage years there had been just a little resentment whenever she was referred to as "the baby of the family" even though poor Hugo couldn't even feed himself. But as she matured and continued to watch Hugo struggle with even the most basic of tasks, she managed to banish her unkind thoughts and promised herself she would take any "baby of the family" comments with good grace.

She also promised herself she wouldn't let one minute go to waste in her attempts to prove to everyone that she was no baby. That was why she put in every ounce of effort she could at school, and took an interest in Papa's work, helping him repair shoes, carrying out some of the more nimble-fingered work that he struggled with, and even taking an interest in the business paperwork. It also brought the two of them closer, and he rewarded her on some of those lonely afternoons at the workbench with stories of how he'd met her mama. Klara never forgot those tales, retelling them over and over again in her mind for years, each time imagining his clear bass voice, almost smelling the cut leather, feeling the fine sawdust catching in the back of her throat, and touching the soft wax that somehow found its way onto every object in the workshop.

Albert and Greta had met at a Bar Mitzvah held halfway between their houses in Leopoldstadt at the height of summer 1908. Albert, a railroad attendant, always maintained that Greta's smile captivated him so much that he couldn't stop talking in her presence, that he somehow thought that if he as much as paused to allow her to reply it might give her the chance to say something negative about him, which would cause her blissful expression to falter.

"You misunderstood," she was to tell him many years later. "I wasn't blissful, I was struggling to prevent myself laughing at you — you with all your boasting about your fancy job on the railroad carrying luggage for Vienna's rich and famous."

Hugo arrived in 1910, a boy with the lungs of an opera singer and even as a baby a broad-shouldered frame. That was all Papa said about him, and Klara didn't ask further about how they had found out there was something wrong with the boy.

After the birth, Greta insisted their son would be her first and last child. "It's your turn to have the next one," she would say to Albert with not one twitch of that famous smile whenever he suggested she would feel different in a few months' time. Two years later he proved to be correct, and Greta's memories of a difficult birth conveniently vanished and gave way to the urges of nature. Likewise, Albert's urges complied and Alicia came along in 1912.

To feed his family Albert took on as much railroad work as he could get, and supplemented that by helping out at his uncle's shoe repair business, and the result of that labor was the new and larger apartment – with their own bathroom – that they moved into just before Greta fell pregnant again in 1914.

"People will always need others to carry their luggage," he would say most mornings as he left Greta and their two children. Likewise, he would say, "people will always need shoes," as he left for his part-time job. And on the way there he would more often than not be frightened by the sound of one of those wheeled contraptions that would inevitably thunder along beside him, and he would curse the potential loss of business to both the railroad station and the shoe repair business, immediately reviving his spirits with the thought that common people would never be able to afford such complex and expensive machines.

Yes, he thought the good times would last forever and his family would be safe and well-fed for many years to come.

Klara learned that he fought against Italian forces in the Great War and that in the days and weeks following the amputation of his legs – when he should have been yearning for home – he actually dreaded returning because he thought of himself as only half a man. She gleaned very little else from that part of his life, but learned that before that cruel moment, while he was fit and well, Giselle was born in 1915, and on a rare home visit from Army duties the following year, he and Greta had gotten so carried away that nine months later her "absolutely and definitely last" child was born.

After losing his legs, and with six mouths to feed, Papa's ambitions couldn't have been more different to those when he'd met Greta and boasted of providing handsomely for her and however many children they chose to have.

He moped around for a few months before Greta told him he had to do something otherwise the whole family would starve. In time, he talked of plans to use what few skills he still had to set up a shoe repair business. Neighbors would joke that one man stitching leather was hardly going to create an empire to make the Rosenthal family rich, but Greta offered constant encouragement, telling him it was as good a way as any to put food on the table, and after beavering away for many years the jokes stopped and he did, indeed, earn enough for the family to get by and a little more besides.

As for Greta's enigmatic smile, well, that was now only occasionally displayed, mislaid during tougher times rather than gone forever, Albert maintained. "If only," Greta would lament in good humor more than bitterness, "my husband would talk as much as he did on that night we first met."

As Klara and her papa repaired shoes together beneath work lamps that highlighted the floating powder of sawdust as much as the shoes, Klara simply listened attentively, not daring to ask questions about Hugo, and definitely not wishing to make Papa talk about his days of fighting against the Italians during the war. If he ever wanted to share more details, then he would.

She was young. Papa wasn't very old. They had the rest of their lives to talk. They had plenty of time.

Chapter Two
1934

Alicia was standing outside her parents' bedroom, her hand held up, her knuckles poised to tap on the door. She took a deep breath for courage.

It was the summer of 1934, the Rosenthal family were preparing to attend the Bar Mitzvah reception of Emil Samach, the youngest son of a local restaurant co-owner and business contact of Papa. Papa had assumed that the whole family wanted to go, but he was wrong.

Alicia had already checked that Mama was in the bathroom helping Hugo wash. She knew Giselle was in the girls' bedroom fussing about what dress to wear, and had seen Klara sitting at the dining table, obviously unable to tear herself away from the book she seemed wedded to. So Papa was alone. She knocked on the door.

She heard her papa let out a grunt of surprise and entered. He was sitting on the end of the bed buttoning up his shirt.

"I have an idea, Papa," she said, and tried to ignore the brief but telling shake of his head.

"I'm sorry," he said. He patted the bed next to him and she sat with great care, feeling the hairs on his arm tickle her shoulder as he gripped her for balance. "I shouldn't tease you, Alicia, but I know all about your ideas by now. Tell me, what's the problem?"

"I've been thinking about this Bar Mitzvah. It'll be very busy there. It's going to be awkward enough for you to get around, let alone Hugo. Why don't I stay at home and look after him while . . .?"

But Papa was already shaking his head again. "We've been through this, Alicia. For one thing, we are a united family, Hugo is your brother, and I won't allow him to be left out. For another, we all need to attend as a mark of respect to the Samachs. And you know Emil has two brothers, don't you?"

"I did know, but I've never met them."

"Well, now is your chance. It's about time you started looking for a husband."

Alicia could feel her skin reddening. "Oh, I can't see either of them liking me."

"Why not? You're a beautiful young woman. You have an elegance about you, and you should have a little more confidence in yourself." The firm glare of his eyes was balanced by a softness in his voice that Alicia couldn't ignore and had no words to counter. So she said nothing, just inhaled the tar oil aroma of the soap he'd been using. It was then that she noticed a sadness invade his eyes.

"Is there something else I should know?" she asked.

"Well, there are other events happening – political issues I wouldn't expect you to understand, things I'm not at all sure about myself, come to that. But one thing I do know is that the way things are moving, family ties and relations with our friends are more important than ever."

"I'm not stupid, Papa. You think Klara is the brains of the family but I have ears and eyes too. You're talking about that horrid man in Germany. I know. We all know."

"And I'm talking about some of his friends who live over here." He gripped her hand tightly. Papa always had strong hands from hauling himself around and working with hammers and cutters all day. "Your mama is scared, Alicia. We need to show solidarity. You must attend."

"I understand that, but . . ."

"Let me tell you something else, Alicia. When you put makeup on your face, you look even more beautiful than you already are, and you tell the world you're proud of yourself. Well, that's what our family needs to do – what *all the families* around here need to do in these worrying times. We need to put on a face even if we don't feel like it. So please, come with us for Mama's sake if not for mine, yes?"

"But nobody will talk to me."

Papa pulled her to him, and she felt the wiry scrub of his beard on her cheek followed by the warmth of a kiss on her temple.

"Why is it that my oldest daughter has so little confidence? You haven't the bookish nature of Klara. You don't feel the need to flaunt yourself in front of every eligible young man in Vienna like Giselle does. And yet somehow, Alicia, whenever you open your mouth, your words give me joy."

"And when Giselle opens her mouth?"

"You know, I feel joyful too, but I also feel, *here we go again*, and then I get the urge to tell her not to appear so eager, that it comes across as desperation. That's not a quality any papa likes to see in his daughter."

Alicia couldn't suppress a laugh.

"But you, Alicia. You have something about you that you are yet to realize. You remind me of that painting in Paris, I think it's called the Mona Lisa."

"The Mona Lisa?"

"Yes. You should see it someday. You might learn that you don't need to be full of knowledge for a man to be attracted to you, and you don't need to throw yourself at his feet either. Sometimes a quiet, reserved smile says more than a thousand words."

"Oh, Papa. What a lovely thing to say."

"Just you think on it, my dear." He took a deep breath. "Listen, I'll make a deal with you. Put on some makeup and your best dress and come along with us. Look after Hugo. Stay for an hour. If you aren't enjoying yourself after that, we'll say Hugo is feeling tired and you have to take him home. Come on, one hour for the sake of your old papa? How does that sound?"

"That sounds good," Alicia said, now grinning. "Thank you, Papa."

§

In the girls' bedroom, Giselle had just put the finishing touches to her makeup and was checking her hair in the mirror. The door opened silently and her mother stole in. Giselle turned around and smiled. Her mother didn't return the smile but silently closed the door behind her.

"So, is Hugo ready?" Giselle asked.

"Hugo's just fine. Klara's looking after him." Her mother strode over purposefully and sat close by. "Giselle, could I ask a favor of you please?"

Giselle tried to smile again but apprehension caused it to falter. "Of course, Mama."

"You know this event is important for the family, don't you?"

"You mean, for Papa?"

"I don't. I mean for *all of us*."

"I understand, Mama. So what?"

"So I just want you to be on your best behavior, that's all."

"Whatever do you mean by that?"

"You know what I mean, Giselle."

There was resolve in Mama's voice. But Giselle simply couldn't give in that easily, and forced a puzzled frown onto her forehead. "I'm not sure I do know," she said.

"If you want me to spell it out, I hope you aren't going to spend the evening trying to talk to every unmarried man there."

"What's wrong with talking to men?"

"This is a Bar Mitzvah, Giselle. It's not about you, it's about Emil Samach, and it's supposed to be a solemn occasion."

"It's only the reception, and isn't it supposed to be a celebration? A happy event?"

"Well . . ."

"And anyway, I wouldn't need to talk to men if you allowed me to bring Gustav."

"Your papa told you about that. He wants us all to go as a family, and Gustav isn't part of the family. And besides, what would Gustav think of you talking to other men?"

Giselle looked in the mirror and touched the palm of her hand gently to her hair. "That's a fair point. But he won't be there, will he? And what he doesn't know won't harm him."

"But he might find out."

"Then I'll ask him whether he talks to other women. Or I'll tell him I don't answer to his command."

Mama tutted. "How did a daughter of mine turn out like this?"

"You make me out to be so terrible," Giselle said, her eyes narrowing at her mother. "I just like talking to people, and I get along with men more than I do women, I find they pay me more attention. Can I help that?"

"As long as talking is all you do."

"Mama!"

"Oh, I'm sorry, Giselle. Just . . . don't embarrass us by trying absolutely every man there until you find the best one. Please behave yourself out of respect for your papa and the Samachs if nothing else."

At that moment the door opened and Alicia came in. "I need to get ready," she said, her eyes swapping between her mother and her sister like a timid animal. "I mean, if you don't mind."

"This is your bedroom too," Giselle said.

Mama gave Giselle a last stare, a hint of a nod to reinforce her message, and left.

§

In the living room, Hugo was sitting next to Klara at the table that dominated one end of the room.

Mama had sat him down there a few minutes before and asked Klara to look after him, saying she needed to have a few words with Giselle. Klara had a good idea what form those words might take, and hoped her sister wasn't in any sort of trouble. Yes, she talked to men a lot, but it was harmless, and it was just the way she was.

Klara was busy making sure Hugo didn't mess up the pieces of paper she'd carefully laid out on the table in front of her, so hadn't noticed Papa come out of the bedroom. But now she looked across and spied him adjusting his tie and checking the shape of his beard in the mirror by the front door. She often found herself absent-mindedly staring at him when he made the effort to dress up. She was proud of him, and he knew it.

He nodded approvingly to his image in the mirror and looked to the side, catching her eye. He smiled a slightly sad smile and wheeled himself over, gliding up to her.

"Do I look good?" he asked.

"You look very handsome, Papa."

"Thank you." He looked Hugo up and down. "I see that Mama has done an excellent job on your brother."

"Yes. He looks as handsome as his papa."

"And what about you, Klara? Aren't you going to get ready?"

"I only need to put my dress on. And I don't like to wear too much makeup."

"Oh, yes. Of course." He stretched his head up to scan the books and scraps of paper on the table in front of her, squinting to read the nearest ones.

"I've been doing some calculations," Klara said. "I think I've found a different supplier for our leather, wax and nails. Walters has offered to undercut Schneider for our business if we commit to buying only from them."

"Yes, but what about their quality?"

"We need to check that, of course, but they promise me it's as good as any other, and everyone knows they deliver anywhere in Vienna within a day. I was thinking of visiting them next week and putting a formal proposal to them. What do you think?"

"I think . . . I think you should get ready for the Bar Mitzvah reception."

"Oh yes, Papa. I will. But I had some spare time and I was just thinking about how to improve the business."

"And you should, Klara, you should. I think changing supplier could be a good idea. A couple of extra groschen in our pocket and—" Papa stopped talking on seeing Klara shaking her head. "What's wrong with that?" he said, puzzled.

"I have a better idea, Papa. I was thinking about one groschen in our pocket and one in the customer's pocket. That way they'll tell their friends, we'll get more business, and in the longer term our profit will be much more than a couple of groschen. Do you see?"

He stared at her for a moment, his eyes flitting between her face and the pieces of paper in front of her. "I see very well," he said. "I see my business in good hands and the Rosenthal name being worthy of respect in future. But could I ask that we talk about this tomorrow?"

Klara came to her senses. She'd been too preoccupied with improving Papa's business to realize that this was his big occasion. She remembered the look of excitement on his face when he'd received the invite. And also the expression of disappointment – which he struggled to hide – on discovering that the family had only been invited to the reception, not the Bar Mitzvah itself. And in an instant she was reminded of Papa's frustrations at being confined to a wheelchair, the indignity of him having to look up to everyone, the frustration of him usually meeting condescending gazes of various veiled implications. And she promised herself that for the sake of Papa she would strive to improve the status and reputation of the Rosenthals in the local business community.

But perhaps not now. Now there were more pressing matters.

She hurriedly gathered up the books and papers, placing them into the old leather briefcase Papa used for business documents. "I'm sorry, Papa. We can discuss this tomorrow. I'll get my dress on right now." She leaned over to kiss him on the cheek. They embraced. It was awkward, but it would never be anything better than that. Still, it was wonderful.

§

An hour later, the Rosenthal family approached the venue for the Bar Mitzvah reception: The Restaurant Samach-Bettauer.

For Alicia, it had been a frustrating walk.

She made a point of grunting, as if to vent her feelings, as she pushed Papa's wheelchair over the restaurant's threshold. She might as well have pushed him all the way from home for what little help she'd been given.

At one point on the journey, Papa – who seemed to be lecturing his family on the state of various European nations – had asked Giselle to take a turn pushing him, and hadn't noticed what Alicia had: an undisguised roll of the eyes from Giselle accompanied by a brief but disdainful flick of her head. Giselle took her time putting out her cigarette, and then, without a word, and while Mama's back was turned, she shoved Alicia out of the way and grabbed the wheelchair handles.

Alicia took the hint and kept her distance, so much so that she was the last to notice that Giselle and Papa were lagging behind the rest of the family.

Yes, it had taken no more than a few minutes for Giselle to tire of the chore. Alicia bit her tongue rather than cause trouble by scolding her sister. For a moment Alicia almost went back to take over again, but thought, *no, why should Giselle get away with such behavior?* Alicia had already pushed Papa some way and now it was Giselle's turn. So she ignored her sister's petulant behavior and walked on.

And then the inevitable happened, and Alicia knew she should have seen it coming. Giselle wasn't paying enough attention and hadn't noticed one of the wheels catching in a rut in the sidewalk, and before anybody had time to warn her, the wheelchair was on its side and Papa was in a heap on the ground, rubbing his elbow, which had taken the brunt of the fall.

Giselle laughed at the incident, Mama scolded her for being so uncaring, and Alicia was so incensed at her sister's behavior that it took her a few moments to control her urge to say something nasty before she came to her senses and started tending to Papa. She struggled to lift him up and back into the wheelchair. "Can't you help me?" she hollered to Klara. And Klara did help, apologizing for having to be asked. She should have apologized for being in a world of her own, Alicia thought, probably with her mind still stuck in one of those stupid books she was always reading.

Giselle positioned herself to push again, but Alicia quickly grabbed the handles and took over. She braced her shoulders, half expecting Giselle to shove her out of the way again. That wasn't happening *this* time; it wouldn't be fair on Papa.

"I'm sorry," Giselle whispered once they were all on their way again. "But Papa's lectures on politics bore me."

"He's not asking you to debate with him," Alicia replied. "Only to listen politely and . . ."

But even now, Giselle wasn't paying attention to her. She was busy asking Mama whether she knew who was going to be at the reception party.

And Alicia knew exactly why she was asking that. Well, *everyone* knew.

Half of Alicia's mind was still incensed at Giselle's obsession with men, and half was listening to Papa drone on and on about politics. Apparently, the new man in charge of Germany had banned all parties apart from the one he controlled, had banned trade unions, and had prevented regions of the country making their own laws. She didn't really understand the details, but knew Papa was worried. And if he was worried, so was Alicia.

All of Papa's concerns only added to Alicia's frustrations as she crossed that threshold. An area in the center of the restaurant had been cleared of tables, presumably as a dance floor, which Alicia would only use if coerced, and so for the moment people were merely standing around, catching up on gossip. And once the Rosenthals were mixing with friends, neighbors, and associates of one sort or another, Alicia became acutely aware of the bonds between her family members. Yes, they bickered among themselves. Yes, there were petty jealousies and occasional hurtful comments. Yes, they criticized one another daily. But they were family. They were the Rosenthals.

And that meant that Klara and Giselle, however irritating their behavior, were her sisters.

She knew she'd been a little harsh on Klara – especially in the thoughts she'd kept to herself. Klara, as usual, had been given the difficult task of looking after Hugo on the journey, making sure he kept out of the way of passers-by, nudging him away from the road, and calming him when noises unsettled him, which often happened.

And Giselle? Well, there was no excusing Giselle's behavior, but Alicia had to admit – only to herself, of course – that there was a hint of jealousy involved. If she possessed only a fraction of Giselle's confidence when talking to men, she would be a happier woman, she was sure.

§

By the time the Rosenthals had taken their coats off and were mingling with the other guests, Giselle had lit up another cigarette. It was usually the first thing she did on these social occasions. She assumed the pose that came so naturally to her: head tilted up to show off that *Helen of Troy* face, one hand casually resting on her hip, her lips pouted in readiness to blow the smoke up and away in a manner that would attract the right sort of attention.

She was sure everyone thought the pose and attitude came naturally, but it didn't; it required considerable practice and effort.

As the guests fell silent and Rabbi Benisch started his introductory speech, she scanned the room, her eyes never resting on anyone in particular just in case they thought she cared too much. Soon, Herr Samach took over from the Rabbi, and Giselle let out a considered laugh at each joke he dropped into his speech. And after the speeches there was food. A piece of latke here, a crispy morsel of wiener schnitzel there, some fluffy kaiserschmarrn or a slice of gleaming strudel to finish, all eaten at a leisurely pace, punctuated by polite smiles to the other guests.

By now, Giselle had homed in on one particular man, who was chatting on the far side of the room, almost facing her. Dark hair in tight-knit curls, broad shoulders, a slightly lost expression on a handsome face – a face which exuded boredom and was almost begging for new company. *Perhaps begging for the company of Giselle?*

But there was no point in rushing. That would give him the wrong idea. Alicia had told her enough times that to appear desperate was counter-productive. Dear Alicia. In spite of her extra years, she didn't possess a fraction of Giselle's considerable experience with men, but to give her credit where due, she occasionally produced words of wisdom. And on this occasion, despite there being a touch of jealousy behind the advice, Alicia was right. So Giselle stayed back and let the man's casual interest develop into an irresistible desire for her.

This time she would wait for her moment.

Timing was everything.

Another few minutes would do.

She drifted out of the room, staying in the man's field of vision for as long as possible, and slipped into the restroom. A check of her teeth in the mirror. No food scraps. Good. A check that her makeup was intact. Also good. She took a deep breath and returned to the room in those unhurried, confident steps she'd practiced so much.

Once back among the throng, she looked straight ahead, below and slightly to the left of the ornate chandelier – to where the man had been standing only a few minutes ago. But now he wasn't there. She cursed – but almost silently – and resisted the urge to stamp her feet. Somehow the man had wandered away. But where to? And furthermore, *how dare he!* She scanned the crowded edges of the room, her eyes hopping along and stopping at every dark-haired man to check.

And there he was. Herr Handsome.

But – and she had to stare to be sure of what her eyes were telling her – he was now talking to Alicia – *Alicia*, of all people. Yes, the man really had contrived to strike up a conversation with the most boring woman in the room. Why on earth would he do that?

And there was her answer. *Now* she knew why Alicia was always telling her not to appear desperate around men: it was so that *she* could elbow her attentions in first. The harlot! Then again, was Alicia that clever? It was unlikely.

But Giselle wasn't going to give up that easily. She headed over – but not too quickly, noticing as she approached that the pair had stepped a few paces to the side and were now with Klara and Hugo.

For some time, Klara had been staring across vaguely in Giselle's direction with a vacant expression. Giselle had noticed this, but hadn't thought anything of it. And now, as Klara started talking to Alicia and Herr Handsome, her face held onto that same vacant expression. It was probably because she'd been spending so much time looking after Hugo.

Poor Hugo. He should really have stayed at home. Preferably with Alicia to look after him.

§

Klara had been watching Giselle for some time. She'd been listening to the speeches, then feeding both herself and Hugo, all the time keeping one eye on her sister.

And she'd noticed Giselle observing the man who was now talking to Alicia. Giselle's staring had been subtle, not constant, but obvious to anyone who paid attention and knew what Giselle was like. It was clear that Giselle intended this man to be her next conquest. But her reaction on returning from the restroom and being unable to find the man was more than slightly amusing. Klara was also a little embarrassed for her sister.

And there was yet another feeling lurking in Klara's mind: just lately, observing Giselle's behavior had plucked at Klara's heartstrings, and it had taken her some time to understand why. Yes, Giselle was older than her, but at times like this it didn't seem that way because of her apparent desperation to latch onto every available man in Vienna. Klara kept telling herself she wasn't yet interested in men; there were much more important things she needed to concern herself with, such as developing Papa's business and working out why so many Austrians were taking an interest in the new regime in Germany. But then again, once in a while her heart ached to be just a little bit more like Giselle, to have the confidence to even *consider* having a boyfriend.

Klara had been looking after Hugo all the way to the restaurant and even now was barely able to do much socializing as she had to stay with him and help him eat and drink and wipe his mouth. Mama was wheeling Papa around the room, both of them chattering away to friends and people who they hardly knew but clearly aspired to be friends with, both of them casting occasional glances to check that their children were safe – as if they really were still children. Even the good and reliable Alicia had moved away, talking to nobody in particular, standing alone, looking slightly lost, as if preparing to excuse herself and return home.

But then, a few minutes later, Alicia wasn't alone; some strikingly good-looking, black-haired young man had taken pity on her and approached her. The two started talking, and then were walking over to her and Hugo, and only then did Klara realize who he was: the very same man her other sister had spent the last half hour eyeing up. She almost laughed out loud, but at least that put a smile on her face for the introductions.

"This is Ludwig Tannenbaum," Alicia said, gesturing to the man. "Ludwig, this is my youngest sister, Klara, and my brother, Hugo."

Ludwig first held a hand out to Hugo – held two hands out, in fact: one to shake with him, one to hold his wayward forearm steady, assisting him. What a lovely, considerate gesture. The kindness made Klara's heart flutter for a moment. And the man didn't react as Hugo's face twitched and twisted to one side, the sign that he was embarrassed and his face was about to turn red, which it did within seconds.

Then Ludwig turned to Klara and guided his hand – jet black forearm hair attempting to escape from his cuff – to gently hold her fingers as he leaned down and kissed the back of her hand.

Klara took the opportunity to raise her eyebrows suggestively at her sister, who giggled but quickly regained control as Ludwig stood tall again.

"Ludwig was telling me he works in the finance department of the hospital," Alicia said.

"A well-paid and reliable job," Klara replied, nodding agreeably.

She was trying to think of a way of saying he was both handsome and clever without sounding jealous of Alicia, but before she formulated the words, Giselle arrived, standing closer to Ludwig than even Alicia had dared get.

"I'm Giselle," she said, with that familiar pose, head dipped slightly, forcing her eyelids wide, exaggerating the size of her eyes. For a moment Ludwig froze like a frightened rabbit, which made her add, "I'm another Rosenthal sister."

Ludwig smiled, now understanding who this woman was, then took her hand and kissed it, but with a little less enthusiasm than he had done for Klara.

"Tell us more about your job," Giselle said.

"I work at the hospital."

"Oh, really? Are you a doctor?"

Ludwig took a step back, but Giselle matched him, so he was forced to talk primarily to her.

"No, I'm not a doctor. Only a clerical worker."

"Oh, well, uh . . . tell me more," Giselle said, before having one of her rare moments of self-consciousness, adding, "I mean, tell *us* more."

"Well . . . I collect copies of all the weekly wage slips, then I add up the amounts, department by department – the department is on the piece of paper, you see, a number on the top left corner – and then I cross-check the total amount for each department against the weekly budget of that department."

Klara was listening to him, but discreetly held a sideways gaze at Giselle, watching her face drop just a little more with every few words that came out of Ludwig's mouth.

"And what do you do if you find a discrepancy?" Klara asked.

"Oh, I have to fill in a form – it's a different form depending on whether the departmental budget is higher or the wages bill for that department is higher."

Giselle nodded slowly, almost imperceptibly distancing herself from him. Klara found herself enjoying this, almost laughing at Ludwig's explanation and Giselle's reaction of disappointment.

"They're different colors, you see," he added.

"Uh . . . pardon?"

"The forms I have to fill in. Two different colors."

"Ah, yes, how interesting," Giselle said, her previously beaming smile now crooked. "Anyhow, it's been lovely talking with you, Ludwig, but I must go now and, uh, meet the other guests." She flashed her smile at her sisters too, then stepped back hurriedly, her thigh knocking a table at one point.

Klara watched her turn and strut away, knowing it wouldn't be long before she found another man to talk to.

When she was out of earshot, Ludwig said, "Your sister Giselle, isn't she rather . . . forward?"

Klara was about to say that was being kind, but Alicia spoke first.

"She is," she said, "But she's still our sister and we love her, don't we, Klara?"

"We do," Klara replied. It was an easy thing to say because it was perfectly true. She found Giselle's behavior entertaining, sometimes irritating, often annoying, occasionally funny. But there was always an underlying fondness in her heart.

"If she finds that interesting," Ludwig said, "I should find her a job in my department."

Klara and Alicia giggled at the idea.

"Is that *really* what you do?" Klara asked.

"I'm sorry to say it is. But enough about boring old me." He turned to Alicia. "Tell me, are there any more sisters I should know about?"

"You're safe for now, Ludwig, there are only the three of us. Not forgetting Hugo."

Ludwig stepped back to give Hugo a center stage of sorts. "Who could forget good old Hugo?" he said, passing his long arm over Hugo's hunched shoulder and gently patting his back.

And that was the moment Klara knew. This was a *good man*. Most people ignored Hugo, either out of embarrassment or simply not knowing what to do or say. Not Ludwig. Ludwig was different. Moreover, despite her initial physical attraction to him, she reminded herself that he had walked over to Alicia, not her. He was also a much better match for her older sister. Alicia had never had much luck with men, and she deserved her chance.

As Klara listened to the continuing conversation between Alicia and Ludwig, she felt as if she were witnessing a rosebud unfolding with a measured caution, letting its color and fragrance gradually radiate into the surroundings.

Soon, her heart was aching, not due to her own love for a man, but in the hope that Ludwig would ask to court her sister.

Chapter Three
1935

It was late summer, the Rosenthals had just attended a synagogue service to celebrate Rosh Hashanah, and the sound of the shofar was still fresh in Alicia's ears, as were the bible verses she and the whole family had been listening to.

But now there was a little respite from the formalities, a relaxed get-together in the adjoining function room to eat dates, pastries, and chunks of fresh apple drizzled with aromatic honey. The phrase "Wishing you a sweet and successful year" was to be heard all around the room.

Alicia looked on as Mama and Klara stayed with Hugo to help him eat, Papa discussed business with an old friend, and just for once Giselle wasn't talking to every man in the room because she appeared to have settled on one man, which was pleasing.

None of that mattered to Alicia, because Ludwig was by her side. They both ate in a relaxed fashion, arms occasionally brushing together, few words necessary, doing little more than admiring the convivial scene before them. She had now known Ludwig for just over a year, and it had been the most blissful period of her life. Also, according to Ludwig and Papa, the political situation in Austria had improved. Alicia didn't take much interest in the details, but it was good news for their future. Yes, there were still political problems that needed solving, but as Papa said, life must go on as normal because otherwise the people who wanted to force "their sort" out of Vienna would win.

And these days, normal life for Alicia was joyful in most respects.

She'd been courted by few men in her brief adult life. Most of them had been a little too short for her, which wasn't surprising as she was the tallest member of her family – even taller, according to Mama, than Papa had been before the horrors of the Great War had cut him down. She'd originally been attracted to Ludwig due to his height and, of course, his handsome features: broad shoulders, a shock of solid black hair and thick eyebrows to match, a square jaw filled with strong teeth. But that soon faded away; he'd been kind to her and confident in her company right from the start, and as their relationship blossomed, those physical things mattered less and less – and now, not in the slightest.

So she and Ludwig now seemed to chat like best friends would, they shared the same interests for the most part, and he got along just perfectly with the family. Both Klara and Giselle had approved of him – the latter begrudgingly at first. He had developed a rare affinity with Hugo, and perhaps because of that as much as anything, Mama and Papa had quickly warmed to him. Papa didn't say as much, but clearly liked the man because he never pitied him or Hugo, never mentioned how terrible it must have been for him to have to get around without legs, or how difficult coping with Hugo must have been.

Also, Ludwig never pried, just tried his best to treat Papa and Hugo like normal men. In fact, he was a little *too* polite about those obvious issues, never even asking Alicia how her papa had lost his legs or how Hugo had become the way he was. Earlier in the year, puzzled as to why he hadn't even shown an interest in that side of the Rosenthal family's history – even when he'd known them for almost six months – Alicia's curiosity got the better of her.

They'd gone to the cinema to watch "Spring Parade," a comedy starring Franciska Gaal, and during the intermission Alicia broached the subject over a glass of wine.

"You get along well with Papa and Hugo, don't you?" she said.

Those teeth appeared to sparkle as he let out a short laugh. "Who could fail to like Hugo? The man has so much to put up with, yet he's never sullen. He's a lesson to us all."

"And yet . . ." Alicia tried to suppress her blush; it seemed almost insolent to ask him. "And yet, in all the time I've known you, you've never once asked me how he became the way he is."

"Are you upset I never asked?"

"Not at all."

He shrugged. "And does it matter? He's the way he is." He looked up, scanned the scene before them, then held her hand. "All right, if you want me to be completely honest, when I first met him at that Bar Mitzvah I did wonder what had happened to him, but it seemed rude to ask, and now it simply doesn't matter to me."

"And Papa?"

"Your papa's a good man, an inspiration to any husband or father. He's hard working, doesn't complain about his predicament, doesn't complain about his son's situation, and most importantly he has a beautiful daughter I've taken quite a fancy to."

Alicia tried to ignore the heat of blush on her cheeks. "But you've never asked me about his . . . problem."

Ludwig shrugged. "I don't see the importance. Your papa is a proud man, and a proud man doesn't invite pity into his world."

The words softened Alicia's heart. Ludwig had poured praise upon Papa's character, but in his kind words there was an honor between men that showed Ludwig's true nature was every bit as good as Papa's.

"But if I were to hazard a guess," Ludwig then said, "I would say the Great War is to blame."

Alicia nodded. "You're right. I could tell you the details, but . . ."

"No, don't." Ludwig leaned across and held her hand tightly. "My papa fought in the war too. He was lucky, but he told me more than I could ever want to know about the conditions, about what happened to those not so lucky. I know that war should be avoided at all costs."

"Thank you, Ludwig. It's not a very pleasant subject to talk about."

"And, uh . . ." He flicked a thumb toward the poster advertising the movie. "It's supposed to be a night of comedy."

There was a pause in the conversation. They both took sips of wine and glanced around at the other members of the audience, all dressed up, some clearly reliving the first part of the movie by aping some of Hans Moser's on-screen antics.

Alicia was relieved she didn't have to tell Ludwig more about those dark days that Mama had mentioned but Papa couldn't bear to bring up with his children: coming round to find his leg muscles full of bullets, listening to the medics arguing over whether they could save the legs, waking later to find he was only half a man, months and years of getting used to moving around on his hands. She knew that whenever Papa even *hinted* of those days, it was usually to deflect attention away from Hugo – away from the grief of what had happened to his only son. She was certain he'd always wanted Hugo to take over his shoe repair business, and after the shock of what had happened to Hugo – although Alicia didn't know precisely what that had been – there must have been the long, drawn-out disappointment of the fact that that was never going to happen, that realistically his only son was never going to amount to anything.

Only once had Papa talked to Alicia about what might happen to the business when he got too old, mentioning in passing that perhaps it would fall to her – *her* – as the next oldest child to learn how to repair shoes and take over the business. She laughed as though he were joking. She saw things differently: yes, she was the oldest sister – the future head of the family due to Hugo's condition – but felt more responsibility in the area of looking after people than repairing their shoes.

Mama seemed to know everything there was to know about cooking and clothes, but needed company as much as anything on those days she was unable to start her daily duties – when she resembled a strong horse that was fully capable of pulling its cart but had been put off by a car horn or a raucous shriek of laughter and needed settling. So Alicia regularly needed to help her.

Hugo, of course, needed help with everything from getting dressed to eating and with – as it were – the bodily necessities that women regularly had to deal with but polite ones never discussed.

Giselle also needed Alicia's help, usually to calm down because she seemed to have inherited most of the exuberance exhibited by Hugo, albeit without the bravado that affects males.

Only Klara, the baby of the family, didn't need Alicia's help. She was clearly uncomfortable being the center of attention, but was too polite to mention it and withdrew into a shell of studiousness. From an early age she excelled at the schoolwork that Alicia struggled with, that Hugo was incapable of, and that Giselle dismissed with contempt.

Alicia was on the verge of telling Ludwig about all those thoughts that were tumbling around in her head, but was hesitating because if she did, Ludwig might – despite his apparent disinterest – ask whether Hugo had been born the way he now was, and if she started talking about that, it would remind her of those days when Hugo was her happy, normal big brother, and her darkest suspicions would start a conversation that would do nothing less than ruin the whole evening.

But Ludwig – dear Ludwig – appeared to detect her discomfort and stopped her even starting to talk about Hugo.

"Why don't you tell me about how your Mama and Papa met?" he said. "You don't have to if you'd rather not, but they seem very happy together and it sounds like it would be a more cheerful story, more in keeping with a comedy movie."

He was right; that would be a much happier story. So she relayed everything Mama had told her over the years, and he stared at her as though mesmerized throughout the potted history of their meeting, their courtship, the growth of their family, and the change in employment forced onto Papa.

And the discussion that day at the cinema showed Ludwig for the understanding man he was: knowledgeable about what went on within families, but aware enough to know when not to delve deeper. Alicia wasn't the most experienced of women, but could recognize that rare virtue in a man. Ludwig might not have been the doctor or the lawyer or the scientist that she knew her Papa had wanted her to fall in love with, but he made her happy, and there was something between them – some sort of unspoken understanding – that she didn't fully understand but even early on knew would be their foundation.

So now they sat at the table, so close she could feel his warmth, few words passing between them as they ate, and Alicia wondered whether the years to come would be anything like the early years Mama and Papa had enjoyed and endured.

And she felt blessed to have found Ludwig. This was especially true when she considered the tribulations of Giselle.

No matter how many men Giselle got to know, she seemed unable to find the kind of happiness Alicia was experiencing with Ludwig. Even now, Giselle couldn't help herself. Alicia knew she'd long since dropped Gustav and had started seeing a man she'd met at the Bar Mitzvah where Alicia had met Ludwig. His name was Eric, but whatever had gone on between them was irrelevant because Giselle was now seeing yet another man, Norbert. There might well have been others between Eric and Norbert; it was hard to tell with Giselle. But Alicia would often pray that Giselle could settle on one man. On the face of it at least, Norbert seemed better than the others – friendly and reliable yet at the same time full of charm and passion. And Giselle seemed to be content with him.

She hoped and prayed that now Giselle had found a man she enjoyed the company of, she might finally stop passing herself around eligible bachelors.

§

For Giselle, these Rosh Hashanah celebrations were bringing back memories of the Bar Mitzvah where she'd chased Ludwig but ended up with Eric. The people here were mostly the same. But thankfully Eric was nowhere to be seen.

It hadn't taken long for Giselle to tire of Eric. He was a pleasant enough man, and took her out a dozen or so times. They went to the cinema, or to the theater, or just for a meal. At the cinema and theater Eric always asked if they gave discounts for this or that profession or membership, insisted on buying the cheapest seats in the house, and feigned a coughing fit if Giselle so much as suggested buying a drink during the intermission.

The final date was at a local restaurant – one where Giselle was well-known. They'd been to other restaurants in the city, and each time the story was similar: he chose the cheapest item on the menu and suggested Giselle did likewise. But on that final occasion, Giselle decided that just for once she was going to ignore his advice and order what she wanted: the tenderest – and most expensive – steak on the menu. Subsequently, Eric spent the entire meal complaining about how she hadn't followed his lead, and how they charged extortionate prices for vegetables and animals that grew naturally and so shouldn't really cost the restaurant anything. She persevered, ordering what she wanted for dessert despite his huffs and reddening face, but halfway through she could take no more and ran out in tears. What made it worse was that she halted a few doors down from the restaurant and was dismayed to see that Eric hadn't chased after her. No doubt he was eating the rest of her dessert rather than waste good money.

For a while Giselle didn't have a boyfriend, thinking perhaps she would never find the man of her dreams. She knew what she wanted. Her man would be one who was wealthy but hadn't become wealthy simply by not spending money, and one who was happy to show his love for her by pampering her and showering her with gifts. Or, in her more sober fantasies, he would merely be a man who wouldn't be so obsessive about saving money. She often thought perhaps such a man didn't exist.

She'd met Norbert precisely when she least expected to find love. She was lining up at the local Kosher store. He was at the counter, and clearly not infected with the skinflint bug that Eric had caught and couldn't shake off. This man was reciting items to the shopkeeper seemingly at random, requesting whatever delicacies his eyes settled on. He became stuck on the final item, unable to decide between two different types of apple pastries.

That was when Giselle pounced.

"Why don't you have both?" she piped up. There was no "excuse me" or "perhaps I could suggest," only the blunt question. For a moment, she was about to apologize for her brashness, but a smile as sweet as those pastries told her that would be unnecessary.

With barely a thought he nodded a couple of times and said, "Sounds like a good idea. Yes, I'll go with the pretty girl's suggestion."

While the shopkeeper collected both items from the display cabinet, the man flashed Giselle a *thank you* smile and she tried to reply with a *you can do better than that* glare through her fluttering eyelashes. As he left the counter he hesitated, she kept looking at him, and what Giselle assumed to be their unspoken mutual attraction was only broken by the shopkeeper butting in with, "Hey, do you want something, lady?"

Giselle came to her senses, bought the bagels Papa had sent her to the store for, and was disappointed when she turned away to find the man had left the store.

Moments later she stepped outside, and was about to curse the fierce rain that had just been unleashed by the heavens when an umbrella appeared over her head.

"I'm Norbert," the man said.

"Giselle."

He frowned, clearly moved. "What a beautiful name, if you don't mind me saying so."

"I don't mind at all. Thank you for the shelter." She fixed a lazy stare onto him as though she was never going to let go.

"Could I buy you a coffee, Giselle?"

And that was how she met Norbert.

An intense romance followed. Norbert promised her the world and all its riches. He was charming. He was handsome. And he was passionate.

And there lay the problem.

Norbert was *very* passionate about *everything*. For instance, now, at the Rosh Hashanah celebration, he had abandoned her and was sitting with another man – a man who was also ignoring his wife or girlfriend. All Giselle could do was listen to the ping-pong conversation between the two men and occasionally let a sigh go to waste.

"Don't you think the situation has improved?"

"I think it's worrying our National Socialists agreed a pact with like-minded people in Germany."

"But now they're in prison."

"Only after attempting to overthrow the government."

"But they failed. And our government has insisted that Austria should be no ally of Germany and that no union between the two countries is going to happen."

"And they haven't imprisoned them all; the attacks are still happening. Many Austrians insist they want this union with Germany and will stop at nothing to get their way."

"But even Hitler himself has publicly announced he has no intention of interfering in Austria's internal affairs."

"Pah! *If you believe him.* The man is a monster."

"That much we can agree on. But I concern myself with my country, not Germany."

And so on and so on, while Giselle waited patiently in the wings for her turn to speak with Norbert. Well, she wasn't going to put up with being ignored. Yes, she wanted a man who was passionate. Didn't every woman? But Giselle wanted a man who was passionate about *her and her alone.*

Oh, how Giselle hated, detested and abhorred boring old politics. And, by association, she was starting to resent Norbert.

§

Klara looked on knowingly. Sometimes she despaired at her sister's frustration.

Giselle seemed to chop and change boyfriends more often than most women changed dresses. There had been two serious boyfriends before she'd made a play for Ludwig. Then there had been Eric, now there was Norbert, and Klara was certain there had been other dalliances between them that hadn't been serious enough for Giselle to tell the family about.

Klara had been so pleased when she'd first been introduced to Norbert. Norbert was a good man for Giselle, a stable man who everybody hoped might dampen down Giselle's wayward tendencies. But now her body language showed that she was getting tired of him.

Much as Klara cared for both Giselle and Norbert, something else had been distracting her while she'd been watching them:

whenever she'd absent-mindedly turned her head away from her sister's romantic difficulties, she'd caught a man looking at her. He wasn't a large man – more the studious type with a clear complexion, a clean-shaven chin and round glasses. At first she'd thought nothing of it, but there was a pattern to his behavior that concerned her. She looked at him and he turned his head away from her. She looked away from him and at the indistinct edges of her vision saw him staring at her again. She turned to him once more and he looked away, engaging the woman sitting next to him in polite conversation.

Klara had tried this a few times and the result was always the same. And she had to admit that the man was vaguely familiar. In her mind she revisited the Bar Mitzvahs, the birthday parties, the Hanukkahs – all the gatherings of family and friends she'd attended recently, becoming increasingly desperate to remember where she'd seen this man before. *A neighbor?* Not that she could recall. *A distant relative?* She looked more closely. The man had an oval face and short-cropped fair hair with a ginger hue to it, nothing like any relative she knew of.

Hugo, sitting next to her, grunted at her, and she immediately turned her attentions to feeding him, dismissing thoughts of how she might be acquainted with the fair-haired man who was staring at her. She held a small slice of apple honey cake up to Hugo's mouth, the other hand waiting patiently underneath to catch the fragments his distorted mouth would reject.

And then Hugo froze, his gaze locking onto something over Klara's shoulder. She quickly twisted her head back to look, only to see that mysterious man looking back at her for a split second before turning away. Yes, even Hugo had noticed, so she wasn't imagining it.

Klara quickly fed Hugo, and with him still happily chewing away, decided that the time for pleasant manners had gone. She stared at this man and would stare for as long as it took – either for him to come over and introduce himself or for her to realize who he was. Of course, he didn't dare look at her now, he just chatted with the woman next to him. Klara was just about to give up when the woman said something to him in an animated, theatrical manner, and he rewarded her with an equally colorful roll of his eyes, an exaggerated raise of one corner of his mouth, and a languid shake of his head.

And that was the moment Klara realized where she'd seen this man before – where she'd *met* him.

A few months ago, Ludwig had casually mentioned to her that the staff at the hospital walked an awful lot in an average day, and consequently regularly needed their shoes repaired. She thought perhaps she could meet the staff manager there and offer reduced repair rates in return for preferential status. Papa was very much against such a move, but she convinced him that the volume of business would make it very much worthwhile, and they could increase their standard prices slightly so that the discount wouldn't be quite as much as it seemed.

Another obstacle was in their way: the fact that, as Papa put it, large buildings and wheelchairs were seldom good bedfellows. So Klara gritted her teeth and went there alone. She ended up in a small office across the table from two men, and got around to pitching for business straight away.

The deputy staff manager was interested; his sidekick – a man of modest stature wearing round glasses – less so.

"Do you own the business?" the sidekick very quickly got around to inquiring in a strange, soft accent that threw Klara momentarily.

Klara wanted to retort: *you think I can't own a business because I'm a woman?*

But she didn't. "It's legally my papa's business," she replied. "But I'm—"

"So why are we talking with you?"

"Because I represent the business."

But the sidekick was already scratching his head of short-cropped, slightly ginger hair. "I would have thought, with such a large amount of business at stake here, that at the very least we'd be talking to the owner."

"It's effectively a family business, Herr . . ."

That was a regular negotiating ploy Klara had worked out for herself: discreetly find out the customer's name, use it a lot, and act like a friend. But this man clearly understood the game she was playing because he ignored the question.

"Listen, lady, no disrespect to you, but we should be talking to someone with authority here."

Klara ignored him and addressed the deputy staff manager. "I can assure you I have the authority to offer your employees a very good deal."

And there it was. The sidekick rolled his eyes, lifted up one corner of his mouth, and shook his head as if to say to his co-worker, *What the hell do we have here?* To his credit, he didn't actually speak, but the inference was clear.

"Is that okay?" Klara continued.

The deputy staff manager said it was. His sidekick said nothing. So she continued.

"I notice you have a lot of noticeboards along the corridors. Do you also have some sort of magazine for the employees?"

"We do," the deputy staff manager said. "It comes out once a month."

"In that case, I'm prepared to offer anybody who can prove they work here a ten percent discount on repairs at Rosenthal Shoes in return for ten exclusive advertisements placed on the noticeboards and one free and exclusive quarter page advertisement each month in your magazine."

Both men were nonplussed for a few seconds.

"You get straight to the point, don't you?" the sidekick said.

"I'm a busy woman."

"Twenty percent discount." Now he was staring directly at her, unblinking.

Klara shook her head. "Ten percent off our standard prices is a good offer. And that won't actually cost you anything – only that no other shoe repairer is allowed to advertise using your noticeboards and magazine. Do you see?"

"Ten percent isn't much discount, though."

"Look," the deputy staff manager interjected, "how about we meet in the middle. Fifteen percent."

"We can't do that. Even our *standard* prices are very competitive."

"So how about we meet at twelve and a half percent?" the sidekick said.

"Ten percent is a good offer. In these hard times ten groschen in the schilling is a worthwhile saving, better than you'll get elsewhere. And remember, we have to make a profit ourselves. The cost of leather and nails isn't going down, and—"

"We can't do that. You have to give in just a little. How about we speak to the business owner?"

"How about you accept a good deal when it's offered?"

That prompted a distinct scowl.

"I've decided," the deputy staff manager said. "We'll accept. Ten percent." He held his hand out to Klara.

She could almost see and feel the steam coming out of the sidekick's collar. Eventually he swallowed as if it were painful, then nodded, and mumbled, "okay."

Klara's thoughts that the same horrible man was now sitting at a table just a few yards away from her vanished when Alicia walked over to join an old school friend, whereupon and an unusually anxious looking Ludwig shuffled up to Papa.

"I'm sorry, Herr Rosenthal," he said. "But I need to talk with you."

Klara deliberately averted her eyes, looking in the opposite direction while taking a sip of sweet kiddush wine. It was rude to eavesdrop; it was also hard not to, especially with those two baritone voices easily audible above the hubbub.

"Of course, my dear Ludwig," she overheard her papa say. "Sit here. Have some more food, some more wine."

"Oh, I've had enough wine, believe me. That's probably why I'm talking to you."

"What do you mean by that?"

There was a long pause. Klara turned her head slightly, and out of the corner of her eye saw Ludwig scanning the room.

"Do you think we could go somewhere more private?" she heard him suggest.

"I find going anywhere quite awkward."

"Of course. How stupid of me. I'm so sorry, Herr Rosenthal."

"Oh, don't apologize. Just tell me what the problem is. Nobody will hear us."

The words made Klara turn her head a little more so that her right ear was facing the two men. She put her left elbow on the table and rested her chin on her palm, one finger plugged into her left ear.

"Well . . ."

Klara took the briefest of glances and caught a glimpse of a very frustrated Ludwig. She stilled herself to listen further.

"You see . . . I want to marry Alicia. Would you please give me your permission?"

"And you needed to get drunk to ask me that?"

"Yes. No. I mean . . . I mean . . ."

"You mean you're nervous?"

"I've never done this before."

Papa's throaty laugh cut through the tension. "I should hope not."

"Oh, of course. I didn't mean . . ."

"I'll let you into a secret, Ludwig. It's my first time too. This is the first time anyone has asked me that question."

Another long pause followed, and Klara was on the verge of turning to look when Papa spoke.

"Tell me, Ludwig, will you treat her as your equal in marriage, as in a true partnership?"

"Oh, better than equal, Herr Rosenthal. I love Alicia so much that I would put her interests above my own every day for the rest of my life."

"I can't fault your answer, Ludwig, but one piece of advice if I may: equal is good enough. You have to look after yourself too. I think you're an honest, hardworking, and caring man – a fine man to be our son-in-law. So if you want my permission to ask Alicia to marry you, then you have it."

"Oh, thank you so much, Herr Rosenthal. You won't regret this. I promise I'll do whatever it takes to—"

"I see what you mean about these pastries, Ludwig. These are the best I've ever tasted."

"Uh . . . I beg your—"

"So light and delicate. So full of flavor. I must get Greta to ask for the recipe and . . . Ah, hello Alicia, my dear."

Klara turned to see Alicia now standing next to the two men, her hand resting on Ludwig's shoulder. It explained Papa's sudden insistence on changing the subject; Alicia had obviously just approached on Ludwig's blind side. Klara smiled a hello to her.

Alicia peered over and said, "What are you grinning at, Klara?"

"Oh, nothing," Klara replied, straightening her face. "Nothing at all."

Chapter Four
1936

It was a spring wedding.

On the morning of Alicia's big day, she sat at her dressing table, Giselle and Klara helping her prepare while Mama kept Papa and Hugo well out of the way.

While her two sisters fussed over her, Alicia's mind had the opportunity to wander, and she couldn't help but consider the life of almost twenty-two years that she was leaving behind. Of course, she was overjoyed at the prospect of her new life with Ludwig, but there was also sadness at leaving her parents, her sisters, and especially Hugo.

She'd mentioned this to Papa but he'd laughed off her concerns and assured her they would cope with two fewer able hands. Alicia wasn't so sure of that. Also – and she knew it was a strange thing to dwell on – there was the matter of what had happened to Hugo all those years ago, and whether the memories Alicia had of his early days would somehow leave the family with her; she was certain Mama and Papa would never talk about what had happened.

With a few months to go before the wedding, Alicia had expressed these concerns to Ludwig, and he'd suggested that as he was now going to be a part of the family, he would like to know as much as Alicia wanted to tell him.

He was to be her husband, so she told him as much as she knew.

Hugo had been about eight or nine, she guessed, and was always joking, tugging her hair when she wasn't looking, playing on the streets of Leopoldstadt, sometimes fighting when the need arose – often when some other child had insulted the family. She didn't know exactly what had happened, and at the time was too shocked to ask, but knew that one afternoon a neighbor had come to the door, that there were tears and words of shock, and that Mama and Papa had left, leaving the neighbor to look after the three sisters.

They were gone until the evening, and the next few days were the most horrid, the most depressing, and the most worrying of Alicia's life. Mama and Papa took it in turns to leave – visiting Hugo, they'd said, and both their faces were relentlessly dour. It was another week before Alicia saw Hugo again, and the boy who had been so protective, occasionally boisterous, and full of energy could now hardly walk, and seemed to have completely lost the ability to talk. He tried – everyone could see the contortions of his jaw and lips – but the only things that came from his mouth were painfully won grunts.

At first, she thought Hugo might recover – that he had some disease that might one day be cured. But it was not to be. Mama and Papa accepted his situation and planned for it, so she felt she had to do the same.

As Alicia and her sisters grew up, it became apparent to her that they had been too young to remember their big brother in his days of full physical glory. Mama and Papa obviously chose to go along with the pretense that he'd always been like that. And Alicia knew from an early age that it was the pain of the memories that prevented them talking about it. And as the years rolled by, it was easier for them all to pretend that Hugo had been born that way, passing off his problem as palsy.

So Alicia had unwittingly taken on the mantle of the oldest child of the family, and as such, decided that if her sisters couldn't remember the Hugo that she did, and if Mama and Papa chose not to tell anyone, then it was better that everyone be left to their comfortable ignorance.

But she never forgot the playful soul who would creep up behind her, tug her ponytails at the most inopportune moment then run off, the strong-willed boy who would dare to shout back at fellow Viennese children when they hurled insults in the street, and who would even argue with Mama and Papa when they told him that he shouldn't engage with those sorts of children but should simply walk away.

And now, all these years later, the lie that Hugo had been born that way might just as well have been true.

Alicia had found a release in telling Ludwig all of this. By the end she was in tears, part of her relieved to be able to confide in someone for the first time, part of her still worried about what would happen to Hugo when Giselle and Klara also got married and left home. Ludwig promised never to talk about Hugo's history with anybody else, but made it clear that there was a small place in his heart for dear Hugo, swearing to always do his best to ensure he was taken care of.

They hadn't discussed Hugo since that day of Alicia's emotional release, something that pleased Alicia because the conversation had felt more like a confession.

There had, however, been other changes since then that took Alicia's mind to another, better, place: both Giselle and Klara now had steady boyfriends. Of course, Giselle had to be different and was very secretive and cryptic about the identity of her man, but it was quite possible that very soon both of them were also going to get married and leave home. So Alicia started to worry all over again about Mama. Could she cope alone with both Papa and Hugo? And what would happen when she became old and infirm? Many people said they would play their part in ensuring both men were looked after, but that didn't stop Alicia worrying.

Alicia looked at herself in the dressing table mirror. She told herself that Ludwig was an honest, loving man with a reliable job and would be true to his word, that one way or another he would ensure Hugo was looked after. She also tried to convince herself that today of all days, Hugo would want her to concentrate on her momentous event and not worry about how he would cope without her. And she did need to concentrate. She and Ludwig had chosen to fast on their wedding day, so she hadn't eaten and her stomach groaned with displeasure. But she looked at her white, lace-trimmed dress, at her modest but immaculate make-up, and tried to imagine Ludwig – who she purposely hadn't seen for a week – in his purple tie and smart morning suit, and her mind drifted to dreams of a happy and meaningful life with the man she loved.

The preparations had seemed endless, but the ceremony was over before she knew it. Ludwig was more handsome than ever, they both signed the Ketubah – he to promise to look after her, she to accept his promise – and he didn't take his eyes off her as he placed the veil over her face to symbolize how he would protect her for the rest of her life.

And that was it. Alicia was married. Celebrations followed in the adjoining function room: food, wine, and dancing, punctuated by speeches, including one by Papa in which he joked – well, half-joked – about when his other two daughters might be getting married.

Alicia's dream had come true: Ludwig was her husband. She eyed Giselle and Klara with a fondness that had bloomed with her own happiness. They were both dancing: Klara with her new boyfriend, Giselle with the rather elderly uncle Viktor. But both appeared to be enjoying the day every bit as much as Alicia was.

She hoped and prayed that in time *their* dreams would also come true.

§

The music ended. Giselle made her excuses to uncle Viktor, curtsied to him to thank him for the dance, and headed back to her seat, casually glancing at the large clock on the wall as she sauntered by.

She knew she had to sit down, compose herself, and most importantly, keep an eye on the time.

She was as happy for Alicia as any sister would be, but at the same time was conscious that she was the only one of the three sisters who was at the wedding unaccompanied.

Earlier in the evening she'd joked that at least there would be someone there to take care of Hugo, but as the festivities wore on, she became more and more aware of the attention her sisters were getting from Mama and Papa – attention she was missing out on. At first, she told herself not to be so self-conscious, that the lack of attention was to be expected. After all, she wasn't the one who had just become a wife. But the more Mama and Papa talked to Alicia and Ludwig and Klara and her new boyfriend, the more she felt ignored. Yes, she was sitting at the large table seating family and close guests, but she might as well have been alone. Only Hugo, now needing a little help to drink, seemed grateful for her presence.

It was just as well that she had other plans.

Again, she checked the clock, willing that lazy minute hand to move faster.

Twenty minutes later, the wine had clearly had time to percolate into Papa's system, because he tapped his spoon on his glass and ordered those at the main table to listen. He raised a toast to Alicia and her new husband. Everybody cheered, the happy couple smiled and blushed, and Ludwig stood and praised his new father-in-law, then raised a toast to his health. There was more cheering from all sides of the table. Giselle did the dutiful thing and joined in with the toast.

Then Papa tapped spoon on glass again and said he was proposing another toast, this time to his youngest daughter and her boyfriend, proudly grinning at them both as he asked them cheekily whether there would be another wedding soon. Neither of the them replied, clearly not wanting to give anything away or make any commitments they couldn't keep; Giselle wasn't sure which one it was and told herself not to care. But they all cheered yet again, and Giselle smiled politely at Klara and her boyfriend then raised up her glass.

It was then that Papa turned his attention to his middle daughter.

"And what about you, Giselle?" he said. "When are you going to meet a man who can make you happy?"

There were giggles from around the table. All faces turned to her – to the woman without a man. She knew what they were thinking: how ironic it was that the sister who had had more boyfriends than all the other women around the table put together was now on her own. But there was more: a lull in the conversation, an implicit prompt for some sort of reply from Giselle. At that moment she detested Papa. Yes, he was drunk, and understandably so, but how could he put her in the spotlight like this?

She decided to treat the question like the joke it was.

"Oh, I've met plenty of men who've made me very happy indeed," she replied, attempting a coy smile to disguise her anger.

"Giselle!" Mama blurted out. "Do you have to be so coarse?"

"Papa asked the question. Perhaps you should blame him."

Her mother's face cracked with pain. "Please, Giselle, don't make a scene at your sister's wedding."

"That's okay, Mama," Alicia said. "I'm sure she didn't mean it to sound the way it came out."

And wasn't that just like dear Alicia? Always playing the big sister, always trying to calm the family waters. Giselle felt the urge to tell her that it had come out *exactly* the way she'd meant it, but resisted because Alicia was her sister – regardless of how dull she was – and this was her big day. So she said nothing, merely took another slug of wine.

It was then that Ludwig – the perfect match of her boring sister – made the unwise decision of adding his ten cents' worth. "Don't worry, Giselle," he said. "I'm sure you'll find a worthy man and he will probably come from the most unlikely of sources when you least expect it. I mean, look at what happened to me and Alicia."

"He's right," Papa said. "You'll find a good man in your own time; I have faith in that. I'm sorry. I didn't mean to poke fun at you."

Again, all eyes were on her, but this time not waiting for a reply, just pitying her – pitying poor Giselle, the pretty sister who had somehow become the ugly duckling. She couldn't accept that.

"Actually, I do have a new boyfriend," she announced to them in a measured tone somewhere between casual and confident. "I've been seeing him for a few months now."

Many puzzled glances were exchanged around the table. The majority settled on Papa, and he clearly felt a weight of expectation on his shoulders.

"Are you serious?" he asked her.

"Of course."

"And . . . do we get to hear the man's name?"

"His name is Kurt and he's a police officer."

"Well, why didn't you invite him to the wedding as a guest?"

"Oh, he wouldn't want to come."

"Did you ask him?"

She checked the clock again. It was nearly time anyway, so it hardly mattered what she said. And they had to find out at some stage. Most importantly, it would wipe the smiles off their faces.

"He's a Gentile," she said.

Nobody around the table uttered a sound.

"Oh," Papa eventually said. "Oh, I see. Well . . . I guess that doesn't have to be a big problem."

"You don't mind?"

"Mmm . . ." He looked to Mama for guidance, but she just shrugged. "I can't say I . . . *like* the idea, but if he's a good man at heart and he makes you happy, then why not? Tell me, do we . . . do we get to meet this Kurt fellow?"

"All in good time." She stood, surprised at how a little nervousness had made her unsteady on her feet.

"Are you going somewhere?" Klara asked.

"I need a cigarette."

"You don't need to leave the table to do that," Papa said. "Please stay."

"I need some cool air on my face. I won't be long. Klara, you'll need to look after Hugo."

Klara obliged without comment, and a few minutes later Giselle was outside the synagogue, where she'd arranged to meet Kurt.

Just like Ludwig, Kurt was tall and broad-shouldered, but there the similarities ended. Kurt was fair-haired, wasn't at all boring, but more importantly showed an intense sense of want – want of love – whenever Giselle was around. And this time was no different. There were few words, which suited her just fine. Kurt led her down the unlit side of the building, behind two large trash cans, and within seconds his hot mouth was pressed against hers, and the back of her head was scraping on bare bricks.

They kissed hard and long. She felt his hands mauling her breasts, kneading her bottom, quickly moving back up, caressing her neck. She groaned as his fingertips pressed against her throat. It was painful, but it was exquisite because it was the pain of passion. He pulled away from her and she dragged him back by his hair, pressing his mouth back onto hers, feeling the sharp graininess of the brick wall almost cutting into her scalp.

Once more he pulled away, this time resisting her attempts to keep him close. It made her laugh.

"Stop it," he grunted. "Or I won't be able to control myself."

His words only excited Giselle even more, but before she could act on her urges he spoke again while reaching for his inside jacket pocket.

"Time for a cigarette," he said. He jammed two of them between his still moist lips and lit both at once, passing her one.

"You can come inside with me," she said. "It's not too late."

"Why would I be interested in a load of Jews celebrating two more Jews getting married?"

"But *I'm* a Jewess," she said, tilting her head bashfully to one side.

"You're not like any Jewess I've ever met before."

"I try to be different."

"That's why I had to see you again tonight, because you definitely are different."

"And how would your family react if they knew about me?"

He blew smoke between his clenched teeth. "They'll never find out, I hope."

"Are you that ashamed of me?" she said, grinning.

"You're my vice, my opium, my secret passion. You're a forbidden fruit that tastes like no other." He sucked in a last lungful of smoke and let the half-used cigarette fall from his fingers to the dirt below them. "You're a forbidden fruit, and I want another bite."

He moved in to kiss her again, gripping her head in his hands, the rough surface of his palms like sandstone against the tender skin of her cheeks. Her hands, outstretched, went limp, losing grip on her own cigarette. As it fell, the hot tip briefly touched her little finger, making her squirm even more.

This was wonderful. This wasn't merely existing; this was a life being lived to its fullest.

§

Just a few yards away from Giselle, but on the other side of the wall, Klara had finished giving Hugo another drink and was wiping the dribbles from his chin. Her thoughts were miles away from Giselle: mostly with Alicia.

She looked at her oldest sister – as she regularly had for the entire evening – thinking how beautiful and elegant she looked in that flowing white dress and pretty veil flecked with tiny flowers of all colors. Most importantly, Alicia hadn't stopped smiling for hours.

Klara's gaze moved along to Papa, and she thought of his drunken inquisition only minutes ago, which made her mind turn back to her own situation, to the whirlwind that had been the last few months of her own life.

It had started at that Bar Mitzvah last year, with that man in the round glasses who had spent so long staring at her. When the eating had given way to music and dancing, she'd excused herself and visited the restroom. It was late, and she knew Mama and Papa wanted to get home, so she was rushing back to them, along the corridor, through a doorway, then around a corner, which was where she nearly bumped into him. Yes. *Him.*

They both apologized, but the words from Klara were instinctive, nothing more, and she assumed the same was true of him.

They stood opposite one another for a few awkward moments before he took a pace to the side.

She hurried past but he called out to her, "Excuse me?"

The words made her turn around, but she kept her distance and said nothing.

"Do I know you?" he said in that strange accent of his.

"Of course you do," she said, attempting a clear, no-nonsense voice. "I'm the woman you've been staring at for the last hour thinking I wouldn't notice."

"Well, I was doing that because you seem familiar and I was trying to work out whether we've met before somewhere."

"Perhaps you should ask my papa."

At that, he showed her a confused frown. It was clear he was going to need more clues.

"My papa owns the business, so of course I'm not worthy of answering questions on my own behalf. I don't have the authority, you see."

His face twitched as if a firecracker had gone off in front of him. He clicked his fingers and pointed at her. "You're that hard-nosed shoe lady. Rosen . . . Rosenberg Shoes."

"Rosenthal."

"Yes. Rosenthal."

Klara considered for a moment asking his name, but quickly decided it would bestow more importance on their casual encounter than she thought appropriate. Instead, she turned without uttering another word and returned to her family.

A few minutes later she and Alicia were helping Hugo leave the building while Ludwig did the gentlemanly thing and wheeled Papa toward the door. She made a point of avoiding even a split-second of eye contact with that man, which explained how he was able to approach her unawares.

"Excuse me again?" she heard him say.

A knowing glance was exchanged between her and Alicia, and Alicia took control of helping Hugo through the lobby and out of the building, leaving just her and this man, who was now clearly trying to smile but not quite achieving that goal.

"Excuse you for what?" Klara said.

"Uh, well, quite a lot, I guess." He opened his mouth, but his throat seemed to stall.

"Go on," she said.

"Well, I'd like to apologize for calling you hard-nosed earlier, for staring at you all evening, and for being impolite to you during that meeting at the hospital."

"*Impolite?*"

"Okay, downright rude."

"Why do you speak like that?"

"Oh, my accent? I'm American. It probably explains why I come across as a little blunt."

"Tell me, are all Americans horrible to women in business meetings?"

He narrowed his eyes at her. "That word's a little harsh, don't you think? As I remember, I was up against quite a shrewd negotiator and lost hands down."

"And are all Americans so rude they think it's okay to stare at people so much?"

The man paused while he fidgeted with his shirt cuffs, as if the sleeves were too short. Klara was starting to see a little boyish charm in his uneasy behavior. He wasn't too tall, was sinewy in build more than muscular, but he stood up straight with his chest puffed out as if trying to impress her. And above all else, Klara was starting to find his excuses amusing.

He cleared his throat. "I guess if I'm being completely honest, I was staring at you because I think you're beautiful."

The more Klara tried to stop herself blushing, the warmer she felt her skin become. And for a second she hated the body that betrayed her.

"Have you said all you need to say?" she asked, intoning the question with a hint of impatience.

"Not quite." He took a deep breath. Discomfort shadowed his face and he moved from foot to foot a few times.

Klara was starting to feel just a little sorry for him.

"Look. My name's Felix – Felix Goldberg – and I genuinely am sorry for being rude to you in that meeting."

"Perhaps we were both a little harsh."

He shrugged. "It was business."

"Of course."

"I can assure you I don't behave like that all the time."

"Me neither," Klara heard herself say, now feeling confused at the fluttering in her chest.

"Could I buy you coffee and a slice of cake sometime to apologize properly?"

By now Klara's throat was dry and sticky. "Tomorrow, Hitschman's, one o'clock," she said. "I'm sorry, but now I have to go." She stepped away, and the last thing she saw before she turned was his face, jaw open but holding onto a faltering smile, shock in his eyes.

And that had been the start of it. The next day, they were only slightly nervous of each other at Hitschman's coffee bar. Surrounded by the homely aroma of sweet milk and hot chocolate, they were soon talking like best friends, like a foot and a made-to-measure boot as Papa would say.

Felix was a radiographer – he had to explain to Klara what that was, and she listened intently. He was visiting from Texas on a one-year contract in order to gain experience before someday returning to his home near a city called San Antonio, where he would hopefully find a permanent post. One set of his grandparents had been born in Austria and so he felt he had ties of some sort to Vienna. He'd learned a little German from them as a child, more recently had taken lessons from a local professor who had fled Berlin many years ago, and was keen to learn more. Hence the move to a Vienna hospital.

Klara told him that she liked him and wanted to see him again, but also that her focus for the moment was on developing what she referred to as "the family business," which sounded grander than "her papa's shoe repair shop." He also asked her whether she was worried about the political situation unfolding in Germany and how it might affect Austria and her family. She replied that she didn't take much interest in politics, that those affairs were left to Papa, but that Germany was a different country and she took even less interest in what happened there.

Very soon they started talking about their respective families, and Felix told her about his brother Larry and what he called his "Ma" and "Pa" back at the ranch, which made her laugh. Before Klara knew what was happening, they were talking about what food they liked, what books they'd read, what movies they'd seen, and what they wanted to achieve in life, both of them glossing over the fact that Felix was due to return to Texas a few months down the line. To Klara, at that moment, that seemed half a lifetime away.

They met again for coffee, after which Felix asked her whether she minded if he held her hand. They met a third time and went to the cinema, and after he'd walked her home he asked whether he could kiss her. She said she would like that, and the experience almost made her faint, although she knew she wanted him to do it again.

A few weeks later, Felix told her he'd negotiated an extension to his contract at the hospital, telling her he hoped that didn't seem presumptuous. She said she didn't mind, that in fact, she was quite pleased. And neither of them mentioned the hospital meeting again. To anyone who asked, they'd met at a Rosh Hashanah party.

And that was how Klara had now ended up sitting at her sister's wedding celebrations, side by side and hand in hand with the man she knew she loved and thought she might just perhaps want to marry.

Chapter Five
1937

By the spring of 1937, Alicia's wedding was a pleasant memory, albeit one that never failed to warm her heart.

But her joy at living with Ludwig in their own comfortable apartment was gradually becoming overshadowed by concerns about the political situation in Europe.

Until recently, much like the average Viennese man or woman, Alicia had felt insulated from the new regime to the north – somehow protected from its anti-Jewish sentiments by a border and a buffer hundreds of miles wide. But now there were genuine worries for the future. Now she was starting to take an interest, often discussing matters with Ludwig. They both listened with concern at the news that political activists sympathetic to the National Socialist cause had been released from Austrian prisons in return for Herr Hitler's assurances to respect Austrian sovereignty. Ludwig, like many friends and neighbors, sensed the feeling that more and more Austrians were seeing their country as a Germanic state.

Alicia had endured long conversations between Ludwig, Felix, and Papa on the politics of the day. Felix was the calmest of the three, yet the other two frequently pointed out that he could afford to be calm because he was an American citizen and so could leave the country at a few days' notice, thus escaping the whole dangerous continent that Europe was becoming.

Papa, with his painful memories of the Great War, was the most worried of the three. He told them all that he was the only one who could remember how complex international treaties and imperial tensions had erupted into a conflict spanning half the globe.

Ludwig maintained in front of them that he had faith in Austria's leaders and trusted the ability of intelligent men to act for the benefit of the people they were supposed to represent. In private, however, it was clear to Alicia that his inner thoughts were darker and there was an undercurrent of naked fear. Just lately, whenever she brought the subject up, he put on a sickly smile and told her not to worry, but there was a moodiness at odds with his words of reassurance.

There had been another development which should have brought joy but only made them both worry more. And that was yet another bittersweet memory for Alicia, because she would often look back to that day the previous year when she and Ludwig had been lying in bed together and she said those words with the deepest kind of joy. She'd been quiet for a few days, waiting until she was certain, so much so that Ludwig had probably guessed. Still, it was something she needed to say.

"Lay your head on my belly," were her words.

"What do you mean?" he said, confused.

"Go on, please," she said softly, running her fingers through his hair.

He did as she wanted, cautiously at first.

"Can you hear anything?" she asked. "Anything that sounds like a baby?"

He immediately lifted his head and gave her a sideways stare. "You're not . . . joking?"

"It's true, Ludwig. The doctor told me this morning."

A gleeful, slightly mad smile erupted on his face, then he threw his head back and laughed to the ceiling. He kissed her – a lingering kiss that took her breath away – then started humming and dancing naked around their apartment, which made her laugh uncontrollably. For the second time that day, Alicia shed tears of joy.

Months later, once that news was no longer news, there was little happiness when there should have been endless quantities of it. Whenever they lay in bed together and he rested his hand on her ballooning belly, there was love, there was tenderness, but there was nothing that Alicia would call unrestrained joy.

Nevertheless, Ludwig's words of reassurance continued. He told her that whatever was going on in the world outside, he would look after both her and their baby. But his demeanor became increasingly defined by intense frowns and deep contemplation.

In a moment of helplessness, Alicia asked him whether he thought the coming years might be simpler if they remained childless.

He thought for a moment, shrugged, and said, "It's far too late to consider that option."

"What do you mean by that?" she asked.

"I mean that the deed is done. We just have to accept the way things are and manage as best we can."

At that, she was unable to hold back the tears.

"Oh, I'm so sorry," he said. "That was a horrible thing to say." He smiled awkwardly and apologized once more. "We'll do whatever it takes, Alicia, I promise you. And *I'll* do whatever it takes to make you happy."

Those big, strong arms enveloped her, and for a few moments it felt as if Ludwig alone could protect her and their baby from anything treacherous armies might do.

"You *have* made me happy," Alicia replied through sobs. "And I'm sorry too. I should trust you more. I have what I've always wanted and I should be looking forward with joy."

But in the weeks that followed that conversation, the reality of the world outside gradually wore them both down again. Ludwig was still pleasant, his mood only spoilt by occasional bouts of melancholy he couldn't disguise, but he was never angry toward Alicia. His words were always encouraging, but Alicia knew her husband well enough by now to see through his mask. He was clearly worried for their future, and Alicia figured that if he was worried, she should be too.

By the time baby Sarah was born in April, Ludwig's position as the voice of realism halfway between Papa's unrelenting pessimism and Felix's unshakeable optimism was forgotten.

For Alicia, concerns about politics and what went on hundreds of miles away would just have to take a back seat, because her life was simple but hard. She would feed little Sarah, bathe her, wash her little clothes, and tease smiles by tickling her or singing. She would also try her best to keep the apartment clean and tidy and to cook and wash for her and Ludwig. She would even – very occasionally – find the time to rest her weakened body. And with Ludwig working extra hours at the hospital to earn more money, with him insisting on spending time with Sarah whenever he was at home – something he said gave her more time to do the housework, concerns about politics and what might or might not happen in the coming months and years hardly entered her mind.

When those concerns did bother her, she told herself that it was likely to be all bluster, and nothing would come of all the serious and somber discussions between the big men in power. No, she had a healthy daughter, a loving husband, enough money to survive and afford one or two luxuries, all wrapped up in a cozy apartment.

That was all that mattered for the time being.

And when Klara and Felix announced that they would be getting married later in the year, the worries about political issues drifted even further into the background. The news gave the whole family yet more cause for optimism. Nothing would stop them living their lives to the full. And helping Klara plan her wedding made Alicia's life even fuller, if that were possible.

Even Giselle had now been seeing the same man for five months – a record for her, and Alicia was so pleased that she might finally be settling down. His name was Maximillian, and he'd been introduced to the family at the last Hanukkah celebrations. He was a jeweler – something that pleased Papa no end – and even Alicia had to admit (although only to herself, never to another living soul) that she was a tiny bit jealous of the life of luxury being married to a jeweler promised. Yet again, this was something to be happy about. More importantly, it was one less thing to worry about.

§

Giselle sat opposite Maximillian in the Hofmann coffee bar, just as she did most lunchtimes, taking in the aroma of baked fruit and molten butter, waiting for her favorite: a slice of the richest, most delicious Sachertorte in all of Vienna.

It was true that her old dresses and skirts would no longer fit because her regular visits to Hofmann's had filled out her figure, but she was safe in the knowledge that just as Maximillian could afford to buy her expensive coffee and cake every day, he could also buy her new clothes. And he didn't let her down in that respect.

Today, like most days, while she luxuriated in the intense flavors of tangy apricot jam, silken cream, and the smoothest milk chocolate, she listened to him talk about where he'd invested money, the house he'd just bought, and where he was going to store his diamonds safely just in case the government "turned," as he put it. To all of that, she simply smiled demurely and nodded at appropriate points in his explanations, even though her thoughts were miles away.

It would have been cruel to let on that she wasn't interested in his "contingency plans" (whatever that meant) or his talk of how his fellow Jewish jewelers in Germany were being given a hard time by the authorities. Shoes interested her, handbags easily held her attention, and she could discuss new dresses and hairstyles all day long. Absolutely none of what was happening in Germany or the world of business remotely interested her.

But settling for Maximillian was for the best. He and Papa got along famously – well, Papa had made it clear from the outset that he approved. Giselle had a suspicion that Papa didn't actually *like* him as such, but put up with him because he was wealthy, and because ultimately a wealthy man marrying his daughter could only be a good thing. Maximillian and Mama always shared a joke: even on the first occasion he'd met her he said he now realized that Giselle was only the second prettiest Rosenthal in Vienna. Mama pretended to blush at the flattery. Likewise, Maximillian also got along well with Hugo and Giselle's sisters.

And in her more reflective moments, Giselle was pretty sure what Mama and Papa would say to each other when they were alone: that they were never in any doubt that she would one day come good and find a fine and wealthy young Jewish man to marry.

So here she was in Hoffmann's coffee bar once more, listening to Maximillian talking again about minimizing his tax liabilities or something or other she wasn't remotely interested in, just keeping vaguely in touch with the gist of what he was saying, just catching enough to be able to ask the occasional vaguely relevant question.

But she was so bored it almost hurt. Again, her mind drifted away, and she wished her body could go with it.

And there was a bigger problem, one she didn't dare tell anyone. Yes, she'd been regularly seeing Maximillian for five months now. The trouble was, she'd also been seeing Kurt for the last three.

"You've grown bigger again," Kurt would say with a lascivious grin whenever they met up. "More for me to get hold of," he would add with a deep and threatening growl. He was only half-joking, Giselle was sure. And within minutes he would lead her to another dark alleyway or shadow-filled corner, where he would lock his lips onto hers so tightly that his sharp-bristled skin would sting her face. And he would maul her with what appeared to be the imagined skill of a hormonally-charged sixteen-year-old boy, his roving hands squeezing and pressing every part of her body.

And the sensation of being wanted and needed would excite her and make her feel alive the way nothing and nobody else could.

It was sometime in August – on a warm and sunny day a few weeks before Klara's wedding – that Kurt drove her out into the countryside and they made love for the first time, on a blanket laid out on the flattened corner of a barley field. They lay together in the calm and quiet afterglow, his head nestled on her shoulder, the blanket flipped over to cover both their bodies, and now Kurt was different, not his usual assertive self.

"Are you going to marry him?" he said, twirling his unseen fingertip around her belly.

At first, all she could do was giggle and reach down to stop him tickling her. He did stop, and she gazed up to a sky as naked as she was – as they both were.

His hand rose to hold her chin gently, turning her face to look directly at him.

"What?" she said, puzzled.

He raised his eyebrows at her. She knew what that meant: stop playing for time and answer the question.

"Papa wants me to. Mama too. He gets along with everyone. It makes sense to marry him."

"I can understand that. They always say you Jews stick together and shut everyone else out."

"I haven't shut *you* out."

"No. But neither would you marry me."

She let out a light laugh. "You haven't asked me."

"And you haven't quite answered my question. Are you going to marry him?"

"I might have to if . . ."

"If what?" Kurt lifted his face to hers, their noses almost touching, his eyes narrowed in intense curiosity.

Maximillian hadn't actually asked her to marry him, but her mind's eye saw the plan unfold, and it would be easy: she would seduce him, soon after that tearfully tell him she was pregnant, then play the poor innocent until he asked her to marry him. So it wouldn't be underhand to simply let Kurt believe that that had already happened and that Maximillian *had* proposed.

"If what?" Kurt repeated. "You might have to marry him *if what?*"

"If you've just made me pregnant."

"Oh."

"You sound surprised."

"I'm sorry. I wasn't sure whether you knew about such things."

"Alicia told me many years ago about what men do and how it happens. It sounded so strange that I didn't believe her at first."

"Of course, even if you *are* pregnant, you don't have to marry him. You could marry me."

She laughed again, then stopped suddenly because Kurt's face was as still as granite. "So . . . are you asking me? Seriously?"

Now his expression broke, revealing an air of sentimentality that was rare for him. "I am," he said. "Will you marry me, Giselle?"

For a few seconds Giselle's mind was dizzy with confusion. She wasn't sure if it was love, but there was definitely something between her and Kurt that she didn't have with Maximillian – something important to her. On the other hand, perhaps she'd put her parents through enough. Perhaps it was time to grow up and do the responsible thing. Whichever way she jumped, someone would be dealt a poor hand. It was an impossible choice to make.

"Let's wait," she said, tilting her head to one side and stroking the side of his face to soften the blow to his pride. "Let's see if I'm pregnant, then we can talk again."

A softened blow is still a blow, and Kurt looked away, hiding his expression, letting his silence give away his disappointment.

Giselle spent the next week wondering what she would do if it turned out that she *was* pregnant, and came to no easy conclusion. But by the end of that week, she knew she wasn't expecting. She'd been lucky, but she took it as a warning: she knew fortune wouldn't always be on her side. It made her think, however. What would she have done if it turned out she *was* pregnant? Marry Kurt or settle for marrying Maximillian? And did she really have to wait until pregnancy forced her into a decision?

Over the weeks that followed, the answer started to crystalize. It was time to grow up. She had to take Maximillian more seriously. After all, he would make a good husband, everyone said so. He was good looking, didn't upset anyone, and provided for her handsomely.

And wasn't that what every woman wanted?

§

Klara had agonized for months about Felix leaving Vienna. He'd extended his hospital contract last year, but she knew it was only a matter of time before he would have to return home to Texas. She secretly hoped he was applying to extend his contract again, but didn't dare say anything for fear of an answer she didn't want to hear.

She even asked him whether he might be interested in joining the family firm of shoe repairers as a way of staying in Vienna. He declined, saying he loved his job too much, but as it turned out, he got the underlying message.

Soon after that conversation, he asked her out to a local restaurant, and asked her how she felt about him, whether she would like him to stay. She was almost tearful at the idea that he had to ask. When he told her he'd been offered a permanent position at the hospital, she knew he'd been toying with her. She was a little angry at that. But when he produced the engagement ring, all anger subsided and her heart melted.

They invited many of Felix's relatives from America to the wedding: his parents, his brother, and a few close uncles, aunts, and cousins. At first, they all said it was a long journey; Felix said he'd traveled it and survived so it wasn't that bad. Then they said it would cost too much; Felix offered to pay for the trip. Finally, they said it wasn't convenient to be away from their farms for so long. Felix asked once more, but they dug their heels in.

The news that nobody from Felix's family would be attending upset Klara at first, but over a series of phone calls – with Felix as interpreter – the truth was gradually teased out of them: they feared for their safety in "that part of Europe." Felix's parents convinced Klara that it was nothing personal, that they were very happy their son had found love, and made her promise to visit their ranch just outside San Antonio as soon as possible after the wedding.

The episode made Klara reconsider her wedding plans – not whether to get married, merely the scale of the celebrations. Felix and Papa both offered to fund an extravagant celebration, but she declined, telling them that the simple fact she was marrying Felix made her happy enough, and in any case, one day they would have the other half of their celebration in America.

She dared not let on the real reason for what she called their *financial restraint*: the creeping feeling that very soon they might need all the money they could scrape together, so shouldn't spend it unless absolutely necessary.

Hence, the wedding was a more basic affair than Alicia's had been the previous year – fewer guests, a less elaborate dress, and plainer food and drink. But for all of that modesty, the wedding was just as joyous an affair as Alicia's had been. The success of the function vindicated their decision not to attempt to match that one for splendor. Even Giselle, who deigned to bring Maximillian – her final boyfriend, Klara hoped – seemed to enjoy herself and appeared genuinely pleased for her sister.

Their honeymoon was a short break to Klagenfurt, staying at one of the finest hotels on the edge of the vast Lake Worthersee. Felix had insisted on that extravagance in return for agreeing to Klara's wish of a modest wedding. Away from their routines of Leopoldstadt and the stresses of the capital city, they relaxed, they visited the museums that Felix so wanted to see, and they took boat trips on the lake. They dined on air-dried bacon, pasta pockets, brown trout, and pastries generously laden with local honey.

They also talked.

Klara felt that perhaps the distance from their regular lives was having a liberating effect on their conversation. They talked of their childhoods in more detail than they ever had before, they discussed not only how many children they wanted, but also what their names would be and what sort of house they would bring those children up in. Yes, for now they would be happy in a small apartment in Leopoldstadt, but they agreed that when the children came along, only a house would be acceptable.

It was on the final night at the hotel before their return home, while lying in bed together, bodies entwined, that Felix brought up the question of where that house might eventually be.

"I know I should have brought this up before," he said. "And please don't take it the wrong way or get upset or anything . . ."

She eyed him curiously, apprehension in her voice. "What is it, Felix?"

"Well, have you ever considered leaving Vienna? I mean, leaving *Austria?*"

She shook her head immediately. "It's my home. And I have to say, even *talking* about the idea of leaving frightens me like nothing else."

"It needn't frighten you," he replied. "I moved here, didn't I?"

"Has this got something to do with your parents' reluctance to come to Vienna?"

"A little, I guess."

"Do you think they were right to be scared?"

He hesitated to reply, and she glared at him.

"Please, Felix. Let's start how we mean to go on. Be honest with me."

"You want honesty?" He let out a long sigh and spent a few pensive moments twirling her hair into curls around his fingers, all the while avoiding eye contact. She stopped him, grabbing his hand and holding it still.

"If you want honesty," he said, "my parents have a good point. Perhaps I understand politics more than you – I don't know – but what's going on in Germany frightens the heck out of me. And I don't mean like a fairground ride or walking along the top of a high building. What's unfolding there is . . . almost inhuman. There are rumors that the hospitals there are firing all Jews. It's a purge, just like forcing us out of the judiciary, the police, the legal profession – all the professions. It's happening in every organization directly controlled by the state up there, and . . ."

"And what?"

"And the worst thing is that many of the people I work with would welcome the same laws in Austria – even if it led to union with Germany."

"But could that happen? Surely our government has ruled out any kind of union? That's what they've said, isn't it?"

"Klara, whatever you read in Austrian newspapers and hear on Austrian radio, what I'm telling you is exactly what the German government wants – to align the rules in both countries, to form a union between the countries in the name of uniting the German speaking regions of Europe."

"That sounds like you agree with your parents."

"I have to say that I do. It makes me so sad, Klara. That's why I turned down the chance to join your family business. I earn good money at the hospital – money we might need if my worst fears come true and they fire me. We have to be careful with our finances."

Klara slid her arms around him, pulled his bare flesh next to hers, and held on tightly.

"Are you scared too?" he asked.

All she could do was nod.

"I'm sorry," he said. "But listen to me, Klara. I can tell you with all my heart that you'd feel safer living in Texas, away from this uncertainty and the worry of what's around the corner; that you'd settle and be happy there, given time. But also with all of my heart, I promise you that I'll stay in Vienna for as long as you want us to – forever if need be. Do you understand?"

"Yes," she whispered hoarsely. "Perhaps the wine is affecting my imagination."

"Perhaps. But try to relax for now. I'm just enjoying the time we have together, and rejoicing the fact that you married me. Please, it's late, let's just sleep."

They kissed and held a passionate embrace, then Felix turned the light out.

For Klara, however, sleep was a long time coming.

Chapter Six
January to March 1938

Alicia left the doctor's surgery and focused all her effort on getting home as soon as possible. She was hurrying partly due to the early morning bite of winter, but mostly because she had to tell Ludwig her good news as soon as possible.

But no, there was a third reason for her haste – the most important one, although it pained her to think that. Even as she wheeled little Sarah's baby carriage along the sidewalks toward home, she could sense change on the streets. She had always left the politics to Ludwig, but today she could almost taste the bitterness in the atmosphere. Faces turned to look, and the looks turned to glares. A few of the burlier men drew their shoulders back, puffed out their chests, and spat on the ground. There had been occasional tales of Jews being attacked in the streets, but over the last few months the frequency had increased. *How could people change so quickly?* Alicia asked herself as she rushed along.

Still, these people kept their distance, and as long as they did that, as long as they allowed her to go about her daily business, it was bearable.

As she approached home, she shook those concerns from her mind and tried to think of nothing but her good news and, hopefully, a better life to come. She opened the door, wheeled the baby carriage inside, and stopped still.

Ludwig, Papa, and Felix were all sitting around the table, and she saw grave expressions on each of their faces as they all turned toward her.

"What's happened?" she said. "What is it?"

There were glances between the three men, but no words.

"Ludwig. Tell me what's going on."

Papa said, "We were just . . ." but his sentence was curtailed by a shake of the head from Ludwig.

Then Ludwig stood, smiled as though the expression was a stranger to him, and gave her a kiss. "It's nothing," he said. "We were just talking and the conversation became a little . . . *heated*, you might say. But it's nothing for you to worry about. Did you have a nice walk? Has that morning mist lifted yet? Did you manage to see the doctor?"

You hardly needed to know Ludwig well to see through him. And Alicia knew his common ploy: ask lots of questions, place lots of words and thoughts between her and her worries.

"Tell me what you were talking about," she said.

"It was only politics. Nothing for you to worry about, honestly. Why don't you relax? Or make yourself a coffee? Does Sarah need a feed?" He placed a hand on Sarah's head and tousled her gossamer hair. "And how's my little princess? Glad to get out of the cold, I bet."

Alicia admitted defeat. For now. "I'm sorry," she said. "I'm a little stressed." She exchanged kisses with Felix and Papa. "It's lovely to see you both. I notice Ludwig hasn't offered you drinks. Coffee?"

A few minutes later she was in the kitchen, waiting for the kettle to boil, but also standing right next to the doorway, straining to hear the conversation going on only yards away. She immediately latched onto the subject: the recent riots by members of the Austrian National Socialist party – people who had been imprisoned but then freed under the terms of the agreement with

Germany. The words were coming out so fast she was never entirely sure who was speaking, but each word was loaded with anger.

"I told you Schuschnigg should never have let them out of prison."

"But you can't lock people up for their beliefs."

"Oh, come on, it was never about beliefs. These people are National Socialists – Hitler's unofficial ambassadors in our country, they're nothing less than agitators."

"I agree. They want the whole of Austria to be under Hitler's jackboot."

"Exactly. They want another country to control Austria, so they're traitors of the worst kind."

"And that's why they're rioting."

"Riots, I understand. By all means, prosecute people for rioting."

"But they're the same people, supporting each other, deliberately stirring up trouble, and most importantly of all, they'll stop at nothing to get their way."

"So perhaps a vote on union with Germany is the answer after all. We all know the government is considering it. And why not?"

"I'd go with that. Let's all vote on whether we want to be an independent country or live under German rule. Surely that will shut them up."

"And what if they win the vote? What then?"

There was a long pause. *Had Ludwig realized she was eavesdropping?* But no. They continued.

"If those monsters win the vote, then . . . then God help us all."

"I agree. We've all noticed the changes. Places that used to welcome us are now turning us away."

"But only a small number of places."

"Yes, but an increasing number, and smiles are gradually being replaced by scowls or sneers. Every Jew in Vienna knows that. I feel the tide is rapidly coming in."

"And when it does, we're going to be trapped."

"Well, I'm sorry, but I can't believe a minority can somehow force through this unholy union with Germany."

A whistle of the kettle drowned out the rest of the conversation. Alicia made the drinks with boiling water, cream and cocoa powder, then placed three fingers of the honey cake she'd made the previous day on the same tray as the drinks.

Before she had a chance to pick up the tray she heard footsteps behind her, felt warm hands on her shoulder, was heartened by the moist kiss on the side of her neck. She instinctively turned and hugged her husband, holding and squeezing him for all he was worth.

"Hey, hey," he whispered. "What's all this about?"

Still, she held onto him, the side of her face nestling against his chest. "I'm worried," she said. "This city – the whole country – is changing, and I don't like it."

"We'll be fine, Alicia. I promise." He stroked her hair tenderly.

"You don't understand," she said. "I'm . . . I'm pregnant again."

She tried to pull back to read his reaction. Two years ago, when she'd told him she was expecting Sarah, he'd had a look of amazement on his face – joyful eyes, a wide grin, and he'd let out a sharp and loud laugh as if he'd trodden on a nail but didn't care. Now his reaction couldn't have been more different. The hand that had been stroking her hair halted. He held her close, as if he wanted to hide his face until he'd prepared an acceptable expression.

"Did you hear what I said," she asked, knowing it was a pointless thing to say but wanting to fill the cruel silence.

Now he released her and they stood, face to face. He was smiling, but it was a flat, lifeless smile.

"Aren't you happy?"

"Oh, Alicia. Of course I am. The timing isn't perfect, but . . ."

"Perhaps I'll give you a son this time."

"Yes. Perhaps."

It took every ounce of Alicia's strength not to burst into tears. She drew in a few long, calming breaths and reached for the tray. "I'll take the drinks in."

"Yes."

And as she took the tray of coffees and cakes in to Papa and Felix, Alicia wondered whether her sisters were similarly being kept under a dark veil of optimism, or whether their men were being honest with them. At least Felix had been party to this discussion so she could ask Klara whether he'd shared his concerns for the future with her. Maximillian – probably because he wasn't yet a part of the family – hadn't been invited to the men's talk.

If the future was going to be as turbulent as the men at her dining table clearly feared it was, she hoped Giselle would hurry up and marry Maximillian.

§

Giselle hadn't told any of her family – not even one sister.

Maximillian seemed to fit in so well. A nice Jewish boy with a very profitable business and manners beyond reproach. She was sure Mama and Papa were counting the days down to the inevitable – to when they would finally be able to say that all three of their daughters had been handed over to good men.

But now Giselle realized it wasn't going to be. That wedding was never, ever, going to happen. And it tortured her that she had to let everyone down. But the sorry fact was that however many riches Maximillian bestowed upon her, however much he promised her for the future, and however much cordiality there was between him and her family, she loved another man. Maximillian was the sort of man she'd spent years dreaming about marrying; everything about him was right. Almost.

By February she hadn't even seen him for almost three months. Whenever she told her parents she was going to the coffee bar to meet him, she was, in fact, meeting Kurt. They couldn't afford to visit expensive coffee bars as often as she was used to, so instead they went for walks along the riverside, or in parks at the other end of Vienna – far enough away so that no friends or neighbors would spot them.

The final meeting with Maximillian had been difficult to say the least. She told him that she knew he was a good man at heart, but not the right man for her, and that she didn't deserve him. He was almost in tears, telling her how much he loved her and worshipped her. He asked her if she'd discussed their future with her parents or sisters. She told him it was nothing to do with them. Because it wasn't; *they* wouldn't have to spend the rest of their lives with him.

Of course, Kurt was overjoyed when they met in a park one afternoon and she broke the news that she was no longer seeing Maximillian. That afternoon, in the quietest corner of the park, and despite the cold, they made love once more. Again, luck was on Giselle's side; she didn't fall pregnant. And again, she knew she wouldn't be lucky every time. Something in her life had to change.

A few weeks later, when Kurt wanted to make love again – and, to be fair, Giselle's own urges were hard to contain – she insisted on simply going for a walk along the riverbank and having a conversation about their future.

"I remember when you talked about marrying me," she said as they strolled alongside the glacier-like ribbon of bluish silver that cut through the city.

He grinned. "Nothing more than a moment of weakness, I assure you."

"Kurt. Be serious. We can't go on like this."

"But why not? You stopped seeing Maximillian some time ago."

"And I can stop seeing you just as easily."

"You can? Honestly?"

A lengthy, frustrated sigh overcame Giselle, and she held her head in her hands for a moment before answering. "Honestly? It would be hard, but yes, I can. You know how I feel about you, Kurt. But equally I have to think about the future. How long can we keep doing this for? A year? Five years? The rest of our lives?"

"So, you want us to get married?"

"Well, you *did* ask me."

He gave his head a dismissive shake that almost brought a tear to Giselle's eye. "The reality is more complicated. My family would never accept me marrying a Jewess. And who can blame them?"

"Kurt! Don't say that!"

"I'm sorry, Giselle. I know there is good and bad in all groups of people, but Jews as a whole? Well . . ."

"Go on, please."

"You do cause a lot of problems."

She was on the verge of storming off, but it was as though Kurt had glued her feet to the spot, so all she could do was say, "What does that mean?"

"I'm sorry, Giselle. Forget I said that. Whatever my personal beliefs are, I know that I love you. So, let me think about marriage, yes?"

A tender kiss on the cheek, a meander behind a nearby hedge, his hands maneuvering themselves into her coat, then a firmer – almost harsh – kiss on the lips. Clearly he'd decided the conversation was over.

She disagreed, and pulled away from his kiss. "I have an idea," she said.

"I have a better idea," he said, letting a deep laugh explain.

"Why don't we visit your parents?"

He stopped. "I told you my family lives in Linz, didn't I?"

"Yes, but I'd like to meet your parents, see what happens, see if they like me, if they can accept me."

He chewed the idea over for a few moments, then said, "Okay. If that's what you want."

"Do you promise?"

"I promise. But it's a long way from here. We'll have to travel there on the train and stop overnight."

"And so?"

"So, what will you tell your parents? They don't know about our little liaisons, do they?"

"Oh, they think I'm still seeing Maximillian. I'll simply tell them I'm seeing *his* family and staying overnight there."

Kurt shook his head, laughing. "You're a woman in a million, Giselle."

"I like to think so," she said, and winked at him.

A week later, after a two-hour train journey that held Giselle's attention but that Kurt clearly found less interesting than the newspaper he'd bought at Vienna, they arrived at Linz. A cab ride took them to the outskirts of the city and beyond, and eventually, after fifteen minutes, they wound their way down a country lane to the Hinkel family home.

The size and location of the house took Giselle by surprise. It was a very classy timber over brick affair with green shutters to the sides of all windows and a small balcony on the top floor – presumably leading off of Kurt's parents' bedroom. The house was surrounded by a well-trimmed lawn dotted with bushy oak trees. Behind it were acres of open farmland, across the road from it was a rolling meadow. Kurt had told her his father was a construction worker by trade, but he was clearly no mere carpenter or plumber.

"Just one thing," Kurt whispered as he reached for the rope hanging from a large bell outside the front door. "We're not going to let on that you're a Jewess, and we won't mention what part of Vienna your family are from."

"Why not?" she asked, slightly hurt, but also a little confused at her hurt as she hadn't felt close to her family for some time.

"Just don't say anything about it," he replied. "Not unless you want to make a scene. Accept my parents the way they are."

She was about to say that perhaps *they* should accept *her* the way *she* was, but he rung the large bell above them and by the time the pros and cons of arguing the point had come and gone in her head, the door was opened and a rotund, smiling, middle-aged woman with a floral apron was greeting her.

Herr and Frau Hinkel seemed pleasant enough and very welcoming, an hour later laying on a selection of cold meats, cabbage, and buttered potatoes for their guest. Giselle picked herself a modest amount, but in time, after some polite conversation about what her parents did for a living and how many brothers and sisters she had, the plate of meat was thrust toward her by Kurt's mother.

"You haven't tried the pork sausage, Giselle. It's my own recipe and delicious. Everyone says so, don't they, Kurt?"

Giselle glanced at Kurt, who simply said, "You should try a few slices, my darling. Better than any you might find in Vienna, I'd say."

Giselle hesitated, the back of her throat now dry with nervousness, then shook her head and said, "I'd rather not, if you don't mind."

"But I insist," Kurt said. "My mother will be offended if you don't try it."

"Nonsense, Kurt," his mother said. "Leave the poor girl alone."

Giselle tried to suppress her sigh of relief. She had been far from the most devout Jew in Vienna, but somehow she felt like she was on the verge of betraying her parents and had just managed to pull away from that verge.

But then Frau Hinkel added, "Although you could just try one slice, my dear. I promise you won't regret it."

Kurt took control of the plate from his mother, holding it still in front of Giselle. He spiked one of the thickest slices with his fork and held it to her lips. "Well, go on then, my darling," he said. Then he winked at her, and for a few seconds she despised him.

She opened her mouth and he guided the slice in. A very quick chew, a gulp, and the thing was gone. Then there was the inquisition to undergo: three pairs of eyes and ears eagerly awaiting her verdict.

She nodded and forced herself to smile. "Very nice," she said.

"And it's very nice to have you here," Frau Hinkel said. After a short silence, she added, "It's only a shame you couldn't meet Helga."

Giselle looked to Kurt to explain.

"My little sister," he said. "I say *little*, but she's twenty-one."

"Is she at work today?" Giselle asked.

"She's busy with the party," Herr Hinkel explained. "She's very active that way. We're all very proud of her."

Giselle didn't feel like delving further into what that meant, and the conversation turned to Herr Hinkel's job. Giselle's assumption that he was no carpenter or plumber turned out to be correct: he was a construction manager for a local building company, responsible for hiring and managing laborers and tradesmen. It explained the large house.

Also, of course, she'd just learned that Kurt had a cruel sense of humor, something she brought up with him later that day as they took a stroll through the meadow across the road from the house. The late winter chill was still holding onto the hillside, so they stayed close, his arm around her shoulder.

"I'm sorry," he said when she told him it was a horrible thing to do. "Yes, I have no doubt you found eating that meat very unpleasant, but—"

"Unpleasant?" she said. "The problem is that you were forcing me to—"

"*Giselle!*" He stopped walking and shoved her away, jerking her whole body. "Don't interrupt me." He gave her a dark stare, then started walking again and tugged her hand to follow. "As I was saying, however you want to put it, I know you didn't want to do it, but it was necessary."

"So, you're going to keep the fact I'm a Jewess a secret forever?"

"Not forever, but for now. And anyway, it was only one tiny slice. What difference does it make?" He let out a long sigh and drew a hand toward the scene around them. "You should come here in early summer, this meadow is full of wildflowers, it's very beautiful."

His words signified that the subject was closed, and Giselle accepted that for now. "Also, much warmer, I hope," was all she could say. She consoled herself with the thought that perhaps there was something in what he was saying, and that at least a little cruel streak made him interesting.

They stayed in the big house overnight and by the next afternoon were back in Vienna.

Giselle and Kurt met up again three days later.

Over a drink in a local tavern, Kurt suggested going to the local park again.

"Isn't it late?" Giselle said, before his sly grin told her his true intentions. "Not again, Kurt," she said. "It was too cold last time."

"Well, my apartment?"

She wasn't keen; she'd been there only a few times because it was such a squalid, dirty single room that reeked of sweat and alcohol – a complete contrast to the family home in Linz.

But it was warm and private, which was exactly what she wanted right now.

"As long as we light the range to warm the place," she said.

Kurt finished his beer and nodded toward the door. Twenty minutes later they were there, and ten minutes after that, Giselle had opened some windows and he'd lit the range.

As the first flickers started to swirl, he hurriedly washed his hands, and seconds later he was kissing her passionately. He picked her up and carried her over to the bed, onto which they both fell. This was the passion Giselle wanted to experience for the rest of her life, regardless of how she got on with his parents or what her family might think of him, but just for now she had more important things on her mind.

She'd never thought of herself as naïve. They had to talk, so she pushed him away.

"What is it?" he said.

"I have to know," she replied.

"Know what?"

"Whether you want to marry me."

His vise-like grip slowly released, and moments later they were both sitting on the edge of the bed. There was an awkward silence, which Giselle simply let flow away. Eventually Kurt spoke, but his words were nothing like the ones she expected to hear.

"They say the vote is definitely going to happen."

"*What?*" she said.

"There's going to be a vote on whether Austria should form a union with Germany."

"What the hell are you talking about?" she said, shooting out every word. "This is *important*, Kurt. I want to talk about our future, not your stupid damned politics."

He tutted. "You don't understand, do you?"

"Don't treat me like an idiot. Just explain."

"If the vote goes in favor of union with Germany, then Austria will enact many German laws. And if that happens . . ."

"Go on."

"Well, marriages between Jews and Aryans will be banned."

She gave the matter some thought, nodding. "You mean . . . if we want to get married, it has to be very soon."

"Exactly. Within weeks, I suggest. And, of course, I have to consider my parents and sister."

"What about them?"

Kurt gave a disconsolate shrug. "They won't be able to come."

"Won't that seem strange?"

"Of course. But if they come, they'll know I'm marrying a Jewess. They're not ready for that. Not yet."

"Well . . ."

"I'm sorry it has to be like this, Giselle, but it's now or quite possibly never." He held her chin, for once quite gently, and gazed into her eyes. "Giselle, will you do me the great honor of becoming my wife?"

She fought back a few tears and nodded. "I would love to," she said, and pulled him toward her, smothering his face in kisses, her fingertips passing through his thick hair. Then she broke free, wiped the tears from her face and composed herself. "But how will we explain why we're getting married so suddenly?"

"Oh, I've thought of that. You can tell your parents – privately, of course, and with a very somber and regretful expression – that in a moment of great passion we made love and you became pregnant, and I insisted on doing the honorable thing."

"Well . . . I guess that would be a reasonable explanation."

Kurt's fingers reached out for the buttons on her blouse. "Of course, the best way to make our plans sound genuine would be for you to actually *be* pregnant."

She snorted a laugh.

His lips met the side of her neck.

She closed her eyes.

§

Klara kissed Papa goodbye and left the shoe repair shop, pulling the lapels of her coat around her neck to keep the chill wind at bay. She hurried home, satisfied she'd done a good morning's work helping Papa out, but also happy that she had the afternoon free to do some housework before Felix came home from work.

Yes, marriage was working out just fine. It was fine. No marriage was perfect, but theirs was fine.

She got home to find a grim-faced Alicia waiting on her doorstep.

"What's happened?" she said, her heart skipping beats, her mind racing with the possibilities. "And where's Sarah?"

"I had to get a neighbor to look after her. Did you speak with Giselle?"

"Giselle? No. Why? What's going on?"

Alicia shivered and motioned for her sister to open the door, and soon they were in the relative warmth of the apartment, trying to stamp the cold out of their feet.

"So?" Klara said.

"Yesterday I went around to Mama's and Papa's. Giselle whispered a message to me. She told me to be here at noon today."

"And that's all she said?"

Alicia nodded.

"In that case I guess we just have to wait for her." She shivered. "And I need to start the fire."

"I'll help."

The two sisters talked as they loaded the fireplace up with small pieces of paper then some kindling wood.

"How's the pregnancy going?" Klara asked.

"Oh, I don't feel any different just yet. I don't even have the sickness I had with Sarah. And what about you?" She flicked her eyes to Klara's belly. "Any signs that you're . . ."

Klara shook her head. "We're trying, but I'm not worried. Often these things take time. Felix says he wants four eventually, two of each. He also says in some ways it's fortunate that nature is making us wait. He says that at the moment the country is far too unstable to bring a child into." Even as the words tumbled from her mouth, she regretted them. "Oh, Alicia, I'm so sorry, that was a terrible thing to say. Please forgive me."

Before Alicia could respond there was a knock at the door.

Moments later, Giselle was inside, and all three sisters gathered around the beginnings of a fire, now with a single split log on top.

Klara waited, not daring to ask Giselle the reason for the meeting. Broaching that subject was the job of the oldest sister, and they all knew it.

"So, how are you?" Alicia said to Giselle. When that didn't bring an immediate response, she said, "Klara and I are worried about you. Is anything wrong?"

Giselle hesitated, almost as slow to start as the fire had been. "I . . . I should be happy. I know I should be happy, but . . ."

"We're your sisters," Klara said, holding her hand. "You can tell us anything."

Giselle looked her in the eye, then did the same to Alicia before continuing. "I know I haven't been the best sister in the world, not exactly loyal, and I know I'm annoying and I always let the family down and bring shame upon Mama and Papa."

"No, no," Alicia said. "Please don't say—"

"It's no good, Alicia. You know that's all true." She glanced at Klara. "Both of you know what I mean. And although I don't deserve your support, I need it now more than ever. I need you to promise me that you won't be angry and you'll help me smooth things over with Mama and Papa."

Klara's mind was racing with all sorts of salacious and distasteful thoughts, but she dismissed them; this was her sister, the older sister who had shown her how to put on makeup and before that had played with her in the street. It was true that Giselle had become a little distant of late, but the love of a sister was for life, come cold, rain, or tempest.

"Of course we'll help you," Klara said. "But you have to tell us what's wrong."

"Thank you both." Giselle gave one firm nod, as if it were a starting pistol. "You know I told you I'm still seeing Maximillian?"

They nodded.

"Well, I haven't seen him for months."

"You mean it's over between you?" Klara asked.

"What about all those times you said you were going to the coffee shop?" Alicia added.

"I lied." Giselle's head hung low. "I lied to both of you and, more importantly, to Mama and Papa, and I'm so sorry. The fact is that I've been seeing another man."

"And that's your news?" Alicia asked. "That's what you wanted to tell us?"

Giselle shook her head. "There's a problem."

"Go on," Klara said.

"He's the man I told you about at your wedding. Kurt."

"The police officer?" Klara asked.

"The Gentile?" Alicia asked, a deep frown suddenly appearing on her forehead.

Giselle nodded. "And the thing is . . . I'm going to marry him."

Alicia let out a gasp. Klara suppressed hers by gulping, then said, "And you haven't told Mama and Papa yet, I assume?"

"No. Not yet. I'm telling them tomorrow when I can be alone with them."

"But . . ." Alicia opened and closed her mouth a few times, then hugged her sister. "But this should be a joyous occasion, Giselle. You should be happy, not troubled like this. We can promise you that we'll support you, isn't that right, Klara?"

"Of course we will," Klara said. "We're sisters, and we'll always support each other. But do you have to tell Mama and Papa so soon? Could you not think it through first, perhaps drop a few hints to pave the way?"

"There isn't time for that," Giselle said.

"Why not?" Alicia asked.

"Because the wedding is next Saturday."

When Klara heard that, there was a small part of her that wanted to laugh, that couldn't accept that Giselle was being serious, that thought this whole act could be one of her sister's cruel stunts to seek attention. She very quickly came to her senses, her mind turning to the practicalities.

"Have you met his parents?" she asked.

Giselle nodded sheepishly. "It was that weekend I told you I was seeing Maximillian's parents. I actually went to visits Kurt's parents."

Again, Klara felt a little hurt at being lied to. She could tell by Alicia's expression that she did too.

"They have a big house in the country near Linz," Giselle continued. "They were very welcoming."

"Good," Klara said, still too shocked to say anything more substantial.

But she also realized that the deception and subterfuge couldn't have been easy for Giselle to cope with, that she wasn't harming anybody after all, and over the next few minutes both she and Alicia assured their sister they would stand by her, whatever she decided to do.

Klara decided not to say anything even remotely uncharitable about Giselle's wedding, and made Felix promise not to either when she told him the news later that day. Giselle was a sister and sisters should support one another – especially when they were getting married, and above all else should never fall out.

Of course, she (and probably everyone else) thought it such a strange affair. A March wedding only announced earlier that same month sounded suspicious. She didn't want any of her unpleasant thoughts getting back to Giselle, but still thought she should bring the subject up in private with Felix.

"There's something going on that we don't know about in all this," Felix said. "I don't want to be unkind, and I pray to God I'm wrong, but I don't like what I hear about this Kurt fellow."

Klara agreed with him, but told him that whatever was happening, Giselle was her sister and nothing – definitely not marrying a Gentile – would change that fact. But even as Klara uttered the words, she felt awkward at celebrating such a strange occasion. The arrangements were cobbled together: only a few people were to be present at the ceremony from the Rosenthal family, and none at all from Kurt's side, and also – abandoning tradition – there would be a small party at a local tavern after the ceremony.

Klara asked Giselle why none of Kurt's family would be attending, and was told that they couldn't afford to travel. But that was odd; she remembered Giselle describing their big house in the countryside just outside Linz, so they weren't short of a schilling or two. But she decided to let the matter drop; there was no point questioning Giselle further, she was stressed enough as it was. The bigger question was why they were getting married so quickly. Again, she confided in Felix.

"I think she's pregnant," she told him. "That must be why they're in such a rush."

Felix tilted his head from side to side, as if half agreeing.

"It must be," she insisted.

"Not necessarily. There is another good reason for them to get married so soon."

"What's that?"

"The vote."

"The vote?" Klara thought for a few moments. There was only one vote she knew of – now officially announced by the Austrian chancellor, and she couldn't work out any connection with it.

"The vote on the union with Germany that's taking place on Sunday."

Klara waited, just staring at him.

"If, heaven forbid, the vote goes the wrong way, they'll impose German laws on us, and one of those laws is the banning of marriages between Jews and what they call *Aryans*."

Klara was in shock. But at least it explained the urgency.

Even at the wedding itself, most guests seemed to be in shock. Papa, Ludwig, and Felix hid it well, Mama and Alicia hardly spoke. The celebration after the ceremony was only slightly better, and that was mainly due to dear Hugo. By far the most cheerful person in the tavern, his crooked grin, the sparkle in his eyes, and even his guttural grunts all brought some much-needed levity to the proceedings. The few other guests who'd been invited – assorted uncles, aunts, and neighbors – had been prewarned not to ask too many questions about the groom's family, and accordingly were polite and measured in their observations.

At the mid-point in the proceedings, Papa raised a toast to the happy couple and gave a very short speech in which he wished Giselle and Kurt eternal happiness, and everyone applauded. From that moment, at least, Klara noticed that there were more smiles, more polite conversations, and it was . . . it was *nice*. Not the most joyous wedding ever, but pleasant.

Despite the muted atmosphere, Mama and Papa did seem genuinely happy for Giselle, and toward the end of the evening, when Ludwig and Felix were alerted by banging on the doors and went outside to see what the commotion was all about, Klara and Alicia got a chance to talk with their mama and papa.

"We all know it's not ideal," Papa told them, "but that man has a stable, well-paid job with the police force, and as long as he makes my daughter happy, I'm happy too." He laid a hand on Mama's knee and glanced at her.

Mama looked at both Klara and Alicia in turn. "I'm happy for her too, but she isn't making life easy for herself. We must all promise to help her in the years to come, and we can't treat Kurt as if he's an outsider."

"Of course," Klara and Alicia replied, almost in unison.

"And I am a happy man, believe it or not," Papa continued. "I've now managed to get all three of my beloved daughters married off in the last three years – all to strong, healthy men with pleasant manners and good jobs. I tell you, I'll sleep well tonight."

It was then that Ludwig and Felix returned from outside, marching straight toward them with faces like overhead thunder.

"There's news," Ludwig announced, looking – *glaring* – at Papa.

Papa held his hand up. "If it's bad news, please keep it to yourself for now. Tonight is a night for celebration."

"But this is important," Felix said.

"Is the building on fire?" Papa asked.

"No, but—"

"In that case, whatever you have to say isn't important. Not now." Papa gestured toward Mama. "*This* is important." He waved a hand in the direction of Giselle and Kurt, both of them smiling and chatting to guests. "*That* is important. If you have bad news, tell me tomorrow morning. And please, gentlemen, don't spoil my daughter's wedding by telling anyone else. Whatever it is, just sleep on it."

Now Klara noticed a sheen of sweat on the reddened faces of both Ludwig and Felix. The men exchanged glances. Felix turned back to face Papa. He opened his mouth as if to speak, but no sound emerged.

Ludwig let out a sigh. "As you wish," he said to Papa.

"I need a drink," Felix said, looking around for a bottle of wine that wasn't empty.

Klara stood up and said she would help him find one. She didn't care that her motives were transparent. He was her husband, and even if he hadn't been, he didn't look like a man who should be left to his own devices; he looked like a man who desperately needed to get something off his chest.

"Tell me what's wrong," Klara said when they were out of earshot of the rest of the family.

"I promised your papa I wouldn't say anything to—"

"*Tell me*, Felix."

He shook his head. "Oh, Klara, it's terrible. It's the worst thing that could have happened."

She said nothing. Just stared at him. Didn't even blink.

"The news is that the northern border has been broken. German troops are streaming into the country. *Our country is being overrun*."

Klara gasped. Her heart started to thump wildly, all thoughts of the wedding and its subdued but pleasant atmosphere banished from her mind for a moment.

"And the worst part – the very worst part – is that there is no fighting. *No fighting.* They say most towns are welcoming the German troops, even celebrating their arrival. There is absolutely no resistance from Austrian troops or police or . . . or anyone else."

Klara glanced over to her papa, a loose laugh falling from his lips as he joked with a neighbor who had sauntered over to congratulate him.

She thought that the evening might be difficult from now on.

But she knew for certain that tomorrow was going to bring a frightening new dawn.

TALE TWO

A Bitter North Wind
March 1938 to May1945

A cruel and unforgiving tempest sweeps through Austria, bringing far-reaching social changes, and the Rosenthals have to contend with the whims of a new regime as well as their own personal challenges.

Chapter Seven
March to December 1938

Alicia considered telling them she was pregnant. She decided quite quickly that not only would that not have helped her, but it might have spurred them on to be even more brutal.

Every time she paused to ease her aching back, there were ten people shouting at her to continue, five people shoving her or kicking her, and a few threatening much worse.

She'd been on her way to her parents' apartment. Ludwig was at home keeping an eye on Sarah, and that turned out to be a blessing of sorts. Ludwig was anything but a violent man, but even he would have fought back, almost certainly getting himself into more trouble because of the sheer number of them. In fact, he'd pleaded with her not to go, but she'd insisted on going mainly for Hugo's sake, because he'd said he was missing her, and she simply couldn't let her dear brother down.

And on the way there she'd been set upon by those angry sorts, and there was no reasoning with them. They'd started to call them "Scrubbing Parties" – impromptu street events where Jews were forced to clean the sidewalks and walls. Swastika flags were proudly held high, insults were hurled like icy snowballs:

"Finally, you Jews are doing work worthy of your people."

"It's no more than you deserve."

"You've had everything your own way for far too long."

"You're lucky we don't lynch you all."

As Alicia scrubbed, her knees bruised and cut, her fingers bleeding, she glanced around, not daring to let her hands stop that tiring circular motion. She saw Doctor Solomon, who had looked after her during her first pregnancy; Herr Frankel from the same apartment block; Frau Adler, who she'd played with as a child; and many people whose faces she recognized from the synagogue but whose names she didn't know. All of them, like her, were on their knees and washing sidewalks or cleaning the slogans off the walls – the anti-National Socialist slogans that only days before had given Jews hope, but now were sad reminders that their hope had come to nothing.

And crowded around were people who mocked and jeered as they waved their flags and spewed out those cruel taunts.

She'd tried to escape once already – to get to her feet and run off toward her own apartment or any place she might find respite – but she'd felt the leather of shoes push her back down onto the ground, and had been ordered to carry on cleaning.

And now, worried that she was bleeding too much from her bare skin catching on concrete, her aching hands and arms somehow giving her the courage, she tried again. She stood up and stumbled a few paces. A young man – little more than a boy – blocked her path and told her to get back on her knees and do the dirty work that only dirty Jews were fit for. Through tears of despair or physical pain – she wasn't sure which – Alicia shoved the boy back and he fell. A young girl appeared out of nowhere, slapped Alicia's face, called her a filthy pig, and told her she would be allowed to return home only when all the streets were clean. A few adults behind the girl shouted support for her, but Alicia forced her way through and managed to break into a run, hearing nothing but laughter and jeers from behind her.

She hesitated as she spied four policemen casually leaning against a wall, all watching the fervent crowd have their way as if they were watching a soccer match, but then her pace quickened as she dipped into a side street and found her way home, thumping her bloody hands on the front door, too panic-stricken to search for her own key. She only stopped thumping when Ludwig opened the door and she fell inside. He spoke, but at first she couldn't listen, and a few minutes later, while he washed her cuts and grazes, she explained what had happened.

"Where are they?" Ludwig said. "Tell me!"

She grabbed his arm. "No, Ludwig. Don't go after them."

"But I can't let—"

"Please, Ludwig. Stay with me."

He cursed under his breath. "That's why I didn't want you to go. I should have put my foot down and stopped you leaving."

"I'm sorry, Ludwig."

"Don't you dare apologize."

"But . . . but I didn't expect that. Things here have changed so quickly."

"Oh, yes. People have changed ever since that visit from Herr Hitler a couple of days after he and his henchmen took over." Ludwig's fist hit the table. "I tell you, that man has stirred something up in this city that I simply do not understand. I heard stories that mobs were roaming the streets, looting Jewish shops and businesses, forcing any Jews who happened to be passing by to clean the sidewalks with their bare hands. I didn't expect my family to be involved in it."

"They caught me by surprise."

"And they're not going to catch you by surprise again. From now on you don't go out alone – and we have to be particularly careful with Sarah."

"But I don't understand. The police were just watching it all happen."

"It's like you say, things here have changed. The police are outnumbered by the mobs. Some say if they interfere, they fear for their lives; some say they simply turn a blind eye."

"*Turn a blind eye?* Hardly that. They seemed to be enjoying the spectacle."

"Whichever is the case, the National Socialists have only been in charge for a few days and it seems we're not welcome in our own city – the city we were all born in and have worked to support. We're not even allowed to call our country 'Austria' anymore."

Alicia remembered being told off in a store for not using the new word for what now appeared to be some sort of property of Germany: Ostmark.

Ludwig continued: "And the worst thing is that I have absolutely no idea what to do about it." He glanced at her cuts, bruises, and red-raw hands. "If they do this to women and old men, what would they do to young, fit men?"

"I don't know, Ludwig. And I don't want to find out, do you hear me?"

"I'll take care out there, I promise, but . . . we have other problems."

"Such as what?"

"At the hospital two of our most prominent doctors have gone."

"Gone? Gone where? And why?"

"Oh, I think I know the *why*. They were both Jews and they were outspoken about their distaste for Hitler and his policies. As for where they've gone, nobody knows. Also, a lot of unpleasant slogans supporting the new regime have been painted on the walls of our synagogue. Like I told you, I can't see an end to it. The most frightening thing is that the new regime has so much support from the people of Vienna."

"Support for us being attacked and spat at in the streets? For us being made to scrub the sidewalks with our bare hands?"

"It would appear so. The only positive thing is that they've announced a new vote throughout Austria on whether to accept German rule."

"Well, that's good news, isn't it?"

"We'll see."

Alicia had never taken much interest in politics. To her it seemed perverse in so many ways. The original vote on whether to accept union with Germany had been postponed when German troops had strolled through the country unopposed, and now the new regime set up by the Germans was going to ask exactly the same question.

All became clear a few days later when their voting cards were delivered. At first Alicia didn't understand the instructions, or, at least, she did but they didn't make sense. When Ludwig came home from work he sat down and studied the details, letting out tuts and groans as he did so. Eventually he stood up and told Alicia he needed a coffee – a strong one.

"And so?" she said.

"The instructions on the cards are clear. If you are a Jew, you are to return your card, and not use it to vote. There are heavy penalties for those who do not comply."

"But . . . I don't understand. It's a vote."

"For God's sake, Alicia. It's not difficult to understand. The bastards have banned us from voting on the future of our own country." He let out a long groan and shook his head. "I'm sorry. I snapped. Forgive me." He kissed her and held her close, then they stood still in an embrace for a few minutes.

"But why would they send us a voting card and then tell us we can't use it?"

"I don't know. Perhaps because they want to rub sharp salt into already inflamed wounds."

"What are we going to do, Ludwig?"

"I've been discussing it with people at the synagogue. We don't have much choice. For now, we need to have faith that somehow people will see that we're no threat, that we can be good for Vienna and good for Austria if they give us a chance. We let people see that Jewish doctors cure people, that Jewish bakers bake good bread, that Jewish tailors make fine clothes. And we hope."

"And if that doesn't work?"

"Then . . . I don't know. But God help us."

Alicia laid the palm of a hand – still stinging from the cuts and grazes – on her belly, and tried to imagine what life in Vienna might be like a year from now.

Was it wise to bring another child into this city?

§

Giselle had moved out of the Leopoldstadt district of the city soon after marrying Kurt.

He'd made it clear that there was no way he was going to live anywhere near *that area*, and was renting an apartment for them in the fashionable Margareten district, so it was quite a walk for her to see either of her sisters or visit the family home.

At first, the distance didn't stop her. But then she'd seen the crowds of people forcing Jews to scrub the streets clean, she'd seen angry mobs vandalizing stores with Jewish names above them. By the summer of 1938 the whole area had become dirty, run-down, and quite unpleasant. It was all very off-putting, but she persevered – long enough to congratulate Alicia on her second pregnancy.

But it was becoming clear that life for the Jewish community in Vienna wasn't going to improve anytime soon. The vote on the union with Germany had seen to that. Almost every man and woman had apparently voted in favor of the union, which only made the National Socialists tighten their grip on the country and confirm plans to adopt German laws.

"Why don't you just forget about them?" had been Kurt's reaction whenever she complained about how hard her visits were becoming.

"They're my family," she would always reply. "And Alicia's expecting her second child."

But now her words were starting to have a hollow sound.

She was about to leave home late one Saturday morning when he suggested she didn't go.

"Why do you keep visiting them?" he said. "You're always complaining about them. You never enjoy it."

"I told you," she said, sitting in front of the mirror, lipstick in hand. "Whatever happens to them, it doesn't stop them being my family."

His head appeared in the mirror next to hers. He grabbed her roughly – a little too roughly – by the hair and turned her around to face him, then he kissed her, pressing his mouth hard against hers. Then he spoke with a softness at odds with his actions.

"You don't need your family anymore," he said. "You've got me."

She smiled coyly. "Of course, but I can have both. I like seeing them. It's important to me."

"You look particularly beautiful this morning," he said.

Then he kissed her again, massaging the back of her neck. She felt the core of her body react, warming her like nothing else could. His hands snaked their way around to her front, down to her breasts, beyond. She felt herself being lifted off the floor and carried into the bedroom.

This was pleasure. *This* made her happy. And life was all about pleasure and happiness. Perhaps Kurt was right; perhaps she didn't need her family after all.

Later, with the midday sun highlighting the patterning on the bedroom curtains, Kurt lit two cigarettes and they both lay back in bed.

"So, you're not going today?" he said.

"I'll give it a miss, just for once. But don't you think it's horrible, what's happening to them?"

"I already told you I voted for the union with Germany, didn't I?"

"You were honest with me, Kurt. I appreciate that. But surely you can't agree with how the government is treating our Jews?"

Kurt gave the matter some thought. "I'm not sure. I know a lot of people for whom the Jewish problem is simply not an issue. They see Germany becoming successful in so many ways – a powerful economy, strong leadership, a country the rest of the world takes notice of – and they want to be a part of that. Others are happy to see the Jewish problem finally dealt with."

"*The Jewish problem?* What do people mean when they say that?"

"Well, people have seen Jews taking all the top jobs, having business agreements between each other to shut non-Jews out, monopolizing the professions, keeping everything to themselves, favoring fellow Jews in every way possible. I guess a lot of people smell revenge."

"And you? What do you think?"

"Me?" He shrugged. "I guess I'm somewhere in the middle. I married you, didn't I? And I met your family."

"But would you help them if the need arose?"

"*Pah!* I married you, not your family."

"But do you like them?"

"Mmm . . . the point is that Austrian people are Germans at heart."

"My papa is Jewish *and* Austrian."

"I don't believe you can have two masters."

"But he fought for his country in the Great War."

"Perhaps he was given little choice in that matter."

"But what about me, Kurt? What if those people on the street attack me or force me to scrub the sidewalk with my bare hands? Would you care about that?"

He took a long suck on his cigarette, still staring up at the ceiling. "Isn't that why you married me? For your own safety? You know they've applied German law, don't you? We couldn't get married now; it would be illegal."

"That's not why I married you, Kurt. I married you because I love you."

"Either way, you had a lucky escape by marrying me when you were able to. Now you don't have a Jewish surname, so nobody would ever know that Giselle Hinkel used to be Jewish."

"*Used to be* Jewish?"

"Yes. I don't see you as Jewish now."

"But my mama and papa are both Jewish, so I am too."

"Not any longer, you aren't." Kurt stubbed his cigarette out and sat on the edge of the bed, facing away from Giselle. "And I've been thinking about something for some time. Perhaps now is a good time to tell you. I think it would be good for you to break your ties with your family."

"What?" Giselle jumped up and sat next to him.

He stared straight ahead. "I'm only thinking of your safety. You've seen the treatment Jews are getting out there. Do you really want to be a part of that?"

"Well, no, I guess not. But . . . it's not my fault I'm Jewish."

"I know that, my darling. All I'm saying is that perhaps we should forget the unfortunate circumstances of your birth."

Giselle thought back to the first and only time she'd met Kurt's parents in Linz, how he'd persuaded her not to let them know about her background, how she hadn't liked the idea of deceiving them but had gone along with it because there hadn't been time to discuss the issue beforehand. So his family didn't suspect a thing. But now Giselle was starting to think perhaps the event had planted a seed in her mind. Perhaps it was what Kurt wanted all along, for her to start believing she didn't need her family, even to somehow sever her ties with them.

But that was what Kurt wanted; now Giselle had to take some time to work out what *she* wanted.

§

By Summer, Klara and Felix were also facing tough decisions.

They'd had the same argument more than once. Earlier in the year, Felix had told Klara that it was clear for all to see what direction the government was moving in. He said that because he was an American and hence an outsider of sorts, he had a better appreciation of the changes happening in Europe, of how Germany was treating the Jewish population there, and of how Austria was clearly moving in exactly the same direction, albeit a few years behind.

Those words were now ringing true, but still, just as before, Klara insisted there was absolutely nothing they could do about it. She said she had faith that somehow the situation would eventually improve, and that they would stay in the city near her family, would start a family of their own in time, and then would live a normal, peaceful life.

In truth, her mind was in turmoil. She and Felix had been caught more than once by a street mob and made to scrub the streets with their bare hands, so now they only went outside when it was absolutely essential. She'd lost count of the number of Jews Felix had told her had been fired from the hospital – doctors, nurses, surgeons, specialists, administrative staff – and that it was only a matter of time before it was his turn. Papa's shoe repair shop, where Klara still worked most mornings, had been broken into twice. Each time, nothing had been stolen, but a lot had been ruined beyond repair. And each time, the police expressed no sympathy – even, on the second occasion, telling them not to complain again.

And then there were the rumors that thousands of Jews, along with others such as Jehovah's Witnesses and Roma people, had been forcibly removed from Vienna – taken to where, nobody knew.

So although Klara knew she was stubborn, she also knew that her insistence on believing the situation would improve was becoming a hard argument.

Talk of how long Klara should continue working at the shoe repair place and why she hadn't yet managed to become pregnant had long since fallen by the wayside. Those mere details of life hardly seemed important now.

Toward the end of summer, Felix said he had the answer. He said that as an American citizen he could move back to Texas and take Klara with him, and that there wasn't a thing the authorities could do to stop them. He told her it was the right thing to do. It wasn't ideal, it wouldn't be a permanent solution, but in the short term it would solve their problems at a stroke. It was, Felix insisted, clearly *the best thing to do.*

Klara held firm. She was going to stay in Vienna. He told her again she was being stubborn.

And he was probably right.

Even after the embers of summer had died, they were still having those arguments. By now, Felix was clinging onto his job, but Ludwig had lost his, and with a child and a heavily pregnant Alicia to feed, he'd started working full-time with Papa at the shoe repair business to make ends meet.

But Klara still held firm.

The events of November changed Klara; they changed Austria much more.

One evening early that month, Klara and Alicia and their husbands were with Mama and Papa. It was a gathering to celebrate the birth just a few days before of Alicia's new baby boy.

As it turned out, the celebration was short-lived. The savagery of that night blew through the Rosenthal family like a bitter north wind on a moonless night. To Klara, the whole thing hardly seemed real.

As darkness fell, shouts from outside caught Klara's ear. Soon, crashing glass stilled everyone's breath. Klara was about to look out the window, but stopped when she heard the noise.

It was an insistent banging on the apartment front door. And a voice of desperation. Ludwig opened the door. It was Elie, the baker from the apartment above.

"They're smashing up the synagogue."

Ludwig was speechless.

"It's chaos, it's hell. Every window broken, the pews smashed with hammers, the Torah ripped apart and burned, the whole building set alight. And not just ours. They're attacking every synagogue and prayer house in Leopoldstadt."

Even Hugo couldn't raise a smile, because even he knew something evil was stalking the streets tonight.

"Our businesses are being smashed up, our shops looted, our people attacked."

Papa spoke, just the one word: "Police?"

"Fire trucks?" Felix asked.

Elie shook his head. "They're all there, to make sure only *our* businesses suffer and only *our* places of worship burn. Anyone who interferes is arrested or . . . or worse."

"What can we do?" Mama said.

"Lock the door. Put out the lights. Close all windows and curtains. Don't answer the door. Do you understand? *Do not answer the door.*"

He left to tell other residents while Felix and Ludwig locked the door and barricaded it with a sideboard and a table. Alicia and Klara ran to the window to see what was happening outside. Yes, the sky bled with flames, swirling smoke carried people's livelihoods to the heavens, breaking glass and celebratory cheers punctuated the roar of a hundred fires. Flag-waving mobs had risen onto the streets like malevolent spirits.

Then a woman looked over to the window – at Klara. She pointed, she shouted. The mob outside, now alerted, threw stones. Alicia screamed as the window shattered. Klara shrieked, cursing the fact they weren't higher up. A man attacked the window with a wooden baton. Others were also close. Klara thanked God that Ludwig and Felix were with them; they fought off the mob by throwing anything at hand at them and pushed a wardrobe in front of the window. The mob gave up and moved on.

The immediate danger over, they all gathered on the far side of the living room, huddled together for safety. All the time, little Sarah was crying. Somehow, her tiny brother slept on.

But then.

Again. A hammering came on the door. More shouts of desperation – this time even worse.

"Don't answer it!" Papa shouted. "It could be a trick!"

"But it's Lev," Mama said.

Klara knew Lev. About fifteen. The tailor's son. Sweet boy. Big teeth. Now he sounded different.

"I said don't answer it!"

"But he's crying. He's *pleading*."

"I don't care!"

"Please let me in!" the voice shouted. "They're chasing me. Please let me in! Let me in! Let me in!"

"But they'll kill him," Mama screamed, her face rosy and glistening with tears.

She looked to Felix and Ludwig for help. They pulled the table and sideboard away from the door and opened it, each armed with kitchen knives just in case.

Lev fell inside, blood streaming from his mouth and nose, a black gap where those prominent front teeth once were.

"Thank you, thank you, thank you." He couldn't speak properly; his missing teeth.

"What happened?" Klara said while the men replaced the barricade.

"They were throwing bricks through the shop window. They woke up Papa and me. We tried to stop them. But they took what they wanted, ripped up what they didn't."

"Where's your papa?"

Lev started to cry, his tears fighting with streaks of blood.

Then a large crash came from outside. Sarah let out a scream.

Alicia put an arm around Lev and led him to the bathroom, telling him she would clean him up.

Klara picked up Sarah and rocked her, shushing her. It should have been a moment to cherish – a time to rejoice in her sister's two healthy children, perhaps a time to look forward to having her own babies one day. But all she could do was weep.

So they all stayed there, for a night and a day and a night, together on one side of the living room – away from the carpet of broken glass near the window, so scared that none of them slept, and none of them daring to leave the apartment.

The next day they gave in.

Klara found the city she loved had become unrecognizable in the passing of two moons. Her world had soured as quickly as milk left in bright sunlight. The carpet of broken glass wasn't merely in the living room; it also covered most of Leopoldstadt. She passed the little prayer house at the end of the street, now a smoldering wreck. She saw smashed up buildings that had once been greengrocers, bakers, shoemakers, tailors, barbers.

And soon they all found out that this was no rogue loss of temper quickly brought under control, no single wrong note in a piano concerto. What happened in Vienna was just a copy of the events that had happened throughout Austria and Germany. And the faces on the streets told them to expect more of the same.

This was a taste of the future.

November changed Austria. Klara had no choice but to change too. But did that mean she should flee her country? Or that she should stand and fight?

Chapter Eight
1939

Alicia was finding it hard to concentrate on feeding her new baby boy. Having Klara on hand to look after Sarah should have helped, but Klara had been so moody and sour-faced lately that she often secretly wished she was alone with her two children. Klara had occasionally mentioned the possibility of leaving Vienna – worse still, had suggested Alicia and her family could leave too. Every time it was mentioned, Alicia deliberately avoided discussing the matter, simply saying that her life was already too busy.

So she knew she shouldn't have been surprised one evening when Klara insisted on staying to help put the children to bed, saying they could have a talk together afterward. Alicia's heart was tired enough as it was, but it still managed to thump with apprehension at the prospect of any sort of disagreement with her sister.

They were settled at the kitchen table with a cup of warm milk each. All Alicia wanted to talk about was how she was coping with the extra motherhood duties or whether she'd recovered from the birth or how Sarah was coping with not being the center of attention anymore. The atmosphere – Klara's severe expression – told her that wasn't going to happen.

"Have you given any more thought to what we talked about last week?" Klara said, casually sipping her drink as if she'd merely asked the time.

Last week? Much as Alicia loved Klara, it felt as if Klara had been asking her the same question every day since the start of the year. Alicia had resisted her on every occasion, and told herself to keep her nerve, that this time would be no different. In fact, no, this time she was going to be even more determined.

"I don't want to fall out with you, Klara," she said, "but . . . could you please stop asking me about that?"

Klara's face cracked as though in pain. Alicia couldn't have that. Only a month ago Felix had been fired from the hospital and so Klara was obviously fragile.

"I'm sorry, Klara. I didn't mean to snap at you. I know you have my best interests at heart, but I've told you many times that I won't leave Vienna, let alone Austria."

"Have you talked it over with Ludwig?"

"Of course I have. He agrees with me."

"And what about the people disappearing?"

"I know. We've all heard the stories, but—"

"They aren't just stories, Alicia. They aren't the product of someone's twisted imagination. The railroads have taken thousands away every month. And if you stay here, you'll find out exactly where they've been taken to. You do realize that, don't you?"

An image flashed through Alicia's mind: that first day Klara had told her through a flood of tears that Felix wanted to return to America. She assumed he still wanted to go, which explained why Klara was still nagging her to go too. And she had to accept that recent events in the city had softened her stance, and they both knew it.

She sighed. "Oh, Klara. I can't pretend I'm not worried, but Vienna is my home, and I have two little ones to think of. Besides, if we all go, who will look after Mama, Papa, and Hugo? Do you think Giselle will suddenly appear and help them?"

"But Felix has said we can all go. He can arrange it with his family. They have a big ranch house we can all stay at until we arrange something better."

"And have you thought about money? There's the cost of the journey and also this extra tax we have to pay to leave Austria."

"We could help out, pool our resources."

"I couldn't let you do that. Even if I could, some people wait hours in line only to be told they don't have the correct details and have to start over."

"But it *can* be done. I know they're not making it easy, but thousands are going to America and Great Britain and other places."

"And what about the practicalities? Let's say we convince everyone to go – even Papa. And we give up pretty much all our assets to the state in return for them *so graciously* allowing us to leave. And we scrape together the money to buy travel tickets. What then? Who helps Papa and Hugo on and off trains and ships? How do we all settle in another country? How do we learn another language? What do we do for a living?"

"I know it sounds—"

"We both know how it sounds, Klara. It sounds impossible. It sounds impossible because it *is*. Now please, I'm getting tired of this. Stop being so stubborn. By all means do what's best for you and Felix. If you go to America, nobody here will think any worse of you. But this is my country and I want to stay."

"But I can't just leave you here. Felix keeps asking me, and I keep telling him the same thing. Mama, Papa, and Hugo depend upon us three sisters. And, as you say, it's a long time since we've seen Giselle, so it's up to you and me. If I left, it would be too much of a burden on you – especially now you have two children."

"If you feel that way, why not take them with you?"

"What? Take who with me?"

"Mama, Papa, and Hugo. Take them to America with you."

Klara strained to reply to that, her mouth opening and closing a few times with no payoff. "That would be even worse," she eventually said. "It would . . . it would feel like we were all abandoning you and your family, and I'm not prepared to do that."

"Likewise, I'm not prepared to give up on my friends, my neighbors, and my city."

"Even if you can't eat? You know how hard it's been for us since Felix and Ludwig lost their jobs at the hospital. Many of those friends and neighbors you speak of have been taken away – and for good, it would seem. So, is there anything worth staying for?"

Now it was Alicia's turn to struggle to answer a hard question. Both Ludwig and Felix had tried to find employment, but had effectively been blacklisted. Both were now working for Papa's shoe repair business, but what with Klara also working most mornings and the shrinking base of Jewish customers having less money to fritter away on repairing their shoes, the business was barely surviving. Moreover, more and more Jewish businesses were being confiscated by the authorities, so it was only a matter of time before they would all have to live off of the state rations and what little extra that begging provided.

The worst thing was that there was no prospect of improvement in the near future. Alicia had started to take more interest in the politics of the day since the German takeover and the explosion of anti-Jewish sentiment in Vienna. She eagerly read of the news that Germany had now also occupied nearby Czechoslovakia, and soon after that she listened – the hairs on her neck prickling – to the radio broadcasts of Britain guaranteeing safety to Poland should that be Germany's next target. It seemed that nobody – not America, France, Great Britain, or any other country – cared about Austrian Jews.

So Klara's question was difficult to deal with; once pride was stripped away, there really was very little worth staying for.

"I'm right, aren't I?" Klara said, as though reading her thoughts. She was, but still Alicia couldn't come to terms with any upheaval on that scale. And yes, there was also her very real pride to deal with. Vienna was her home and always would be. She shook her head, leaned across the table, and drew breath.

"You're usually the stubborn one, Klara, but now it's my turn to stand firm. I witnessed the National Socialists wrestle control of this country. I stood by when German troops invaded as if they were taking a Sunday stroll through the countryside. I felt the humiliation of being forced to scrub the streets. I comforted my husband when he lost his job for no good reason. I listened to the glass smashing and the buildings burning on that horrible night last November. And do you know what? I'll be damned if I'm going to run away after all that. This is *my city* and I won't be bullied out of it."

"But . . . but . . ."

"But nothing, Klara. I've made my decision."

Klara stared at her and nodded slowly. "And . . . and I respect that decision. And I'm sorry for asking once again."

"Come here." Alicia beckoned her over and they embraced. "I know you're only trying to help, and it's not something we should fall out over. So let's not."

"Of course. We need each other like never before. And I know my big sister will cope somehow."

A few minutes later, after Klara had left, Alicia sat and thought. She wrestled with the whole matter again and considered that perhaps . . .

But no. She didn't want to think *that*.

And it was time to check on the children.

They were fine, sound asleep. She looked at their clear skin and their peaceful faces, thought of their innocent souls.

Was she really doing what was best for them?

Deep down, was there a little regret that Klara had given up trying to change her mind? The truth was she'd been close to caving in; her little speech had been aimed at herself as much as at Klara.

But life had to go on. She'd made her bed.

She went back into the kitchen to wash up the two cups.

She picked up the cup Klara had been drinking out of and stared at it for a moment. Then she knew.

Klara had been right and she had been wrong.

She flung the cup against the wall, damning herself for refusing to listen to reason, and sat, sobbing.

§

Over the past year, Giselle had made a pleasant home for herself and Kurt in the Margareten district of Vienna, and initially had enjoyed the novelty of the walk of almost an hour each way to visit her family back in Leopoldstadt. But that novelty had gradually turned into a guilt-ridden chore. Her lifestyle was hardly sumptuous, but she was fully aware that she and Kurt enjoyed many little luxuries that were completely out of reach for the rest of her family.

And by now she hadn't visited them for almost six months, and was sure their situations had deteriorated further.

Kurt kept telling her to keep a low profile – even to the extent of banning letters to and from Leopoldstadt – just in case they gave away her background in these dangerous times. So as well as being able to indulge in soap, coffee, alcohol, and fresh food, she also had the luxury of time on her hands. But that spare time was no luxury; she used it to think of her family, of those carefree early childhood days playing on the living room floor with Hugo, Alicia, and Klara, and of the later years joyfully chasing each other around the streets and parks of Leopoldstadt.

She wondered what had gone wrong, why she'd gone full circle, why she now thought so much about the older sister she'd once considered the most boring woman in the whole of Vienna. How she now craved some of that boring company. By now Alicia would have given birth to her second child. Just to know whether it was a boy or a girl and to be assured mother and baby were healthy would settle her nerves.

And what had become of her little sister Klara? Were she and Felix parents yet? Was Klara still helping Papa out in the shoe repair business? Was the business even still open and making any profit in the face of government actions to squeeze even more Jews out of the city. Yes, even the goings on at a shoe repair shop were now of interest to Giselle.

Hugo would always be just Hugo; he would never change. Perhaps she shouldn't have poked fun at him so much, but he had grinned at the time. And she missed that grin as much as she missed his innocent laugh.

And how were Mama and Papa – the people who must have felt so let down by her behavior in the past? Well, they could survive anything, couldn't they? Or was that just wishful thinking?

Two months ago, she'd plucked up the courage to leave her Margareten apartment – while Kurt was at work, obviously – and venture into Leopoldstadt to seek out her family. She told herself they would be in each other's pockets as they always had been, so if she managed to talk to any of them, she would learn about all of them.

But the place turned out to be barely recognizable. Beggars lined the streets. Stores she used to run in and out of as a child and leisurely peruse as an adult were now smashed-up shells or burnt-out husks. Groups of flag-waving National Socialists – often no more than boys and girls accompanied by party officials or even German soldiers – would appear from around street-corners, making any rag-clothed Jews who dared to hang around the streets scatter.

And whereas she'd gone there hoping to meet someone she knew, she now became worried that someone from her past life would recognize her in front of soldiers – soldiers who would ask her where she was from and how someone so well-dressed knew people in this Jewish area. She worried for her own safety.

So she returned home, reassuring herself that at least she'd *tried* to contact them.

But she wouldn't try again; the risk was too great. Instead, she busied herself cleaning and cooking for Kurt at home, and occasionally meandering the streets of Margareten pondering how this city of hers had become so divided.

She also had plenty of time to sit at home and wonder what had become of that strong-willed adventurous woman who felt as though she could go wherever she wanted, with whoever she liked, and could attract the attention of any man at will. Why had she changed so much? She now missed the family that she'd never really cared for, which was confusing. Had the cold hand of loneliness laid itself upon her heart?

She was deep in thought trying to unravel these conundrums one afternoon when the door opened and Kurt announced his arrival. Years ago, the thought of being an attentive housewife kissing her husband as soon as he crossed the threshold and asking him about his working day would have disgusted her. Yet here she was, doing everything she hated but hating the alternative even more.

"Sit down," Kurt said. "I need to talk to you."

"What is it? Have I done something wrong?"

He said nothing, merely sat and pointed at the chair next to him.

Thoughts rushed through her mind like a cold stream around hot feet. Had someone in Leopoldstadt recognized her? She hadn't been there in two months, so surely he would have brought the subject up earlier if that were the case.

She sat down, a bitter taste chasing up her throat.

"You know times are hard, don't you?" he said.

"We survive," she replied. "Many are much worse off."

"But the economic situation in this city isn't so good since they got rid of the schilling. The rent on this apartment. Food for the two of us. It's costing too much."

"What are you saying? This is our home, so what else can we do? If you want me to buy cheaper food I can try, but—"

He held up a silencing finger. "I know this is going to be difficult for you to accept, but I've been offered a transfer back to my old job in Linz."

"But . . . but . . ."

"And I've talked to my mother and father. They say we can live with them until we get settled and can afford a place of our own."

"But that's on the other side of the country."

"I know where it is, Giselle; I was born there. But why does the distance matter?"

"Well . . . what about my family?"

Kurt shrugged. "What about them? You've done without them for months, so you don't need to be so close to them. And they clearly don't need you."

Giselle went to speak but he held up that finger again.

"Let me finish. One other thing. You're lonely here, I know that. But if you lived with my parents and my younger sister it would be company for you. Doesn't that make sense?"

It did make sense, Giselle had to admit, but only for Kurt. Not for her. Never for her.

Her mind raced, hunting for some fragment of argument as to why she should stay in Vienna. "The neighbors," she blurted out. "I'll miss the neighbors if I leave here."

"Neighbors?" He laughed. "Who do you know? Come on, name them."

"Well, I . . . I don't know them by name."

"You'll meet new people in Linz." He lifted his chair and nudged himself closer to her, placing an arm around her shoulder, kissing her on the lips. "I promise you'll be fine." There were more kisses, and his spare hand caressed the back of her neck, slipping around to the front and undoing the top button of her blouse. "How about we . . . talk this over in bed?"

"Oh, I've prepared a meal for us. Aren't you hungry?"

Now he held her head tightly and gave her one of those hard, strong kisses that once up on a time had excited her. "Oh, I'm very hungry," he said. "But not for food."

She pushed him away. For once he accepted, although he grabbed her chin between thumb and forefinger, saying, "Ah, what's wrong now? Don't you love me anymore?"

"Kurt, I'm pregnant."

His whole body relaxed in an instant. "Oh," he said. "Well . . . are you sure?"

She nodded. "Two or three months."

"I see." He took a deep breath and let it out slowly through twitching, flared nostrils. "Mmm."

"Aren't you happy?"

"Of course I am, my darling, but . . . I'm afraid that settles things."

"What do you mean?"

"There's no way I'm bringing up my son or daughter in this city. Tomorrow you start packing. At the weekend we leave for Linz."

Giselle was unable to utter one word, her mind a haze of hot red, her throat as parched as sun-dried straw.

§

Klara had spent the last two months of the previous year trying to decide whether to flee Vienna.

Her stubborn nature prevailed. Alicia was right: running away would be letting the authorities win. So she and Felix stayed, fearful whenever they left home, watching and listening to the events unfolding week by week.

Klara and Felix often talked during their evening meals, but more often of late they simply listened to the radio broadcasts, because these were such worrying times. They'd learned that after capturing parts of Czechoslovakia last year, Germany had now taken over the rump of that country almost as easily as they'd walked into Austria. The next country on their list, apparently, was Poland, and Klara and Felix had listened with hope to news that Great Britain had assured Poland it would not allow Germany to do the same to that country.

But then, in early September, the unthinkable happened: both Germany and Russia invaded Poland, and despite armed resistance had quickly overrun the country.

Days after that news had broken, a scared Klara and a sullen Felix sat down to their usual meal, both more concerned with the news on the radio than the food in front of them. Because tonight, the news was that Great Britain and France had declared war on Germany.

"I don't quite understand," Klara asked Felix once the broadcast had finished. "Does that mean we're at war with Great Britain and France?"

"Mmm . . . yes. Perhaps. I don't know. I guess we're officially part of Greater Germany. Austrian troops fight in the name of the Third Reich. We can only hope that if those powers attack, then they target Germany and leave Austria alone."

Felix cut his slice of boiled potato in half and stuck his fork into one of the pieces, but before it reached his mouth Klara's cutlery clattered on the plate. She glared at him and shook her head.

"Did I say something wrong?"

"You keep using that word: hope. But do you know what, Felix? I'm so, so tired of simply *hoping* that the situation will improve. I helped you and Ludwig breathe life into the shoe repair shop after it had been smashed up by those mobs last November. I remember how sick I felt when I found out they'd stolen anything worth taking, shattered anything that could break, bent anything that couldn't, and painted horrible words and swastikas on the walls."

Felix let down his cutlery. "You think I've forgotten about that? I worked hard too. And I also remember how rebuilding the business itself was even harder work because of the lack of customers. But now we make some money to supplement our rations, don't we? And that's something to be proud of."

"Yes, and now Papa stays awake every night hoping those people don't smash it up again. Ludwig says he hopes people don't forget how long-lasting our shoe repairs are. And you keep saying you hope the business continues to bring in enough money so we don't have to rely on rations and begging for food. I can tell you this, Felix, I'm getting tired of relying on hope."

"Does that mean you've reconsidered leaving?"

Klara's mouth opened. But all she did was chew her lip.

"We can still go to Texas. We'll have none of these problems over there."

"I'm not so sure about that."

"We can build new lives for ourselves over there and—" Felix halted, mouth open, narrowing his eyes at Klara. "What did you just say?"

"Nothing. It was nothing."

"You said you're not so sure. What did you mean by that?"

"Forget I said it, Felix. Come on, let's eat. The vegetables are getting cold."

"Never mind the damned vegetables. Tell me . . ." He halted, put a hand to his forehead, let out a long sigh and massaged his temples for a few moments. "I'm sorry, forgive my anger, Klara. Please, do you know something? Or have you been talking to someone?"

"Well . . . no, really, I shouldn't have said anything."

Felix reached across the table and held her hand, squeezing it gently. "You can be honest with me, my love. I promise I won't be angry."

Klara's face contorted; a confused frown above uncertain eyes. "I had a conversation a few months ago while I was lining up to buy bread."

"What kind of conversation? An argument?"

She shook her head. "If you remember, you mentioned moving to America in January and I refused to talk about it, then you asked again in April and it erupted into a shouting match and I told you I never wanted to hear about it again. Well, it was the morning after that argument, and I struck up conversation with another woman, and I know I shouldn't have said anything, but so many thoughts were spinning around in my head that something had to come out, I couldn't help it."

"What are you saying? Just that you told someone you were thinking of moving there?" Felix shrugged. "You know I'd rather keep it quiet, but . . ."

"You don't understand, Felix. It isn't what I said to her, but what she said to me."

"I see. Go on."

"It turns out that this woman's nephew went to America a couple of years ago – to New York. He told her that Jews aren't always welcome over there – particularly in the southern states. And that confused me because you said Texas is in the south and they were nice people and we would be safe there. I don't want to think you're lying to me, but . . ."

"Mmm." Felix nodded thoughtfully.

"I'm confused, Felix. Is Texas really the pleasant place you say it is? I'm not sure I want to go there if the people are going to treat us like they do here."

"Now just hold on there."

"I think I'd rather—"

"I don't often tell you to shut up, Klara, but now you need to shut your mouth and listen."

Klara said nothing. Felix stood up and paced the room, his face reddening by the second. He drew breath and began wagging a finger at her, but no words came at first. Then he nodded, thoughts gathered, and spoke.

"Okay. Texas. Are there stores there that refuse to serve Jews? Well, that's happened to me twice in my lifetime, so I guess there are. Do people say unpleasant things about Jews? Occasionally, yes, I guess they do. And is Texas the most welcoming state for Jews? Probably not if I'm perfectly honest. But is the government happy to let people burn synagogues to the ground and smash up Jewish businesses? Do angry mobs force Jews to scrub the sidewalks while the police look on and do nothing? Do the government stop Jews marrying non-Jews? Do they fire thousands of people just for being Jewish? Do they deny Jews the vote?"

"Felix, I'm sorry, I—"

"Just hear me out, Klara. I'm sorry too, and I know it's not your fault, but it annoys me when people say things like that. And it annoys me because I'm a proud Jew and a proud Texan and a proud American. You see, you're allowed to be all three of those things over there. I know it's hard for you to understand the way things work in America, but people can say things I don't like, and guess what? *I can say things they don't like.* Because Americans have a thing called freedom, and hearing things you don't like is the price they pay for that freedom. Is it perfect? Hell, no. But is it anywhere near as dangerous as it is here? I guarantee it's in a different league. Almost everyone accepts Jews and we all get along just fine because we're all proud Texans and proud Americans. And I'm sorry for the lecture but Texas is my home and I love it and you need to know these things. You won't come over with me and see for yourself, so telling you is the next best thing."

"Oh, I know you're right, but it's still hard for me to leave Vienna because . . ."

"Your sister again, yes?"

Klara nodded.

"Mmm." Felix sat back down, picked up his knife and fork, and nodded for Klara to do the same. They both started eating. "I can understand you wanting Alicia to come over with you. I can't promise never to mention it again, but I won't bully you into anything. You know that, don't you?"

"I do, Felix, and I'm glad I married you."

A smile – all too rare in recent months – grew on Felix's face. "I'm glad you did too."

Klara was proud of Felix. He was a good man, decent enough to listen, caring enough to accept her decision. He was only human, and nobody could be expected to hold their tongue forever, but he had knuckled down and tried his best to make the business work, had done odd jobs on the side for people, and had gone out begging – anything to earn a few more of those new Reichsmarks that had replaced the Austrian schillings.

Felix had also been very understanding on the subject of fatherhood. The fact that Klara hadn't yet become pregnant had turned into the mystery that only once had they dared discuss.

Klara told him she was upset about the past, emotional about the present, fearful for the future, and worried every time she set foot outside. She also said she wasn't sleeping or eating properly. In short, she tried pretty much any excuse she could think of. He tried his best to put on a smile, kissed her softly, said it was hardly the most important thing to concern herself with in these difficult times, and that they had plenty of years left to start a family.

Other than on that occasion, whenever the subject came up it was dismissed by one of them saying, "it will happen eventually" or "as long as we keep trying" or "it's part of God's plan."

Klara had many things to worry about and few things worth hoping for. The most upsetting aspect of the past year was that despite her consistent refusal to move to America, she now realized she was wrong; the abuse in the streets and the cruel new laws and her despair at every news report had all, in time, brought her to that conclusion.

She'd always insisted she would go to America only if Alicia came too. But now Alicia was doggedly refusing to even discuss it, so Klara let Felix believe that the matter was closed. And it definitely wasn't.

During many sleepless nights, she cursed her own stubbornness – her short-sighted pride in always being right. And in her darkest moments, she prayed that Felix would try yet again to persuade her, or even would insist on leaving and force her to go with him.

In time, she came to accept that Felix was never going to do anything remotely as cavalier as that. She'd made her feelings plain, and he'd accepted her position on the subject.

Chapter Nine
1940

When Ludwig first started working at the shoe repair shop, Alicia would always ask polite questions on his return from work. "How was business today?" or, "How much did the shop take?" or even, "Did you meet anyone interesting today?"

Those days had now gone; she knew such questions would only infuriate him because he'd said so many times that it was hard work, that it was hardly worth going there considering what little money he made, and that he hated it but that there was nothing better to do. She also knew that the "little money" he brought home was actually important to them; it was the difference between starvation rations and something close to a basic lifestyle.

So these days, when he returned home, any words she wanted to utter would always lodge in her throat until she got a sense of his mood. He would, however, still give her a kiss on the cheek and ask whether the children were well. She appreciated that.

Today was typical. A tired expression weighed his face down, and after kissing her, he slumped into a chair and rested his head back, closing his worried eyes. Then came the hand exercises. Hands that were calloused caressed each other, bending tired fingers back slowly, then closing into fists. The ritual was repeated many times – a product of relentless manual labor. Alicia thought he should have been used to it by now, but didn't dare say such a thing.

"Are you well?" he eventually asked, opening his eyes just a fraction.

She nodded.

"The little treasures?"

"Asleep."

"I wish I didn't have to work so late." He let out a long yawn. "Did you have a visit from your sister today?"

He meant Klara; nobody had seen Giselle for over a year. It was as though the family had forgotten her – or were pretending they had.

"Did Felix tell you?"

"I've been stuck in that damned workshop with him all day. We had to talk about *something*."

Alicia took a moment to think about what to say next, trying hard not to look at his slouching form, trying not to think about how much weight he'd lost over the past year.

"You must be thirsty after working all day. I'll get you a cup of water."

"No." He lifted his head with a start and eyed the chair next to him. "Sit down. Please."

She did. He held her hand and the brushing of his callouses against her skin unnerved her; when they'd first met his hands had been strong but soft. He laid his head back again, eyes closed.

"I need to talk to you about Felix and your sister."

"Oh? What about them?"

"Felix is becoming more bitter by the month. He . . . he keeps asking why you and I refuse to go to America with him and Klara. Whatever I say, he won't let go of the subject."

"I find it hard to believe Felix is bitter. He's such a placid soul."

"Oh, he hides it well when he wants to, but you can only push a man so far. I was wondering . . ."

"What?"

"It sounds as if I'm trying to get rid of Felix, and I'm not; it's just that I fear for their marriage if he carries on like this."

"I'm guessing you want me to talk to Klara again about her and Felix leaving for America without us."

"You read me like a book, Alicia. Except that I had something a little more forceful in mind. I'd much prefer them happy in America than unhappy here, and you've expressed much the same feelings to me. I think you should tell her she has to go."

"Tell her? I couldn't do that."

"You're the oldest sister, as you keep saying. If anyone can tell her, you can. And it would be better for everyone concerned if they went and left us here. Unless, of course, you've changed your . . ."

Alicia was already shaking her head.

Ludwig held up a dusty hand. "I know. You can't leave your parents and Hugo. I'm sorry I mentioned it."

Alicia knelt down at Ludwig's feet and lay her head on his torso, hugging him, feeling his weary heart pulsing. She wanted to question him about Felix – to suggest perhaps he'd misinterpreted Felix's words – but there was no point in her pretending; the two men had come to know each other as well as brothers since working together.

"You realize that if I ask her, if I tell her to go, then we might never see them again?"

Ludwig caressed her, his hands stroking her hair with a gentleness that belied their gnarled appearance. "Could you accept that?" he asked.

"I want to do what's best for my sister. As you say, I'm the oldest and it's my job to care for the others. But even if she agrees, then it'll take some time, won't it?"

"Oh, Felix has every detail worked out, he often talks of it. They have to pay their permission money to the government, get the paperwork arranged, and then gather together the money for the journey."

"So it might be . . ." Alicia gulped back the tears. ". . . a matter of days or weeks?"

"Yes," he whispered hoarsely. "But we can meet up after . . . I mean, when this mess is all over." He groaned then breathed in through his nose, probably sniffing away a few tears of his own, Alicia thought, then said, "I'll miss them just as much as you will, but it's the right thing to do."

And Alicia could take no more. After balancing on the edge for so long she tipped over and convulsed in sobs of the pain she'd been trying so hard to contain, her mind a bitter blur of hatred, regret, conflicted loyalties and confusion. She was vaguely aware of hands on her shoulders, a head gently touching hers, but no words. Ludwig clearly knew that no words would help. He gave her a handkerchief, and although it took a while, the tears stopped coming.

"I know it's difficult for you, Alicia."

"You don't, Ludwig. I love you more than anything, but I can't expect you to understand what you're asking me to do. The last time I spoke with her, she begged that we should all go together – you, me, our children, my parents and my brother. I had to tell her that was impossible. I keep thinking she's right and we should go, but I always end up telling myself it's the wrong thing to do, that the practicalities are against us. We can't afford our own passage – the four of us – let alone the fee we have to pay the government to leave, and also the same for Mama, Papa, and Hugo. We simply don't have that kind of money – even if Klara and Felix were to help us. And, of course, it's only fair to consider your parents and Giselle."

"Giselle? Don't you think she's happy and safe with Kurt?"

Alicia shrugged. "That's just it. I don't know. I already told you what happened a couple of months ago: I walked all the way over to Margareten only to find that someone else is now renting their apartment, and Kurt had told them not to tell anyone where they'd gone. And Giselle didn't even tell any of us that she was moving. That's worrying enough, but I dread to think what would happen if we went to America; I would never see her again and I can't bear that thought. It's all too complicated, Ludwig. It's too much to think about and I can't cope with it."

"But if we went – just you, me and the children, and your parents stayed where they are now, then at least you'd know Giselle wouldn't be alone. You could write your Mama and she could tell you Giselle's new address when she gets it and—"

"No, Ludwig, no!" She shook her head violently. "There's no way I'm leaving Mama, Papa, and Hugo to fend for themselves against these monsters. I won't do it. I *won't!*"

"All right, all right. I was only asking."

"Well, don't. But I do agree with you about Klara. I promise I'll talk to her; I'll tell her she and Felix should leave Vienna without us. I'll stress to her that we can stay in touch, and that if our situation gets desperate, we can always change our minds. And who knows, the situation here could improve."

"Mmm."

"What do you mean by that? Have you heard something?"

"Improvement isn't impossible, but people are saying . . ."

"What, Ludwig? What are people saying?"

"Well, Germany is getting stronger, not weaker. They've taken Belgium, the Netherlands, Denmark, most of Norway, and now the rumor is that Italy will side with them. And while Germany is strong, we all know they will gradually apply more German laws here. Did you know that Jews over there must wear yellow stars sewn into their clothing when in public? Can you imagine that here?"

"Let's hope that never happens," Alicia said, looking up to Ludwig. "Isn't there always hope?"

Ludwig smiled, but his eyes were blank and lifeless. "Yes," he said without even a trace of enthusiasm. "Of course there is."

§

A heavily pregnant Giselle left Kurt's parent's house, crossed the road, and started walking through the meadow, pacing herself.

She treasured this walk; it was ever present, didn't threaten, didn't question. Even in her condition, it was a wondrous experience. Ahead of her was a dazzling blend of white, yellow, red, and violet wildflowers. A small area of woodland ran along on her right, verdant pastures spread out along the valley below to the left, with wooded hills on the other side. It always soothed. It was a walk that had become her friend over the past few months. Perhaps her only friend.

Today she couldn't walk too far due to backache, so she settled down on her favorite spot: a hillock that served as a natural viewing platform. There, she soaked up the sun, absorbing the view of the meadow almost flowing in front of her. Then she cast a glance back toward the house and saw the flag flying above the front door. She remembered – with the indulgence of just a little self-pity – the first time she'd seen it, almost six months ago, when that simple rectangle of dyed cloth fluttering in the wind had set her nerves on edge.

With most of their possessions traveling separately, Giselle and Kurt had just endured the two-hour journey along the railroad that seemed to entwine itself with the Danube, and were approaching his parents' house, a suitcase in each hand, when Giselle stopped, staring upward, mouth agape. It took Kurt two or three more paces to realize he was walking alone.

"Why have you stopped?" he said.

Giselle said nothing, just continued staring up. Kurt looked too.

"The flag?" he said, puzzled.

It was only one word, but one that frightened and confused Giselle at that moment. It was high above her, at the end of a tall flagpole, fluttering in the chilling breeze. It boasted a solid blood-red background, a pure white circle, and a dark black swastika. She'd seen the symbol a thousand times in Vienna, so it shouldn't have shocked her. But it wasn't the welcome she expected.

"So what?" he said. "It's not as if you haven't seen one before. Come on." He grabbed her upper arm with his spare hand and pulled her. "Most houses around here have them."

Still, she stared. "There was no flag last time I came here."

"*Giselle! Move!*"

She said nothing, just followed as Kurt pulled her toward the front door.

She'd met his family just once, and been told not to mention or even imply that she was a Jewess. On that occasion it had been easy; a few hours, some polite conversation about what everyone did for a living, about how many brothers and sisters Giselle had, and about the relative merits of living in Vienna and Linz. Giselle knew this was going to be much harder; she was now going to be *living* with them.

His parents – both still quite stocky and looking as healthy as they had been on Giselle's last visit – were very welcoming, taking her suitcases up to the bedroom and offering her coffee or wine, both of which she refused on account of feeling queasy after the journey.

I'm so pleased to have you living with us," Frau Hinkel said, rubbing her hands on her apron with an excitement Giselle found uncomfortable.

"And we're both very grateful," Kurt said. "Aren't we, Giselle?"

It took a moment for Giselle to react. "Oh, yes," she said. "It's very kind of you."

"I've been looking forward to it so much," his mother continued. "Having another woman around the house is a good thing, but as it's my daughter-in-law it's going to be wonderful. When Kurt told us you'd married in secret because you didn't want any fuss, I was so disappointed, but now we can get to know each other properly, can't we?"

"Of course."

"Do you cook, my dear?"

"I try," Giselle replied, her mind squirming with thoughts of what they would or wouldn't consider typical Jewish food.

And while Kurt's mother reeled off a list of her house specialties, it occurred to Giselle that perhaps all of this deception was a bad idea, that perhaps she should calmly explain that she came from a Jewish family and offer to leave and return to Vienna if they objected to her staying in this house.

But if she did that, where would she go? And how would Kurt react? She decided to say nothing just for now and talk the subject over later with Kurt.

"We have some news," Kurt said once his mother had exhausted her repertoire of recipes.

"News?" his father said.

Kurt held Giselle's hand and tilted his chin up proudly. "We're expecting our first child."

That was the cue for his parents to come even closer – far too close for Giselle's liking – but at least she couldn't fault their enthusiasm and the hugs and kisses made her feel welcome despite the distasteful backdrop to the pretty picture they painted for her. For a few moments it occurred to her that perhaps she might be happy here after all.

"Would you prefer a boy or a girl?" Herr Hinkel said.

"I'm hoping for a son," Kurt said.

They all looked at Giselle, waiting for her opinion.

"I, uh . . . I don't mind," she said, trying to smile.

She was about to speak again – to say she could see advantages in both, so either would do as long as he or she was healthy – when they all heard the front door open.

"That'll be Petra," Frau Hinkel said, her eyes aglow with excitement.

Kurt had talked only a little about his young sister, how they used to tease each other as children but didn't have much to do with each other as adults.

Then the door to the living room opened and Petra walked in. She rested a tall flagpole on the wall, it's familiar flag limp, but still recognizable to all. She removed her jacket, replete with swastika armband.

"How was the rally today, my dear?" her father asked.

"Very good," she replied, nodding. "More people than last time."

"I'm sorry I couldn't come with you, but I was welcoming Kurt's new wife."

Petra turned to Giselle, looking her up and down. "His new wife?" she said. "What happened to the old one?"

Kurt and his father laughed.

His mother didn't, but she did smile and didn't try to disguise it. "Ignore them," she said. She tapped Giselle on the knee. "Are you a member, by the way?"

"A member?" Giselle asked.

"The party. The NSDAP."

Those letters. Giselle instantly knew. In an independent Austria it had once been the DNSAP, but had been subsumed into the German equivalent. Either way, it celebrated and promoted the National Socialist cause.

She hesitated to answer, which was answer enough.

"But you should join. We're all members in this household."

"You support Adolf Hitler?" Giselle asked.

Kurt coughed. It was a loud and raucous cough clearly designed to distract.

"I was only asking," Klara said.

"But it's an unfair question, my darling. We support *the party*, not Herr Hitler himself."

"You too?" Giselle said, her heart now fluttering.

"You didn't tell her?" Kurt's mother asked him.

"I didn't think it was important," he replied. "A man's politics is his own affair, besides which, it's hardly unusual, is it?"

"Quite normal around here," Herr Hinkel said. "Although plenty of Austrians are yet to be convinced."

"Convinced?" Giselle took a gulp, conscious of the tremble in her voice. "So ... so you agree with how the government is treating the Jewish population?"

"It's not as simple as that. Why do people concentrate on the Jewish question? We all need to see the wider picture. Look what Hitler has done for the German nation – a country, like Austria, broken to pieces and humiliated after the Great War, with weak politicians squabbling over what to do but with no real strategy. Now it's productive, the people are healthier and better off, the government is seen as strong on the world stage. I tell you, that man has galvanized that country, made it a place to be proud of. All we want is for him to do the same for Austria."

"And the Jews?" Giselle said.

"Well ..." He huffed and puffed for a few seconds. "... I guess the problem is that Austrians are Germanic people at heart and the Jew ... well, he isn't. He always has his own agenda, which is to help other Jews and nobody else. These people are Jewish first and German or Austrian second if at all."

"The Jew doesn't belong here," Petra chimed in.

"So where do they belong?" Giselle asked.

Petra shrugged. "That's not a problem for the Germanic people to solve."

"The Jew will be fine," Herr Hinkel said. "The Jew always survives one way or another. Jews in this country have had everything their own way for far too long, and it's time other people were given a chance to run the show."

"Do you know any Jews, my dear?" Frau Hinkel asked Giselle. "There are rather a lot of them in Vienna, so I hear."

"I . . . well . . ."

Giselle's throat locked. Images galloped through her mind. She saw her family – the family she hadn't been terribly kind to in the past. In her mind's eye they were wagging their fingers admonishingly at her.

"Giselle?" Kurt said. "My mother asked you a question."

"I . . . uh." She lowered her gaze to the floor. "No, I don't know any Jews."

"Lucky you," Petra said. "So, why are you concerned about them?"

"I never said I was," Giselle replied.

"By God, Kurt." Herr Hinkel casually pointed a thumb in Giselle's direction. "You've hooked a feisty one here, haven't you?"

Giselle, catching a sharp look from her husband, said, "I'm sorry, Herr Hinkel. I'm talking too much because I'm nervous."

He offered her a cheerful laugh, his belly quivering. "I understand, my dear, but in time you'll see what good Hitler can do. In the meantime, perhaps you should leave the politics to the men."

Kurt joined his father in smiling, and turned to Giselle, saying, "I didn't know you were so political either."

"I'm not," she replied quickly.

It was only then that she realized what she'd done, how she'd argued for her family's sake. Kurt was right, it was probably the first time in her life she'd expressed strong political beliefs.

She got to her feet. "Will you excuse me? I think I need some fresh air."

"I'll come with you," Kurt said.

She shook her head. "That's okay, darling. You catch up with your family. I've a headache I need to get rid of."

A few minutes later Giselle had crossed the road and was striding straight ahead through the meadow. The tears had started the moment she'd set foot outside of the house. She turned back to look, but her vision was blurred by sorrow, so she couldn't quite make out the flag outside the house waving at her.

That was a blessing of sorts.

She found a hillock with a particularly beautiful view of the meadow, and let the tears flow.

She'd come to Linz not knowing a soul except Kurt, expecting her first child, and surrounded by the paraphernalia of an ideology that numbed her senses and threatened her existence.

After that inauspicious arrival, it took only a month for the arguments with Kurt to start. They would normally be ignited by her being unable to hold her tongue when he was preening himself in the mirror.

"Are you going somewhere?" she would typically ask.

He would usually sigh, his shoulders would drop an inch, and he would glare as he said something like, "I'm just meeting a few friends" or, "I can't stay in this house every night" or, just lately, "No, I've dressed like this to dig up the garden."

And it would ratchet up from there. She would say she was carrying his child just in case he hadn't noticed, he would say that he could hardly fail to notice but that they didn't have to spend every waking hour together, that he wasn't doing any harm, and that she could come along if she really, really wanted to.

And just to call his bluff, on one occasion she did. But in the beer-soaked atmosphere of a local tavern she was probably the only female customer – definitely the only pregnant one – and it turned out to be such a horrible experience of sweat and masculine boastfulness that she insisted on leaving after ten minutes. To his credit, Kurt, in turn, insisted on walking her home and stayed with her, although he didn't talk to her for the rest of that evening.

And now, almost six months after arriving, here she was again, sitting on exactly the same hillock. The view had changed with the seasons, but Giselle had changed much more. She'd started doing something she never thought she would do: listening to political radio broadcasts and reading newspapers. She was *taking an interest,* as Papa had once said she should. She often had the urge to get involved in discussions, although she had to bite her tongue to avoid dangerous arguments that might give away her background.

Yes, Giselle had changed. However, the biggest change in her was yet to come. She laid a hand upon her distended belly, unsure and afraid of the world she was bringing life into.

§

Klara lay back in bed with Felix one morning, her hand clamped firmly around his.

Making love was out of the question, and would be until the demon of regret raging around her mind was freed. And there was only one way that could happen.

It was always going to be hard for her to put her pride to one side and tell Felix that perhaps, in the light of the way Austria was changing, leaving was the best thing to do, that she'd now had more than enough time to think it over. And she *had* thought it over. She'd thought of the loss of employment, the random acts of violence, the many Jewish community leaders who had suddenly disappeared never to be seen again, the "scrubbing parties" as they had come to be known, and, most importantly, the international situation that seemed to hold no prospect of any other country standing up to Germany in any tangible way.

Her mind had been flipping one way and then the other for months, but a few days ago, while Felix was at work, Alicia had turned up and talked to her – had *told* her that she and Felix should leave for their own safety. That had made up her mind. But even then, it took a few days of deliberation to decide on the right moment to tell Felix and how to word it.

One afternoon, while Felix was at work, she rehearsed what she was going to say that evening, still not completely sure she was doing the right thing.

In the event, none of her planning helped. Despite her skills with explanations and negotiations, all she could do was speak the words plainly as they sat down to eat.

"I've been thinking," she said. "Thinking an awful lot."

"Oh?"

"And you're right. We should ..." Palpitations threatened to overwhelm her. She took a long breath. "We should leave for America. Just the two of us."

There. It was said. She immediately felt woozy with relief.

"What?" he said. "Are you ... are you joking? I mean, for heaven's sake."

"But I thought you'd be pleased."

His knife and fork clattered onto the plate. Klara let hers lay idle too as he gesticulated wildly, his words coming out slowly.

"But why?" he said, glaring at her. "I mean, why *now*? Why not last year or a few months ago?"

"Because I ... I don't know, because I was scared. You know what America's like; I don't. I've never been abroad in my life."

"You're scared of America but you aren't scared of what's going on all around us in Vienna? In Austria? In the *whole of Europe*, for God's sake?"

"I've admitted I was wrong, Felix, and I'm sorry, but—"

"Oh, you were wrong. You were *very* wrong. All this time, we could have been gone a year or more. We might have been settled there by now, safely away from all this danger and rebuilding new lives for ourselves."

"Please, Felix, don't make me feel bad, don't keep making me apologize."

"I don't want your apologies. I just want . . . oh, I just wish we could turn the clock back."

"And it need only be for a short time."

He shook his head. "Oh, Klara. It's a long way. We can visit here, for sure, but I don't want to mislead you. We won't be able to hop back and forth."

"But my friends, my families, my history – my whole life – all belong to Vienna and always will."

"I know that. How many times have we had this argument? I feel like Vienna's my home too and I'll miss the place, but we can't deny the fact that every time one of us goes out that door we fear for our lives. We need to get the hell out of here while we still can."

Klara let her head drop, one hand massaging her brow. "I know all that, Felix. But it doesn't stop me being scared of leaving it all behind."

Felix let out a long sigh. Neither of them spoke for what felt like an hour. Eventually Felix reached out and held her hand. "Oh, I'm sorry, Klara. I guess I'm not in your position. I wasn't born here like you. I, uh . . . I over-reacted. It was just a shock to hear you say that, and I'm sorry."

"I understand," she whispered.

"And I'm grateful you had the courage to say it. I feel happy. I really do."

She squeezed his hand. "Let's carry on eating while we talk. It's not right to let food go to waste."

"Of course. And you won't regret this, Klara. I know you won't. I told you that life would be good in Texas, and it will be.

I've always promised you that one day we'll come back to Vienna, and we will."

"Are you sure about the work?"

"Like I always said, if I can't get hospital work I'll help out on Pa's farm and he'll support us. Anything has to be better than what we have here."

She wiped her eyes, then nodded. "Now I've said it, I feel happier. I'm not changing my mind again. I've had enough of Vienna. Let's go. Please, Felix. Let's go as soon as we can."

Saying goodbye to Alicia, Ludwig and their two small children was hard – a tear-filled affair on all sides.

Breaking the news to Mama and Papa was harder – if only because they both pretended they were pleased she was going somewhere safe. The fact that they asked for nothing in the way of explanation or excuses or reasoning should have made it easier for her to take. But no, it broke her heart to see them both blinking away the tears and wiping the wetness away when they thought she wasn't looking. Like all caring parents, they were both accomplished liars and deceivers; just not quite good enough on this occasion.

She assumed Hugo wasn't going to understand, that he would be incapable of doing so. She was wrong. Unable to speak properly or write, his thoughts would be forever trapped in that prison of a mind of his, but somehow the solemnity of the occasion got through to him. His arms – under only a rudimentary form of control but as strong as any man's his age – appeared to get the message that this might be his last ever contact with her. He held onto her until Papa suggested he let her breathe, then let go and stared at her as if he knew something she didn't. And just when Klara's tears were about to breach the banks, just as she thought she had her emotions under control, he aimed a shaky arm at her and tapped her nose with his wandering fingers. It was a completely inappropriate gesture, it touched Klara's heart, and she started to cry.

She would miss Hugo's sense of fun.

But hardest of all was Giselle. Nobody had seen her or heard from her in such a long time. They talked to Rabbi Benisch, the police, even her old schoolfriends and the people who now lived at their old apartment in Margareten. In desperation and with great trepidation and heavy hearts they even enquired at the mortuary, and were relieved to find no record of her there.

Klara insisted there was no way she could leave Vienna until she'd tracked Giselle down and told her she still loved her and would see her again one day, but after five days of searching, her insistence had to yield to reality: if Giselle had any intention of being found, it would have happened by now.

Klara and Felix left Vienna with no fanfare, no tearful farewell, and no fuss, reaching San Antonio, Texas almost three weeks later.

She'd been quiet and reflective throughout the endless journey – deliberately so to keep thoughts of loneliness and fear to herself – but as she was being driven through streets devoid of swastika flags, she dared to dream of a happier life. Here there would be nobody telling her to scrub the sidewalks, no random arrests, no wrecked and burned-out synagogues, no visits from police in the middle of the night leading to disappearances.

They soon reached the family ranch just outside of city limits. Just as Felix had described, it had a low-slung roof, was wide, and stretched back some distance too. All windows had shutters, those on the sun-side were closed, and along the front – again just as Felix had told her – it boasted a slightly raised porch with a swing bench and a wicker lounger.

The front door was not only unlocked but left wide open. Moments later Klara told herself to hold back while Felix met the mother, father and brother he hadn't seen in over five years. There would be a language barrier to overcome, but Felix's family were so welcoming that she relished learning English if only to be able to talk with them.

As they all sat and the family continued talking in English, with Felix occasionally translating to keep Klara involved, she succumbed and nodded off to sleep in her chair. Soon, she felt herself being picked up and carried to the far end of the ranch. She stirred a little more as she was settled between cool cotton bedsheets, and then felt Felix's warm body next to hers.

"Go back," she said. "Catch up on the news with your family while I sleep."

"No," he said. "I told you on the journey I'll stay by your side for the first few days, and I will; anything else wouldn't be fair." He yawned – a forced one, Klara thought, which made her smile inside. "Besides," he continued, "I'm every bit as tired as you are."

They lay back in bed together, her hand firmly clamped around his, but her grip very quickly loosened as she started to drift off to sleep again. She was in a house, a city, a whole country that felt alien to her. But she was with the man she loved, and knew her feelings were reciprocated, so she knew she would sleep better than she had done for years.

Sometimes the full weight of a burden only becomes apparent once it's lifted. Klara – however lonely she felt and however much she would miss Vienna and her family – had just lost a lot of weight off of her shoulders.

She slept soundly until late the next morning.

Chapter Ten
1941

By the summer of 1941, Alicia, Ludwig, and their two bewildered children had twice been forcibly moved to other properties within Leopoldstadt, first because the owner had suddenly decided he no longer wanted Jews as tenants, and then because the Vienna authorities were reallocating their block to "Aryans."

On that second occasion, they were forced into the same apartment as Mama, Papa, and Hugo. They had originally been allocated a slightly larger room on the second floor with absolutely no regard for the practicalities, but a small family at ground level took pity on Papa's predicament and swapped so he would have no stairs to climb. That family also got a larger apartment, so Alicia and the rest of them had to share what was effectively a single room intended for a couple with one child, with a kitchen area at one end and a communal latrine down the corridor. Bathing had become a real problem since Jews had been prohibited from using the local public baths that most Viennese relied upon for washing facilities, which only added to the embarrassment of seven people living in such close quarters.

But beyond those six relations who lived in Alicia's pockets, she hardly knew anyone in the immediate neighborhood. More importantly, she'd completely lost contact with both her sisters. She now hadn't seen Giselle for two years, and had no idea whether she'd written during that time because they'd moved twice and Alicia was sure the new tenants wouldn't pass on any mail. It was a similar story with Klara and Felix; she'd asked Klara to write to let her know they'd arrived safely in America, but either she hadn't written or her letter hadn't been forwarded, leaving Alicia to merely *assume* that all was well, whereas she longed to know for certain. But the biggest tragedy was that Felix had given her the address of his family ranch, but the note had gotten lost somewhere in the two moves she'd been forced to undertake.

All her friends and old neighbors had either emigrated or been removed in one of the many purges of Jews. Entire families that had once had strong ties with the Rosenthals or Ludwig were long gone – to where, people could only guess. All Alicia knew was that she was grateful she hadn't gone with them. And the only reason they hadn't gone was that the authorities had reluctantly given them special dispensation due to Papa and Hugo. For years their condition had been a burden, but now it bestowed a privilege of sorts, albeit it a rather distasteful one.

So there was the isolation and yet also a kind of claustrophobia. It was funny, Alicia thought in one of her more uninhibited moments. She'd never felt lonelier, and yet at the same time she'd never felt so in need of more privacy. Of course, she would never dare voice that sentiment, never hint at humor.

Even the shoe repair shop – which Papa had founded and had once employed him, Klara, Ludwig, and Felix – was now out of bounds. First it had been sequestered by the authorities, who paid the workers a pittance. Then, within a short space of time, Klara and Felix had left for America, and Papa and Ludwig had been moved too far away to reach it.

More changes came later in the year – changes that although subtle, were more worrying.

The family had just been to one of the many soup kitchens that had sprung up to feed those unable to survive by their own means. There, while the rest ate, Ludwig talked to one of the men serving the soup. He returned to eat, while Alicia continued feeding the children. But she quickly knew something was wrong; Ludwig was too quiet.

Back in the relative privacy of their home, Alicia asked him who the man serving soup was.

"Just someone I used to know," he replied.

"From where?"

"Oh, it doesn't matter."

"It looked like it mattered to you."

"Oh . . ." Ludwig huffed and puffed for a few seconds.

"Please, Ludwig. Tell me what you talked about. I'm interested."

"Yes. I might as well. He was a surgeon at the hospital. He's a very skilled and educated man who is now reduced to serving up soup. He joked that the ladle is now the tool of his trade. But he wasn't laughing; I could sense the tears he was holding onto."

"You were talking to him about surgery?" asked Mama, who couldn't help but hear the conversation.

Ludwig glanced around the room, at Alicia, their children, her parents, and brother. "No, we were talking about . . ." He let out a gasp and shook his head.

"What is it?" Alicia said. She could see his lower lip trembling, so sat down next to him and held his hand.

"What's happened now?" Papa said.

Ludwig wiped away a solitary tear that had escaped his eye and was running down his cheek. "They've thought up something else," he said. "You know, I feel sure they have a department – a bunch of funny men whose sole job is to think up new ways to humiliate us."

"What do you mean?" Papa said.

"Well, they've banned us from the public baths and the coffee shops, stopped us owning our own businesses, taken away our driving licenses, given us lower rations and restricted the times we can visit the stores."

"I'm not sure what else they can do to us," Mama said.

"Well, they clearly have more imagination than you or me," Ludwig said. "There is a new law. Now we are officially prohibited from using public transport; we have to walk everywhere."

"I don't wish to steal your thunder," Papa said, turning his wheelchair so that he faced the only window in the room, "but we rarely go anywhere. We go to the soup kitchen, the grocery store during the hours they allow us to. We don't even visit the old workshop since they snatched it from under us. I have to admit – and it pains me to say it – but I'm losing the ability to care."

"That's not the main new law," Ludwig said.

"What else can they do?" Alicia asked.

"Well . . ." Ludwig laughed, shaking his head, despair apparent in his eyes. "From now on, just like in Germany, we all have to sew yellow stars onto our clothes and display them whenever we're in public, just in case people don't realize we're Jews by the fact that we stink and our bodies are wasting away."

"What?" Alicia exclaimed.

But no reply was needed. Alicia and her mama and papa were silenced. Ludwig, however, let out another laugh. Hugo, who until now had been sitting on the floor patiently listening but not having a clue what was happening, started laughing along with him. The sight made Ludwig laugh even more.

"Why are you laughing?" Mama asked in a strident, scolding manner.

"I'm sorry," he replied. "It's just that, well, these stars that we have to wear . . . you see, someone, somewhere has decided that we have to buy them with our own money. I'm sorry, but I just find that funny."

He started to laugh again, but soon let his face fall into the palms of his hands, and Alicia heard sobbing, not laughter.

Alicia put an arm around his shoulder. There was nothing else she could do.

§

For Giselle, the changes had come thick and fast, and she was certain they were not yet over.

That threatening flag still fluttered above the house she now called home. Kurt's family still held the same beliefs. And the government pressed ahead with its plans.

But Kurt had changed; he was at the very least trying to be a better man. His baby boy was now almost a year old. Whether it was due only to fatherhood or some deeper change, Giselle didn't quite know, but he was gentler with her, kept asking if she was warm enough or hungry, pulled her coat around her and buttoned it in inclement weather. More importantly, he was quick to defend her in front of his family. Indeed, if before, sides had occasionally been taken in a discussion and it had felt like four against one, it now felt more like three against two.

And now, as if Giselle were gaining more ground in a battle, Frau Hinkel was more often than not also a useful ally.

Frau Hinkel was the closest thing Giselle had to a mother, and although she felt hurt and confused to admit it, the woman's experience had helped her cope with the sleepless nights, the feeding, the diaper changes and her own physical recovery so much that she almost felt like calling her *Mama*. They would talk about the best ways to feed and wind babies, and Frau Hinkel would reminisce fondly about her own experiences with Kurt and Petra during days that, she said, were the best of her life.

While still pregnant, Giselle had considered writing to Alicia or her mother, but feared a return letter could reveal her cover – her *family background*, as she and Kurt had started to refer to it as. And she figured that simply advising them she was well and pregnant but telling them not to write back – or even not giving a return address – would only alarm them. So, having just adapted to the idea that she only had Kurt to cling to, she now often found even that shred of security taken from her. Kurt's sister was consistently poisonous, his father plain insensitive, and it was left to his mother – who had clearly heard one or two of her arguments with Kurt – to show that there was at least a little empathy within the Hinkel family.

That was never more clearly demonstrated than on the morning Giselle was alone in bed and Frau Hinkel knocked on the door, saying she wanted to have a woman-to-woman talk.

Giselle's belly was fit to burst at the time, and she was hardly sleeping, so talking to Frau Hinkel wasn't high on her list of priorities.

"I feel I should apologize for Kurt," Frau Hinkel said in a whispered tone. "No man is perfect, and us women always find that out when we are in your condition, but I want to assure you that Kurt is a better man at heart than he appears to be."

Giselle considered arguing the point. The woman obviously didn't know her son as well as she thought she did. However, she bit her tongue; it wasn't worth alienating the person who had by far shown her the most kindness.

"I was thinking," Frau Hinkel continued. "What about your mother?"

Giselle gave the only reply she could think of, which was, "I'm sure she's well, thank you."

Frau Hinkel laughed softly. "No, no. I mean, surely you'd like her to see you at this important time?"

"Oh, I'm afraid my parents couldn't afford the train fare to Linz, let alone a hotel to stay in."

The woman nodded thoughtfully. "I've noticed that you haven't even received any letters from them."

"I told them not to write," Giselle snapped, immediately regretting it.

"What? You told them not to write? Why would you do that?"

"It . . . it would upset me even more because I miss them so much."

Frau Hinkel nodded once more and said, "Okay," but thankfully didn't pry any further.

So it was clear to Giselle that this woman possessed tact and consideration as well as empathy. It was a fact most ably demonstrated two days later – on the most momentous day of Giselle's life.

Petra had just returned from a march and a casual comment about Vienna sparked debate over the dinner table – despite Frau Hinkel's insistence that politics and dinner shouldn't mix.

Petra peered at Giselle and said, "The news is that your city is being cleansed."

"Cleansed?" Giselle asked, thoughts of hygiene and tidying running through her mind.

"Of *Jews*," Herr Hinkel said, intoning the second word as if what Petra had meant should have been obvious.

Giselle hesitated. *Did she dare ask for more information?* She'd been too frightened to even contact her family in Vienna, let alone tell the Hinkels the truth about them. She could only glance at Kurt, pleading for help.

"What are the authorities doing with these Jews?" he casually asked.

"I don't think anybody cares," Petra replied.

"But they must be sending them *somewhere*," Giselle said.

It was Petra's turn to ask for help, from her father, who eagerly obliged.

"I think you're focusing on the wrong issue," he said to Giselle. "The important point here is that the Jews have brought all their problems upon themselves, and, let's be honest, they don't deserve such a beautiful place as Vienna. Do you see?"

Giselle felt forced to nod agreement. She was about to give birth and life was – physically, at least – comfortable compared to what might have been. She was starting to become a part of the Hinkel family, and any alternative was unthinkable for the foreseeable future.

"Could we change the subject?" Frau Hinkel said.

It was a perceptive and thoughtful intervention. She obviously could see the discomfort on Giselle's face.

Herr Hinkel, however, had the aura of a dog that had caught a rabbit and wouldn't let go.

"Do I sense a little sympathy for the Jew?" he asked Giselle bluntly, staring straight at her.

So many words squirmed around on Giselle's tongue – about them only being human, about how much they'd brought to society, about the musicians and artists who'd entertained all citizens, the medical professionals who'd saved lives, and the teachers who'd enlightened both Jews and Gentiles alike. But before she could get any of these words out, Herr Hinkel spoke again.

"There's nothing wrong with having sympathy," he said. "But you have to have a sense of proportion. You can tell from a distance that the Jew is clearly only a sub-human species. I mean, I have sympathy with rats that find their way into our cellar. I have sympathy, of course I do, but that sympathy ends at the flat end of my shovel. Jews aren't much different. You do understand, don't you, Giselle?"

Giselle could feel her head starting to spin, acid bittering the back of her throat. All she could do was nod in agreement.

"So, you agree?" Petra asked.

Giselle took a gasp of air. "Oh, yes," she said. "As your father says, the Jew is a . . . a sub-species."

"That's enough," Frau Hinkel said to her daughter and husband.

She was ignored.

While Giselle took more gulps of air, Herr Hinkel continued, "And I've absolutely no doubt that our government is doing the right thing in trying to give non-Jews what they also deserve: a chance to get on and have good jobs and money. And in the end . . ."

Giselle heard no more. The spinning sensation in her head hadn't abated, but now started to get worse. She could feel sweat beading on her brow but felt cold and weak yet also somehow energized. The numb ache in her lower back – a constant companion for months – reached a higher level within minutes. She cried out in pain.

Frau Hinkel sprang into action, telling her husband to shut up then telling Kurt to call a doctor.

The next day, Giselle was mother to a healthy baby boy.

Kurt's behavior continued to improve. It had taken longer than Giselle would have wanted, but being a father changed him for the better. He stopped going to the local taverns with his old friends, stayed with Giselle when not working, kept asking how she was and whether she needed anything, intervened when he thought his father or sister were badgering her about Jews, and, most importantly, the arguments between them all but stopped.

But no sooner had Giselle dared to dream of a brighter future for her family than Kurt received a very official looking letter.

He was being called up to serve as a soldier in the Wehrmacht.

"It's funny," he said soon after that, when more letters detailing his instructions came through, "I have no idea where I'll end up, but my first step is to report to Vienna."

Giselle found no fragment of amusement in the situation. When her baby boy was three months old, Kurt left for Vienna, and she was more alone than she ever had been in her life. Although Frau Hinkel tried her best, there was no family to share her joy, only people she lived with – from whom she would always feel detached and isolated. Moreover, because of her secret, the possibility of harm to her and her baby was never too far from her thoughts. Risks to her own life had never bothered her too much; but now, worries about the safety of her baby often kept her awake at night.

Giselle had never thought of herself as the maternal type, but now she was quite prepared to kill anyone who harmed her baby.

§

Klara had never thought of herself as the worrying type; there seemed no point, it was such a waste of effort. And as far as she knew, nobody else had thought of her in those terms either – especially her sisters. Alicia had always treated her as if she were the brains of the family: balanced and knowledgeable, whereas Giselle had always treated her as though she was staid and boring. Then again, Giselle had usually referred to pretty much everyone else as boring, so Klara could hardly take that as a serious indictment of her character.

But now she felt very different; the mental tug of worry was ever-present. Since arriving in Texas, she'd sent three letters to her parents and also two to Alicia at their last addresses in Leopoldstadt, but she hadn't heard back once. Either the letters had gotten lost and hadn't reached the addresses, or Alicia and her parents had moved on – or *had been moved* on. So the question she'd asked Alicia – whether she'd heard anything from Giselle – was rendered pointless; her guess was that each sister had lost contact with the other two.

Felix's parents were as accommodating as anyone could be; they even insisted Klara call them Ma and Pa, but she missed her family back in Vienna and nothing would ever take their place. She wondered whether a little research might give her some idea of what had happened to them, and concluded that yes, it might calm her nerves, but in a foreign country such research was easier said than done.

By the middle of 1941 her spoken English had come on well, encouraged by the ever-supportive Felix, and helped by his parents and Larry, his here-today, gone-tomorrow kid brother. Larry looked very much like Felix – the same lean frame, the same oval face, the same fair to reddish hair. They might have passed for twins were it not for Larry's extra couple of inches in height. Larry also didn't wear glasses and his hair was longer, almost scruffy, whereas Felix's hair was always neat and short. The other big difference was Larry's accent, obviously purer Texas than that of the more educated and well-travelled Felix. Accent or not, Larry was good for her English as he had plenty of free time and didn't speak a word of German. So her spoken English was coming on well. However, *reading* it was another skill entirely, especially trawling through the politics and international sections of newspapers.

She wondered whether Larry might be able to help her in that regard.

When Klara had originally asked Felix what his brother did for a living, the reply was that he wasn't sure what the word was in German but in English it was "bum." He said the word with a broad smile and a laugh, so Klara knew that whatever it meant, there was no animosity between the two brothers. And while Felix went off with Pa most days to work on the far and wild reaches of the ranch mending fences and checking on their cattle, Larry either stayed at home flicking through newspapers or whittling wood, or met up with what he called his "pals" for a few beers and lots of talk. In time it became clear what Felix had meant: Larry wasn't exactly lazy, but had no great ambition to do anything particularly constructive or onerous and worked toward that goal with the utmost dedication.

It did, however, make it easy for Klara to talk to him.

One warm morning when Larry was taking care of a hangover under the guise of helping her with her English, she decided to ask him whether he knew what was going on in Vienna. They were both on the front porch, she on the shaded wicker lounger, he on the swing bench, a little breeze on his face helping his hungover condition, no doubt.

"You're always reading the newspapers, Larry," she said. "Have you read anything about what's happening in Vienna?"

"Oh, we've all been taking an interest in that," he replied, his sideways stare speaking of secrets as his face flashed in and out of shade.

"What do you mean?"

He huffed a long breath. "I mean . . ." He stopped the bench swinging and leaned toward her, elbows on knees, hands and forearms just slung where they came to rest. "You know I get into trouble for being honest with folk, don't you, Klara?"

She secretly liked the way he pronounced her name, with a long drawl on the first "a." She also liked his straightforwardness. "I can take the truth," she said. "I lived it for many years."

"Course y'did. Sorry. And that's why we've always taken an interest, because Felix was there." He drew breath, thinking, judging her. "My big brother's only being secretive to spare your feelings. You know that, huh?"

The words made the back of Klara's neck tingle. "Of course," she said. "He loves me."

"Oh, his love for you is bigger than the sky, my dear."

Klara almost looked up to try to work that out, but she let it pass. "I still want to know the truth," she said.

"Well . . ." He pursed his lips, twitching them to one side. "Word in the newspapers is that the few Jews still left in Vienna are being slung out pretty darned quick."

"Slung out?"

"Moved out quickly, like rats being brushed off a ship's deck."

"Oh, I see."

"And I, uh . . . I reckon . . . well, it's not a nice thing to say, but I reckon everyone you ever knew has been removed from that there city."

"And put where?"

"That's what you'd call conjecture at the moment." He quickly clarified, "That's to say, nobody knows for certain but there are nasty rumors going around."

An unpleasant taste emerged on Klara's tongue, and she felt the need to cover her eyes.

"You ain't gonna cry, are ya?"

She looked up and shook her head.

"Well, that's a relief."

"And thank you for telling me the truth."

"Ah, it's nothing."

"I won't tell Felix you told me."

He shrugged and said, "Don't spare my feelings, lady." Then he looked left and right and froze as he stared directly at her. "I, uh . . . I have something to say, something I need to tell Ma and Pa and Felix – an *announcement*, you might call it."

"You can tell me, Larry. I mean, if it's a secret, then—"

"Oh, thank you kindly, but it's too late for that. They'll all find out soon enough."

"Find out what?"

"Well, you know how Roosevelt started up a draft last September?"

"A draft?"

"Conscription – the government call you up to join the army, navy, or air force."

"I understand. And so?"

"So my lucky number just came up. I have to leave a week on Monday."

Klara gasped. Now there were a few tears.

"Hey, hey. It ain't no big deal. Why, could even be fun."

"But you could be fighting if America joins the war."

"We're sending arms to Britain, Russia, and China. Our warships have been told to shoot German and Italian warships. We're as good as in this war already. All it needs is a sharp nudge in Roosevelt's back to make it official, and then it's full-out war."

"But I came to this country to avoid war."

He stepped over and sat next to her, putting a brotherly arm around her shoulders. That was just like him.

"Lady, don't you ever be kiddin' yerself. You and Felix made the right decision coming over to Texas, y'hear me? It was *the right decision*. You'll be safe here. Government's spent years preparing for war and arming America up to its eyeballs. No country would be dumb enough to attack us on our own soil."

"I guess you're right."

"Why, o'course I am." He gave her shoulder one last squeeze and stood. "Now, my head and belly are both screaming for breakfast. You in?"

Klara followed him into the kitchen, in truth unsure about the war, despite having agreed with him. But there were two things she *was* sure of – perhaps the only things in this turbulent world: meeting Felix had been lucky; and marrying into his family had been a blessing in so many ways.

All she could do was wait for that "sharp nudge in Roosevelt's back."

And it seemed inevitable.

Chapter Eleven
1942

Like heavy snow falling upon heavily packed ice, 1942 brought nothing but more danger to the Jewish citizens of Leopoldstadt, and Alicia's mind was becoming numb to the misery of her existence.

So, when an official sounding knock on the door came one morning early in the year, she almost longed for it to be news that would make things either worse or better; if it weren't for her children, she would gladly have tossed a coin to choose either of those things – anything but the life of relentless poverty she was currently enduring.

She let Mama answer the door.

"Seven occupants?" the man said, perusing the sheet of paper in his hands.

"That's correct," Mama said.

"I'm here to give you notice to evacuate this dwelling."

"Where are we going this time?" Mama asked. "Another two streets away?"

"You need to be ready in three days, otherwise you will be forcibly removed."

"Even Papa and Hugo?" Alicia said.

"You are each allowed two suitcases, two blankets, two pairs of shoes."

"Will we have jobs there?" Ludwig asked.

"Any assets you can't take with you will be sold and the proceeds put toward the cost of transport to your new home."

Mama stepped closer to him. "But where are we going?"

"Good day," the man replied.

She grabbed his arm.

"*Let go of me!*"

"Can't you tell us where we're going? Is it somewhere else within Vienna?"

"It's somewhere better," he said, pulling his arm away.

"Please have a little mercy. Can't you tell us *anything*?"

The man frowned at her, deep in thought. He glanced left and right. "I can tell you it will be abroad," he said quietly. "But honestly, I don't know where."

"Abroad? My God."

"And I would advise you to take as much warm clothing as you can carry."

"Why?" Ludwig asked. "What's the place like?"

"I don't know," the man sneered. "Why don't you write and tell me?" He ruffled through the sheets of paper in his hands and approached the next door along.

Mama shut the door and they all sat. The only voices Alicia could hear were those inside her head.

Just when she was thinking conditions could hardly get any worse, when she was telling herself that *anything* would be better than this cramped hovel of a home in this dangerous city, she and her family were being forced to move on again, this time much further afield by the sound of it. And for a few minutes she forgot about all the hardships, the maltreatment, the feeling that the souls of her family and friends were being slowly ground to dust; Vienna was her home, all she'd ever known, and for all its problems, she now so desperately wanted to stay. Whereas before, her mind had meandered, hoping to find a good reason to stay put, now it was hunting for some method of avoiding the inevitable.

There must be another way, she told herself, *there must*. She needed to think hard to work out what that way was. *Perhaps solitude would help her find an answer.*

She stood up and headed for the door.

"Where are you going?" Ludwig asked.

She shrugged. "I just need a walk to settle my nerves."

"I'll come with you."

"No."

"*Yes*. It's not safe out there."

She held the flat of a hand up to him. "No. Please, Ludwig. I'm sorry, but I need to be alone."

He bit his lip, then said, "Alone? What do you mean?"

"I need time to think, but I'll be fine. Really."

"I don't like it, but . . . at least tell me where you're going."

"I'm not sure, I just need a walk, but I promise I won't be long."

He sighed, his shoulders relaxing. "Just be careful."

She grabbed her coat and hurried out, having no idea where she was headed, but also very much aware that the feeling of helplessness was no stranger to her.

She passed along streets lined with beggars, crossed to the opposite sidewalk to avoid flag waving groups of Hitler Youth, and couldn't avoid a platoon of fifty or so troops undergoing drill practice in a square. They were ordered to be at ease just as Alicia hurried past.

Then it hit her like a stray bullet from one of those troops. It was a memory – from where, she didn't know. Whatever it was, it made her halt and think, desperately trying to remember. Perhaps she was mistaken because her broken mind was playing tricks, mocking her. It was a face – a face from the past flashing in front of her. She looked around the square, her eyes scanning the crowds of people scurrying past or just strolling or even lingering to chat.

But she saw no face she recognized.

Then a few words came from one of those troops — a caustic remark as they were now at ease — causing the others to laugh. She only allowed herself a glance as it didn't pay to stare at soldiers. And there it was again: the face. This time she did stare, and stepped toward them.

"Kurt?" she said.

The soldiers stopped laughing.

Alicia called out again, this time daring to hold up a hand. He was three rows back, his hair was shorter, and he was gaunt and serious — shocked, even — but it was definitely him.

A sergeant appeared in front of her and asked for her papers. After he'd checked them he faced his platoon. "Private Hinkel," he said, beckoning the man to the front. "Do you know this Jewess?"

Kurt looked her up and down. "I've never seen her before in my life, sergeant."

"And can you explain how she knows your name?"

"I . . . I . . ."

Alicia noticed discomfort on Kurt's face as he struggled to invent an explanation.

The sergeant turned back to Alicia and said, "How do you know Private Hinkel?"

Now she saw stark fear descend onto Kurt's face. And she knew; it just wasn't worth it — for Giselle's sake more than for his.

"I'm mistaken," she said. "The man I know is Kurt . . . *Stadler.* I don't know this man. I've never met him. I'm sorry to cause such confusion." She turned and started walking home, praying that she wouldn't be called back.

After she'd turned a corner she started running, stopping at the next corner to catch her breath — breath that fear was leeching away from her. She leaned against a wall and took a few minutes to recover, then headed home. She'd almost reached her front door when she heard her name being called out from behind her. She turned to see a figure galloping toward her – although not the sort she expected. It was a young boy, hardly a threat, so she waited for him.

"Are you Alicia?" he said, out of breath and sheened with sweat from running.

"Who are you?" she said.

"That doesn't . . ." The boy took a few gasps of air to recover. "That doesn't matter. Is your name Alicia?"

"It is," she said, steeling herself to step away from him.

"Then you have to meet him under the Stuben Bridge at 3pm."

"But . . ." She paused, and by the time she'd gathered her thoughts the boy had turned and was running away.

She went back inside.

Later that day, Alicia made her excuses to Ludwig and left home again, albeit a little delayed, and arrived almost half an hour late, lingering on the shadowy footpath under the bridge. Her nervousness made it easy to ignore the fetid odor.

People strolled and hurried by, her eyes discreetly tracking each man until she was sure it wasn't Kurt. And just as she was considering leaving, thinking that she'd missed him, she heard his voice call her name from the darkness at the back of the path, and edged closer.

"Take care," he said. "There's a step."

As she got closer, a hand appeared from the darkness and held her arm for support, guiding her.

"I'm sorry it has to be like this," he said. "But I can't be seen meeting you." He handed her something soft wrapped in paper.

"What's this?"

"Some cake for you and your family."

"Cake? Have you . . . I mean, is it . . .?"

"It's perfectly safe. I would never do anything to harm you. It's to thank you for not telling them I was your brother-in-law; that would have caused problems for me."

"Thank you, but . . . aren't you ashamed of denying that you married a Rosenthal?"

"A little."

"How's Giselle?"

"She's good. Well, she's safe in Linz, but perhaps not good. Only now do I realize how trapped she is. She has often talked of returning here but knows she can't. And we have a son."

"Oh, Kurt. She must be so happy."

"I wish she was, but . . ." He let out a long groan. "Alicia, I have to tell you that I haven't been the best husband to her. I think of Giselle a lot these days. Time and distance bring me a more considered view of the time I spent with her. I miss her. I realize I haven't been kind to her and I've made lots of mistakes. She always wanted to keep in contact with you all, but I . . . I persuaded her not to. That's why I wanted to meet you. When you see Giselle, tell her I love her, and that I wish I had been a better husband. Tell her I always loved her, despite the way I treated her. Will you please tell her?"

"Don't speak like that, Kurt. Don't speak as if you'll never see her again."

"I might not; don't you see the uniform?"

Alicia tried to force a laugh. "You'll see Giselle someday, I'm sure of it, and when that day comes, you can tell her yourself."

There was no answer. Now her eyes were adjusting to the darkness, and the first thing she noticed was the sadness drawn on his face.

"How are you?" she asked.

"Oh, I survive, like you, like many, but it's not much of an existence. You and Ludwig?"

"We survive too. We have two children now, one of each."

"Good. I'm happy for you. Your mama and papa and Hugo?"

"Life's hard. All seven of us live in a small apartment. But they say soon we're being moved on – out of Austria. I don't know where to."

She heard a sound that smelled of despair, then, "Oh, Alicia."

"What? What is it?"

"I've heard such unpleasant stories of what's happening in some of the camps they run – stories that worry me. They're horrible. I hope you don't go to one of those places."

"But don't you think what's happening in Vienna is horrible?"

"I wasn't sure, but now, looking around, remembering how the place used to be, the answer is yes. But I can't say it openly."

"And your fellow troops? What do they think?"

"It's like I say. We don't talk about it. We're not allowed to, and punishments are severe. Alicia, I have to go, but just promise me you'll try to leave this place, get out now on your own terms, emigrate if you can and take as many people as possible with you, don't wait for them to move you where *they* want you to go."

"I'll try," Alicia said. "Take good care of yourself, Kurt."

Alicia briefly felt his long arms brush against her, was powerless to stop his strength gather her in, and then smelled his earthy manliness as he embraced her.

"I'll see you again one day, Kurt," she whispered to his ear.

He said nothing, and a few seconds later she saw the shadow of a man she had perhaps misjudged quickly disappear into the daylight.

She waited, a little in shock, then started to walk home, her mind fizzing with Kurt's final words, telling her to get out now, to emigrate instead of waiting to be moved on. As she walked, the words haunted her. *He must know something*, she thought.

So instead of returning home, she headed straight for the main police station in the city center, and joined the line for emigration visas. They were spilling out onto the streets, but within an hour she was inside the building. Now she could count the number of people between her and the desk at the front – all of them Jews applying for permission to leave Vienna for London or New York or Zurich or just *anywhere* that wasn't controlled by the German regime. She counted over a hundred. And the place was due to close in just over an hour. Nevertheless, while there was a chance of her speaking to someone in authority – while she could smell freedom – she would try. Perhaps it would only be for her and Ludwig and their children, and if Mama and Papa and Hugo preferred to stay and take their chances with whatever the authorities had in store, that was up to them.

She waited in line for another twenty minutes, regularly checking the clock on the wall, eagerly shuffling forward whenever someone left the desk for home and a new applicant stepped forward. By now she'd been in line for almost an hour and a half; it was long enough for her back to ache, but it proved to be more than enough time for her to consider how Mama would cope on her own with Papa in his wheelchair and with the bundle of random contortions that was Hugo.

She cursed her own weakness and rubbed a weary hand up and down her face, holding a palm over her mouth to stifle any stray words of self-disgust.

Because she knew.

Even if she were to reach the counter; even if, by some miracle, she were to receive all the correct paperwork; even if she were able to hold the travel permits and tickets in her hand; even if she and Ludwig and the children could wait on the platform for their train to arrive – even if all that went right, Alicia knew that her heart wouldn't allow her to do wrong: there was no possibility of her being able to walk away, no way she could abandon Mama, Papa, and Hugo.

She left the emigration office and returned home.

There had been many changes to Alicia's life over the past few years – too many of them damaging to her existence – but now she feared that the worst was to come.

§

Giselle's son was now almost two, and had started walking. He was her focus, her everything. Letters from Kurt had been frequent and caring in his early months away from Linz, but now they were only occasional as well as being confused and rambling. The blessing was that in his last letter – a very melancholy one in which he apologized for his behavior yet again – he also mentioned Alicia, and that she was well. Giselle was heartened by this news but still worried about Kurt, although looking after their son helped take her mind off the worry.

It also helped that her friendship with Frau Hinkel had now deepened. The fact that Herr Hinkel seemed to be forever beavering away in the study accompanied by sheaves of paperwork only made it that bit easier for the two women to become closer.

So one day, after Giselle had just washed some blankets, and an even more cheerful than usual Frau Hinkel emerged from the study, Giselle felt emboldened enough to ask why she was in such a good mood.

"Oh, it's nothing," she said, her grin indicating the opposite.

Giselle just smiled and was about to dismiss the subject and take the blankets outside to the mangle when Frau Hinkel grabbed her by the arm.

"I can trust you, can't I, Giselle?"

"Oh, of course."

"Well, I'm not supposed to say," she whispered. "It's a secret, but it's such good news I don't think I can keep it to myself." She glanced over her shoulder and lowered her voice even more. "You know that we own the land behind this house?"

Giselle didn't know – and didn't really care either – but she nodded and whispered back, "What about it?"

"He told me he's been working on it for weeks."

Giselle immediately made the connection with the amount of time Herr Hinkel had spent in the study, although she'd thought nothing of it at the time.

"He's now heard it officially," Frau Hinkel continued. "We have permission to build houses on that land behind us and sell them."

"So . . . you're going to be rich?"

She nodded hurriedly. "Very much so. He tells me he even has some laborers lined up to do the physical work. Isn't it all exciting?"

Giselle smiled. If nothing else, seeing someone grin with so much feeling was infectious. "I'm very happy for you," she said. Then she thought of the contents of the house: the fine furniture, the oil paintings on the walls, the number of cabinets and closets, the large, patterned rugs on many of the floors. These people were already very wealthy. Giselle wondered how they would live with even more money. Either way, it wouldn't affect Giselle; she had blankets to deal with.

She tried to move away toward the back door, but Frau Hinkel laid a hand on her arm and continued talking about what she would like done to the house. Then the door opened and Petra walked in.

Frau Hinkel straightened her face, instantly excising all traces of excitement. "Did you have a good meeting?" she asked her daughter.

Petra nodded, and soon a smirk appeared on her face.

"What's funny?" her mother asked.

"Oh, nothing."

"Come on, Petra. I know my daughter too well. What's going on?"

"I know what you and Giselle were talking about, that's all."

"What do you mean?"

"The houses that father is planning to have built by men from the camp. We're going to be rich."

Her mother frowned. "Who told you?"

"People in the party who work at the camp. It's happening everywhere. It makes no economic sense to waste the labor, so they're being used on farms and in factories – construction sites too, it seems."

Frau Hinkel turned to Giselle, widened her eyes and tutted. "It looks like I have no secrets from my family."

"Camps?" Giselle said. "What camps?"

Frau Hinkel and her daughter exchanged puzzled glances. "Didn't Kurt tell you? There are camps not far from here, at . . . uh . . ."

"They all come under the name of *Mauthausen*," Petra said.

"Yes, thank you, my dear. It's a series of camps set up recently to house all of the undesirables of Austria and a few other countries."

"What do you mean by *undesirables*?" Giselle asked.

"Exactly what she says," Petra interjected. "Political agitators, unpatriotic types, criminals, some Polish and Roma types too. Now they're also taking in a lot of Jews."

"And about time too," Frau Hinkel said. "After all, there are rather a lot of them to deal with."

"Far too many," her daughter added. "It's so encouraging that the government is making progress." She smiled at her mother and Giselle in turn, saying, "Anyway, I'm thirsty after all that work. I need a drink."

While Petra got a drink, Giselle once again tried to take her blankets outside to the mangle. But Frau Hinkel stopped her yet again.

"Giselle, my dear, there's something else I've been meaning to say to you."

Giselle waited, the wet blankets now soaking her clothes.

"It's about your mother – well, both parents if you wish. If you remember, I asked you to write and tell them that they're welcome to stay here. I'd like to meet them." She looked to the side. "Wouldn't you like to meet them, Petra?"

Petra took a break from gulping water to nod agreement.

Frau Hinkel turned back to Giselle. "If I remember, you said they wouldn't be able to afford the train fare here or the accommodation."

"Yes, but—"

"But nothing, my dear. I'm determined to meet them one way or another. And bearing in mind our good news . . . well, the thing is, we can pay their train fares and they can stay in one of our spare rooms."

Giselle was baffled, instinctively shaking her head to turn down the offer but unable to come up with any excuse.

"What's the problem, my dear? They won't need any money. Don't you think they'd like it here?"

"It's . . . it's not that," Giselle managed to say. "I mean, it's a generous offer and I'm very grateful, but I think . . . well . . . my father would have too much pride to accept."

"Oh." An awkward silence filled the air for a few moments, then Frau Hinkel said, "Surely it wouldn't do any harm to ask next time you write them a letter?"

"Perhaps I'll do that," Giselle replied, her nerves starting to settle. "First I need to get these blankets dried." She headed for the door to the back yard, and a few minutes later was feeding the blankets into the mangle.

But she wasn't alone for long. The door opened and she turned to see Petra sidling up to her, gazing up to the sky, holding a glass of water and a smile that spoke of mischief.

"Hello again," Giselle said.

"Hello," Petra replied.

Petra busied herself sucking in a few lungfuls of fresh air, then said very slowly, "You're hiding something, aren't you?"

"What?" Giselle stopped turning the mangle and looked around to see if anyone else might be listening, before adding, "What do you mean?"

"You're hiding something about your family."

"No, I'm not."

"Are you really from Vienna?"

"Of course. I was born there. Why would you think I'm not?"

"I don't recall you getting any mail from them."

Giselle prepared her face to lie. "I get letters from them all the time."

"Do you?"

"Of course I do. Petra, I don't wish to sound rude, but half the time you're not here, so you wouldn't know about what mail I get and who it comes from."

"What's on your passport?"

Giselle knew full well what was on her passport. Yes, it would have proved she came from Vienna. But it also had a large red "J" stamped on it courtesy of the new regime that had taken over in 1938.

She'd heard Herr Hinkel comment on the progress of the German army, saying attack was the best form of defense. She decided to take a leaf out of that book. There was no way she was going to let anyone see her passport.

She threw the blanket she was holding back into the basket and planted her hands onto her hips.

"I've had enough of this, Petra. I know you don't like me, and that's your choice. But if I'm good enough for your brother to marry, I should be good enough for you. And if I'm not, then please keep your ridiculous accusations and theories about me to yourself. Do you understand?"

Petra swilled the water around in her glass for a moment, her eyes fixed on it. "Yes," she eventually said. "I understand perfectly. I won't question you about your background again."

That evening, over the family meal, Giselle saw more opportunity to put Petra off the scent of a kill.

"I completely agree," she said when Herr Hinkel yet again started talking about Jews being a sub-species of the human race.

"Does that mean you've come around to our point of view?" he said.

She nodded. "I'm sorry. I've been a little weak-minded. I wasn't thinking properly."

"Good girl." He laughed. "At least you've come to your senses now. The creatures are vermin, don't you think?"

"Oh, absolutely. As you've said before, it's an unfortunate situation, but they've had too much power for too long. They need to be eradicated from Europe – well, preferably from the whole world."

More words of hatred against her own people stung Giselle as soon as they left her lips, but they were necessary words. It took all of her willpower not to glance at Petra to check her reaction. All she could do was pray that her little speech had done the trick.

Giselle hardly slept that night for the chill creeping up her spine. It might have been caused by the worry that Petra would see through her little act, that she would discover the truth and expose Giselle's secret. It might have been caused by her confused feelings toward Kurt and concern for his safety. Or it might just have been due to the words she'd used to describe Jews, and thoughts of how upset her family would have been to hear her spit those words out.

There was little sleep, but there were plenty of tears.

§

For Klara, 1942 might not have been a dangerous year, but there was little respite from dark thoughts. She'd escaped the dangers of Vienna, but late the previous year Roosevelt had received that "sharp nudge in the back" Larry had hinted at, and Klara listen to the news reports with fear crawling up her own back.

Hundreds of Japanese fighter aircraft had brought thousands of bombs and bullets and a hell full of surprises to the American nation. Unprepared for the attack, a dozen US ships were sunk and many more were badly damaged. Nearly two hundred aircraft were destroyed. Thousands of people were killed or injured.

Pearl Harbor might not have been mainland America, but as far as the American people were concerned, those bombs might just as well have rained down on New York or Los Angeles or Washington DC. America declared war on Japan. As a show of solidarity with Japan – and some said in retaliation for the tacit American support of Britain and Russia – both Germany and Italy declared war on America.

Klara was, once again, in a country at war. The number of countries not at war was shrinking rapidly, but that was no consolation.

In the early months of 1942 there was little change to Klara's day-to-day life. At least, any changes were minor and more significant in their portent than their immediate effect: she'd heard via Felix that Larry was in the navy undergoing basic training, so was not – so far – at any risk; Felix and Pa worried about meeting the food production targets set by the government; and she'd just about given up on hearing anything from her family back in Vienna – or wherever they were.

But one goal was achieved: thanks to Felix, Larry, their parents, and one or two neighbors, Klara's English was now very good – good enough to hold down a job. And the government made it clear that every citizen had to play their part. If "Victory Gardens" were springing up in every town and city for people to grow their own fruit and vegetables, then output from the ranch had to increase dramatically to feed the nation.

The days were long. Weekdays, Klara and Ma worked in a factory across town that made boots and helmets for soldiers, because the men who normally worked there had been either drafted or moved to new armaments factories. The factory floor was the largest room Klara had ever seen, with an array of workers stretching in both directions, all equally spaced.

Pa and Felix grafted all day long on the ranch, with Klara and Ma joining in when they weren't on the boot production line. It seemed that the whole country was at breaking point. People were encouraged to eat leftovers, to save any waste fat so the glycerin could be extracted and used to make ammunition; similarly, sugar was used in the production of gunpowder and dynamite, so was rationed to civilians; scrap metal was salvaged from anywhere for the war effort – so cars that had been abandoned ten or more years before now suddenly had purpose; likewise, when the Japanese overran Malaya and surrounding countries and subsequently cut off the supply of new rubber to their enemies, old rubber was recycled and synthetic rubber production was ramped up; taxes were hiked to pay for it all; more and more people volunteered or were drafted, causing labor shortages.

It was all the kind of drama Klara thought she'd left behind, but on the positive side she was learning a lot in the factory. At first the scale of the operation had been intimidating, but soon it became her own little enclave of reasoning in a world getting less sane by the day.

The factory used production methods that were strange to Klara; Felix told her those methods had been pioneered by car plants. When she and her family had worked at Papa's shoe repair place, everyone had been capable of carrying out every task. She, Felix, Ludwig, and Papa had all known how to cut and shape leather and wood; how to nail, sew, and wax; and how to judge the size of components to minimize waste. But here, the jobs were split so that people specialized in a particular part of the production process. One group of workers would make the outer soles, a different group the heels, different groups the insoles, the toecaps, the tongues, the outers – and they would pass the boots along a line that would separately take care of any nailing, gluing, sewing, waxing, packaging etc.

And despite the stories of horror in other parts of the world, most days for Klara were ones of drudgery and boredom, so her mind drifted, and she started dreaming of opening up her own shoe factory – not a million miles away from what was going on in front of her eyes, except that she would own and control what Larry would refer to as "the whole shebang." Yes, Klara knew it was selfish. But it was a harmless pipe dream. A few people joked that the war would be over within a year now that Uncle Sam had gotten himself involved. Others urged caution, pointing out that government plans had been ongoing for years so they were obviously considering the long-term situation.

The day Larry was due to come home on leave was keenly anticipated at the ranch. In Klara's mind he would regale them all with tales of meeting people hailing from all corners of America and frighten them all with the dangerous – but not too dangerous – situations he'd found himself caught up in.

When it came, however, it was all too fleeting a visit; understandably, he spent most of what little time he had with Ma and Pa, leaving Klara somewhat left out whenever Felix wasn't around. And with the added fact that Klara was now busy most days at the boot and helmet factory, the days of her and Larry taking walks across the family land were replaced by short and sweet talks on the porch out front.

One exchange in particular was to stick in Klara's mind. It happened on a warm evening while Pa and Felix were out harvesting, and Ma was cooking. She was resting on the swing bench on the porch when he turned up with a small bottle of beer in his hand and sat next to her.

"Still looking swell, Klara," he said. He took a swig of beer before adding, "Must say, a little too *slim* for my liking."

She giggled. "I don't want to be overweight, do I?"

"Ah, you know what I'm talking about, sure y'do."

And she did. He'd mentioned it in passing the previous year. Twice. And each time she'd ignored it, quickly changing the subject to avoid the issue. This time he had a more persistent air to him – perhaps he was more bullish after mixing in that military environment.

"Say, how long exactly have you and Felix been married now?"

"Oh, five years."

"And you ain't expecting yet?" He screwed his face up and shook his head. "Something wrong there, I reckon."

In panic, Klara snapped, "That's none of your business, Larry. Please don't mention it again."

She glared at him. He blushed like a schoolboy caught smoking, then shrugged his shoulders and got up and left. She felt a little sick in the stomach. They were all to have dinner together that night, the men would have a few beers and talk about football or baseball (because talk of war was off-limits by decree of Ma), and early the next morning Larry would return to the naval base. Yes, it was probably the last time she would be alone with him, and now she'd upset him.

And so, late that evening, when she and Felix and Ma and Pa had gone to bed, she told Felix she'd forgotten to say goodnight to Larry and was afraid she might not see him before he left in the morning. She crept back out to find him taking in the night air on the porch.

Before she could speak, he said, "I owe you an apology, Klara."

"You don't," she replied.

"No, no. It was forward of me, asking a question like that. It's the beer. Or it's just me being dumb. Either way, ain't none o'my business."

"Well, I owe you an apology too. I was rude to you and I'm sorry."

He gave her his broadest smile and said, "How 'bout we call it quits?"

"That would be nice." Klara took a step back toward the door, saying, as a parting shot, "If I don't see you in the morning, please take care of yourself."

"Ah, you'll see me. But hey, thanks."

She returned to bed, but the conversation had served to bring the subject into focus for her. And with that in mind, she brought it up with a tired and slightly drunk Felix, speaking in German for privacy.

"Can we talk?" she said.

"Only if it's in English," he said in English.

She shook her head. "It's private. I'm wondering if there's something wrong with me."

"Wrong? In what way?"

"You must have thought the same thing, Felix. We've been trying for a baby for so many years now, something's wrong. I should be pregnant. Realistically I should be expecting my second or even third baby by now."

"Oh."

"Perhaps I should visit the doctor."

She felt his hand – rough-skinned through months of manual labor but gentle as ever – caress her neck and the side of her face. "I don't think that's a good idea," he said quietly.

"But what if there's something wrong with me?"

"There's nothing wrong with you, Klara. You're the way God made you and that's perfect for me. Besides, what can anyone do to help?"

"I . . . I don't know."

"More importantly, now would hardly be the best timing. We're both still young, Klara. It'll happen in time if it's meant to, so please stop worrying."

"But haven't your parents asked? Don't they want grandchildren?"

He sighed. "Oh, I can deal with Ma and Pa and their questions."

"So they *have* asked?"

"Couple o'times. They wouldn't be normal parents if they didn't."

"And what did you say?"

"That it's something we'll get around to in time. But it doesn't bother me and it shouldn't bother you." He turned and switched out the bedside light. "Now I'm exhausted, everything aches and I need some sleep." He leaned across and kissed her, long and tenderly.

She could still taste the beer on his lips, her nose approved of the tar-like aroma of carbolic soap that clung to his skin, protecting him. Above all he tasted and smelled of Felix, her man. She held onto him, deepening the kiss he was giving her. He responded, those toughened hands roaming firmly down her torso.

In the warm September Texas air, they made love. And for a while, until the scent of morning woke Klara, there was no war, no fear of the future, and no worry about her family.

Chapter Twelve
1943

Alicia and her mama sat at the table, each holding a cup of cold water, and wished each other a happy new year.

They'd already celebrated the Jewish new year the previous September, but there was so little happiness of late that any reason to celebrate was grasped and held tightly. The year they were bidding farewell to had been the worst of Alicia's life, and there was little prospect of 1943 being any better.

The signs when they'd left Vienna many months ago were ominous. They'd all been shepherded to the train station – each of them carrying the crucial two suitcases, two pairs of shoes, two blankets, and all the warm clothing they could carry – and then ordered by soldiers onto waiting train carriages that were more like cattle trucks.

Papa made the mistake of asking one of the soldiers how he was expected to get onto the carriage. Ludwig offered to carry him on, but it seemed to be a matter of principle for Papa to show his anger the only way he could at being removed from the city he'd always called home.

The soldier clearly didn't care much for Papa's principles. A few words were exchanged between him and a fellow soldier and then Papa was manhandled out of his wheelchair and bundled onto the carriage's bare floor. His wheelchair was given even less consideration, thrown to the far side of the carriage where it shattered into a heap of splintered wood and forlorn hinges.

Papa was already red-faced with pain, rubbing his sore stumps, but stared in horror at his broken wheelchair. Ludwig shouted out, "Couldn't you be more careful?" to the soldiers, and had the muzzle of a rifle pressed to his neck until he apologized, followed by a crack on the head with the butt even when he did.

They still had no idea where they were going or for how long they would have to endure the discomfort of this dirty carriage.

Alicia fell asleep, but guessed a few hours had passed by the time she woke up to find the train had halted alongside a deserted field, where they were given bread and water, and shown to an area of sandy earth for natures other imperatives. The train set off again, and a few hours later pulled up at a station, where Alicia readied herself to set eyes upon her new home

It wasn't to be.

They were transferred to another train, which again stopped after a few hours for food and nature's calls.

She lost count of the number of stops and changes, but two dark and cold nights had passed by the time they were finally told to get off the carriage and line up outside a gate between barbed wire fences.

Like everyone else, Alicia shivered in a coldness she'd rarely experienced in Vienna and scanned the surroundings. "Riga," she said aloud on seeing the sign. "Where are we?"

A kind man offered to help Ludwig carry Papa off the train but it was a struggle as they were both stiff and tired and were also carrying their own luggage. Mama was busy carrying the broken wheelchair as well as keeping an eye on Hugo and carrying *their* luggage. And Alicia was carrying luggage for herself and her two children, who were so frightened that they were holding onto her arms, pulling her down. Understandably, Alicia's question went unanswered.

Over the next few days they learned that Riga was far to the north – which explained why it was so much colder than Vienna –

and was in Latvia, a country that had once been independent, had been taken over by the Soviets, and very soon after that had been occupied by German forces. Of course, those fenced into the Jewish sector were never going to find out much about the wider country.

The sector was divided into Lithuanian and German areas, and even the German area was subdivided according to city of origin: Dortmund, Hanover, Berlin, Hamburg, Vienna etc. The place was all very well organized, Alicia thought, with each city having a representative on the Jewish council, which did as much as it could to make life comfortable. Nothing, however, could stop the place feeling like a prison, with access in and out being only through a single gate, involving searches and occasionally beatings of people found trying to smuggle in food.

There was water, there were very basic food rations, there were jobs with occasional pay in the way of extra food, and there were schools. The single room the seven Rosenthals and Tannenbaums occupied was cramped and dirty to say the least. There was no lavatory – they had to line up in the cold to use the communal facilities – but at least the room had a fireplace, whereas many weren't so lucky.

Within days of arriving, all able-bodied people not looking after children were told to report for work duties, and Ludwig was allocated a job in an armaments factory. Soon after that, the remainder of the family had a visit from the authorities, a smartly dressed man accompanied by two armed soldiers.

"You have seven people living here," the man said. "But only one worker."

Alicia gathered her two children close by, holding them to her body. "I have my children to look after."

The man looked them up and down, then turned to Mama.

"I'm looking after my husband and my son," she said.

The man's brow furrowed in confusion. He looked to the side –
to Hugo, grunting and twisting his head, and to Papa, balancing on
his stumps and knuckles.

One of the soldiers explained: "This one is unable to work due
to being sick in the mind, and this one because he has no legs."

Because he lost them fighting for your country, Alicia wanted to add.

The smartly-dressed man looked closely at Hugo and Papa for a
few moments, occasionally sighing and shaking his head. "The one
who is sick in the head we can do nothing about," he announced.
"But the other, has he a wheelchair?"

"Broken in transit."

"Repairable?"

A shake of the head. "Too badly damaged."

Damaged by thoughtless idiots like you, Alicia felt like explaining.

"Mmm," the man said, rubbing his clean-shaven chin, swapping
his gaze between Papa and Hugo, who was now widening his eyes
and displaying a gleeful smile that everyone knew simply didn't
belong in a situation like this.

"Put them on the list," the man said to one of the soldiers.

"What list?" Mama asked.

"We have easier work for these kinds of people," the man
replied. He turned back to Alicia. "Perhaps for the children too."

"No!" Alicia shouted, forcing the objects of the man's
attentions behind her.

"Perhaps not the children," the man said. "But definitely these
two."

"I don't want them to go," Mama said. "They're not doing any
harm. I'll look after them."

"We can't carry people," the man replied. "Children and
women caring for children are the only exceptions; everyone else
must pay their way. And once you no longer have to care for them,
you can work too."

The men left, but a few days later soldiers returned and read out Papa's and Hugo's names, ordering them outside, saying they were going to be transported to a special work compound called Dunamunde.

Mama was in tears. Papa consoled her, saying they had no choice, but that he would make sure Hugo was well looked after. And so they left, and a now unburdened Mama was told to take up her new job in the armaments factory. At first she refused, but eventually Alicia persuaded her to put aside her grief and do as she was told. Even then, it took a threat and a final warning before she did so, leaving Alicia alone at home during the day with her two children and her thoughts. Much as Alicia loved her children, she would long for the hour Mama and Ludwig returned from work, only to be disappointed everyday as they both arrived tired and lifeless, Ludwig not even in the mood for talking.

It wasn't long before they heard the truth about Dunamunde.

Alicia and Mama had gone outside to give the children some fresh air, and a pair of guards seemed eager to talk about the two missing family members – eager to tell them about the place.

"You were told it's a factory?" one asked.

"Or a workshop of some kind?" the other asked, half-laughing.

"What do you mean?" Mama said. "Tell me. Tell me what you know!"

"If you want to know the truth, old woman, the truth is that it doesn't exist."

"Well, it exists," the other explained. "But it's no factory or workshop."

"What do you mean?" Alicia asked.

"You want to know? You really want to know?"

The guard stepped closer and lowered his head near theirs, so he could whisper. "It's a beautiful place, deep in the forest not too far from here, where we take all the sick and elderly."

"And what happens there?" Mama said.

"What do you think happens?" The man started laughing. "They all get shot, that's what happens."

"Otherwise they're nothing more than a burden," his fellow guard explained.

Mama ran indoors as fast as her ageing bones could carry her, and Alicia followed.

The next day, other residents of Riga confirmed the story.

Papa and Hugo were gone; there hadn't even been a chance to say goodbye.

Mama became as quiet as Ludwig; neither wanted to talk, they just wanted to eat and rest.

Later in the year, Ludwig was given new duties helping to construct buildings at a complex known as Salaspils.

After what had happened to Hugo and Papa, they feared the worst, but were eventually persuaded that it was a genuine construction project – not that they had any choice in the matter. Ludwig was away most of the summer, and when he returned, Alicia felt the closest thing to joy she had felt for many years.

Her joy was short-lived. Like other occupants of the Riga Ghetto, Ludwig had been losing weight even before he left for Salaspils, but he returned a shadow of a man – a sunken chest, injured hands and fingers, a persistent cough, constantly complaining of fever and headache.

On the rare occasions that water cleared the dirt from his skin, Alicia noticed many patches of small spots. She didn't get the opportunity to find out what they were caused by; one morning late in the year she woke to find he had passed away in this sleep. If the killings of Papa and Hugo had taken a knife to Alicia's heart, the death of the love of her life had given the knife a sharp twist.

But here, mourning was a luxury, and Alicia's mind was numb to luxuries as well as pain; any feelings beyond caring for her children were wasteful. Fleeting thoughts of the cake Kurt had given her in those final days in Vienna would still visit her. She'd taken a few bites on the way home, just to ensure it hadn't been poisoned, she told herself. Then she'd kept it secret from Mama, Papa, Hugo, and even Ludwig, eking it out only to her children in secret. For a time, she'd felt guilty about that deception, but not now. Now there was no guilt – hardly any feeling at all, in fact. Now, survival of herself and her children was the only thing that mattered.

So it was that 1943 fulfilled its promise of being worse than 1942. Alicia had now lost her papa, her brother and her husband. There wasn't much more trauma for her and her mama to take, so it seemed.

But in November of that year there was more turmoil: they were told they would be leaving Riga. For where, nobody would say.

§

By the summer of 1943, Giselle's son was developing into a boisterous little thing, and with Frau Hinkel's help was being cared for better than Giselle could ever have hoped for when she'd become pregnant.

Frau Hinkel's help also meant that Giselle was starting to have more free time and taking an interest in her surroundings. Once a day, Frau Hinkel would keep an eye on her grandson while Giselle went for a walk through the meadows just across the road from the house; that was the only place to go for a walk since the area behind the house had been turned into a construction site, with regular deliveries of materials, and men working throughout the daylight hours with very few breaks – a world of mud and noise and sweat and more mud.

Giselle's meadow walks lent her regular opportunities to detach herself from the Hinkels and reflect on her situation.

On Frau Hinkel's insistence, conversation over the dinner table had largely been steered away from politics, so it was less stressful for Giselle. And because of that, she had the presence of mind to consider her husband. Yes, Kurt's shell had softened even before he'd joined the Wehrmacht. Yes, his visits to local taverns with old friends had become less frequent as he'd chosen instead to spend more time with his wife and baby son. So yes, he was definitely becoming a better man. However, the wounds from the many years of Kurt's unsavory behavior ran deep in Giselle's mind, and the years she'd been separated from her family didn't help either, so in the year before he'd left, although the two of them had shared the same bed, they might has well not have done.

The only certainty in Giselle's mind regarding Kurt was that her feelings were confused.

On her walks through the meadow, sitting on her favorite hillock, there were times when she told herself that she and Kurt were husband and wife, that they had a lovely, healthy son, and that once the war was over they would always be together. Yes, he would have witnessed horrors, and would need respite from those experiences, but there was hope within her heart that when the war was over, he would still be that better man and they would be as happy together and as much in love as they had been in Vienna all those years ago.

But there were also days when she wondered whether those feelings she'd had for Kurt had completely withered away and could not be revived. Perhaps in all honesty she'd never been that happy with him in Vienna anyway. It wasn't that she wished she'd married Maximillian instead; she hadn't been in love with him and what had happened to him in the intervening years was anybody's guess. And at least she and her son were safe, warm, and well fed. Yes, such issues were boring – as boring as the many things she used to complain about in her younger years – but they were what mattered most to her now.

She felt no shame that the safety of her son was now the most important thing in the world to her, but it didn't stop her thinking about her family back in Vienna, and on her walks through the meadow she would wonder what had happened to them. The news reports she'd listened to and the half-truths that came from Petra's mouth put thoughts in her mind that were too horrific to dwell upon; Jews from all German-occupied countries were being treated like cattle, shunted from one area to another with no regard for their desires or even their basic needs. Giselle had heard whispered rumors that even worse was happening – things that amounted to nothing less than slaughter. Counter rumors said those stories were merely unpatriotic lies. Perhaps they were indeed lies, but perhaps, Giselle thought in her more critical moments, certain people chose to believe they were lies.

But today was one of her better days. The sky was clear blue, the sun was kind and enlivening, and she strolled through the meadow just as childhood memories of playing with her sisters and brother in Vienna strolled through her mind. There had been tears when she'd thought of them over the years, but today she was confident she could hold her sorrow at bay; she had hope that one day they would all be together again. And on that day, she would apologize for her behavior – for all the times she'd poked fun at Alicia for being boring, bickered with Klara, and laughed at poor Hugo.

Only in hindsight – and with a child of her own – did she realize that Mama and Papa had done their very best under difficult circumstances. They must have sacrificed so much and worked so hard to bring up four children.

That last thought was a little too much for her. She'd now reached her favorite spot again and settled down onto her hillock. She'd promised herself that today would be a better day, but the image of her family in her mind's eye upset her, and alone on the hillside she allowed herself to weep, as much as anything in regret at her own childish and selfish behavior when she'd been with them.

Perhaps even that was a self-indulgence – a selfishness – because she should have been more concerned with what was happening to *them*, not her. For a moment she wondered whether Alicia had given birth to a boy or another girl, and whether Klara was expecting yet. Yes, she was curious, daring to celebrate on their behalf, but there were more important considerations. The authorities were sweeping Jews out of Vienna like dust out of a house, but did that include her family too? Mama, Papa, Hugo, her two sisters, and whatever children they had? And if it did include them, where exactly were they being swept to?

She tried to dry her tears, and promised herself that one way or another she would visit Vienna – and as soon as possible – to discover what had happened to them, to help in whatever way she could, to make her own peace.

Her thoughts were interrupted by a heavy panting sound – lungs on the edge of exhaustion. She turned to see a man running straight toward her. Her first instinct was to bolt, but fright paralyzed her and she stayed still, half sitting, half curled up into a ball. As the man closed in on her she could see he was hardly a man at all. Very short-cropped hair, a dirt-streaked face almost sunken in on itself, eyeballs as full of fright as she herself was, rotten teeth on display through a mouth that gasped as if it were its final attempt. His body was stick-thin, his chest concave.

She let out a shriek as the man set eyes upon her. His husk of a mouth uttered a few words to her. She didn't understand the words, but some meaning was clear: this man was pleading with her – for what, she had no idea.

Distant shouts came from behind the man and he jerked his head back to see. Then he set his eyes upon the wooded area behind Giselle and set off for it. Giselle crawled back a few paces and lay herself down behind the hillock and tall grasses – hidden, but still able to watch the man stumble and race for the cover of the trees.

He'd reached the shadow of the nearest trees when a shot rang out and the wreck of a man took one more step before slumping to the ground. For a few seconds he grasped out toward the trees, but then relaxed.

Two more men – both fit and healthy, one holding a rifle – ran toward the now still figure. Both started kicking and stamping on him. Then the one with the rifle took aim and put another bullet in the fallen man's head. The other man dragged the corpse into the wooded area, hiding it behind a large tree.

Giselle's heart was still thumping, but she watched as the two men lit a cigarette each, then appeared to be talking to one another – joking, even. They sauntered back in the direction they'd come from – back toward the road and the house Giselle lived in, but not before they'd passed by close enough for Giselle to recognize one of them.

The man holding the rifle was Herr Hinkel.

§

By 1943, Klara's English was fluent, albeit still heavily accented. She was now a supervisor at the boot and helmet factory, responsible for making adjustments to the working environment, where every second or cent saved contributed to the war effort.

And that helped take her mind off her rarely expressed concerns for Felix.

For a couple of years all men had needed to register for conscription. Only a few healthy men of that age were exempt – those doing jobs vital to the war effort in other capacities such as medicine development or weapons research or certain farming jobs. That latter example might have deferred drafting for Felix, and in January he was due to meet with the local draft board for them to assess his case.

A week before the meeting was due, on a cold but sunny afternoon, Felix took Klara out for a walk across the dormant cornfields and sat her down by a shaded creek they'd often cooled off in during the warmer months.

"Do you worry much about Larry?" Felix asked her as they settled onto an old log.

It was an odd question. Klara didn't answer, but instead tried to figure out what was coming next. Felix continued.

"He seems to be enjoying navy life, doesn't he?"

"Mmm . . . I guess so. He doesn't complain. Why are we talking about this?"

Felix picked up a handful of flat pebbles and launched a couple into the water, watching them bump and skim along the surface. "I, uh, I'm trying to soften the blow for you. It's stupid, I should know I can't fool you."

"What do you mean? What are you trying to tell me?"

Felix discarded the pebbles and drew breath. "It's kind of hard for me to say. You know I have this meeting lined up with the draft board?"

"Yes."

"Well, I'm not going."

"Why not?"

"Because I already enlisted. I'm joining the navy, just like Larry."

"Oh."

"Is that all you can say? You're not angry?"

"Angry?" Klara tried to smile sweetly, tried to ignore the knot in her stomach. "I guess I'm a little upset that you didn't tell me earlier, that you didn't feel able to discuss it with me before you made your decision."

"I know, I know. And I'm sorry. But I couldn't take the risk you'd try to talk me out of it."

Klara shook her head. "I don't like it, but if that's what you have to do, I'll support you. I would like to know your reasons, though, and also how you expect Pa to manage on the farm without you."

"Well, that was one of the reasons I've waited till now. I've arranged for a couple of sixteen-year-olds – kid brothers of old schoolfriends of mine – to help out here." He nodded at the fields in front of them. "And as for the reasons, well, I've seen for myself what those jokers have done to Vienna. If I didn't do my duty, I couldn't live with myself. And if . . ." He glanced at her – at her torso.

"And what?"

"Well, if we ever have a son, and if this war ever ends, I want him to be proud of me and of what I did to help."

She smiled. "You mean, *when* we have a son."

"Yeah. Of course. And thanks for being so understanding."

"Oh, I get the war drummed into me at the factory. Posters on the wall, announcements, pep-talks – all reminding us why we're doing it all. I feel like telling the managers that I know more about the war than they do."

"About that," he said. "Your job. Have you ever thought about moving on within that business – I mean, moving *up*."

"But, I'm a supervisor."

Felix gave her that flat smile he shared with his brother. "I'm sorry. I didn't mean to belittle your achievement, but I know you're capable of a whole lot more than the shop floor. Product development, accounts, sales, purchasing – I know you better than anyone else in this world, Klara, and I know you could do it all."

"Stop it. You'll make my head big."

"Fine by me so long as worrying about that stops you worrying about me."

"Oh, believe me, Felix, I'll have sleepless nights about you. I know you don't think of me as a worrier, but I just hide it well." She tried to keep her composure, despite the barbed wire pulling itself around her heart. "I'm proud of you, and I promise that one day I'll give you that son, and he'll be proud of you too."

"That'll please Ma and Pa no end."

She frowned. "What did you say?"

"I'm sorry. It's just that they've been asking again. Have they dropped any hints to you about wanting grandkids?"

"No, but if they do, I'll give them the same answer I'll give anyone else, that we're planning it properly, that we're waiting for the war to finish." She shivered in the breeze that had just picked up.

"Of course," he said. "I completely agree. Come on, let's get back inside."

Later that year, as planned, Felix left the farm and joined the navy, following in his brother's footsteps.

Klara had cried the night before he left, and over the next few days wondered why she hadn't cried more often in her life. Alicia and Giselle had both remarked upon it over the years. They were also much more predisposed to emotional outbursts than Klara, who seemed to be able to control her feelings. And in her bleakest, most lonely nights alone in bed she started to wonder whether there was something wrong with her – something that was preventing her becoming pregnant.

Then she remembered Felix's words, and decided – very characteristically, she noted – that she was the way God had made her and nothing would change that. She set her mind to the job of controlling and improving the factory production line, spent her evenings and weekends helping on the farm because Pa was still struggling to meet the government-set yields, and locked away her dreams for the future.

Toward the end of the year, Larry came home on leave again. That helped Klara. It helped enormously. He wasn't Felix and never would be, but he was fun to be around, and during some long, rambling conversations on the porch, he told her not to worry about Felix, that Felix would be just swell and would return with a chest full of medals and a smile as wide as the Colorado river. It made her laugh, and he told her that in all seriousness Felix would be safe and home on leave soon.

Klara believed him – she *made herself* believe him – and sure enough, as though Larry had cast a spell, she soon received news that Felix would be coming home on leave early the next year.

Chapter Fifteen
1944

By the start of 1944 the Riga Ghetto was a mere memory for Alicia, albeit one that made her cry because her papa, brother, and husband rested there in one of those sacrilegious mass graves.

She promised herself that when the war was over she would return, find their bodies, and give them the respectful burials they deserved. But for now she had to concentrate on ensuring survival for herself and her children. And she still had Mama, which was something else to be grateful for; apart from anything else it was another adult to share the grief with.

In the previous November, while Alicia had still been grieving, while she was still regularly explaining to her children why their papa had gone away, the four of them had been moved on again. Alicia went gladly because Riga held too many bad memories. The only things she would miss were those bodies of loved ones – wherever they had come to rest.

The journey was déjà vu; herded onto trucks like livestock, then a long, cold trek with few breaks and little in the way of food or drink.

At the end of the journey Alicia realized how naïve she'd been to think they could be going someplace better than the prison-like camp in Riga. From the moment she stepped off the train it was clear that this place was far worse than anything she could have imagined. At least Riga had held the pretense of being a town, albeit a fenced-in one. Here, the stench of burning meat – although not any meat Alicia had ever smelled before – made every breath uncomfortable, the throngs of half-humans in striped rags scared her more than any ghost could, and those prominent words about *work giving a person freedom* erected over the main gate were just plain cruel.

Unlike Riga, Auschwitz had no pretensions of normality. It was a brutal prison steeped in rumors of worse to come. Food at Riga had been strictly rationed – the bread usually stale, the morsels of fish or meat well past their best and barely edible. It had been just enough to live on, but it *had been enough to live on.* Here, the hunger was constant. People stole anything from anyone to survive, they ate food however rotten or contaminated or maggot-ridden it was, and often resorted to drinking rainwater from puddles as there was no alternative.

As the weeks passed by, Mama became increasingly frail, and would keep complaining that someone was stealing her food. By the start of 1944 she was little more than skin and bones, and usually bedridden, and Alicia was trying her very best to care for her, as any dutiful daughter would.

These days Mama was reminiscing a lot about her life – or, at least, she took a long time to say what she wanted to say, each lazily exhaled breath carrying only one or two words. But Alicia had time – there was little else to do here – so she listened intently whenever Mama spoke in that delirious fashion, her mind tuning in and automatically stringing together the widely separated words.

"Did they give me any food today?" she asked Alicia one day when snowflakes clouded the air outside.

"Same as usual," Alicia replied. "They say if you can't line up to collect your ration, you go without."

"But whenever I do manage to get to my feet and collect a little bread, I take a bite, I store the rest for safekeeping inside my sleeve, and the next thing I know, it's gone."

"There are many thieves in here, Mama."

"Well, I hope they can live with their guilt. Tell me, how are my grandchildren today?"

"They're over there, asleep on the other side of the cabin." Alicia glanced across to the huddle of six or seven children – it was hard to tell exactly how many – all sharing each other's body warmth.

Mama, her eyes only half-open, her lips cracked from dehydration, the corners of her mouth caked in white gum, shuffled an arm toward Alicia. "Hold my hand, my dear," she said.

Alicia did, feeling an iciness that normally would have shocked her, but not now, not here.

"I'm too tired to lift my head up to look at them," Mama said. "If you say they're fine I believe you."

Alicia was now kneeling at the bed her mama shared with two other women, holding her mama's hand but in truth hardly caring. She concentrated, and told herself she *should* care. She told herself she should force herself to talk to her mama, to give her encouragement. Then she noticed a jaded smile playing on her lips.

"What are you thinking about, Mama?" she said.

"Your papa. I miss him so much."

"Me too. I'm proud of my papa. He was a brave man to fight in the Great War."

"Your papa was no warrior, Alicia. He was a good man, but he had no choice in that matter. I remember him telling me he had absolutely no intention of volunteering for the army. I was expecting Giselle at the time and I was so relieved he said that. And, of course, I was even more pleased when the birth turned out to be so easy. Giselle. Easy birth, difficult child."

"So, why did he end up fighting?"

"In the end he felt he had to. When he told me he'd enlisted, I didn't talk to him for two days. There were many tears – some from him. But he told me about the finger pointing, people saying Jews were avoiding their responsibilities. Like many men at our synagogue, he wanted to prove them wrong, so he went. I didn't like it, but I understood, and I gave him my blessing. By the time he joined up with the army I was expecting again."

"Was he back home when you gave birth?"

Mama gave her head a tired shake. "Klara was born in summer 1917. By then it was many months since I'd heard from your papa. I hoped for the best – that perhaps he was involved in some siege and couldn't get a letter out, but I feared the worst. By then, your brother was a precocious seven-year-old, but as big and strong as many ten-year-olds, and would insist on asking me every day where his papa was and when he would be returning home. I didn't have the heart to tell him that I just didn't know."

"But he did return. You had a happy life together, didn't you?"

"We did. My mind was a mess in those few days after they told me what had happened, but when he returned he was just the same old Albert – apart from his legs – and my worries soon melted away. We were just as happy as we had been before it happened. He used to joke about being a shoe repairer who didn't need shoes. He found that funny. I didn't, but I laughed."

Alicia pictured the scene. "I can imagine my brother laughing at that too."

"Ah, Hugo. I miss my boy so much. He never harmed anyone in his life and they did that to him."

"Did what to him? What do you mean?"

Alicia felt her mama's hand grip hers with the strength of a small child.

"I never did tell you what happened to him, did I? I mean, how he became the way he was."

Alicia sensed her heartbeat quicken. "No. No, you didn't."

"Your Papa and I promised each other we'd never tell you, but that seems a pointless promise now."

A minute ago, Alicia had hardly been listening, had been merely going through the motions, because there was nothing else to fill these endless days with. She was being the dutiful daughter on the outside, but in reality was too weak, too tired, and too hungry to genuinely care. But now her ears were alert. An image of Hugo as a normal little boy was buried at the far end of her mind. Now she needed to know the truth.

"What happened to him, Mama? Please tell me."

Now Mama's speech became even slower, her words slurred and delivered with little of the emotion Alicia thought they deserved.

"It's not a long story. There were some . . . older boys who used to tease him – especially whenever he wore his yarmulke – but he didn't care. They used to call him . . . the same names their parents called all Jews, and he turned the other cheek. But one day, one of the boys whipped the yarmulke off his head . . . and told him to chase him if he wanted it back."

"And he started a fight?"

"Not until the boy knocked a little Jewish girl over – one of our neighbors . . . and she started crying because her hands were cut. The boy laughed at her . . . and called her names as she was crying. Hugo couldn't ignore that; he chased the boy . . . around the streets and down an alleyway."

Mama's head lolled back further, her mouth gaped.

The story – the sorrow – was sucking what little life was left out of her.

But Alicia had to know. She shook her mama's arm. "What happened next, Mama?"

It took some time for the words to come, but they did, delivered even more slowly.

"The alleyway . . . it was a trap. Witnesses who broke the fight up . . . said there were about six of them. They jumped on him, beat him, broke his skull. We thought . . . we'd lost him, but he survived. And that's how . . . Hugo became . . . Hugo."

Alicia was speechless. It shouldn't have mattered now, not in this hell-hole where survival seemed to be decided by the toss of a coin or even by how ruthless and selfish people could force themselves to be.

But that didn't matter. Alicia had become closer to her mama than she ever had been before. She fought against the tears, knowing each one would deprive her body of vital water. She held her mama's hand tightly, not speaking, thinking of Papa and how he must have struggled to hold his tongue about the incident involving his only son for all those years.

While she thought on, Mama's hand gradually relaxed; minutes later it was completely limp, as was her whole body. She was utterly still. Alicia tried to rouse her but that proved to be impossible. She fought the urge to cry because that would have been wasted effort, but she thought it fitting that the final word Mama would ever utter was the name of her only son.

Still keeping hold of her dead mama's hand, Alicia glanced over at her two children. They were safe – by the standards of Auschwitz. They were as well fed as any children in here. The extra food Alicia provided made sure of that.

The thought of that extra food brought Alicia's thoughts back to the lifeless hand she was still holding, and she wondered what sort of a woman would steal precious food from her own mama.

In a cloud of confusion that she knew was partly of her own making, she lost control and wept in silence.

§

Giselle hadn't slept for days after witnessing the shooting incident on the hillside the previous year, and had been on edge for many months, always fearing for her life, hardly daring utter a word to Herr Hinkel, who – until that incident – she'd never thought of as a violent man.

Yes, at the dinner table, or while sitting in his favorite armchair reading the newspaper, or when making polite conversation with his family and occasionally smiling agreeably to Giselle, the man had given off an aura of going along with the acts of the German-backed regime with only a degree of reservation – accepting those acts as unpalatable but necessary so long as other people committed them. But what was the story behind the man who'd been shot? Had he attacked someone? Stolen something? Tried to break into the house? Giselle kept coming back to the same answer: that he was one of those men working on the construction site a short walk away behind the house, and that his only crime had been trying to escape.

The incident had become something of an obsession with Giselle, and even as 1944 dawned, she would spend many sleepless nights wondering whether to tell Kurt about the incident when he finally returned from wherever the Wehrmacht had sent him. Her conclusions didn't make sleep any easier to come by: if Kurt already knew that sort of thing was happening, would he be angry that she'd found out? Would he even believe her? Would he tell his father what she was accusing him of? And if that were to happen, how would his father react? And what about Frau Hinkel? Did she know what kind of a man her husband was? Could Giselle confide in her?

Ultimately, due to stark fear, Giselle kept her thoughts to herself. And throughout all this mental turmoil, another obsession had burrowed into her mind: had she done the right thing leaving Vienna? The thought that she'd made the wrong choice had never completely gone away, but now, five years after she'd left, she would often dream of a parallel life where she'd stayed with her sisters in Vienna, perhaps married Maximillian even though she hadn't loved him, and not felt as lonely and isolated as she was right now.

Was it worth living? Only caring for her beautiful and innocent son answered that question. But could life get any worse?

Early in 1944 the issue of exactly how much she should confide in Kurt became irrelevant. Giselle came downstairs one morning to find Frau Hinkel in tears and being comforted by her husband, who also looked ruddy around the eyes. On seeing Giselle she became engulfed in her sorrow for a few moments, unable to speak, before beckoning Giselle over. And in those same few moments, their horrid opinions and what Herr Hinkel had done melted away, to be replaced with a feeling of plain compassion that Giselle couldn't put aside.

Frau Hinkel tried to utter a few words, but they all knew it made no sense.

"We heard first thing this morning," Herr Hinkel managed to say, as if the message wanted to stay in his mouth. "It's . . . news about . . . Kurt."

Giselle felt the skin on her face tingle, her heart thumping her whole body awake.

"He's dead," Frau Hinkel whispered, immediately convulsing again into tears.

Giselle couldn't hold back, and started crying too. "What . . . what happened?" she said, stuttering.

Herr Hinkel took a few deep breaths and explained.

"Kurt was fighting in Russia as part of the push to capture Leningrad. They'd been forced to retreat to a place called Narva. He was about to be captured by the Red Army, but instead, he . . . well, he shot himself. It must have been awful for him, but at least the end was quick."

Giselle said nothing, but took a step back, then turned and ran to her bedroom, all the while telling herself she was only crying because of the shock, not for her loss. She scooped up her son and curled up on the bed with him, her mind engulfed with memories of the good times with Kurt. There had always been a realistic possibility that he wouldn't come back, but it was a fact she'd denied to herself – perhaps because she'd fallen out of love with him a long time ago. None of those considerations stemmed the tears.

There might not have been undying love for Kurt, but there was concern. He wasn't perfect, but possessed many good qualities and had mellowed with fatherhood. And, of course, there had been that time when she *had* loved him so much, when the passion between them had been like an inferno. But now they would never meet again, and the possibility of rekindling any of that love and passion had evaporated. It might have been the sorrow in her heart for Kurt or his parents, or disgust at the sheer waste of war, or the self-pity that came with knowing she and her son were now truly alone, but she couldn't cope. All of these things were too much, and after letting her son go, she wept for an hour or more.

After the funeral, Frau Hinkel was at pains to stress to Giselle that she was still the mother of their grandson, so she could stay at the family house for as long as she desired.

So there was no need to leave, but the house definitely felt colder, and there was still a longing in Giselle's heart to return to Vienna. She started to take more notice of events there, and when she heard stories of sporadic American bombing raids on the city, her mind was made up: it still wouldn't be safe for her to return to the city she thought of as home. The news also made her worry even more about members of her family who might or might not still have been living there, but there was nothing she could do for them except pray.

In time, one or two smiles found their way onto the faces of Kurt's still grieving parents, and perhaps Giselle too was starting to make a recovery of sorts. She took yet more interest in the progress of the war, which had started to turn against Germany and its allies around the time of the failure to capture Leningrad.

Giselle had also started to take more interest in the construction project still in full swing to the rear of the house. Whenever she knew Kurt's parents had gone into Linz, she ventured over there, taking care to hide behind storage sheds, and was both impressed and shocked. A lot was happening there: huge channels of earth were being dug out, concrete was being mixed and laid as foundations, brick walls were going up, road surfaces were going down. Most of the men working there weren't at all up to the job of hard labor, being not merely slim, but little more than skin stretched over bone.

On one occasion she got close enough to a worker to see bloody bandages around his hands; it was obvious that constant shoveling had worn his skin away. The vision made her run back to the house and up to her bedroom, past her confused son playing on the floor, where she collapsed onto the bed and shut her eyes, trying to catch her breath, and desperately trying to forget the horror of what she'd just seen.

"The site?" she heard someone say.

She opened her eyes with a start and turned to see Petra in the doorway, her face impassive.

"Hello, Petra," she said, her voice trembling.

"You've been to the construction site, haven't you?"

Giselle just nodded; she was in no fit state to make up some sort of lie.

"You know you must keep it secret," Petra said with a superior smirk. "Father doesn't like to make it public that he uses prisoners from the camp."

"I'm sure he doesn't. Do the men get paid to work out there?"

Petra laughed. "Don't be stupid. Father pays a fee to the government for each worker. But no, those vermin don't get paid."

"They look like they don't get fed either."

"Oh, they get fed. A farmer feeds his animals so they have the energy to work, doesn't he? Well, he does for a few months. And what else are we supposed to do with these people?"

While Giselle was thinking how to respond to that, Petra took a step closer, causing Giselle to keep a cautious eye on her son.

"I won't tell Papa that you know, as long as you promise to stay away from there. Do we have an understanding?"

Giselle nodded, her mind now picturing the man she'd witnessed being shot on the hillside the previous year – the man Petra's father had murdered, although he wouldn't have used that word.

Petra left the room. Giselle sat on the edge of the bed and watched her son tug wooden blocks across the floor.

She had a lot of thinking to do.

§

For Klara, most of 1944 was a lonely vigil. Felix came home on leave in Spring, and it was a magical week that neither of them wanted to end. On the last day he broke the news to her that he would have to wait until much later in the year for his next leave period. Klara didn't complain; there was no point.

But the long wait was arduous in every sense. There was work at the ranch, there was her job at the boot and helmet factory, and then there was the hardest time of all: spending every night alone in the bed she longed to share once more with Felix.

She spent much of her spare time reading about the numerous and lethal bombing raids on Vienna, searching for as much detail as possible on exactly which streets had been bombed and the extent of the damage. The targets were clearly military and industrial sites, but inevitably there were errors and fatalities. Klara prayed for her family.

The next bright spot was when Larry returned on leave in summer. By now she looked upon him more as a friend than a brother-in-law, and hoped the visit would help her forget how much she was missing Felix.

She was very wrong.

She was wrong because the time she had with Larry reminded her all the more of Felix and the time he could have been at the ranch house with her instead of away fighting in this damned war.

Nevertheless, Larry was a welcome respite from the drudgery of work, work, and more work. They went for walks, and spent most evenings after dinner sitting together on the porch – he drinking beer, she just lemonade – and talking. Klara even learned a few more words of English – including one or two she wished he hadn't told her.

And when the family gathered around the table at mealtimes there were four of them, not three, so Klara could – for the occasional moment – imagine that the man sitting opposite her was not Larry, but his brother.

Like Felix's visit earlier that year, Larry's leave was over before Klara had gotten used to his presence. Parting wasn't painful, as it had been with Felix, just sad.

But before he left, Larry told Klara and Ma and Pa two important pieces of information "straight from the horse's mouth," as he put it.

The most important one was the rumor from inside the forces that the end of the war was in sight. Pa asked exactly what he meant, and he replied that it could well be over before the year was out.

The second thing he said was that he'd asked for his next leave period to coincide with Felix's, hopefully for the first day of Hanukkah in December, so the whole family could be home together. He left Klara and Ma and Pa with the thought that by the grace of God maybe – just maybe – those two things would combine, that the war would be over in a matter of months and so both men would come home for good.

Toward the end of the year, however, Larry's words were shown to be foolishly optimistic. Yes, the axis powers were on the back foot in many battle locations, but, as a radio commentator put it, those back feet were dug in deep and hard. It was clear that the war would stretch well into the following year.

Larry's hope for the leave periods of both brothers to coincide also came to nothing. Felix did indeed come home for the first day of Hanukkah, but Larry's leave was set for two weeks later.

It didn't matter to Klara. She had a whole week with the man she loved and was determined to make the most of it. She didn't work for that entire week – either in the factory or on the ranch – and she made sure Felix didn't get roped into work either, making Pa promise not to allow that. At first Felix was stiff-shouldered and over-polite to Klara – a hangover from the regimented environment he'd spent so much time being a part of, she figured. But within a day or two he'd relaxed and was his usual self again.

They took slow walks along the nearby creek; they talked of life after the war, when Felix wanted to resume his career as a radiographer and Klara wanted to start a family; they made love most nights – not to mention a few afternoons when they had the ranch house to themselves; and they even took an overnight stay in Houston, watching a show and visiting a couple of museums and more than a couple of stores.

It was only on the final day of his leave that the tension in Felix's shoulders returned, as if his body were preparing itself to return to battle.

"Some people say the war will be over soon," Klara said on their final night, in bed, the side of her face nestling on his ginger-blond chest hair.

"Some people have little grasp of reality," Felix replied.

211

Klara said nothing; she was, after all, only repeating what she'd heard, desperately wanting Felix to confirm it, if only for the sake of her feelings.

"Hey, I'm sorry," he said, combing his fingers through her hair. "That was a little blunt of me. If you want the truth, yes, we're winning, but the end could take a week, it could take two years. Nobody knows for sure."

"There's no point in you going back if it could only be a week. You might as well stay here."

He laughed. "You mean, here in San Antonio or here in bed?"

"I'm serious, Felix." She lifted her head and kissed him slowly on the lips. "Can we kid ourselves that's true, just for tonight? Can we dream that the war is over and you're not going back, that you're staying here forever?"

"Of course we can, if that's what you want."

"Oh, it is, Felix. It really is."

And so, they spent the next half-hour planning what they would get up to during the next week – a train ride to the coast, a baseball game, a day browsing the stores and historic sights of San Antonio, a couple of days exploring some of the rivers and old towns of the Hill Country, and a visit to Canyon Lake.

Then, as they fell asleep in each other's arms, Klara told herself that the next morning, after Felix had gone, she would sit down with her notebook and write down every detail of their imaginary week, so she would have a record of it, so when the war was over and he returned home for good, they would have that week for real.

And after saying farewell to him the next morning, that was exactly what she did.

Klara felt reassured and a little more relaxed about the future after Felix's home leave visit. It had been a wonderful week and held the promise of many more of the same. Also, Larry was due the next week, so that prospect took her mind off her longing for Felix.

There wasn't much to do to prepare for Larry's visit; Ma and Pa merely left up the "welcome home son" banner they'd put up for Felix, and Ma baked another cake. On the day he was due home all three of them waited inside doing chores around the house, having little idea what time of day he would arrive because this was Larry, the patron saint of bad timekeeping, as Pa had often described him.

Early that afternoon, they heard a car draw up and its doors open and shut. Ma was first to the front door, and while Pa and Klara waited just behind, his arm around her shoulder in shared excitement, Ma beamed a broad grin back at them and opened the door.

But it wasn't Larry with his wide smile and some sort of apology for being late. Two men stood there: one in full naval uniform, the other in a dark suit and a dark blue tie. The thing both men had in common was grave expressions on their faces.

"Mrs. Klara Goldberg?" one of the men said.

Ma and Pa shot looks at Klara, who said nothing, just nodded once.

"We're from the Naval Authorities, Mrs. Goldberg. Could we come in for a moment, please?"

They instinctively knew what this was about; such men only visited for one good reason. Ma gasped, put her hand over her mouth and took a step back, almost toppling over.

"Oh, dear God," Pa said. "Not this. Anything but this."

After that, Ma and Pa didn't speak – didn't even offer the men refreshments, and Klara led the men to the kitchen table, where they all sat, and one of the men spoke.

"I'm Lieutenant Maldini and this is Chaplain Jones. I'm afraid we have some very bad news for you." He glanced at the chaplain, who took over. "It is my unfortunate duty to inform you that your husband, Felix Goldberg, recently serving his country in the battle of Leyte Gulf, was involved in . . ."

Klara only managed to hear a few phrases after that, and she felt them thump her in the stomach more than she heard them. There was "bravely fought" and "died fighting for his country" and "passed away at the scene" and "should be proud," after which she ran out of the front door, heading for anywhere and nowhere, eventually finding herself on the edge of that dormant cornfield next to the creek in which she and Felix had cooled down during better times. She sat cross-legged on the muddy banks and wept at the prospect of never hearing Felix speak again, never being moved by that broad, genial smile, never being able to confide her worries in him, never getting enveloped in his comforting arms, never starting a family with him, never getting to have the week she'd only recently written about in her notebook, and never growing old and crotchety with the love of her life.

It was two hours before she returned to the ranch house, chilled to the bone, to find that Larry had now turned up safe and sound. He didn't greet her, just showed her a face full of pain and said, "I'm so sorry, Klara, for you more than us."

Next to him were Ma and Pa, both reddened under the eyes, both with heads down and shoulders hunched over. Nobody spoke for a few minutes. Eventually Ma blew her nose and cleared her throat.

"What can we say?" she said to Klara. "He was our son, but we've had the best years of our lives and you two still had yours to come."

Pa held her hand, squeezed it, and turned to Klara. "There's one thing we *can* say, my dear. It might not be any comfort to you at the moment, but we want you to know you'll always be our daughter-in-law, nothing will change that, and you can stay here as long as you want to. And that's not just a promise, it's a cast-iron guarantee."

"It's what Felix would have wanted," Ma added.

But Klara's mind had started reeling all over again. It made her feel sick. She said nothing, didn't even thank them, just went up to her and Felix's bedroom, curled up into a ball on the bed, and prayed for now to go away.

Chapter Fourteen
January to May 1945

If it hadn't been for her children, Alicia would have given up long before the start of 1945.

In the purgatory that was Auschwitz, people slept in huddles – friends and strangers, male and female, old and young – all together to keep the killing cold at bay. But disease and hunger were not cured by warmth, so despite those measures, corpses had to be removed from the cabins most days.

Alicia had no idea where her mama's body had been taken. She should have cared, but there was no enthusiasm in her mind for anything that wasn't going to help her children survive; they had become the sole reason for her own survival. If she could take food, she took it. When someone died, she would try to get there first to take their blanket and any spare food. If the person was alive but too weak to hold onto their food or blanket, Alicia would still take what she could. And throughout all of that, she had to deal with questions from her children.

"Mama, when are we leaving this place?"

"Mama, I'm still hungry."

"Mama, is Papa coming back to take us away from here?"

"Mama, I'm so cold."

"Mama, tell them I need more food."

All, of course, were perfectly reasonable requests. But Alicia had no answers.

The cold was hated, but snow brought just a little relief for Alicia; she could give it to her children, telling them it would fill their bellies. Beyond that, there was no food. Neither was there any order, control, mercy, or a hundred other things she'd taken for granted back in Vienna. All she could do was tell her children to come closer. To huddle together. To share body warmth. To stay safe. The three of them lay down as one, hours drifting into days, their togetherness punctuated only by Alicia's journeys outside – all hard-fought against a body that didn't want to move – to gather snow or water to keep the three of them alive. She went on her own as the children were too weak to walk, drifting in and out of either sleep or unconsciousness, she wasn't sure which.

Alicia knew all three of them had only days left – perhaps even hours.

All she could do was hunker down with them. She'd lost so many people who'd been close to her that it was hard to care.

If this was going to be the end of her own personal journey, then so be it. At least she and her children would die together.

A day had passed since she last fetched water. Perhaps she would never fetch water again.

And then the peace was disturbed. An explosion jolted her, and then a crash made the whole cabin shake.

Couldn't she and her children even be allowed to die in peace?

She lay back, a child under each arm pressed against her shrunken torso, and tried her best to blot out the crashing noise and also now the smell – a smell that reminded her of the synagogues of Vienna burning back in November 1938.

Then she heard shouting from outside, then more shouting, closer, not far from her bed. She lifted her leaden eyelids to see. Three guards were in the room, two using their rifle butts to rouse the prisoners, ordering them all to get out of bed, while the third stood at the doorway also shouting. Perhaps it was her state of mind, but to Alicia the guards appeared to be arguing with each other.

"We have to get them all out."

"We don't have time."

"But what about our orders?"

"Never mind orders. We have to leave *now*."

"Go on your own. We'll follow."

Then Alicia felt the rifle butt nudge her chest, heard a voice directly above her say, "Come on. Get up."

She lay there, unable to do anything except look up at the guard, who was only half-dressed.

"Get up! Stop playing dead!"

There is no playing, Alicia thought.

He was about to speak again, but the guard at the door shouted across, "Leave them!"

The order was ignored.

"Everyone must leave the camp," the guard standing over Alicia said. "All staff and all prisoners must come with us. If you stay, we have to shoot you."

Then shoot, Alicia thought. Because she wanted respite from this air that was alive with the thunder of explosions and the roar of fires. Because she wanted peace.

The man raised his rifle. "All of you! You get up and march or you die here!"

Alicia's vision was blurred, but somehow her eyes made out the dark hole at the end of the gun barrel, beckoning her to mercy of a sort.

"We don't have time!" the guard at the door hollered, now shouting desperately.

"He's right," the third guard said, grabbing the rifle barrel that was poised inches from Alicia's face, then pulling the guard away by the shoulder.

The guard who had just held Alicia's life in the balance of his trigger finger hesitated, resisting the tugs for a moment.

"Come on. They're five kilometers away, probably less by now."

That persuaded the man. All three guards ran out of the building.

In time, the explosions and crashes stopped, and despite the low roar of the fires burning outside, Alicia quickly drifted off to sleep.

The next sensation she experienced was being rolled around, as if adrift on a calm ocean, but she felt powerless to open her eyes or move or speak. There were voices, but they weren't speaking German. The voices, the movement, and her consciousness all seemed to melt into one another until she fell asleep again.

Alicia awoke to silence, and the first thing she sensed was cleanliness – no disgusting smells, clean sheets against her flesh, her fingers washed, her mouth and nostrils no longer caked in mess. This time there was silence, so she felt it was safe to open her eyes and look around. She was in a bed. All around her were more beds, arranged regimentally. Everything was so clean. Like heaven. She looked down, to the small body lying next to her.

One body.

She checked the other side again.

Definitely only one child.

"My . . ." She croaked the word out, her throat dry and painful. She coughed, sticky mucus splattering her lips. "My daughter," she said. "Where's my daughter?" She said it again and again, each time louder.

A door opening. Women. One either side of her. Talking to her. Talking in a language she didn't understand.

"Where's my daughter? What have you done with Sarah?" She tried to sit up but her body was too heavy and she slumped back.

A third nurse appeared. Alicia asked again. More foreign voices. Then a sharp prick in what little flesh remained on her upper arm. And then nothing.

§

In Linz, Giselle had promised Petra she would stay away from the construction site, and she did – for a while.

But those images haunted her – images of the man she'd seen shot dead and of the gaunt figures she'd seen toiling away. So she did the only thing possible to meet those images head on: one afternoon, while her son was safe playing on the bedroom floor, and ensuring that Herr and Frau Hinkel and also Petra had gone out, she visited the place again.

By 1945 the visits had become a secret habit. Whenever Giselle and her son were left alone in the house, she knew it would be safe to leave him for ten or fifteen minutes, so slipped out.

In her first few visits she'd been shocked to see Herr Hinkel and others beating the workers with their own shovels merely for being so exhausted they needed to rest, all the time ranting about timescales and the need to speed up work. And from what had become her regular hiding place behind one of the storage sheds, she'd vowed to do something to help.

That was when she started stealing food from the house. She would place whatever she could take – often bread, cake, or pieces of chicken – on a low wall near her hiding place, then listen to the men find the food, whisper in amazement, and devour it. Once or twice she had to toss the food into the dirt to avoid being seen, but still the men wouldn't be put off, and would eagerly brush the dirt off the food and eat it.

In time she started to care more that the supply of food should continue and less about getting caught; after all, she was the site owner's daughter-in-law, the mother of his only grandchild. What would they do – prosecute her for stealing from the house she lived in? She did, however, ensure that the food she stole only amounted to *some* of the chicken, or a *quarter* of the loaf of bread, or a *few* chunks of cake or cheese or potato or pastry or indeed just *anything*, but never everything. It was just enough to make it worthwhile for the men, but not so much that Frau Hinkel could be certain food had been stolen. And occasionally – just in case Frau Hinkel had suspicions – Giselle would tell her she'd felt hungry and had taken food for herself or her son.

By March, while her methods had become slick and quick, her concentration was inevitably starting to lapse. One morning she was busy filling a paper bag with food when she heard a familiar voice quiz her from the kitchen doorway.

"What are you doing?" it said sternly.

The words made Giselle jump. "Petra, I didn't realize you were still in the house."

"Clearly." Petra strode up to her and peered into the paper bag at the chunks of meat, cake and cheese.

Petra knew she'd been to the site before, so there was no point in Giselle lying; Petra was too sharp for that.

"You know exactly what I'm doing," Giselle said.

"My suspicions are correct. You must have been doing this for months. Mother is always asking me if I'm taking food."

"Is that why you're here – to catch me? Is that why you told me you were going into Linz and left the house half an hour ago?"

Petra tutted. "*You* are accusing *me* of deceit?"

"The war will soon be over."

"The war will be over when the Third Reich says it is."

"But what does Herr Hitler say about Italy, Russia, France, or Belgium? I know you follow the news and you can read between the lines. You must know in your heart that the end is near for your precious National Socialists. Just let me do this. Please. Those men are starving. If only some of them live a few weeks more, they could live to be seventy."

Petra didn't reply, just continued staring at Giselle. It was the stare of someone whose dream was slowly slipping away.

Giselle grabbed the paper bag. "Well, I'm going. I'm asking you not to tell your parents about this, but it's up to you. Perhaps for once you'll do the right thing."

Giselle hurried out, leaving the door swinging in her wake, and ran all the way across cold, compacted earth to the site. She left the food on a low wall, where the men had come to expect it. She would usually wait awhile, but today was cold and in her haste she'd forgotten her coat. She took a few steps back toward the house, hugging herself, and then a horrible thought congealed in her mind.

It wasn't only her coat she'd forgotten about.

Her son.

She'd left Petra alone in the house with her son.

She fled, for once not caring if anyone spotted her, back to the house, running straight through the kitchen door that was still open. She thumped upstairs and didn't stop running until she entered the bedroom, where her son was sitting on the floor, playing with wooden blocks. Startled at her sudden and breathless appearance, he started crying, and her heart felt each bawl. But she picked him up, held him close, shushed him, rocked him slowly from side-to-side as if she were on a dance floor, and eventually his crying subsided, as did her anxiety.

He said she was hurting him. She apologized, kissed his forehead, and let him down, telling him to carry on playing.

And then, straight ahead of her, on the far side of the room, she saw her suitcase – the one she kept padlocked – split open with all her most treasured possessions spewing out of it. She looked at her son, then the case, then her son again.

She heard his little voice say, "Aunt Petra said she needed something from it."

She dropped to her knees and sorted through the history of her life, her hands a blur, tossing clothes and old letters and notebooks and papers into the air, desperately searching for her passport. The passport only *she* knew had a large red "J" stamped on it.

She thumped the suitcase in anger, got to her feet and thundered out of her bedroom – into Petra's. "Where's my passport?" she shouted from the doorway.

Petra, lounging on her bed, grinned. "Your passport is safe, Jewess."

"Give it back to me."

"You know, I always had a suspicion something was wrong with you."

Giselle felt her face flush, her legs weaken, her head buzz. For a moment she struggled to breathe, then she took some deep gasps and turned her back on Petra.

A plan of sorts came to her from nowhere – probably from thoughts of desperation. She'd become tired of this place. She had no idea where to go, but knew she couldn't stay here; she couldn't bear to see the faces of Kurt's family ever again.

She plucked the key from its hole, stepped outside, slammed the door shut, and locked it.

Petra was still hammering on the door when Giselle and her son, hand in hand, hurried out of the house with a change of clothes, as much food as they could carry, and what little money she possessed.

§

Klara's shock at being widowed had quickly turned to bitter thoughts of what Felix would now miss out on, but by 1945 this had softened to an acceptance that perhaps she'd had her run of luck in meeting him and escaping from Vienna.

There was also more guilt in her heart than she ever thought possible.

Since that horrible day last year when the two men from the naval authorities had turned up, there had been another important development, and now, almost three months after the visit from those two men, and ten weeks after her husband's funeral, it was time for Klara to share it.

On a bright March morning that promised more warmth than it was ever likely to deliver, Klara sat Ma and Pa down to break the news to them. She spoke quietly, wanting no fanfare, no celebration, no cheer at all, just that the unvarnished fact – although not the complete truth – be out in the open.

"I'm having a baby," she said to them.

Their jaws fell open. They stared at each other for a few seconds.

"Are you serious?" Pa said.

"And are you certain?" Ma said.

She nodded. "Three months gone."

Pa started crying first, the sags under his eyes catching and holding the tears. But when Ma started, she was easily the noisier of the two. They hugged her, Ma saying she was so pleased, Pa saying she'd made him as happy as a hog in a mud bath. Then they hugged each other, Ma saying they were going to be grandparents, Pa saying they would have a permanent reminder of Felix in flesh-and-blood form.

"We promise we'll look after you," Ma said.

"And our grandchild too," Pa added. "So long as there's a cent in this house you'll want for nothing. Y'hear me?"

"I don't want too much fuss," Klara said, trying to smile innocently.

"But we can tell people, right? It's no secret, is it?"

"I'd rather we kept it to ourselves just for now."

Ma and Pa consulted each other with a glance.

"Any particular reason, my dear?" Ma asked. "Times like these, we could do with sharing good news."

Klara shook her head. "Not just yet, please. It just feels like . . . tempting fate, if that's the right phrase."

Pa shrugged. "Whatever you say, Klara."

They accepted Klara's wishes without further questioning, going about their daily business, not even mentioning it again.

And it wasn't the only thing they hadn't mentioned.

They'd stopped talking about Larry some weeks ago. It was clearly too painful for them.

Soon after that horrible day the men from the naval authorities had visited, Larry had disappeared in the middle of the night without explanation. Ma and Pa had assumed that returning early to the naval base was the only way he could handle the death of his brother, and they agreed that he should be left to come to terms with the tragedy in his own way, in his own time, and return home only when he was ready. But when the naval authorities contacted them again a few days later to say that Larry hadn't returned from leave and was thus officially AWOL, it only heightened their anguish at losing Felix.

Now, well into the new year, Larry was still AWOL, so Ma and Pa had stopped even mentioning his name. The last talk of him that Klara could remember was when Pa had tried to drown his sorrows in a few bottles of beer and had smashed one against the wall, shouting out from his bunker of self-pity that one son had gone to God, the other had gone to "God knows where."

He'd been taking the beers from that crate that lived on the floor in the coolest corner of the kitchen, the crate that had been there ever since Klara had arrived from Vienna, and seemed to automatically replenish itself no matter how quickly the beer was drunk. And more often than not it was drunk by Larry. Or, at least, it *had been*.

And that beer had an awful lot to answer for.

Klara spent most of March in her bedroom, cursing both the beer and herself, her mind running over and over the events of the days following that visit from the naval authorities the previous December, wondering how she could have done such a thing.

Klara had been unable to sleep that chilly night, doing nothing more than praying for history to change, asking God to go back and make it so that Felix hadn't died.

In desperation, she'd had a waking dream where it had been Felix coming home on leave to find out that Larry had died on that ship. She felt awful for wishing such a thing on poor Larry, then told herself not to feel sorry, that she didn't care about Larry or Ma or Pa – or even Alicia or Giselle or Mama or Papa or Hugo; she cared about *herself* and her wretched condition, and she was going to hold onto any damned dream that made the truth easier to accept.

Having not slept all night, the next day was a blur. She didn't eat all day, went for long walks around the areas she and Felix had frequented, with that optimistic but crazy part of her mind hoping to find him there. After the final walk, she gave up and returned to bed, but was still unable to sleep.

It was then that she thought of the beer. She hated the stuff. No, she *usually* hated the stuff. But she also remembered the taste of it from Felix's lips. She thought perhaps a taste of it might – in some ethereal way – bring him back to life.

She crept out of the bedroom, found the house silent, so snuck into the kitchen and picked up a bottle. She eyed up the opener, hanging on a length of string, then used it. She lifted the tip of the bottle to her mouth and inhaled the aroma. To most people it probably smelled of barley or corn or hops or whatever the hell the stuff was made of; to Klara it smelled of Felix making lazy and beautiful love to her on a humid midsummer's night.

She lifted the bottle and gulped down half of it before stopping to draw for breath.

Guess what? she told herself, *it doesn't taste so bad after all.*

She finished the bottle and opened another. Halfway through that, her head was dizzy and her feet became unsteady. She'd forgotten how wonderful the feeling was – how it somehow promised to dissolve heartache, so she finished it and opened a third bottle, taking a few gulps, this time savoring it, already feeling a little of the pain in her chest seeping away.

It was then that she noticed him, and for a moment her heart grew stronger.

He was in the same room. It was Felix. *It was Felix.* Her beautiful husband hadn't died after all and was—

But no. It wasn't Felix; it was Larry.

He was standing by the kitchen doorway, leaning against the doorframe, an empty beer bottle in his hand, his cheeks ruddy.

She put her bottle down and ran past him, along the main corridor and into her unlit bedroom, where she jumped onto her bed and lay there, listening to the unhurried thump of his footsteps outside. Soon, she sensed him sitting on the edge of the bed, right next to her.

"Never meant to scare ya," he said. "Just wanted another beer."

"I'm sorry I took your beer," she snapped.

"*What?*" He edged himself along, taking her hand, making her sit up next to him. "Relax, Klara. You can have as many beers as you want. You can drink the goddamned lot if it dulls your pain. I just wouldn't recommend it, is all."

"I'm sorry," she said. "I just feel so confused at the moment. Where are Ma and Pa?"

"Oh, they've gone to see the rabbi in town. They'll be a few hours yet. They're cut to pieces. And I'm the same, way madder than a wet hen is what I am. But *you*, Klara, I can't even *begin* to think how *you* must feel."

"I don't know what I feel anymore," she replied. "I feel . . . I feel I have nothing."

"But that's not true."

"I know you mean well, Larry. But I really do have nothing. Now I have no relatives to talk to; I don't even know which of them are alive. I still love Felix, but now there's a voice inside my head telling me I should never have left Vienna, I should have stayed with my family."

Larry shook his head. "Hey, truth here is that you had no realistic choice, and we all know that. You're not thinking straight, and I get that, but hell, don't blame yourself. It's just the way it was over there with those goddamned lunatics in charge. So don't you ever kid yourself about coming here. I'm glad you and Felix came back, and d'you know what? So is everyone else."

A part of Klara knew he was right. The larger part couldn't see that; every thought in her head was overshadowed by the idea that she wanted the world to take a different turn, wanted Felix to still be by her side. She took a breath and tried to rationalize, to explain to Larry. All she had was, "I can't disagree, but also I can't stop being bitter and angry and worried."

"Hey, c'mere." He pulled her toward him. They sat side by side and he put a consoling arm around her. "Listen to me, Klara, and listen good. Be bitter by all means, be as angry as you want to and take it out on me if you feel like it, but hell, don't worry. This is your home and we're your family. So don't worry. Y'hear me?"

"I wish that helped me, Larry."

"Well, how about *you can't change what's happened*? How about *booze isn't the answer*? Do they help?"

Klara shrugged. "Something has been ripped out of my insides. I feel so sick and so alone."

"Whatever else you are, you ain't alone. *You are not alone.* You have us, y'hear me?"

"Larry, could you please do me a favor?"

"Of course. Anything."

"Could you please lie down with me for a moment, just to hold me?"

He said nothing, but she lay back on the bed, and moments later, hesitantly, he joined her, cradling her in his arms, as though protecting her from the world outside and its cruel truth.

Klara shut her eyes and started to believe in her own truth. When she opened them and looked up to his face, in the half-light it was Felix's broad chin and red-rimmed eyes, framed by those ginger-hued locks of hair, that looked down upon her.

"Could you please kiss me?" she said, lifting her face up to his.

"Uh, what?"

"Just give me a kiss. Please."

"No, Klara. No, I really—"

It was too late. His lips tasted of her lips and of Felix's lips. She could feel him pushing her away, resisting, but she held on.

Then his arms overpowered hers.

"I can't do this, Klara. It's wrong. It's *very, very* wrong."

"I love you, Felix," she said.

"No, Klara. I should leave you alone."

She ran her fingers through his hair, kissed his soft neck, his stubbly chin, his lips, his cheek, his lips again, all with the tenderest of touches.

He hesitated, said no a few more times, but she could hear and feel his heavy breathing.

"Damn you, Klara."

She feathered her fingertips over his face, touching nose, cheekbone, forehead, then closing his eyelids. She kissed him on the lips once more and he responded, now using his strength to hold their lips together. She felt his hands caressing her neck, her chin, sensed his fingers being trailed down her breastbone.

It was then that Klara knew she could enjoy her husband's company again, even if it would be for the very last time. There was no sense or justice in the world, so this was her dream to have, and it was only fair that she should grab it and hold it close. For a time that felt like a season, all of her senses melded into one glorious experience that she could not control.

And then, like any other dream, the next thing Klara knew, she was being woken up by a noise. It was a car or truck pulling up outside. She was in total darkness, naked, and for a moment confused about what she thought had happened. Her hands reached out to feel, but she was alone in her bed.

She was alone. Felix must have—

No. Now she remembered. There was no Felix. The men from the navy. There was no Felix.

And there never would be.

She thought again, then reached both arms out on the bed, searching. She was alone – alone but for the fragrance of a desperate sorrow shared as passion.

Then she heard the sounds of doors opening and closing out front, then voices: Ma and Pa returning home.

She looked over to the doorway and saw a strip of light appear at the bottom. Good. She'd shut the door. Or someone had done it for her. Yes, good. She didn't want to speak to anyone right now. She was tired, light-headed, fragile like a trip-wire.

She curled up and went to sleep.

Morning came, and with it a realization of something horrible and unholy having happened the previous night. It was one more thing to shed tears about.

A knock at the door jolted her. She lifted her head and pulled the covers up around her neck.

"Come in."

"Sorry to disturb you, my dear," Ma said. "Have you seen Larry? He's not in his room."

Klara shook her head. It hurt. Her head hurt and so did her heart. But she had to reply – if only out of guilt. "I came to bed yesterday afternoon. I only went down for a drink of water last night, and I didn't see him."

And that was true. She hadn't seen Larry last night. He hadn't been in her bed. That had been Felix. For one last time, *it had been Felix.*

Then Pa appeared at Ma's shoulder. "He's taken his stuff with him," he said. "Poor boy can't cope with being around here, I guess. Must have gone back to report for duty early."

Klara said nothing.

Days later, Klara came out of her bedroom to find two more men from the naval authorities being shown out the door. She waited for them to leave, then asked what had happened.

"He hasn't reported for duty," Ma said to her.

"I'm pretty sure the boy's safe," Pa added. "He's just so cut up about his brother that he's gone AWOL – that's away without leave." He gave Klara a sideways quizzical stare. "Say, Klara, are you sure he didn't say anything to you before he left the other night?"

"I'm certain," she said.

Even by March, Klara had still said nothing; it seemed easier all round to let Ma and Pa believe the obvious: that their remaining son had gone missing due to being upset about losing his brother.

And why not? Klara told herself. *What else did he have to be upset about?*

None of that stopped her being worried for his safety.

She started to worry a hell of a lot more when May arrived and there was still no news of him.

TALE THREE

Salvage and Legacy
May 1945 to June 2012

In a world close to peace and looking forward to new beginnings, Austria is once again free from German shackles. Dirty clothes are washed and washed, some stains fade, but some persist.

Chapter Fifteen
San Antonio, Texas, USA. June 2012

The décor – or lack of it – was the first thing that struck Hugo about the place, and his nerves wouldn't let him be quiet about it.

As he sat down in the waiting room with Eleanor, he leaned toward her and whispered, "Isn't this place a little bare and minimalistic for an Estate Attorney's office?"

She whispered back, "You mean, as in *uncluttered and stylish*, or as in *cheap and basic*?" She didn't even try to conceal her smirk.

He saw the smirk and raised her a crooked grin. "Thanks," he said.

"What for?"

"For not being sensitive and understanding and all that garbage. I get the urge to stick a finger down my throat when you do that."

"I do sensitive and understanding? Really?"

"Only on your off days. But I forgive you."

A gentle laugh escaped from her lips, then she playfully bumped her shoulder onto his. "You know I'm just trying to humor it out."

"Like you always do."

"Like I always do. It's really affected you. Even the girls can see that."

"Girls? Are we still calling them that? Even when they're all over thirty?"

"Don't try to change the subject. We all know it's thrown you off balance."

Hugo stared at his wife's face for a few seconds – at the warm blue-gray eyes that had represented his closest companion for over forty years. He screwed his own face up into a grimace before replying.

"Mmm, I wouldn't say she *threw me off balance* exactly. Caught me off guard, is all. Like a sniper would. Part of me thought she'd be around forever. I know I spent the last ten years saying 'this could be her last birthday,' or 'she might not see another thanksgiving,' or 'let's make Christmas special for her because it might be her last one,' but somehow . . ."

"What?"

"I just never believed those things; I always thought it would happen next year or the year after. Like the *tomorrow never comes* thing."

"I get that. But you were no worse than anybody else. When she hit ninety we all kinda gave up on the idea of the old bird being mortal."

For a fleeting second, another image of Hugo's mother popped into his head – an often-remembered vignette of him bringing Eleanor home for the first time in the late sixties.

Yes, he'd expected the archetypal mother's disapproval of his new girlfriend, but at that stage he wasn't yet mature enough to appreciate exactly how deep his mother's feelings on that or indeed any subject were. While she wasn't exactly rude or offensive, she was unable to disguise her disdain for a hippie girl in faded bell-bottoms and long, red-streaked hair that dragged across a baggy top stenciled with flowers.

It had taken nineteen years to produce that girl, but it would take another two decades, a wedding and three granddaughters for his mother to truly accept Eleanor as her daughter-in-law.

She was in her seventies by the time she apologized to him and admitted she'd been wrong about Eleanor, her only excuse being that she had a stubborn attitude and wouldn't have gotten where she had without it.

A fly – one of many in the waiting room – almost hit Hugo in the face and made him break his gaze away from his wife, and he took another look around the room to clear his mind of those memories.

While growing up in San Antonio he'd never been inside any attorney's office, and back in Dallas – where he'd now lived for forty years – he'd only been in a couple, and their waiting rooms had been expensively and tastefully furnished, with artsy prints on the walls and leather couches strategically placed under subtle lighting. But here, the hard plastic chairs reminded him of his school classroom, and the only prints adorning the walls were maps of Texas and the USA, both out of date and yellowed by the ruthless Texan sunlight.

The desk where a secretary tapped away at her keyboard was badly chipped at one corner, the damage partially covered by an electric fan that appeared to do nothing more than help the flies circulate. More fans peppered the room: one on a windowsill, another on a filing cabinet, and even one on the end chair to his left. It was probably the only attorney's office without air-conditioning in the whole county. The scene made him laugh inside. It was typical of his mother to choose what she would doubtless have called "the most financially advantageous firm" to take care of her will.

"I guess I'm nervous about this too," he mumbled, nodding at the door ahead of them.

"I don't get why you had to come here in person."

"Neither do I. That's why I'm nervous, dummy."

"Hey. Dummy yourself."

They sat in silence for a few minutes. Then the door opened, and a dome carrying a pair of black-framed glasses popped out.

"Guess you must be Hugo, huh?"

"Guess I must be."

"Well, come right on in, sir."

Hugo slapped his palms onto his knees and groaned as he pushed himself out of the seat. Eleanor was only two years his junior, but irritatingly managed to get up without the indignity of groaning, and moments later they were both inside the office of *Ruben Schwartz III, family law with grand service, not grandiose prices.*

"Hello, Ruben," Hugo said as he shook hands. "Good to meet you face to face. This is my wife, Eleanor."

"Uh, sure. You mentioned your beloved on the phone. Good day, ma'am."

They all sat, and Hugo allowed his eyes to wander while Ruben rearranged the papers on the desk between them.

Rickety-looking bookshelves covered one wall of the room, probably held firm only by the masses of legal books weighing them down, he surmised. The air in here was just as hot and sticky as it had been in the waiting room, although at least these chairs were padded. Hugo discreetly pressed his thumb into his, then nodded to Eleanor as if he was impressed. She gave a frown as if to say, *not discreetly enough.*

"Okay," Ruben said, briefly flicking his eyes toward Eleanor before returning his attention to Hugo. "I think I already told you how sorry I was to hear of your mother's passing," he said in a drawl that somehow seemed stronger and more endearing than the Dallas accent Hugo had become used to.

"Had to go eventually," Hugo said.

"Part of our contract with the good Lord," Ruben replied with all the emotional warmth of one of those legal tomes on the shelves. "And once again I apologize for dragging you all the way from Dallas."

"I did wonder why you wanted to see me in person," Hugo said. "I mean, under the circumstances I don't mind, not at all. It's good to visit a few of my old haunts. But I did wonder."

"Mmm . . ." Ruben nodded, thinking. "It's true I could have just mailed you a copy of your dear mother's will; as the named executor that's your right. But due to some of what you might call *the small print,* I had little choice but to insist we do this face to face."

"Oh?" Hugo said, glancing at Eleanor and bobbing his eyebrows up, the usual pre-arranged sign that he wanted some support – support that on this occasion wasn't forthcoming.

The two of them had talked about his mother's will on the journey over. As well as moaning about why the hell he was required to trek over to San Antonio, Hugo said that he assumed his mother would leave everything to him. And that wasn't out of wishful thinking, but simply because he was an only child and he didn't think she'd been close to anybody else in her later years apart from her caregivers, who Hugo had already insisted would be well rewarded for their efforts regardless of the will. Eleanor had espoused in her usual blunt but accurate language that when a person got super-old and outlived all their contemporaries, loneliness kind of went with the territory, so she was equally puzzled about the need for a journey to San Antonio.

Either way, Ruben Schwartz didn't take the bait of Hugo's exclamation of surprise. But Hugo assumed it didn't matter; it would all come out in the wash.

"Without further ado," Ruben pronounced, tapping the sheet of paper in front of him, "I have here your late mother's last will and testament."

Hugo sat up a little straighter.

Chapter Sixteen
May to December 1945

Alicia repeatedly told herself she was safe in hospital, but a part of her mind couldn't settle while knowing she was only a stone's throw from that disgusting camp. It was too close, but then again, anyplace in the world would have been too close.

She'd complained about it, asking to be moved further away, but had always been told that it was safer for her to stay put until she'd recovered, and that the location didn't matter.

And right this second, that was probably true; all her senses were tuned to something more important. She was having a hard time believing what she was hearing.

No. It was more than that: she simply *would not* believe what she was being told.

She'd spent more weeks than she could remember recuperating at a local temporary hospital set up by the Soviets, who eventually brought in an interpreter to explain to Alicia what had happened to her.

The Germans had abandoned the Auschwitz complex of camps when they'd heard that approaching Soviet forces weren't too far away. Their plan had been to raze all buildings to the ground, to destroy all records and documents relating to the camp operation, to march all prisoners toward Germany, and to kill every prisoner physically unable to leave. But in their panic – due to the speed of the Soviet advance – they fled when the job had been only half-completed.

So when Soviet forces arrived soon afterward, they found mounds of rotting corpses, huge quantities of clothing and hair taken from prisoners, but also thousands of emaciated people just like Alicia. She was told that the hospital in which she was recuperating had been set up by the Soviet authorities to care for the survivors and was staffed mostly by Russians and Poles.

By May 1945, Alicia had come to terms with the fact that her daughter had been too ill-nourished to survive. She had her son, however, and both made slow and steady progress, putting on weight week by week and building up muscle by gentle exercise.

She'd just been woken up first thing in the morning when she heard the news. And that news was the thing that she simply *would not* believe.

They were saying that the war in Europe was over, that Germany had surrendered. At first Alicia could get no words to come from her mouth. She just shook her head in disagreement.

"But it's true," the interpreter told her. "They've surrendered."

"It's a trick," Alicia said. "I know that isn't true. It can't be."

"But it is. It's been on the radio broadcasts."

"You're lying."

The interpreter painted a sympathetic frown on her forehead. *Perhaps she was part of the trick. Alicia hated her.*

The woman lowered her voice. "I'm not lying, Alicia. It's true. The rumor is that Adolf Hitler committed suicide some time before the surrender."

"Well, the rumors are wrong. He would never do that. And Germany would never surrender. He has a plan. I know it."

The interpreter smiled sweetly, and explained, "A new German government is in place. The representatives are negotiating with the British, French, Americans, and Russians. They're deciding what happens now to Germany."

Alicia shook her head again, this time wildly, her teeth grinding. "I don't believe you. He'll be somewhere. He'll turn up in time. He has a plan. Perhaps he'll . . . he'll . . . he'll let opposing forces into Germany then ambush them." She pulled the sheets away and swung her legs out to the side. "Where's my son?"

"I'm sure your son is safe."

"What have you done with him?"

"Calm down, Alicia. He's probably eating breakfast."

"I want him here now. We're leaving. You can't fool me. We both know Hitler isn't really finished."

The interpreter laid a hand on Alicia's arm. "Please relax. It's the truth. The war in Europe is over. The people who served in Hitler's government are either in prison or being pursued."

Alicia pulled her arm away and stood up. "I want my son," she said. "I want him here, now. We're leaving." She got to her feet, tottered unsteadily for a few seconds, then headed for the door.

The interpreter shouted out something that Alicia didn't understand, and very soon two strong-armed men appeared from nowhere and stood in front of Alicia, closing in, standing between her and the door. She lunged to the side. One of them grabbed her, and between the two of them they took her back to her bed. She slapped one of them in the face. A whistle cut the air, then more people arrived. Alicia tried again to force her way beyond the two men. She tried to shake herself from their grasp but their strength was too much. One of the men held her arm still while a nurse filled a syringe.

"It's a trap!" Alicia shouted out. "Don't believe it when they say Germany has surrendered. None of you should believe that."

As the nurse jabbed the needle into her arm, Alicia spat in her face. "I know what you're doing. Let me go. Let me GO!"

She heard a soft voice say, "I'm sorry, but this is necessary," and then her eyelids became heavy and she felt the side of her face sink back into the pillow. She cursed the Germans, cursed all the people standing over her, then her whole body went limp, her muscles unable to obey her orders.

The next time she woke up, she was woozy, only able to move slowly, and completely unable to focus. She remembered being in some sort of hospital, but couldn't understand what was happening.

Perhaps it was time to give up. Perhaps it was over.

She fell back to sleep.

§

Since leaving the Hinkel's house in Linz, Giselle and her son had spent many days making their way through various towns and villages, trying to follow the route of the Danube, occasionally crossing over it, sometimes washing in its shallow edges, always assured that this gently sloping valley led all the way from Linz to Vienna.

Their mornings consisted of walking toward that city she still saw as her home. Yes, she knew that bombs had turned parts of the city to rubble. But it would still be *her home*.

Their afternoons were spent begging for food in the streets, sometimes even stealing vegetables and eating them raw. And when darkness fell, there would always be a hay barn, a shop doorway, or occasionally some sympathetic Austrian's shed or outhouse to sleep in. Her son only ever complained when the walking became too much, and she would carry him on her shoulders, adding to her own fatigue, inevitably slowing her own personal march on Vienna. She had no idea what she would come across there, but hoped, at the very least, she would find answers. Perhaps even family.

On one spring evening, when the day had been sunny but the evening skies had quickly become overcast, they were walking along a quiet street on the outskirts of one of the many pretty villages that overlooked the Danube when they heard a loud honk from behind them. Startled, Giselle turned to see a car – a big black monster, so it seemed in the dusk light – lurching to one side to get around them. A shout came from the open window: "For God's sake, get off the road!"

Giselle then heard another voice, the ever present one from closer to home.

"I'm scared, Mama."

Soon there were tears. She picked him up and carried him, telling him there was nothing to be scared of, just some nasty angry man who would probably go home to his nasty wife and nasty children. She turned a corner, then stifled a curse as a spot of rain hit her face.

And then she saw him – clean-shaven, smartly-dressed, coal-black hair neatly combed to the side. Behind him was the parked car, in front of him a door. He held a briefcase and newspaper in one hand, a set of keys in the other, fiddling with them while he mumbled noises of complaint. Then he spotted Giselle and froze.

She walked toward him, telling herself not to even make eye contact, but to continue without even a hint of hesitation. She passed him, conscious that he was looking at her, but ignoring him.

"I'm sorry," he said behind her back.

She turned. "What?" she said sternly.

"I've had a terrible day. I'm sorry I shouted at you."

Giselle wiped some of the raindrops that had fallen onto her son's face and said, "You can't harm me. It's my son you should apologize to."

The man dropped his keys, then bent down and fumbled to retrieve them. "In that case, I'm sorry I upset your son."

Giselle offered him a glare, then started walking again, this time across the road to avoid him.

"You're not from around here," she heard him in a questioning tone.

"We're walking to Vienna."

"Vienna? Why would you want to go there?" Before she could answer he added, "Anyway, you won't get there tonight."

She thought of telling him not to be stupid, that she knew how far it was – probably another week of walking at the very least. She turned and ran her eyes up and down his lean frame, trying to assess his intentions, trying to ignore the rain that was now pouring down on all three of them.

"Would you like to shelter here for a while?" he said, pointing his key at the door in front of him. "I live alone but you'll both be safe and warm. I promise."

She hesitated, but a shiver made up her mind. She'd taken much greater risks and survived. "That's very kind of you," she replied, walking toward him. "As long as you're sure we're not imposing."

He put his key in the lock, but then stopped. "Were you born in Vienna?" he said.

She nodded.

"What part?"

"Margareten," she replied with no hesitation.

"So, you're not . . . Jews?"

In the distance, across the river, a dagger of lightning fell upon a high field.

"No," she said. "Don't worry, we're not Jews."

"Let's get out of the rain," he said.

They warmed their bones by the fire, which also dried their clothes. They ate rye bread and hearty vegetable soup made by the man's mother, but they hardly talked before tiredness forced them all to sleep, the man in his bed upstairs, Giselle and her son in armchairs by the fire.

By the next morning their clothes were completely dry, and after a breakfast of hot milk and buttered bread, Giselle said they had to get going, that there was a lot of walking to do.

As she gathered her belongings, she pointed at the newspaper, folded tightly next to the logs by the fire. "Do you mind if I take your newspaper?"

"How educated of you," he said.

"We put the sheets in our clothes. It helps keep us warm on the cold nights."

"Oh, I'm sorry." He picked up the paper and handed it to her.

It was then that Giselle's world turned inside out, so it seemed. She thought of the pain, the turmoil, the mess that had been happening all over Europe and beyond for the past few years. She could do nothing but stare at the headline:

Germany Surrenders

Tears stopped her reading further, but she couldn't take her eyes away from the headline.

"Is . . . is this true?" she said. "Has Hitler surrendered?"

"You didn't know?" A hollow laugh came from the man's mouth. "Hitler's dead," he said dolefully. "But yes, we've surrendered. Isn't it terrible?"

"Oh, yes. Awful."

"Were you a party member?"

Giselle nodded. "Of course."

She thanked him for all his help, and hurried out the door, keener than ever for her and her son to witness the bright new dawn that she knew lay in front of them.

Just over a week later, they entered Vienna.

For the first hour or so, Giselle wandered around aimlessly, one hand firmly holding her son, gazing at a city that was, in parts, little more than a rubble-strewn wasteland. Then she reached Leopoldstadt, taking her first steps for over six years around the streets of her childhood. This was her birthplace, her home, the site of so many pleasant memories: holding her Mama's hand as she browsed the stores; being taken to the coffee shop by Papa; playing in the streets and parks with her sisters and friends.

But since she'd been away, there had been many horrific scenes for those she'd left behind, and it showed in the houses destroyed by bombs, the filthy and dusty streets, and the disheveled figures that shuffled along the sidewalks. The scenes weren't so different from the last time she'd been here. But no. No, *there was a difference.* The figures were scruffy and skinny, just as they'd been in 1939, but now they chatted, they smiled.

These were people who possessed freedom – people who now held hope of better times to come.

The thought made her remember something Papa had said, something he'd been told after surviving the Great War: however bad things seemed, if there was peace and freedom, there was also optimism.

This great city and its people *would* recover.

She continued to meander the streets, finding the apartment where she'd been brought up – where it was just possible her parents and brother still lived, or even where new occupants might show a little sympathy to a mother and child lost in the confusion of this embryonic renaissance. But no. There was only a rather rude man who said he knew nothing about any Rosenthals.

It was much the same story at the apartments her two sisters used to live at, although one of the new occupants said, "Oh, the Jews. I don't know where they are and I don't care."

She felt like telling them the news over and over again until they understood: *the war is over. Hitler and his government have been defeated. Can't you see the Soviet troops on street corners? How do you think those bridges across the Danube got destroyed?*

There was talk of Vienna, like the rest of Austria, being divided up into areas to be controlled by American, British, French, and Soviet authorities. There was also talk of recrimination by Soviet troops, but for most people the prospect of Austria becoming an independent country again was clearly on the horizon.

Regardless of those considerations, food and somewhere to sleep was of more immediate concern.

The former was sorted out by the various soup kitchens which had been set up by the occupying forces.

The latter was a more complex problem. Giselle had hoped to find Mama or Alicia or Klara here – or just *anyone* she knew who would provide shelter – but strangely she recognized nobody. Still, they hadn't experienced bedsheets around their bodies for weeks, so in the short term any form of shelter would do.

They lined up outside a hostel set up inside a dance hall, and slept on the floor with over a hundred other people. Giselle and her son were warm; even their feet were warm, which they hadn't been for days. It was dry. It was safe. She was back in her home city, and for all its faults, her home city now tasted of hope. Despite the groaning and snoring noises coming from every direction, she slept more soundly than she had done for a long time.

§

On the ranch in San Antonio, the end of the war in Europe was welcomed rather than celebrated.

With one son killed in action and the other missing, Ma and Pa had lost their two most treasured possessions and the loss was still too raw for them to cheer on soldiers, sailors, and airmen returning from the hostilities. But they coped, sharing their grief with Klara, but also sharing a little bittersweet joy at the promise of a new life to come.

Klara was lonely when in her bed, but the rest of her time was largely occupied by planning for her new baby: purchases of clothes and equipment, visits to the hospital for checkups, reading books, and listening to Ma's suggestions. Work at the factory and on the farm had been gradually taken over by men released by the armed forces, so Klara had given up work long before her physical limitations forced her to.

The war against Japan still rolled on, but the outcome was in no doubt. The mood of the nation had also shifted; the constant urgency in every aspect of commerce and society had largely been relaxed when the war in Europe had stopped.

At the end of May they got news that changed everything. It was a phone call, completely out of the blue. Larry assured them he was fine and well – although a little unclean and hungry – and told them he was going to turn himself in to the naval authorities. Because he'd gone AWOL there was a sentence to serve, but they took into account – so they said – his previous good record, the shock of the loss of his brother, and the optimism of the day. He served a month in a military prison before a dishonorable discharge for desertion.

When he eventually arrived home, the first thing he did was apologize again and again to his parents for putting them through the worry. They insisted no apology was necessary, that they understood perfectly his motivations. It was only when Klara awkwardly pushed herself up from her chair that he noticed her condition.

In fact, he couldn't take his eyes off her torso, and his face blushed.

"I forgot to tell you on the phone about Klara," Pa said. "Isn't it a blessing that we'll have more than just memories of your brother?"

"Uh, yeah," was all Larry could say.

Pa let out a slightly annoyed laugh and said, "Well, aren't you going to congratulate the girl?"

"Oh, jeez. Excuse my manners. That's swell news, Klara. I'm real happy for you. It's just, uh . . ."

"Shock?" Ma suggested.

"You could say that."

Klara could almost see his mind counting back the months. "It's due September," she said to help, still judging his reaction.

"Uh . . . so you, uh . . ."

"She what?" Pa snapped at him.

"Oh, nothing. Nothing at all."

"Hey, I know you've had it rough, son, but you could be happier for Klara. Don't you think it's great news?"

"Oh, of course." Larry was clearly trying not to stare, but failing. Eventually he turned his whole body away from her and said, "Hey, can I get food around here?"

The next hour was taken up with them all eating, and with Larry telling his parents about how he'd survived for all those months travelling around Texas and Arizona, offering casual labor in return for food and shelter. It was sometime later that he asked Klara to go for a walk with him over the fields. At first she declined. He insisted, said he wanted to get out of the house and get some fresh air, that they could catch up. She accepted, if only to save Ma and Pa from getting even more confused than they already were.

"I'm sorry, Klara," Larry said as soon as they were out of earshot of the ranch house. "I had to get you alone."

"Why so?" she asked flatly.

"Ma and Pa think I went AWOL because I was upset about Felix. I'm assuming they don't know the truth. Is that right?"

"What do you mean? Isn't that why you ran away?"

"Hey, Felix's death hit me hard, and no mistaking, but we both know why I wasted those months bumming around the minor towns of two states."

Klara kept her head up and stared straight ahead as they walked on. "What other reason would you have?"

He stopped still. She carried on walking until he jumped toward her and held her steady. They stood face to face in the middle of the field. He looked back, but the ranch house was now out of sight.

"Klara, I don't blame you if you hate me. I did a terrible and despicable thing."

"Did you? What was that?"

"Let's not kid ourselves, honey. You're trying to tell me that after all those years of trying, Felix gets you pregnant just before he . . . before he . . . well, look, we both know that ain't the truth."

"That *is* the truth, Larry. It's the only explanation."

"All I'm saying is . . ." He flicked a finger toward her prominent belly. ". . . if you need any help, well, I'm here for you."

"That's very kind of you, Larry. I'll bear that in mind."

"You know I hate myself, don't you?"

"Why should you do that?"

He gave a loud grunt. "Look, can we quit with the charade, Klara? I took advantage of you. You needed comfort and help, but instead of giving you that, I took advantage. I did a horrible, selfish thing that night, and I'm ashamed of myself."

Klara looked him up and down, then stared at him, daring him with her eyes. "I have to say, I haven't the faintest idea what you're talking about."

"Oh, you do. Yes, you do. We were both a little drunk, but you remember, sure y'do."

"I don't want to fall out with you, Larry, so listen to me, once and forever. The last time you were here, I spent the entire night alone in my bed, grieving the loss of my husband, not yet aware that I was carrying his baby. I didn't even *see* you."

"But . . ."

"That's the truth, Larry. *That is the truth. Do you understand what I'm saying?*"

His confused expression faded. He nodded slowly. "Oh, yeah. I think I've only just understood, and I'm sorry."

"Good. Now I suggest we get back inside. I can't stand or walk for too long these days."

Klara gulped, knowing she'd done the hard part – the part she'd rehearsed a hundred times over the past month. But she saw how the confusion on Larry's face turned to acceptance and then perhaps even to disappointment. For a moment, Klara pitied him. A lot of men in his position would have run away, and many would have stayed away, but few would have returned and offered to help. And he was also offering to share the shame too, and that helped her even more.

"Now I understand you perfectly," Larry said. "And I'll never mention it again, so help me God, but if you ever need my help – and I mean in five or ten or even fifty years' time – I'll be here."

She reached out a hand and touched his arm, caressing it for only a second. "Thank you," she said. "You're a decent man, Larry. Don't hate yourself."

He nodded, and they started walking back to the ranch.

"What was Arizona like?" Klara asked as they were in sight of the ranch house.

"Texas," he replied with a shrug.

She laughed. It was her first genuine laugh for some time.

It was good to have Larry back.

Chapter Seventeen
San Antonio, Texas, USA. June 2012

In his office, Ruben Schwartz smiled briefly, but only out of politeness, Hugo thought, and perhaps to prove he didn't charge for absolutely everything. He ran the tip of his pen down the side of the sheet of paper as he scanned it.

"You'll be aware," he said, his voice slipping into dreary, legally-binding mode, "that the majority of the value of your mother's non-business assets including the house were used up paying for her care in her later years."

"That was always fine by me," Hugo said. "I think I already explained to you how I moved away from the area some time ago, and I always wanted the best for her because I wasn't here."

"We both did," Eleanor added.

"I'm sure. Now, the residue amounts to a little under forty-thousand dollars, fifty percent of which is left to various local charities and fifty percent to your good self."

"Again, fine by me."

"Yes, I always found your mother to be a kind, thoughtful woman at heart despite her stubbornness. Now, turning to the—"

"Hey, hey. Back up a little. Did you just say 'Stubbornness'? You do realize you're talking about my mother here, don't you? Meaning that I'm, like, her son, yeah?"

"Hugo!" Eleanor hissed in an admonishing tone.

Ruben held up a hand. "That's . . . that's okay. I apologize for any offense caused, sir, but, uh . . ."

"But what?"

"Now is probably a good time to explain the small print I mentioned earlier. You see, when I was preparing your mother's will, there was one small detail she insisted on inserting despite my advice to the contrary."

"What detail?" Hugo asked.

"Well, she wanted you, as her sole offspring, to be the executor of her will, which was fine, and I told her I would contact you when the sad occasion arose, but she insisted you be here in person with your wife, and that I keep the reason for that stipulation secret until now."

"I don't quite understand."

"With the greatest respect, sir, I think you might be trying to see things that aren't there. She wanted you to be here in person with your good lady wife, is all. She didn't want me to just mail it to you or tell you over the phone."

"Did she say why?"

"Not until I told her again that it wasn't necessary, after which she said she was paying me, so I would do exactly as she said. She could be quite . . ."

"Stubborn?" Eleanor suggested.

Ruben simply coughed and said, "Better we just move on. Point is, she eventually told me the reason for her stipulation. Which is that she feared for your reaction when you found out the details. Hence she didn't want you to be alone when you heard it."

"You mean, I might not like some of the detail?"

"Correct, sir. That was precisely her concern."

Hugo shrugged. "As I say, it's her will, so I'll go along with whatever she wanted."

"I certainly hope so. I reckon we'll see." He tapped his pen halfway down the sheet of paper. "Let's continue with the details, shall we?"

"Yes please."

"Well, the second part of your mother's will deals with her holdings of stock in Rosenthal Shoes."

That was better. Hugo could sense himself flushing with pride at the mere mention of the company. His mother had founded the business just after the war and built it up from nothing into a group of three shoe factories in Texas. Even in her fifties she'd worked tirelessly most nights keeping the production, the marketing, and the accounts on track. Hugo remembered her bitter disappointment when he'd broken the news at eighteen that he wanted nothing to do with the company. Only as he matured and became a little more worldly-wise did he realize that she'd been a woman far ahead of her time, a great role model that he often cited in his later years to his daughters.

"And as I'm sure she told you," Ruben continued, "she diluted most of her stock in Rosenthal Shoes over the years."

"We know she lost overall control in the eighties," Eleanor chipped in.

Ruben nodded. "Very much so, and just lately, even though they closed two factories here and moved production of some of their cheaper lines to China, it wasn't the healthiest of companies."

"It was a *good* company," Hugo said. "My mother took care of her employees, paid good wages and treated everyone equally regardless of color even when that wasn't fashionable."

Then he clamped his mouth shut, lips tight. Perhaps banging the drum for his mother's moral fiber and business skills wasn't entirely appropriate here. He let Ruben continue.

"Uh, yes. How times change. Anyhow, in the end your mother owned just five percent of Rosenthal Shoes, and left one third of that to you."

"A third?" Hugo asked.

"I'm guessing the rest goes to charities," Eleanor suggested.

Ruben gave them both a warning glance before shaking his head. "You'll still benefit from over seventy thousand dollars at the current stock price."

Hugo was shocked – not at all feeling like a man who'd just inherited what his mother would have called "an amount worth taking care of." He struggled trying to phrase the obvious question without it sounding selfish.

Luckily, he could always rely on Eleanor to be more forthright.

"What about the other two thirds?" she said.

Another firm glare came from Ruben.

"That's a reasonable question," Hugo said, his voice not exactly full of anger but certainly tinged with it. "We're talking about my mother's will here, after all."

Ruben turned the yellowing sheet of paper around and placed it on the desk in front of Hugo. He started speaking just as Hugo got out his reading glasses.

"This is the part your mother was concerned about – concerned about your reaction, that is. I'm thinking you might be upset about the identity of those other two beneficiaries. All I can advise is that as the executor of the will you have a legal duty to contact these people and ensure that they get what your mother bequeathed to them."

By now Hugo was scanning the sheet, and toward the bottom a sense of disbelief grabbed him. He read the same three lines again and again, and what he read caused what few hair follicles that remained on his head to spring upright.

He looked up and said, "Is this some kind of joke?"

"What is it?" Eleanor said. "What does it say?"

Hugo ignored her and stared at the man opposite. "Who the hell are these people?"

Ruben shifted his backside as if his seat didn't quite fit and he was trying to make it. "You'll have their addresses, just like you'll have the addresses of the charities."

"No, I mean, *what did they mean to my mother?*"

"I'm afraid I'm not at liberty to divulge that information."

"Is it a client confidentiality issue?" Eleanor asked.

"*Client confidentiality?*" Hugo blurted out. "What does that matter? She's *dead.*"

"Hey, calm down," Eleanor said.

"I'm sorry, but . . ." Hugo tapped the top of the piece of paper. ". . . this will is dated 1981. Do you even know where these people live? Or even if they still *do* live?"

"Your mother kept me up to date with the fine details." Ruben picked up a freshly printed sheet of paper and handed it to Hugo. "They were indeed still living the last time we checked, and these are their addresses. Whether they're still living today . . . well, it's now the executor's responsibility to find that out."

Hugo opened his mouth to speak, but instead found himself wiping the light smear of sweat that had appeared on the back of his neck. There was so much he wanted to ask – so much, in fact, that he didn't know where to start. It was left for his wife to fill the awkward silence.

"Thank you very much for all you've done for my husband's mother all these years," she said.

"That's okay, Ma'am. It genuinely was a pleasure dealing with her. She was a feisty sort – and I mean that in a complimentary way, I assure you. She was one of those clients who stick in the memory for a long time. I'll miss her."

"We'll miss her too,' Eleanor said, immediately glaring at Hugo, who nodded agreement.

"Well, I think that concludes our business, unless you have any questions."

Hugo and Eleanor exchanged glances. "No, we don't," Eleanor said.

Ruben stood. "If you need my help ensuring the correct checks are made and the transfer of stock goes through smoothly, then of course I'll be happy to oblige."

"And that's it?" Hugo said. "You expect me to distribute the monies from the stock sale to people I don't know?"

Ruben let a heavy sigh escape from his lips then sat back down. "If it makes you feel any better, sir, when I told you I was not at liberty to divulge to you who those two people are and what they meant to your deceased mother, I probably should have explained that I wouldn't be able to tell you *even if I knew*. I apologize if my poor phraseology caused any misunderstanding."

"Oh."

Nobody spoke for a few seconds. Eleanor, again, was the one to break the silence.

"I guess there's nothing more to discuss," she said. She got to her feet and looked down at the two men, who eventually stood and shook hands.

"I'm sorry if I came across as angry," Hugo said as he folded up the sheets of paper and put them in his jacket pocket.

"Oh, I kind of expected it. Believe me, sir, I've seen far worse reactions to wills in my time. Perhaps now you understand why your mother insisted on you both being here in person."

"I do, and I appreciate that. I'm just . . . in shock."

"Of course. Now, good luck being an executor."

Hugo, questions still swirling around in his mind, hardly heard a word Eleanor said to him as they left the building and got into their car.

Chapter Eighteen
1946

At the makeshift hospital just outside Auschwitz, Alicia had spent the latter part of 1945 insisting that she was right, that there was some conspiracy going on to convince her the war was over, that she didn't trust the Germans and never would. She was shown newspaper reports and dismissed them as fake or propaganda.

It was hard for her mind to yield to the news, but eventually, as the new year dawned, she had accepted what the hospital staff were telling her – that Germany had surrendered, that the war was over, that Europe was adjusting to peace at last.

She'd felt so foolish about holding onto her fears for so long. The doctors told her not to worry, that her attitude was common among concentration camp survivors, that she'd experienced things that had driven others insane, and that in time the mental scars would heal and she would be able to get on with her life.

They even asked her to talk about what "getting on with her life" might mean for her, and she always had the same answer: that she wanted to return to Vienna, her home, with her son, and live a normal life. Whenever she told them that, there were always more words that followed in her head: *I want to live a normal life with my husband and both children – not just one – and also with my Mama, Papa, and brother close by.* She always had to slam the verbal brakes on when it came to those words; there was always the fear that if there appeared to be even a hint of her still being mentally unstable, they would keep her in hospital for longer. So it was something of a surprise when they told her she could leave.

And there was no doubt in her mind about where she was going.

By 1946, a battered and bombed Vienna had been liberated by Soviet forces and the city – like the rest of Austria – was divided into Soviet, American, British, and French areas of control, with the very center alternating between the four. Alicia felt reassured that Leopoldstadt was controlled by the Soviets, the same people who had rescued her from Auschwitz and looked after her in the months that followed.

And although troops were on the streets, they were invisible to Alicia. She was, however, moved by what *wasn't* there: German soldiers sneering and threatening, swastika flags proudly held high, Hitler Youth marching along the sidewalks as if they owned them. She quickly learned that she could walk the streets without having to display her star of David, she could travel on buses, visit the public baths, visit shops whenever they were open. Yes, this was a very different Leopoldstadt to the one she'd left.

The differences took some getting used to, partly because it had taken Alicia so long to accept that Germany was now a defeated nation and Austria was free of National Socialist control. Now, seeing the reality of Vienna, she felt more foolish than ever about her behavior back at the hospital. It was probably for the best that she hadn't told them about her nightmares: of being locked in a burning synagogue on Kristallnacht, of being taken to the edge of the world on a cold and crowded cattle truck, of being locked inside a room with no food, water, or heat and left to die a slow, lingering death. No, if she'd told them about those nightmares, they really would have thought she was mad.

After coming to terms with the changes to the city, Alicia turned to the practicalities: her first priority was to find accommodation. She and her son were initially housed in a room of one of the lesser hotels just outside the Leopoldstadt area – a room they shared with two other small families – but soon they were allocated a small community apartment only three blocks from where she'd been brought up. It had a living room, a kitchen, one small bedroom, and a lavatory – with a large complex of baths to serve the whole complex. Everything was clean and bright. It was paradise.

With her new accommodation came the next job on the agenda: claiming food rations, which would be so much better than relying on soup kitchens. There had been many riots in Vienna about the lack of food, and Alicia knew as much as anyone that the quantities were nowhere near those she'd been used to before the war, but she kept her distance from the protests and simply took what she was given without complaint. She'd come too far and suffered too much to argue about such things, and found any kind of stress upsetting – upsetting enough to make those nightmares more vivid.

The nightmares still infiltrated her sleep more often than not, but she was confident that once she was fully settled back in Vienna, the problem would go away. As the weeks passed by, however, nothing changed. And just when it seemed the nightmares had every intention of sticking by her like a good friend would through thick and thin, she blotted out those morning memories of nighttime aberrations and just got on with life. Yes, if she ignored the nightmares, they would soon go away of their own accord. And if not soon, then eventually. Time was all it took. Time was the greatest healer; didn't they say that?

The next issue to sort out was schooling for her son, and once that was arranged, Alicia had the days to herself, and settled into a routine. Once alone in the apartment she would start by clearing the breakfast table and doing the washing up, then she would clean the kitchen, thoroughly washing all surfaces with a salt and carbolic soap solution, then she would go over the lavatory, scrubbing down everything and cleaning the tiles until they were as good as new, and finally she would brush the carpet and chairs in the living room and bedroom, also taking the opportunity to wipe all surfaces and especially door handles with that same solution to keep them clean.

Somewhere she'd heard the saying that a clean house led to a clean mind, so after a light meal at midday she would wash some clothes in the kitchen sink, wring them out, then hang them to dry across the kitchen. Sometimes there were no dirty clothes so she would wash the bedsheets and blankets instead, or perhaps wash clothes that hadn't been worn but nevertheless looked dirty.

Of course, all of that would leave dirt and germs in the kitchen, meaning it had to be cleaned again, and if she was cleaning the kitchen, she simply *had* to clean every surface in the lavatory. And if she was going to scrub the kitchen and lavatory again, it seemed somehow not quite right to leave out the living room and bedroom, so they would get another clean too.

Yes, twice a week she had to leave the apartment to buy food, but while at home it seemed to make perfect sense to have that rule: she couldn't clean any one room more or less often than she cleaned the others.

So that was the routine and Alicia was happy with it. Routine became her friend. She was also happy that she only had to leave the apartment twice a week to buy food, and anyone who visited – or anyone who might visit in the future, because she hadn't yet had any visitors – would be impressed with the level of cleanliness.

She'd heard that the one synagogue still standing was once again being used for its intended purpose, but she couldn't visit just yet; there was far too much housework to be getting on with. Yes, leaving the apartment twice a week was enough. In fact, sometimes Alicia thought it was perhaps too much. Walking along those sidewalks and crossing those streets only brought back memories of afternoons and evenings out with her family years before –

those Bar Mitzvahs, Rosh Hashanahs and Hanukkahs that now seemed to have happened to a completely different woman.

And anyway, simply walking outside was a waste of time, especially when there was housework to do. Keeping her son well-fed and clean-clothed was ambition enough.

Yes, a clean house led to a clean mind. And given enough time, a clean mind might well rid itself of those nighttime thoughts of burning inside a synagogue, or enduring a cold, endless railroad journey to nowhere, or being locked inside a filthy cabin and left to rot.

As long as she kept the apartment clean, everything else in her life would eventually slot into place.

Definitely.

§

Giselle had settled into a life of comfortable solitude in the new Vienna.

Soon after she'd returned, as the mother of a young boy she'd been provided with modest accommodation and food rations. With life's basic necessities sorted out, she set about finding out what had happened to her family.

She walked the streets searching for faces she recognized, but found none; she knocked on doors on the street where she was brought up, and was met with blank faces; she inquired with the authorities, but was told there were no surviving records relating to her family.

In those weeks, however, she came to both wonder and fear what Mama and Papa would have thought of her behavior over the years – fleeing Leopoldstadt, cutting ties with them, even denying her faith and her history.

The previous September she'd even attended one of the first services to be held at the Stadttempel – the only synagogue to survive the purge of all things Jewish. Even then, it was far from unscathed, the damage and looting it had experienced not yet dealt with.

It was a strange feeling because she no longer thought of herself as a practicing Jew, but it was a connection with her past, something she had no intention of ever disowning again. The reason for attending, however, was more practical than spiritual: while there, she scanned the faces in the hope of recognizing someone – even a neighbor or shopkeeper of old who she wouldn't have known well but who might have possessed information – just *anyone* who might help with what was quickly becoming an obsession that threatened to engulf her. She was surprised and dismayed to discover that she knew nobody there, and apparently nobody knew her.

She decided that the very least she could do was find a job and take responsibility, because it was what Mama and Papa would have wanted. So, early in 1946, when her son was old enough to be left in the care of her neighbor, she started making clothes in a local factory.

She also took an interest in newspaper stories and radio reports, hoping that they might shed some light on what had happened to her family. What she heard and read about the Jewish population of Vienna explained why she didn't recognize anyone: the estimates were that before the German occupation there had been around two hundred thousand living there, and by the end of the war, after the rushed emigrations and forced deportations to ghettos and concentration camps, only a few thousand remained – almost all of them the old, the infirm, the sick, or those protected by marriage like Giselle.

That last fact was the bitterest pill to swallow: if she'd stayed in Vienna, she might have been relatively safe because she was married to Kurt, she might have regained contact with her family, and might now have a better idea what had become of them. Of course, the stakes had been high; nobody had been completely safe, so she might not have lived to make such speculations.

But the most important pieces of news were the stories of the perpetrators of heinous crimes – in prison camps, in ghettoes, in experimental hospitals, and in ordinary towns and cities all over Germany and occupied lands. Giselle took great personal interest in these stories. They troubled her greatly, making her consider what her parents would have wanted her to do.

Early one morning she made her way to the end of the street, slid herself into a phone booth, and plucked a scrap of paper from her pocket.

She dialed the number on the scrap of paper.

"Yes, hello?" she said when the man answered, her voice breaking with a fear that caught her by surprise because she wasn't doing anything wrong. "I have . . . I have . . ."

And there she halted. She asked herself whether she really wanted to do this – whether those who might soon be her enemies could possibly reach her or her son. She could always leave the task to someone else.

So she put the phone down. And as soon as she did that, she knew it was a moment of unforgiveable weakness, but told herself it didn't matter. She'd been through enough over the past seven years; her son had suffered far too much trauma in his short life. Yes, someone else would have to tell the authorities what had happened.

She left the telephone booth and started walking home.

Yes, someone else would tell them.

But as she walked on, her steps hesitant where years ago they'd been filled with confidence, she thought for the hundredth time what might have happened to her parents, to her brother, to her sisters, and their own loved ones. She couldn't shake off what she'd witnessed in Linz, and thought perhaps she never would.

Yes, there had been the shooting – the murder – that she'd stumbled upon while taking a stroll through the meadow, but that had only been the start of it.

The more recent incident – and the one that now forced itself into her mind – had happened during one of the last times she'd taken food to the men working on the construction site, just a few days before Petra had found her out.

As usual, she'd left the food on top of a wall and was on her way back when she heard shouts. These weren't the common shouts used to order men about, but of an anger and intensity that made Giselle fear for her life. She hid behind a huge stack of timber on the site perimeter, crouching to make herself small and keeping still. Two men were arguing. She recognized one voice – the angry one; it was Herr Hinkel himself, and he was clearly in a foul mood.

"He's completely finished," the other man said.

"But you have *deadlines*," Herr Hinkel said, spitting the last word out. "How many times have I told you about the need to keep to the schedule? We need to get this work done."

"I know, but there's nothing left in him, he's had it."

"Damned useless Jews. Have you tried throwing a bucket of cold water over his face?"

"Trust me, Herr Hinkel. You won't get any more work out of this one."

Herr Hinkel cursed. "So you're telling me I need to fetch another to replace him?"

"No. I'm merely telling you that you won't get any more work out of him."

"Damn!" An exasperated sigh filled the air. "Well, there's no point in him being here, is there?"

"What do you mean?"

Herr Hinkel cursed. "Oh, for God's sake don't sound so timid, man. Luckily for you I brought my rifle. I'll do it."

The voices stopped. Giselle heard only grunts. She carefully positioned herself to see through a gap in the stack of timber. She saw three figures pass by. First Herr Hinkel, rifle in hand, then another man who was struggling to drag the barely conscious third man through the mud to the site perimeter. He let go, and Herr Hinkel took aim. The man on the ground mumbled something she didn't understand, and one arm – a withered thing – reached out to his tormentor. Giselle couldn't bear to watch the rest, but heard the gunshot, and heard the next exchange as clear as ice:

"Get rid of him."

A long pause, then, "Where?"

"Stop dithering. Just drop him in the foundations with all the other garbage."

Giselle might not have believed her eyes and ears had this not been the same Herr Hinkel who she'd seen shoot another slave worker on the hillside. It was half an hour before Giselle had the nerve to come out from behind the stack of timber and run back to the house, where she sat alone in bed, re-running the scene in her head.

And now, on this Vienna sidewalk, the scene returned to haunt her, and she thought again. She thought of the stories about the trials that she'd read in newspapers. She wondered whether anyone else *would* tell the authorities, and even whether any of those men from the construction site would still be alive.

But most of all, she wondered what her estranged family would think of her.

Yes, she was haunted by those scenes.

Did she want to be haunted forever?

She turned and walked back to the telephone booth, this time striding, unwavering, as if some of the old, confident, Giselle had returned.

She dialed the same number again.

"Hello," she said. "I got this number from the newspaper article – the one about the trials. I have some information for you about a man who lives in Linz." She paused to listen, then said, "Yes. I'm prepared to give evidence, to tell you everything I witnessed."

§

By September 1946 the war had been over for a year. America, still booming with the spirit and productivity of a country at war, but unencumbered by the costs of such a war, was very much the safe and free country Klara had expected it to be when she'd first arrived all those years ago.

Her baby, like peace, was a year old when Larry broke the news to her. He waited until Ma and Pa had gone to the country store and then until the sound of baby cries had subsided. Klara was washing her little one's clothes when he casually suggested she take a break and asked whether she'd like a cup of coffee.

A few minutes later they were sitting at the kitchen table across from each other.

"So, how are you?" she said.

That was something she never would have said to him a couple of years ago because she would have *known* how he was. But since he'd returned to San Antonio, their walks and talks had gotten rarer and rarer, because she had less time due to motherhood, and he was always out seeing friends and also trying to start a career in the building trade, so they'd drifted apart. But she still knew him well enough to suspect he'd engineered this situation to ask her or tell her something, so she obliged by making it easy for him.

"I'm swell." He smiled, but it was an awkward smile, not the broad and innocent variety of his that she knew and loved. "I, uh, have some news. I wanted you to be the first to know."

"Oh, really?" She feigned a little surprise.

"You know I've been going steady with Deborah for around eight months, don't you?"

"She's a lovely woman."

"Thank you. I guess that's why, uh ... well, we just got engaged. Haven't even told Ma and Pa yet."

"Oh, that's wonderful news, Larry." Klara's smile came easily. The news was no huge surprise, but she was genuinely happy for him – and for herself too. She'd always had a fear in the back of her mind that he had romantic inclinations toward her, so this was proof – or as close to it as she was going to get – that he'd moved on.

"You don't mind?"

"Of course not. I want you to be happy. Congratulations. I'm pleased for you."

"That means a lot coming from you, Klara. It's a big step, for sure."

Klara leaned back and stared up aimlessly. "I remember our wedding back in Vienna. It wasn't a fancy affair by most people's standards, but I was floating on air for weeks afterward. Now it seems such a long time ago."

"I wish I'd been there. You know Felix wanted all of us to go, don't you? Tried to bribe us, then tried to bully us, finally he tried to shame us into it."

"I know. He told me all that at the time."

"We didn't want to admit it at first, but we all thought it was too dangerous."

"And you were probably right about that."

Larry nodded, and there was a lull in the conversation they both took advantage of, each taking a drink.

Then Larry said, "So, what do you think the future holds for you?"

She thought for a moment, pursing her lips. "Well, my mind is on other things at the moment, but in time I'd like to get a job – well, I feel I *need* to get a job to pay back Ma and Pa."

"You're gonna be one o' them there career women?" His mouth shaped to laugh but he stopped himself. "Hey, I'm not making fun of that. Good luck to you. But honestly, Klara, if you want to work you should train for some sort of profession."

"Profession? Me? I was thinking more in terms of getting another job in footwear – perhaps repairing shoes. It's the only skill I have."

Larry was shaking his head. "No, no, no. It's definitely not the only skill you have. You're way better than that. Way smarter. You should be . . . I don't know . . . setting up your own business or something." He clicked his fingers. "I got it. Why not start up a shoe factory?"

"Oh, sure. Let me just get these diapers washed and dried then I'll do that."

"I'm serious, Klara. Not today or tomorrow, but sometime. It's the obvious thing for you to do."

"Oh, I don't know."

"Come on, you're no production line worker. You're a smart lady, make no mistake 'bout that."

"Felix used to say things like that about me."

Larry thought for a moment, clearly dwelling on the memory of his brother. "Here's an idea, why not do it for him?"

"Perhaps in a few years."

"Oh, of course. You're a mother, that comes first. But while we're talking, just remember what I said last year. I love Deborah like no other woman and I'm going to marry her, but if you need my help – at any time – I'll always be here."

"That's nice to know. Thank you." She couldn't take her eyes off him for a few seconds, knowing what she wanted but unsure how to phrase it – or even whether she should phrase it at all.

But he knew her well by now, and read her expression.

"What is it?" he said, squeezing his eyes and giving her a quizzical, sideways stare. "You know you can trust me, don't you?"

"Well . . ." She took a few breaths. "There is something you can help me with."

"Just you name it."

"I want to find out what happened to my family – my sisters, my brother, my parents."

"Oh, jeez." He exhaled loudly. "That's a big one, Klara. I guess you've been too busy just lately to give that much thought."

She shook her head. "That's not true. They're my family. I think about them every day and always have. And I know I can survive today, tomorrow, and next month without knowing, but I'm not sure if I can live a normal life – job, business, study, whatever – until I know what became of them, until I know whether they're even still alive." She blinked her watery eyes and sniffed a couple of times.

Larry rubbed his clean-shaven chin thoughtfully. "I know it's what Felix would have wanted. When you feel ready to start looking, you just tell me what I can do to help, y'hear me?"

Before Klara could answer, they both heard a baby's raucous cry and their eyes flicked to the doorway.

"I hear you, Larry," she said. "And I appreciate it."

She quickly threw the rest of her coffee into her mouth and stood up. But she halted herself, thought for a moment, and leaned down toward Larry. She spoke quietly.

"Larry, could I ask you, does Deborah know about him?" She eyed the door again, this time lingering for a second. "Have you . . . told her what happened?"

He shrugged, then that broad, warm smile that reminded her so much of Felix crept across his face like morning sun gradually covering a field. "What is there to tell?" he whispered.

"Thank you, Larry," she whispered back.

Chapter Nineteen
San Antonio, Texas, USA. June 2012

In the parking lot outside *Schwartz, Schwartz, and Bindesmann*, Hugo
and Eleanor slumped into the seats of their Mercedes, both staring
ahead at the meat processing plant on the other side of the road
puffing out steam. A low-rent location was obviously another
reason why the firm was "financially advantageous to their clients,"
which made Hugo think of his mother again. He tried to forget
thinking about her and concentrate on what to do next, but out of
the blue wondered whether the plant made chicken soup, her
favorite.

"I can't get her out of my mind," he said.

"Anything else would be surprising. Even for me, it's tough to
accept she isn't here anymore."

"Mmm. Talk about someone leaving a hole in your life."

"Exactly. You're perfectly entitled to be upset."

Hugo cast a puzzled glance at the Estate Attorney building.
"More confused than upset. I guess I'll get over it."

"You want me to drive on?"

"Uh . . . yeah. No. I'm not sure."

Eleanor let out a long sigh and fastened her seatbelt. Hugo
fastened his. Eleanor's finger almost touched the start button, but
she pulled it away. "I could just drive on, or you could tell me what
the hell upset you back in there."

"I'm . . . not sure it would help matters."

"It would help my curiosity." When there was no reply Eleanor added, "Okay, it would help my anxiety. That would be a good thing, wouldn't it?"

Hugo almost smiled. "If you must know . . . well, the two people, the two other beneficiaries named on Mother's will . . ."

"Yes?"

"Sounds crazy but . . . their names are both Hugo."

Eleanor stared straight ahead for a few seconds, then said, "Huh?"

"Exactly."

"And their surnames?"

Hugo plucked his reading glasses from his jacket pocket but immediately replaced them. "Ah, what does it matter? Point is I've never heard of them. I don't know the guys. Never have. Never did."

"Weird."

"Exactly."

"So, what, did the old bird clone you?"

"Would you notice?"

"Would I care?"

"Perhaps there are three of me and we've all been swapping places for the last forty years and you never knew."

Eleanor shrugged. "I figured it out. I told the other two, just not you."

At that, Hugo's face cracked into a smile.

"Seriously," she said. "You're telling me you have absolutely no idea who these guys are or what they meant to your mother?"

"That's *exactly* what I'm—" Hugo stopped and thought for a moment, then said, "You know it's not about the money, don't you? I don't care about the money."

"Shut up."

Hugo laughed at that. She'd stolen the "shut up" habit from their youngest daughter.

Eleanor laughed too. "Look," she said, "I know whatever your mother wanted is fine by you. She gave you the best thing a parent can give any child: self-sufficiency. So we don't need the money. But do you know what? I figure you're just as curious as I am to know what those two other Hugos meant to your mother – why she felt she had to include them in her will."

"But I only have their details so I can send them the proceeds from the stock Mother left to them. That's all. I mean, even if I wanted to know who they are – and, more importantly, what they were to my mother . . ."

"Which you clearly do."

"Okay. *Which I do*. But they might not want to talk to me."

"That's true. What's also true is they might just have a lot to say to you. And there's only one way to find out for sure. And as we're here . . ."

"That's assuming they both live in San Antonio."

Eleanor eyed the sheet of paper poking out of Hugo's pocket. "Well, do they?"

"I don't know. I didn't look at the addresses and I don't want to. I feel sick. Just drive."

"Where to? Home?"

"Out of the parking lot."

"Ah *jeez*! I hate when you're like this, Hugo."

"I can't say it's a bundle of fun from where I'm sitting."

"But it could be. It *so* could be. You have a chance to find something out about your mother that might . . . might . . ."

"Might what? Destroy the respect I had for her? Taint all my sweet-smelling memories of her?"

"Suit yourself, Mr. Grump. We need gas." She screeched the tires as she took off, then again as she pulled out of the parking lot into moving traffic, and neither of them spoke until they pulled into a gas station.

"You need anything?" she said as she opened the door.

"You said we need gas."

"Hugo, if you're going to bicker, at least make a contest of it. Should I get drinks while we're stopped here?"

"Chilled water."

Eleanor slammed the door and Hugo fumed for a few seconds while she put her card in the pre-pay machine. As she filled the tank, he continued huffing, aimlessly looking around. He caught sight of her, she caught sight of him looking at her, and she stuck her tongue out at him.

"Damned self-pump stations," he muttered under his breath.

She finished filling the car and Hugo's eyes locked onto her as she headed for the gas station store. His fingers tapped against the door handle the way a nervous hunter might fidget with his rifle. Except that no, he wasn't hunting. Nothing like it. Nothing at all. It was simply that he had a right to know who his two namesakes were, how they were connected to his mother, and, most importantly, why she hadn't told him all about them.

No.

Just *no*, Hugo. He didn't even want to consider that question, because it would turn into one of those recurrent issues that stopped him sleeping at night however much he tried to forget, ignore, push away, dismiss – hell, just *stamp all over till it died.*

He let out a grunt of frustration and pulled out his cell phone to check the weather, the news, the sports results, emails or voicemails from their daughters – just *anything* that would shove that big, blood-red, horrible monster of a question out of his head.

But he needed his reading glasses to check all of that, and they would only remind him of that sheet of paper with the two addresses on it. Besides, it was quicker to switch on the car radio.

A jingle for a motel played. One he hadn't heard of. Perhaps it was new.

He should have returned to San Antonio more often.

Then another jingle. Pizza parlor. Mmm, sounded delicious.

He should have visited her once a month at the very least.

Then another. Who'd have thought there were so many variations of electric garage doors? And all so reasonably—

"*Goddammit!*" he shouted, thumping the door.

Who the hell were those two guys? And why the hell had Mother kept them a secret all these years?

He cursed at the stupid man trying to get him to move to a retirement village near Galveston and turned the radio off.

Memories of his mother flung themselves at him. How she'd spent so much time running the business that she'd felt the need to smother him with attention whenever she got the opportunity; how she'd bought the best education for him; how she had no hobbies or interests outside looking after him and keeping the business afloat; and how totally dedicated to those two goals she'd been.

There had been vacations to pretty much every country on the planet, except, of course, those on the far side of Europe, where she'd originally come from – places, she always insisted, she didn't want to visit again when there was so much of the world she hadn't yet seen.

There were her expensive clothes. She always said she could afford them so there was no reason why not, but everyone knew she looked after what she had, expensive or not, so even those purchases were infrequent.

She'd been a fine mother – perfect in every tangible way, but also distant in a manner Hugo could never quite put his finger on, punctuated only by those rare close moments on vacation together.

She'd been a doting grandmother too. There were always questions and offers of help, lengthy stays in Dallas to spend time with her granddaughters.

There had been many good times, it was true, but there had never, ever been one time when she'd mentioned anyone else called Hugo.

Hugo had once asked where his name had come from, whether he'd been named after someone else in the family. She'd replied that she just liked the name, but her frown indicated there was more to it. Only once had he pressed her on the subject, and she'd become angry, asking why he couldn't just believe her, telling him not to ask again. So he didn't.

But all along there had been something else, something important enough for her to include in her will, but clearly not important enough to share with her adult son when she was still capable of telling him.

His train of thought was broken by Eleanor rushing back to the car, moving more quickly than he thought wise for a woman of her age.

Moments later the door shut.

"You're right," Hugo said. "And I'm sorry."

"Sorry for being a gigantic ass?"

"Kinda."

"Okay. Good. Let's see those two addresses."

Hugo put on his reading glasses.

Chapter Twenty
1947

Alicia filled the bowl with hot water, lathered the brush with soap, and got on her hands and knees, pressing her cheekbone to the floorboards to assess the cleanliness. She looked long and hard before realizing there was nothing wrong with it – it was merely her bad habit coming back, so she threw the water away, cursing her weakness.

Then she noticed a few specks of dirt here, a smudge mark there, a few breadcrumbs from breakfast somewhere else, so she decided the floor was dirty after all and needed a good scrub. And this time she might try a different cleaning solution. As well as her usual salt and carbolic soap, she'd started using soda crystals, borax, ammonia, vinegar, and pretty much anything that she'd heard might clean and disinfect. She could hardly afford it, but cleanliness was important.

She heated up more water, poured it into a bowl, and lathered her brush up again. But she still wasn't sure whether to give in and continue, probably due to the voice, close by, telling her she was being unreasonable.

A knock at the door startled her, taking her away from her dilemma.

And she knew who it was from the force and rhythm of the four knocks. Well, partly because of that but mostly because Rabbi Benisch was the only person who ever came to see her.

She knew him of old – a good friend of her dear old papa, and late the previous year they'd bumped into each other in the bakery.

"Isn't it ... uh ... one of the Rosenthal girls?" he'd said initially.

"Alicia," she replied.

"Ah, yes. Now I remember. Alicia, Giselle and ... Klara, was it?"

"Your memory's good. And you're Rabbi Benisch."

"Indeed I am. So, how are you, Alicia?"

"I'm fine." She nodded, but knew her smile was fractured. She felt awful. But she felt awful whenever she had to leave the apartment.

"Are you sure?" he said, peering at her face. "Who are you living with these days?"

For a moment it was as if Alicia's mouth had ceased to function. But she stuttered the words out, eventually telling him she lived alone with her young son, who was at school. Her endeavor was rewarded by a look of intense concern from the rabbi.

There were two possible reasons for his reaction: either her appearance and behavior were a lot worse than she realized, or the man in front of her with the bushy white beard possessed some sort of sixth sense granted only to men of divinity.

"Would you like me to come around and see you sometime?" he asked, his guttural voice easily matching his slate-like cheeks for gravity.

She just shook her head, aware she was almost cowering under the pressure, but unable to control herself.

"Alicia, I was lucky. I happened to be visiting London when the Germans took over, so I stayed there. But I know you've been through a lot. I expect you've seen visions of hell. Tell me, what happened to your sisters?"

That made Alicia turn away and head home without another word, her heart thumping in her head all the way, bringing tears of frustration when she got home and shut the door on the world.

It was two weeks later that he found her – when she first heard that distinctive knock.

"How did you know where I lived?" were her first words.

"Don't be alarmed, Alicia. It's nothing sinister or magical; I have contacts. And if you say the word, I'll leave now and I'll do nothing more than say hello when we meet in the bakery or on the streets, but . . . well, I'd like to know how you are, and I'd say you need someone to talk to."

"Haven't you got other people to talk to?"

"Never mind them. Your papa was a good friend of mine, and I know what happened to him. But I'm here for you, Alicia, for *you*."

Alicia stood still, fighting herself, fighting the urge to check that everything was clean and tidy enough for a visitor, that the kitchen chairs were perpendicular to the table, that her three saucepans were arranged in size order with the handles in-line, just as she preferred. Those thoughts made the decision for her.

She stepped aside to let him in, unable to prevent herself staring at his feet, her muscles tightening at the thought of dirt brought in from outside. She wiped the door handle he'd just touched using the soapy rag she kept with her at all times, then led him to the kitchen, where she wiped down the seats of the two chairs and took two cups from the closet. *Don't wash them*, she told herself, *they're clean, they're already clean.*

And that was how the visits had started. Rabbi Benisch could see exactly what Alicia could – the constant cleaning and irrational worrying – but somehow he could see *beyond* those things. Over a dozen or so visits, he managed to tease out of her those experiences in Riga and Auschwitz that she hadn't mentioned to anyone, encompassing not only the toll the years had taken on her personal health, but also her grief at the division and destruction of her once-close family. Every part of that account was an unburdening that brought her to tears.

He would tell her that those days were gone forever, that she now had control. Nobody was going to force her to scrub sidewalks. She had control. Nobody was going to lock her inside her house. She had control. Nobody was going to take her to a frozen wasteland in a train truck. *She had control.*

After those initial few visits, Alicia could sense her nerves settling, as though calmness was a drug slowly seeping into her system. Rabbi Benisch promised her he would visit again, but less frequently because he had other equally deserving cases to deal with. She thanked him and said he would always be welcome.

Alicia knew her behavior wasn't going to change overnight – she and Rabbi Benisch had discussed the obsessions she felt powerless to control. She knew that changes to her behavior would be down to her and nobody else. It helped to look at herself from someone else's point of view, but bad habits would take time to die, and apart from anything else, the time she spent cleaning still soothed her.

She came to accept that in time she would find something better to occupy her mind, and then she would stop washing door handles every time someone touched them, and wouldn't wash clothes that were still clean, and wouldn't be so concerned with chairs being perfectly straight or pans being arranged in a particular order and orientation.

Rabbi Benisch, true to his word, visited her the first Monday of every month.

But today was Friday, although it definitely sounded like his knock. Just in case it was him, she quickly poured away the hot water and opened a window to let out the chemical smell. She opened the door and they smiled at each other. He had his usual walking cane in one hand, and a newspaper under the other arm. They hugged, and after shutting the door, Alicia almost wiped the handle with her rag but managed to refrain. Small victories were still victories.

"I need to talk to you, Alicia."

"Warm milk?" she suggested.

He shook his head. "I haven't time." He glanced at the door handle and around the room, returning his attention to Alicia. "I can see that you don't need my help now. You can work things out for yourself. And I always knew you would; I always had confidence in you."

"Thank you, Rabbi." She looked him up and down expectantly. "So?"

"Yes. To business." He took the newspaper from under his arm, turned a couple of pages and folded it in half. "I could be wrong," he said, "but I think you should read this."

Now confused, she craned her neck to look.

"Here. Take it. Keep it."

She held the paper and read aloud. "Local woman gives evidence in war crimes trial." She pointed. "You mean this?"

"Yes. Read on."

She did, and seconds later she gasped and had to settle on a nearby chair. "But it's . . ."

"Giselle," he said. "I wasn't sure, but from my memory it looks like her and it says she's from Leopoldstadt. It gives her surname as Hinkler. Would that be correct?"

But Alicia's mind was racing ahead. "How do I get in touch with her?"

He lifted a small sheet of notepaper from his coat pocket and handed it to her.

"Her address?"

"I'm reliably informed so."

"How did you get it?"

"As I keep telling you, I have contacts – journalists, in this case. Go see her, Alicia, but don't rush, prepare yourself. This could be your next step to recovery."

"Thank you, Rabbi. Thank you so much." Alicia gasped a few times and flung her arms around him, her fervor almost toppling him over because he was considerably shorter than her. She excused her behavior and let him go, thanking him again.

"It's my duty," he said. "And you're welcome. I hope Giselle is well and you find some solace in meeting her. Please tell me what happens. Now I must go."

Alicia couldn't resist hugging him once more, after which he was gone.

She stared at the address for a moment, thinking hard. Yes, she had a good idea where that street was, it wouldn't be too hard to find. She grabbed her purse and coat. She was two streets away before realizing that thoughts of washing her hands or cleaning the door handle or checking her shoes for dirt hadn't passed through her mind since she'd read the story in the newspaper.

Little victories.

§

Giselle shut the door behind her and dropped like a dead weight onto one of the two armchairs that dominated her tiny living room. She unbuttoned the top of her gray flannel blouse and opened it wide, letting the cool air onto her skin.

This place was her sanctuary. In her weaker, self-indulgent moments she daydreamed of never going the other side of the front door again, of having everything delivered and having someone else take her son to school and back so she didn't *need* to go out.

It was a daydream borne out of frustration. Ever since she'd made that difficult phone call to the war crimes people, her life hadn't been her own.

Her statement of what she'd witnessed in Linz had led to a broader investigation into the construction project, including who else apart from Herr Hinkler was involved and what else Giselle might have witnessed. There had been interviews with the investigating authorities, documents to read and sign, and court appearances where she'd had to stand up and talk in front of hundreds of people. There had also been further interviews – this time with journalists – which had led to stories in the newspapers about her, which in turn had led to people at the clothes factory recognizing her and pointing. She'd eventually had to give up her job in the factory in order to protect her son from unwelcome attentions.

But what annoyed her most was that the memories of the court case filled her head when she had other things to concern herself with.

She sometimes wished she'd never made that call.

And in those moments of regret, she felt even worse than when people were taking photos of her or when clever lawyers were cross-examining her, trying to catch her out by picking on the nuances of every word she uttered. Yes, she hated the life she was living at the moment and wanted to run away and live in a cave, but she kept telling herself that she needed to lock the self-centered part of her personality away until the case was all over. She'd been fortunate in having Kurt take her away from the dangerous mess that Leopoldstadt had become all those years ago, and couldn't help but obsess about the huge number of people who had died horrible deaths while she'd been living a life of relative affluence in Linz.

She kept telling herself that in time the trial would be over and she would have the privacy she craved, whereas those who had died would be dead forever.

Selfishness and guilt constantly leapfrogged each other, swapping the lead so Giselle found it hard to have any firm view on where her future life might lie when this was all over. She told herself she had to concentrate on the ground underneath her feet – one step at a time – but think of the summit.

The problem was that her thoughts were stuck in the past. Why had she taken the decision to make that phone call – to even get involved? Had it really been some simple desire to do the right thing? Had it been for the pleasure of knowing Kurt's father would be brought to justice? Or had she harbored more selfish desires – that what she was doing might soothe the guilt of years of disowning her family? Because in her time in Linz she'd said some terrible things. She'd said them to keep herself out of danger, but the words echoed around her head like flies trapped in a bottle:

Do you know any Jews, Giselle?

Of course not.

The filthy Jew has had everything his own way for far too long, don't you think so?

Oh, I completely agree. They're vermin – little more than a sub-species.

Isn't Herr Hitler doing a good job, standing up for the rights of Aryans?

Yes, he is. He's certainly a man to be proud of, and the sooner he eradicates the Jew, the better.

Yes, she often questioned her motives for that phone call, but there was also a desire to block out the rest of the world – a desire she didn't fully understand.

Giselle had known all along how much her family would have worried through not knowing where she was. Perhaps her need to lock herself away was some sort of payback for those terrible things she'd said about her family.

Those thoughts became even more jumbled in her head during her time in the witness box, testing both her power of recollection and her honesty.

How good would you say your memory is, Frau Hinkel?

And do you swear you saw it all happen?

Did you actually see the accused pull the trigger?

Think carefully. Could you have been mistaken?

Is it possible that you hold some sort of grudge against the accused?

Those were the days she came home, shut the world out and wished she were the only person left in the world. That would solve all her problems.

When did she lose that raw optimism that fueled the younger Giselle? What happened to that confidence she'd always had with men? And what about the belief that once she'd found the right man, her life would be complete and everything that touched her tongue would taste of honey and the air around her would smell of sweet rose and nothing would harm her or make her unhappy?

She eventually accepted that all of those wishes had disappeared long ago, leaving the feeling that she needed nobody, that nothing would recapture that essence of better times.

But she wasn't alone in the world and never would be. There might be more court appearances, she had a son to look after, and then there was the rest of her life to deal with. At least her son had now started school, which perhaps would give her some respite – some more time to herself, some more time to consider what she wanted to do with the rest of her life.

And at that moment what she wanted to do was have something to eat. She put some oatmeal into a saucepan, stirred it with a little water, and left it to soak while she made a fire in the range, loading it with scraps of straw, kindling, and a small log. And then, while her hands were dirty with lichen and wet sawdust, as her mind was occupied wondering where she'd left the matches, there was a knock at the door.

She cursed. She told herself to stay still, to be silent, and then they would go away. She couldn't be alone in the world, but by God she could be alone in her apartment – her sanctuary – where she could at least *believe* she was alone in the world. That was her right.

The knock came again. The lichen and sawdust clinging to her hands was now annoying her – she wanted to wash it off. And she wanted to put match to straw and start up the range. She mouthed more silent curses and told herself to stay still, that she would win, that whoever was outside her door would give up sooner rather than later.

A third knock came, this time louder and with a voice asking if anybody was in. A woman; she would be easy to get rid of. She marched to the door, her head full of *I don't want anything* and *please go away*. But when she opened it, she couldn't speak because of the ghostly vision in front of her. It was a reminder of her past – someone who looked like her older sister.

While she was too shocked to speak, the woman who she suddenly knew was no mere *reminder* of Alicia burst into tears. She felt arms around her, a body pressing itself against hers, squeezing her in desperation. A few moments later the shock subsided, the reality rose up.

"Alicia?" she said breathlessly. "But . . . what . . .?"

Then Giselle's emotions took over. Thoughts of solitude and court appearances and evidence and *everything else* were all forgotten. She held this stranger at arms' length, but the face and the tall elegance were nothing strange. She, too, started crying and the two women embraced again.

Time lost its meaning for a while, but at some stage, a little presence of mind returned to Giselle, and she shut the door and led her sister to the two armchairs.

"I understand that it's a shock," Alicia said, "and I'm sorry for that, but Rabbi Benisch saw the news report about you testifying and got your address, and I had to meet you, Giselle, and I need to tell you it's a wonderful thing you're doing, and perhaps this is your reward, that I've found you, and ... and ... oh, I can't believe it. I can't believe that after all these years I've found you."

Alicia flung her arms around Giselle again, and Giselle responded, her eyes streaming with tears. It had been a long time since she'd felt this close to any adult, let alone one she'd spent so many years wondering and worrying about.

"Come on," Giselle said. "Let's sit down. I have a lot to tell you, but I don't know where to start and I want to know what's been happening to you."

It took almost three hours, but they covered all sides of both of their stories.

Giselle explained how leaving Vienna and her family had seemed the right thing to do at the time, but her denial of being Jewish or even knowing any Jews had left scars. On the face of it she'd led a comfortable life while those in Leopoldstadt had suffered so much. She told Alicia only that she felt bad about what she'd done, because talking in detail about her feelings of worthlessness and how she wanted to cut herself off from the world somehow seemed unnecessary.

Likewise, Alicia told her how Klara and Felix had fled to America but how they'd lost contact due to the upheavals. She told her about meeting Kurt in her final days in Vienna, about the terrible days in the purgatory that was Riga and the hell that was Auschwitz, of how the rest of the family apart from her son had died one by one. It took Giselle some time to recover from hearing those details.

Eventually Giselle realized she had to go collect her son from school and told Alicia.

"Oh, of course," Alicia said. "I forgot the time; I need to collect mine too."

They left together, but had to part on a street corner.

"It's a shame they don't attend the same school," Alicia said as they hugged goodbye.

"We could change that," Giselle said. "It would be nice."

Alicia started laughing, although still wiping away one or two tears. Giselle, smiling back, asked what she was laughing at.

Alicia's shoulders gave a slight shrug. "I think it's funny, that's all – funny that we both remembered that silly talk we had when we were little girls."

It made Giselle laugh along. "Our sons? Of course we remembered. We all promised. I had no idea whether you remembered, I didn't even know you had a son, but for me it was always going to be something to remind me of our brother forever."

"And to keep him alive, in a sense."

"Yes. He deserves that much. And it also reminded me of you and Klara – wondering whether you also remembered."

"Do you ever think about Klara?"

Giselle gave a sad, upturned smile. "All the time, Alicia. All the time." She took a step back. "Anyway, I can't be late."

"Me neither."

The two sisters promised to see each other every day, and parted.

But however uplifting the meeting had been, however much meeting Alicia was going to help mend Giselle's life, some things were never going to change. It was true that she often thought about Klara and dear old Hugo, as well as Mama and Papa. But whenever she did there was always a bitter aftertaste – as if she remembered what annoyed her about them more than what she loved about them, and she hated herself for taking that attitude. That was perhaps why she still wished she were someone else, someone who loved her family, someone who would find it impossible to disown them.

She walked on, because that was all she could do.

§

In San Antonio, Klara thought she'd spent the years since Felix's death settling into a comfortable but lonely existence, and 1947 looked like becoming more of the same despite her best endeavors.

She'd written to the government offices in Vienna asking how she might go about finding missing relatives, but had heard nothing back. Having no idea of the name of the person or persons who could help or even the relevant department, she'd simply addressed the letter to the office of the Chancellor. She lived in hope that the letter would find its way to the relevant department, but in desperation had written follow-up letters asking for names and addresses of rabbis and newspapers because she had no idea which ones still existed and where they were.

By the middle of 1947 none of these had brought any useful replies. Larry was understandably preoccupied with his new wife, but found time to help; he suggested writing to the Austrian embassy in New York, which she did. She got a reply stating that they didn't keep records of rabbis but gave her the correct government department to write to for the information she wanted, also warning her that the authorities had enough work on their hands rebuilding the city and the country in every sense, and that it would probably be a year or so before she heard back.

Undeterred, she sent the letter off and told herself that she simply had to wait and, in the meantime, get on with her life.

Of course, that was easier said than done. Her son was now her main focus of attention – or, as she occasionally thought on those rare occasions she slumped into melancholy – the only reason she existed.

And that wasn't enough. Not for Klara. She felt as if she'd lost one life when Felix had been taken from her; she wasn't going to waste her own now he was gone. Moreover, perhaps she would never find out what had happened to her family, but she knew that wherever they were, they wouldn't want grief to hold her back in life.

So one day, when Pa had gone out to work in the cornfields and Ma was on her own in the kitchen, Klara told her she needed to talk – to ask her a big, big favor.

"I want to start my own business," she said once both women had sat down at the kitchen table with coffees. "I want to start a business doing what I know best: repairing shoes."

Ma thought for a moment. "I certainly admire your courage, my dear, but . . . well . . ." She glanced at Klara's son, crawling around a nearby rug, grasping at the wooden blocks Pa had lovingly cut, sanded, and painted. "What about little Hugo?" she said.

"That's the big favor I wanted to ask you."

"You want me to look after him while you work?"

"I'll understand perfectly if you'd rather not, and, uh . . ."

"Don't say another word, my dear. He's my grandson. The answer is *yes*."

Klara had rehearsed the question and its possible complications for days, and now in the event her request had been granted immediately. Tears of relief weren't far away. "Oh, I'm so grateful," she said. "I know he'll be well cared for."

"You betcha he will."

"You don't think . . ."

"What?"

"You don't think I'm being selfish? Just a little?"

Ma shook her head. "I've been a mother myself. I know what it's like. You spend nine months dreaming of endless days playing with your new baby – and there is a lot of that – but the novelty of it wears off at some point – earlier for some than others – and you just need . . . uh . . ."

"Something more?"

"Exactly. And you know what you want, my dear. So you go for it."

"Well, I don't know what I want immediately; I'm just going back to what I know. But I'm thinking about the years to come – when Hugo's at school."

"Like I said, us mothers are all different. If that's a reflection of what you feel, then what you're doing is a good thing. It's constructive and it'll take your mind off Vienna and your family."

"I know."

They took a few minutes to drink their coffee and watch Hugo crawl and try to stand up and fall over, then Ma put her cup down, faced Klara, and drew breath to speak.

Klara waited, and then, when she heard nothing, said, "Is everything okay?"

"Oh, it's nothing, but . . . well . . . if you don't mind me asking . . ."

"Of course not. What is it?"

"We did always wonder about something. It's not important, but why did you insist on calling him Hugo? We appreciate that you've given him Felix as a middle name, we just would have preferred it . . ."

"The other way around?"

"Well, yes."

Klara nodded thoughtfully. "I should have told you. I should have told you at the time, I'm sorry, but I wasn't quite myself."

"Told us what, my dear?"

"It all goes back to when I was a little girl. It started out as a joke – a silly joke. You see, I must have been . . ." She relaxed back and stared at the ceiling. ". . . I'd say six or seven. Giselle was eight or nine, Alicia ten or eleven. We were all playing with our dolls in the living room, and it was little girl talk – about what sort of men we would marry, what sort of houses we'd live in, how many children we'd have, that kind of thing.

"Alicia started it. She said she was going to have four babies – two of each or three girls and a boy just like our mama. She said she liked Hugo – liked his name – so if she ever had a boy, she would call him Hugo. 'I like that,' I said. 'But I'm going to have six babies – all boys – and I'll call the first one Hugo too.'

"Then Alicia turned to Giselle and said, 'What about you, Giselle? How many children are you going to have and what are you going to call them?'

"Giselle turned her nose up at her and said, 'Oh, I'm not going to have any children. They're too much trouble and they stop you going where you want to go and doing what you want to do.'

"I remember that Alicia and I stopped playing and stared at each other, plain confused. Giselle saw this and added, 'But if I ever do have a baby boy, I promise I'll call him Hugo too.'

"We all giggled at that, then Alicia put her hand in the center between us, Giselle put her hand on top, and I did the same. We all promised on each other's lives that when we grew up, we would each have a baby boy and call him Hugo. We chanted the words as if they were a prayer, and when we called out Hugo's name, he heard it and staggered over to us the way he always did, and grunted a noise that we all knew to mean *pardon?* so we repeated it, told him about our agreement. He cried, and I remember it so well because it upset me. It was the only time I ever saw him cry, even though he had such a big problem to cope with.

"After that it became a running joke between the three of us. As you know, I have no idea what's happened to Alicia and Giselle, whether they had boys, whether they called them Hugo, or even whether they're . . . still . . ."

Klara couldn't bring herself to utter the last word.

"What a lovely story," Ma said

"I only wish I'd told you earlier. I'm sorry."

"Water under the bridge, dear. Now I get it. Now I get why the name meant so much to you."

The next day Larry called around while Klara was alone with Hugo.

"Ma's out at the store," she told him.

"I know," he replied. "It's you I came to see."

Klara hardly had time to ask how Deborah was before he brought the subject up.

"Ma says you're starting up a shoe repair business."

"Well, I hope to."

"You haven't planned it yet?"

"I haven't bought anything yet."

"Good."

"You don't think it's a good idea?"

"You know what I think. I already told you. You're way better than that. I know a place you can start up a small manufacturing business. You should make high quality shoes and boots – top end stuff – there's a lot of demand for that around here."

Klara shrugged and opened her mouth to speak, but was stuck for words.

"You can do this," he continued. "I know you can. Think of little Hugo's future if not your own."

Then Klara started nodding, giving him a suspicious, sideways stare. "Oh, I think I get it now, Larry."

"Ah, no. It's not what you think. It's not that. I'm thinking of *both of you*, not just little Hugo."

"Are you sure?"

He glared at her. She saw an anger in his frown that she'd rarely seen. He lowered his voice to a whisper. "As we both know, Hugo is my deceased brother's child, but I love him as if he's my own. I look out for him. I always will, and—"

"Okay, okay. I'm sorry. Let's move on. The business."

Larry let out an exhausted sigh. "I'll help with the practicalities and the legalities if you're interested. I'll do what I can. And I know people who can help with what we can't do ourselves. Just promise me you'll think about it."

Klara nodded. "Of course I will. I want the best for Hugo – just as much as you do."

"Good."

"Good."

"Listen. I, uh, know how worried you've been about your folks in Vienna. Ma said you've been writing letters."

"I have. I got nowhere."

"And you think this idea of yours is gonna take your mind off of them?"

Klara was already shaking her head, aware of her face flushing, her nostrils twitching nervously.

"Hey, I'm sorry," Larry said. "Of course you can't forget about them. I didn't mean it like that. You know everyone hopes and prays they're okay, don't you?"

"I do. And thank you. But hope isn't enough for me. I know what I'm doing. I'll carry on with my life and my plans for now, but if I haven't heard anything by next year, I'm traveling over there to find them myself."

"You're a tough lady, Klara. If anyone can do it, you can."

Klara thanked him. She'd been slightly disingenuous. She hadn't planned a visit to Vienna at all; the words had come to her on the spur of the moment. But she was grateful for Larry's encouragement, it gave her confidence.

It hadn't been a plan, but now it was.

Chapter Twenty-One
San Antonio, Texas, USA. June 2012

In the passenger seat of the Mercedes, Hugo had his reading glasses on and was holding the pristine sheet of paper in his hands.

"According to this," he said, "one of these mysterious secret Hugos lives just the other side of town, although the other's in Houston."

Eleanor nodded. "Okay. So we know where we stand. I guess that makes the decision easier."

"What decision?"

"Which one to visit first." She replaced the cap on her bottle of water.

"You think we should just turn up?"

She shrugged. "What else? Drive all the way back to Dallas and think on it?"

"I . . . well . . ."

"So it's settled. Put the address into the map gadget thing."

"The GPS."

"That's what I said."

While Hugo brought up the correct menu and tapped in the zip code, Eleanor continued talking.

"Something else I thought about."

"What's that?"

"Your Uncle Larry."

"What about him?"

"Did he ever mention anything to you about other relatives?"

Hugo thought about it for a few seconds. "Not that I recall – at least, nothing to help us with this."

"Okay. It's just that you always said he was like a father to you – you know, because your real father died before you were born."

"Yeah." Hugo removed his reading glasses and focused on the horizon, holding his gaze there. "Like I said to you many times, that guy was as good to me as any father could have been. He took me and Mother on days out, took me fishing and to ball games, never forgot my birthday. I guess being my father's brother he felt he had a duty to help out."

Eleanor glanced to the side and gave Hugo a thoughtful look.

"What?" he said. "What is it?"

"Perhaps I shouldn't say."

"You should. Hit me."

"Well . . . as I recall, your Uncle Larry was just as fond of your mother as he was of you."

"Meaning?"

"Meaning . . ." Eleanor gave a long sigh. "Meaning nothing."

"My mother and my Uncle Larry? You think . . .?"

"Oh, I told you I shouldn't say it."

"No, you shouldn't. Wash your mouth out, and while you're at it wash your mind out."

"Sorry." Eleanor bobbed her eyes upwards. "Sorry, Klara. Sorry Uncle Larry. Sorry, Aunt Deborah."

"I should think so. Guy was happily married, devoted to Deborah. He looked after her when she got ill, even sold the ranch when he inherited it to pay her medical bills. He was one of nature's good guys."

"I know. I'm sorry. Like I said, he was . . ."

"Yeah, like a father to me. There's no other way to put it. And he had so much to put up with."

"You mean, in addition to a sick wife?"

"I mean nothing. You know what I'm talking about." Hugo drew a deep breath and sighed. "Let's get going if we're gonna do this."

Eleanor nodded and set off. Neither of them spoke for a few minutes.

Then Hugo groaned loudly and said, "Ah, what the hell. Why do I have such a problem talking about it?"

"Because you never met your father and you loved your uncle Larry as if he was your father."

"That'll be it." He turned to see Eleanor smiling at him. "I told you he never got over it, didn't I?"

"You mean, his army record?"

"Yeah. My father was held up as some kind of hero for being killed in combat, but Larry had to live the rest of his life with a dishonorable discharge hanging around his ankle like a ball and chain. I even caught a few people referring to him as *the deserter* like it was his nickname."

"Pretty ironic, huh?"

"Ironic?"

"Your Uncle Larry only went AWOL when he heard your father had been killed in action, isn't that right?"

"I see what you mean. Yeah. Mother always said he was just as upset as her – cut to pieces."

"So he spent the rest of his life in the shadow of the same man. He never stood a chance of living up to his own brother's glorious reputation. I think the authorities would be more understanding today, of course."

"Damned well hope so. You know, it was only when I was about twenty or so, and I started to think properly, that I realized something about Uncle Larry."

"What was that?"

"Well, it was a given I was proud of my father – even though I never met him. And everybody told me I should be proud of my mother – the way she built up that business without screwing people over, how she treated her workers fairly and equally and didn't, as we say now, discriminate. Of course, I'd have been proud of her whatever people said."

Eleanor waited, eventually saying, "And?"

"What?"

"You're rambling. What is it about Larry that you didn't realize?"

"Jeez. Sorry. Brain's misfiring. Well, throughout all of that, Uncle Larry didn't bat an eyelid about being . . . I don't know, a kind of anti-hero, almost a scapegoat that people like to point the finger at, almost a pariah. Nobody suggested I should be proud of him – not a one. But I realized when I grew out of being a teen that even if nobody else was proud of him or looked up to him, hell, I did."

"He'd have liked that, your Uncle Larry. He was proud of you too, you know, getting to college, moving to Dallas and getting a good job."

"Did he tell you that?"

Eleanor nodded. "More than once. I got the impression he wanted to be in your life more than he actually was when you got older."

"Mmm, I'd have liked that."

"Anyway, leaving aside life's regrets, do you have any other folks you haven't told me about?"

"Uh, don't think so. You've met all my living relatives and quite a few of my dead ones."

"Humor me. Let's go through them all."

"Okay. I had Uncle Larry and Aunt Deborah. They didn't have kids because of her health problems. And, I guess, there were his parents, who were my grandparents."

"You sure they only had two children?"

Hugo nodded. "My father and Larry."

"And what about on your mother's side?"

"Oh, I figure she had lots of relatives. Just wouldn't talk about them."

"This guy could be one of them. Come on, Hugo. She must have said *something* about them."

Hugo shook his head and went to speak. But it was hard. It sounded stupid. Every time he'd asked his mother about her family back in Vienna, she'd batted the ball back with the ease of Roger Federer returning serve. She would say, "You don't want to know about that" or, "They're all long gone now" or, "Let's think of the future, not the past" or even the downright dismissive, "You wouldn't be interested." So yes, he felt stupid saying he didn't know. And it wasn't as if he hadn't already been through this with Eleanor.

So he didn't reply to her question, and she seemed to sense his answer the way a good wife of forty years would, and changed tack appropriately.

"What about cousins, second cousins, neighbors or family friends? You sure none of them had either of those surnames?"

"You reckon I haven't already thought of all that?"

"No. Just that you might be able to think a little harder. You definitely don't remember knowing any other Hugo when you were a kid?"

"I'm definitely sure I don't remember. Doesn't mean I'm right, of course."

"What about friends of school friends, or just anyone with either of those surnames?"

"Oh, Eleanor, you're making my head hurt."

"You're not being helpful."

"What else can I say? I don't remember much at all from before I was . . . mmm, I'd say about nine or ten. I got vague memories of starting school when I was six, and even then, I can barely remember the faces of one or two schoolfriends and teachers from the first few grades, and no names at all. If one of those kids was another Hugo, all I can say is that he wasn't very memorable."

"And before school?"

Hugo laughed. "When I was five or less? You gotta be kiddin'. I got squat."

"Absolutely nothing?"

"Hey, it was a long time ago. A *hell of a long time ago.*"

They sat in silence. Hugo's mind had run through the whole list of every person he could remember knowing in San Antonio, friends of people he knew, and people whose only connection to him had been that he'd heard their names mentioned. Hugo wasn't a common name in Texas; he'd have remembered knowing another one, wouldn't he? For a few moments he cursed moving away from San Antonio. There must have been someone who his mother had become friendly with in her later years – someone whose identity she'd kept from him and, indeed, from everyone else.

The inescapable conclusion was that yes, his mother had some dirty little secret, something that would soon cease to be a secret if this mystery Hugo on the other side of town was still alive and was willing to talk.

As they drove on, Hugo started to hum a tune; inside, he was bracing himself for a revelation that perhaps he might not like one bit.

Chapter Twenty-Two
1948

By 1948 Alicia's obsession with cleanliness and order was under control. The urges still stalked her, and there were lapses, but as far as she was concerned, she'd started to live a normal life. She was no longer alone in this city – she had Giselle – and the joy of meeting her and the surprise that they'd both named their sons after their brother was the boost she so desperately needed.

More importantly, there was now a fresh impetus in her life: finding Klara.

She and Giselle had talked at length for months about how they might go about the task. They knew Klara lived somewhere in or around San Antonio, Texas. At least, they knew that was where she and Felix had gone in 1940; whether she was still there was anybody's guess, but it was their only lead and they had to run with it.

Their initial idea had been to send a letter addressed to "San Antonio Main Hospital" asking whether a Felix Goldberg worked there. They didn't expect to hear back, and sadly that expectation was fulfilled. The fact that the letters were written in German clearly hadn't helped matters.

Then they had another idea: to ask their local synagogue for the addresses of every synagogue in San Antonio and write to each one. After some research, Rabbi Benisch gave them four addresses, although he insisted it wasn't a complete list. He also reminded them that he'd spent many years in London so spoke and wrote passable English. With his help, Alicia wrote to all the synagogues explaining their predicament and asking if they knew Felix. They got replies from all four, which Rabbi Benisch translated for them. Two said they were sorry but they knew nobody of that name, one had a man of that name but he was in his sixties, and one didn't have a man of that name but suggested placing a notice in one of the local newspapers, three of which they provided addresses and phone numbers for.

Following on from that, Rabbi Benisch helped Alicia talk to those top three newspapers over his phone, during which the woman relayed details of how to place and pay for notices in their classified ads sections. Alicia and Giselle put money aside until they had enough to wire the money to America and place the notices, and Rabbi Benisch not only let Alicia use his phone again, but also allowed his number to be placed in the notice so Klara would contact him in the first instance should she happen to read it.

So, in the Summer of 1948, three small but clear notices appeared in three different San Antonio newspapers, each running for a whole week, each politely asking Klara to get in touch with her long-lost sisters.

Alicia couldn't sleep for two whole days after the notice was due to appear, and on the third day decided that giving the lavatory a thorough clean would tire her out and make her sleep. It didn't, and over the next 24 hours she quickly fell into her old ways, wiping every door handle on the hour every hour – never in between unless a stranger had touched them, arranging the kitchen seats in perfect symmetrical alignment either side of the kitchen table, and scrubbing that table clean after every use – even if it had only hosted a cup of coffee.

On the fourth day she succumbed to tiredness, halfway through scrubbing the lavatory floor yet again, telling herself she was merely resting her eyes for a moment, but waking up four hours later, laid out on the floor, her hand still resting on the scrubbing brush.

Any longer and Hugo would have been left all alone outside the school gates. She quickly grabbed her shoes, coat, and purse, then hurried out, her eyelids still sticky from sleep.

She knew she had to rush because Hugo would be frightened at being left unattended, but her task wasn't helped by the fact she had to pick a route whereby she could alternate left and right turns. She didn't know why; it just had to be that way.

Exhausted and flustered, but now relieved, Alicia found out to her great surprise that Hugo was quite content to sit on his own for a few minutes outside the school and was also perfectly safe. She cursed herself for worrying so much and set off for home again, her hand firmly grasping Hugo's.

On the way back she had to put up with Hugo occasionally asking why they were turning left when they lived to the right or vice versa. Between his questions, Alicia tried her best to put her situation in perspective. It was true that worries about finding Klara should have overshadowed any concerns about cleanliness and tidiness in the apartment or finding a particular route to school, but the worry about Klara seemed to be *fueling*, not diminishing, her behavior.

Still, Klara would see the newspaper notice, the three sisters would be in contact, they could at least plan to reunite, and when that happened things would be different. Her nerves would settle, and all this stupid finicky behavior would cease.

She was certain of that.

§

The courtroom is silent. Giselle stands in the witness-box, explaining for what feels like the hundredth time what she saw –

what Herr Hinkler did. In front of her, head bowed, sits Herr
Hinkler himself. Some distance to his side sits his wife, in tears.

Even after all these years, Giselle remembers the scenes from
Linz in every detail: the clothes, the weather, the smells, the facial
expressions, the shouts, the blood, and every single word and
action she witnessed.

But she stops talking when Herr Hinkler gets to his feet. He is
double the height she remembers. And louder, too. "You betrayed
everyone, Giselle!" he shouts across the courtroom. "You betrayed
your family, then you betrayed us. We looked after you and you
were one big lie. You're a cheat and it's you who should be on trial,
not me."

Giselle asks the judge to order him to be quiet, then turns to the
two burly guards and pleads with them to haul him away. Neither
of those things happen. The judge looks one way and then the
other, rubbing his chin pensively. "The accused has a fair point,"
he says. "The witness here is clearly a fraud, so after due
deliberation I decree that the accused and the witness should swap
places."

Giselle complains, tells the judge that isn't fair, but the guards
approach and drag her from the witness-box. She screams that she
had no choice, but Herr Hinkler, now a free man, his eyes
sparkling with the delight of revenge, just laughs.

Giselle sat up in bed and let out a cry, no words escaping from her
lips, only meaningless sounds.

She wiped her brow – dripping wet – and flopped back down
onto her pillow.

The end of the war crimes trial should have brought her relief,
yet she found absolutely none. Instead, she felt she could never
win, and that she would forever think of herself as a liar and a
cheat who had betrayed everyone. Nobody was on her side.

Nobody understood what she'd been through or what decisions she'd had to make to survive. It was horrible, and always would be. Perhaps she needed a break – of what sort, she didn't know.

No sooner had the meetings and court appearances stopped than she and Alicia had gotten themselves involved in finding Klara. Initially she'd been enthusiastic, but now a little part of her thought that perhaps the authorities should have been doing that, allowing her some time for peace and recovery – for the solitude she craved so much.

In theory, finding Klara didn't take up much of her time as Alicia was the one writing letters and making phone calls and seeing Rabbi Benisch; Giselle did little more than keep in touch with what was happening and make the occasional suggestion. But it just didn't *feel* as if she had more time. It was as if the world was watching her, judging her unfairly because of what she'd done, and what she'd so often denied being.

There had even been that occasion she'd thought would be some sort of epiphany.

It had happened outside the school gates one morning after she'd said goodbye to Hugo and had started to walk back home. One of the other mothers struck up conversation as they walked in the same direction. The woman talked of the work she was doing in aid of the local Jewish support group. Giselle could feel her gut clenching at the thought of talking about such a thing. It was involuntary and all the more confusing for her as she'd briefly attended synagogue just after the war. She asked herself why she was feeling like this, and what she had to hide, but found no answer.

While Giselle's mind was tying itself in knots, the woman asked the question.

"Are you Jewish?" she asked. It was shameless in its casualness, as if the woman were asking whether Giselle had been born in

Vienna or whether she took milk in her coffee or even whether she thought it was going to rain that day.

Giselle's throat became constricted at the question – physically choking her. She could hardly breathe, let alone answer. It was as if she'd been asleep and had just been woken by a loud bang. She stared in all directions, desperately trying to judge if anyone else was looking or waiting for her reply.

"Only, you might know the place if you're Jewish," the woman continued. "It's only three blocks up here, around to the right, and on the left after—"

"Yes!" Giselle blurted out, panting, her brow beading with stinging moisture, her body feeling weak. "Yes, I'm ..." She gulped and needed another breath. "Yes, as a matter of fact I am Jewish."

Those words hadn't passed her lips for so many years. She felt ashamed of that, and now ashamed of her reaction when she'd said it. Still hardly able to speak properly, she took a step back from the woman. "I need to ... to go ..." She pointed in the opposite direction. "... to go this way."

"Well, goodbye then," the woman said. "Perhaps we'll meet tomorrow." She turned and walked off, again as if she'd just been having a normal, polite, everyday conversation.

Giselle had to take a seat to recover. A man sitting at the other end of the bench smiled at her.

"I'm Jewish," Giselle told him.

He returned his attention to his newspaper. Giselle got up and headed home.

"I'm Jewish," she said to two old ladies walking by. "I'm Jewish," she said to the policeman standing on the street corner. He frowned at her and looked the other way.

It was much the same all the way home. A young man hauling a sack of wood, two women carrying babies in their arms, a shopkeeper chalking up his latest prices on a board on the sidewalk. They all got the same news – news that Giselle had been wanting to tell people for years.

Those few minutes should have signaled some form of liberation. But no. When she got home, she shut the door behind her and started crying. The whole affair had been embarrassing and unsettling.

Why had she said that to so many people? And how could she show her face on the streets again?

Even now, months after that event, it felt as if the entire population of Vienna was watching her, talking behind her back about how she'd turned – first one way to save her skin, then the other way to ingratiate herself with the very people she'd betrayed the first time.

Or perhaps, she considered in her more conscious moments, that was a reflection of what she thought about herself. If she didn't have Hugo to look after she would probably deal with the situation the only way she knew: she would leave Vienna and settle somewhere nobody knew her, to start again, so that she might even convince herself, given enough time, that she'd never done any of those things.

But that was all just a pipe dream. She lived in Vienna with her son and that wasn't going to change anytime soon. The best she could hope for was that Klara would be found, that the three sisters would be reunited, and that in time she would feel better about herself.

Alicia had promised to let her know as soon as she heard anything from Rabbi Benisch about Klara. The notices in the newspapers had apparently been printed, and far as any developments were concerned, Giselle would just have to play the waiting game.

Much like every other aspect of her life.

§

Klara had always kept her distance from Deborah.

After what had happened between her and Larry on that momentous night four years ago – and with the legacy of that night's traitorous passion now her constant companion – becoming close to Deborah in any way would have been plain awkward.

It was clear from the few and stilted – although polite – conversations the two women had had that Deborah was fully aware of her history with Felix in Vienna and Texas, of what had happened to Felix, and of how Larry had become a good friend. But there had always been uncertainty in Klara's mind about exactly how much Deborah knew – especially after the conversation Klara had had with Larry the previous year, when she'd said she was planning to visit Vienna but he'd been keener to talk about her starting up a shoe factory.

Larry had been right about the shoe factory, of course. Eight months on from that conversation with him, Klara now employed four people plus herself making shoes and boots by hand, and was starting to win a favorable reputation both in San Antonio and further afield. But her uncertainty about the extent of Deborah's knowledge was like a stone caught inside one of those shoes that refused to be dislodged.

So when a phone call came from Deborah one Saturday evening, it was as though someone had sprinkled hot pepper onto Klara's usually settled nerves.

All she said was, "Oh, hi, Klara. Do you think you could come over please?"

"Is everything all right?" Klara replied.

"Oh, yes. Everything's fine."

"Is Larry there?"

"Larry? Oh, he's out shooting pool with a few pals. Guess he won't be back for a couple of hours. I need to talk to you, is all."

Uneasy thoughts rampaged through Klara's mind.

Had Larry told Deborah? Surely not.

Why would he? Well, perhaps because she was his wife.

If she asked outright what Deborah wanted, it would have sounded blunt and might have aroused suspicion, so she tried a less direct tactic.

"It's a little awkward just now, Deborah. How about we just have a talk over the phone?"

There was a long pause, then Deborah said, "I'm sorry, Klara. It's hard to explain on the phone. It's better that you come over, or I can come see you if you prefer."

Was that a vague threat? If Deborah was going to cause a scene, Klara didn't want it to be around Hugo or Ma or Pa.

"I'll come over now," she replied. "I'll be about twenty minutes."

"Sure. I'll look forward to that."

On the drive over, the possibilities – and the ensuing arguments and counter-arguments – circled around in Klara's mind. To absolutely no conclusion. She would simply have to face whatever music Deborah was going to play her, and work out what to say on the fly.

She braced herself for conflict even as she rapped on the front door of Larry and Deborah's modest wooden cabin, but was confused at what happened when the door was opened.

"I am so, so sorry about this, Klara," Deborah said, ushering her inside. "As soon as I put the phone down, I realized how it must have sounded – like something sinister is going on or I have an unpleasant shock for you."

Klara said nothing, just smiled, relieved, almost feeling the tension that had built up on the journey melt away.

"Come see this," Deborah said, leading the way to the kitchen table, on which a newspaper and a cup of coffee lay side by side.

Klara followed, and could feel her skin tingling with shock as she stared, open-mouthed.

Deborah had circled the notice in the newspaper with thick pencil so there was no missing it. It was a simple box with a long phone number at the bottom and a message above:

> Klara Goldberg, born Rosenthal, last known
> to live in the San Antonio area, is wanted by
> her long-lost sisters, Alicia and Giselle.
> Please call with any information.

"I read this and thought of your sisters. Larry told me all about how you've been looking for them."

Klara said nothing, but collapsed, weakened, onto a chair.

"I couldn't tell you over the phone, I know it means a lot to you and didn't think you should be alone, and I didn't want to wait for Larry to tell you, and I thought you should know as soon as possible so that . . . Klara?"

Klara could do nothing but stare at the notice, reading those words of beauty over and over again. She thought of all the letters she'd written to Vienna, all the times she'd wondered what had become of her family in the cauldron of Hitler's Vienna that she'd run away from. At least Alicia and Giselle were still alive, presumably healthy, and obviously in contact with someone wealthy enough to own a phone.

"I checked and the code is definitely for Austria, and if you want I could . . . Are you okay, Klara?"

Klara dragged her gaze to Deborah, managed a few nods, and said, "So . . . does this mean they're alive?"

"I'd say so, yes."

"I'm sorry. Of course. How stupid of me. And thank you. Thank you so much, Deborah."

"Would you like to call them?" Deborah said, pointing to her phone out in the hallway.

"I . . . I . . ." Klara's mind stalled for a moment, still trying to believe that this wasn't some sort of elaborate and cruel hoax. "Won't it cost a lot?" she eventually said.

"We can afford it. Go ahead. As it's overseas you'll need to call the operator and tell her the number."

Klara looked again at the notice in the newspaper ads section. It seemed to be reaching out to her.

"Do you want me to do it for you?"

Klara shook her head but said nothing more to Deborah, not even a thank you. She stood, steadied herself, and both women went into the hallway, where Klara's trembling finger dialed the operator. She rubbed the sweat that had formed on her palm onto her blouse and took a sharp breath.

"Could you arrange an international call for me please?"

She read out the number, waited for the clicks and crackles to subside, then heard something that sounded like a dialing tone. The palpitations were threatening to make her faint. She almost hung up, dismissing what she was hearing as an engaged tone. She felt herself stagger to one side. Deborah quickly fetched a glass of water and waited next to her, a hand on her shoulder.

This is taking too long.

No, there's clearly nobody there.

It's a wrong number.

It sounds nothing like a US dialing tone.

Then the tone stopped.

"Yes," a flustered and slightly irate male voice said in German.

"My name is Klara," she replied in German. "Klara Goldberg. I saw the notice in the newspaper here in America. Do you know women called Alicia and Giselle?"

There was a gasp. Followed by a long pause. Then the caller's voice changed to one of pure joy.

"*Klara,*" he said slowly, imbuing the word with wondrous qualities. "It's Rabbi Benisch here. You saw the notice? How marvelous! I'm so pleased." He laughed. "And that would explain why you've woken me up at two o'clock in the morning."

"Oh, I'm so sorry, Rabbi. I feel stupid. I should have known. Can I call another time?"

Another laugh. "Don't worry about waking me. I treat these occasions as part of my calling. But your sisters aren't in the habit of sleeping in a rabbi's house, so you will indeed have to call again, I'm afraid. But I can assure you they're both well."

"And the rest of my family?"

There was a very long pause. "Oh, Klara. I think you need to talk to your sisters, but I should warn you it's not good news. You need to know that very few Jews survived the purge of Vienna."

Klara's eyes welled up. She took a moment to pull herself together. "I know. I heard. And thank you for being honest. What about their husbands?"

"I'm afraid they, uh . . . they didn't make it either."

"Neither of them? Oh, how awful. I'm so sorry. Poor Ludwig. Poor Kurt. But . . ."

Klara took a few breaths to prepare herself.

"What is it, Klara?"

"Well, you see, at least that's something we have in common."

"You mean . . . Felix?"

"He was with the navy and died fighting in the Pacific."

"Oh, Klara, I'm so sorry for your loss. I hope it brings comfort to you to know you have your sisters. *The three Rosenthal girls are all alive*, and I thank God for that. I'm thrilled you saw the notice, and I know Alicia and Giselle will be too. You mean the world to them. I'll go around to see Alicia first thing in the morning. I promise."

They talked a little more, Klara mentioning that Felix had given her a son before the war took his life, then she arranged to call Rabbi Benisch the next day at a more convenient time, although she didn't want to leave anything to chance so they exchanged addresses and Klara told him the ranch house phone number.

"I need to go home and lie down," Klara said after she'd hung up.

"I understand," Deborah replied, laying a hand on her trembling shoulder and offering her the glass of water. "I'm so happy for you. I can't even begin to understand what it means to you. Drink this. Just relax for a moment."

Klara took a sip, then downed the rest in two gulps. "Deborah, I'm so grateful for what you've done."

"Hey, I was just browsing the classified ads. I had to read it three times to be sure."

After waiting ten minutes to calm herself down, Klara went home, but her itchy feet couldn't settle, so she went for a long walk. That didn't help, and Rabbi Benisch's words were still rattling around in her head when she returned home. Her stomach rumbled, but eating was out of the question, so all she could do was go to bed.

But she knew she wouldn't be able to sleep until she'd spoken to Alicia and Giselle.

Chapter Twenty-Three
San Antonio, Texas, USA. June 2012

"That's the one," Eleanor said with totally unnecessary cheeriness as she and Hugo pulled up outside a dilapidated concrete shack in a run-down district the other side of town.

Hugo wasn't so sure. He didn't quite *want* to be sure. He definitely didn't want *this* to be it, and knew that distaste was written all over his face. He checked out the boarded-up broken window on one side, the rusting heap of a pickup precariously balanced on concrete blocks on the driveway, and the dented and weathered steel front door.

He unbuckled, took a deep breath, and reached for the door handle.

"Wait a minute," Eleanor said. She held his hand.

Hugo did wait. Quite a while.

"What am I waiting for?" he said, glancing all around.

"We've had a good life together, haven't we, Hugo?"

Hugo let a gentle squeeze of her hand answer the question, saying, "What's wrong?"

"What's wrong is I don't want things to change. Selfish, I know. Truth is I'm as worried as you are about what we'll find if we dig too deep – worried about what it'll do to you."

Hugo took a good look at the eyes that were now just a little sunken, at the cheeks he'd seen gradually transform themselves from tight, fresh milk-skin to a set of wrinkles reminiscent of ripples from a pebble dropped in still water. He'd loved watching every day of those changes in her. She had been and still was everything he ever wanted from life's roller coaster – everything except another turn on that ride with her by his side. It pained his heart to think she might be worried about him – about *them*. So he did what he always did in these circumstances: he stared deep into her eyes and said, "You don't need to worry about me."

"I'm sorry. And I'm sorry I make dumb jokes when I'm nervous."

"And also when you're not."

She laughed, and the wrinkles on her face became even more endearing.

"You know," he said, "Mother used to tell me that once bagels are boiled, they don't change shape much, and once they're baked, they don't change at all."

Eleanor thought for a second. "Yeah, I remember her saying that. I hope she's right."

"Was certainly the case with her. I always figured she was molded by what happened to her in Vienna."

"I thought she never told you what happened there?"

"She didn't. And I never asked. Didn't have the nerve when I was younger, and by the time I got older I'd, uh, *done my research*, as you might say. I knew the sort of thing that went on with Jews back then and thought retelling it would be too much for her. It took me a while, but in time I realized what she meant by the bagel thing."

"I don't want you to change, Hugo. I don't want *us* to change." She closed her eyes for a few seconds. "Oh, forget I said that. I'm being selfish. Let's do what we need to do."

"Relax, Eleanor. Someone in this car has to; hell, I can't. Let's just see what this guy has to say and take it from there. Whatever it is, it can't hurt us, can it?"

"No. It can't hurt us."

"You ready?"

She unbuckled. "Come on, let's do it."

"You make us sound like the mob."

"Didn't I say? I've already sold the movie rights to Tarantino."

"You're funny. I hope we can keep the body count down."

Thirty seconds later they stood at the steel door, nodding at each other, geeing each other up.

"Yeah?" Hugo said.

She nodded. He knocked. It didn't make much of a noise but hurt his knuckles. There was no answer, but they heard music coming from inside, like a TV.

"This had better be worth it," Hugo said, then banged on the door with his palm.

They heard a bolt shoot across, then the door opened.

A middle-aged woman appeared and said nothing, just widened her eyes and smiled warmly to ask what they wanted.

"Does a Hugo Tannenbaum live here?" Hugo said.

The warm smile cooled. "What is your visit in regard to?"

"Uh . . ." Hugo gritted his teeth. "We're not quite sure."

"It's nothing to worry about," Eleanor added. "We're not asking for money or anything."

"So . . . what *are* you asking for?"

"We'd just like to speak to Mr. Tannenbaum please."

The woman's eyes now turned to distinctly unfriendly slits. "Stay there," she said, pointing her arm, rod-like, at their feet. "Don't come in."

She turned and walked through a doorway. After a few distant mumbled words, a man approached them. He was not unlike Hugo – a pretty average man on the second rung of the old-age ladder, a little paunchy, gray wispy hair on a tanned scalp.

"Are you Hugo?" Hugo said.

"Might be. Who are you?"

"Well, my name's Hugo too – Hugo Goldberg, and this is my wife, Eleanor. We, uh, wanted to ask whether you ever knew a woman called Klara Goldberg."

The man seemed to edge away just a fraction at the mention of the name and struggled to speak, then he snapped himself back together and said, "Nobody here by that name."

The accent was faintly foreign.

"I know that much, sir," Hugo said. "She's passed on."

The man's face paled a shade or two. Hugo felt a little on edge, like a wolf sensing its prey weakening, and it was an uncomfortable feeling.

"I'm Klara's son, and I'm trying to find out what you meant to my mother – that is, if you are Hugo Tannenbaum."

The man looked them both up and down, then hooked a glance at their car. "I don't go by that name these days – never really have, to be truthful. Name's Lud."

Now Hugo homed in on the accent a little more. Mostly Texan but tinged with European. German or similar. And there was something else to the way he spoke that Hugo couldn't quite figure out in his mind.

"You call yourself 'Lud'?"

"What I said, ain't it?"

The snarky reply put Hugo off his train of thought for a moment. He hesitated before saying, "So . . . did you know my mother?"

The man shook his head. "Never heard of anyone by that name."

Hugo glanced up and down the street. Three boys on bicycles passed by on the road, and a woman was walking her dog along the sidewalk. "Do you think we could come in and talk please?"

"About what? I told you I never knew nobody called Klara."

"The thing is, in her will she left something to Hugo Ludwig Tannenbaum, apparently living at this address."

The man hesitated, just for a telling second. "I don't care," he said. "I've told you. It's nothing to do with me."

"We're not talking about a hundred-dollar bill here, Mr. Tannenbaum. It's around seventy thousand dollars."

"I don't care. I still don't want anything to do with it."

"But it's been left to you. No strings. It's yours."

"Keep it. Burn it."

"But she wanted you to have it."

"I don't care. I never knew the woman."

Hugo sighed, exasperated. If the mention of free money didn't make the man talk, what the hell would?

"I wonder if I might ask you about your own mother?" Eleanor said.

She might as well have thrown a bucketful of twitches at the man's face, his reaction making Hugo and Eleanor take half a step back. "I'm sorry," Eleanor said instinctively. "I didn't mean to pry or upset you."

"Well, why the hell d'yask?" The man took a tired breath. "I think I've said all I want to say to you people."

"What do you mean?" Hugo asked. "Surely you can tell us something about your own mother?"

"No, Hugo," Eleanor said. Then she addressed the man. "Thank you for your time. We'll leave you in peace."

He went to shut the door on them, but Eleanor said, "Just one more little thing, if I may, Mr. Tannenbaum?"

"What?"

She fumbled around inside her purse for a minute and handed him a card. "It's where I used to work," she said, trying a smile. "Been retired four years now, so don't call the work number. Cell's still the same. If you change your mind, we'd love to hear what you have to say. We're not looking to cause trouble or grief, just to talk, to find out what Klara meant to you."

The man held the card out at arms' length, squinting to focus on it, then looked at Hugo and Eleanor. His features seemed to soften, and he opened his mouth as if to speak, but only looked at the card again. Hugo tried a smile too, but unlike Eleanor he didn't get anywhere near it.

Then they found themselves staring at that big steel slab of a door, listening to the bolt shoot across.

Hugo looked at Eleanor, assessing whether she had the boldness to knock on the door again.

"Let's hope he might think on it and call us," she said.

"Yeah."

"Houston?"

Hugo glanced up and down the street, then said, "Lunch."

As they walked back to the car he added, "Somewhere Houston way."

Chapter Twenty-Four
1949

Alicia didn't bother with the kitchen drawers and closets, but checked inside the wardrobe and all three drawers of the chest beside the bed, then under the bed and in the cabinet by the window.

It was perfect. Well, no, not *perfect*. But things didn't have to be perfect. The four suitcases set in the middle of the room were fit to burst, and there was nothing left here bar the odd sock she wouldn't miss or a scarf she wouldn't need.

This small but modern apartment had been her and Hugo's home for three years, and had seen her undergo a rehabilitation of sorts.

When the two of them had first been allocated the room back in the chaos that had been postwar Vienna, she'd been thrilled at the thought of having a whole apartment – however small – for only her and Hugo, with a door she could lock, a bed to sleep in, and space to prepare food and relax.

Then her priorities had changed; she soon realized she would have to share the place with another force – the one that made her scrub the lavatory floor, the kitchen table and every surface daily; the one that told her every object had to be arranged in an orderly fashion and that the door handles had to be wiped clean within seconds of anyone touching them.

She had subsequently beaten those invisible forces, and so her expectations had changed once more. Yes, she would never again take such luxuries as food, a lockable door and a bed for granted, and yes, with intense effort she had control of her demons, but now she wanted more than that from life. *She wanted what remained of her family.*

And now, due to Rabbi Benisch, that was within touching distance. It was due to his assiduous following of the war crimes trials that she'd found Giselle, and the two of them had become each other's rocks – much closer than they ever had been before the war. And together they also had Rabbi Benisch to thank for making contact with Klara in America.

Alicia sat in the armchair, glancing occasionally at the front door, but mostly watching Hugo pull his wooden train engine by an old shoelace around the room, circling those four suitcases.

He tooted sharply to imitate the horn, then started making chuffing noises. The noises got louder.

"Hugo Ludwig."

The train engine fell silent. He looked up to see his mama holding a finger to her lips.

"Shush. I'm listening out for a knock at the door."

By now he'd gotten used to being called that. Alicia and Giselle had spent an awful lot of time together over the past couple of years, and with two Hugos around it only seemed sensible to include their middle names to differentiate them, the habit sometimes sticking even when there was only one Hugo present.

"Okay, Mama," he replied, but carried on making the train engine noises in whispered tones.

Alicia stood up and wandered aimlessly around the apartment, and every time her eyes landed on an object, she knew it would probably be for the last time. The table by the kitchen sink, the chairs whose alignment she'd needlessly worried so much about, the bed she'd shared toe-to-tail with Hugo Ludwig, the wardrobe and chest of drawers, the clock on the wall, the mirror by the door, the range cooker she'd struggled to keep topped up with logs every winter.

Once that knock on the door came, she would never see any of these things again. It was sad. Her heart would ache for these objects – these silly, lifeless objects that didn't care about her. But her heart ached for Klara even more.

Was she doing the right thing? She could still hear the conversation that had planted the seed of the momentous journey she was about to make. Now she was waiting for a knock at the door, but back then the knock had caught her by surprise. No, more than that, it had shocked her so much she'd nearly fallen out of bed.

It hadn't been so much a knock, more like someone continuously knocking with no break. Alicia's initial thought in the dawn light was that a fire had broken out and the building was being evacuated. Then she heard her first name being called, and the voice was familiar but difficult to place in her half-awake state.

"On my way!" she shouted out, pulling a blanket off the bed and wrapping it around herself in the name of decency. "Stay there," she said to Hugo Ludwig, who hugged a pillow and curled up at the other end of the bed.

"Who is it?" she said, her ear close to the door.

"Rabbi Benisch," came the slightly annoyed reply. "I've heard from Klara. I've been speaking to her on the phone. She's alive and—"

By then, Alicia had unlocked and opened the door and was ushering him inside.

"Tell me more," she said, shutting the door behind him. "Tell me, tell me."

"She called me a few hours ago – in the middle of the night."

"And is she well?"

"She's excellent, Alicia. Happy and still living in San Antonio. Isn't that great news?"

"Oh, of course. Is Felix well too?"

The rabbi's face dropped. "I'm . . . sorry to say that . . . well, sadly, Felix died fighting with the US navy. But she has a son by him and they're settled with Felix's parents."

Alicia flung her arms around him, squeezing the breath out of him until he let out a groan. Then she stepped back and said, "Oh, poor Felix. And poor Klara too. I must talk to her. Could I talk to her?"

"She's calling again at two o'clock this afternoon – first thing in the morning over there. That gives you time to visit Giselle and arrange for you both to come over."

A gasp escaped from Alicia's lips. "Of course. Giselle. I have to tell Giselle." She pulled her attention away from Rabbi Benisch for a moment and stepped over to the open bedroom door, rapping her knuckles on it sharply. "Get up, Hugo Ludwig. Shirt, pants, socks, shoes. We're going out."

He rubbed his eyes and looked across. "Where are we going, Mama?"

"I'll tell you on the way. Now come on. Shirt, pants, socks, shoes."

"I'll see you at two o'clock," Rabbi Benisch said, stepping to the door. "I can let myself out."

"Of course. Yes. I'm sorry. And I won't forget what you've done for us, Rabbi."

"It was nothing." He smiled and left.

Alicia grabbed Hugo's coat. "Put this on too. I'll count to thirty. I want you ready to leave by then."

A few minutes later Alicia was walking briskly through the dawn streets of Vienna, with Hugo trotting alongside to keep up. They rushed past Hermann Frank arranging his grocery store's best vegetables on rickety sidewalk displays, past Freida May opening up her fancy clothes store, around the steam coming out of Steinberg's Bakery, past the beggar accordionist warming up, around a few more street corners, over a bridge, and then they were there. She thumped her fist on the door, only then thinking that she might have been waking Giselle up, not that that mattered.

But the door opened immediately and Giselle was standing there with a slice of buttered rye bread in her hand. "Alicia?" she said.

Alicia walked straight past and into the room, where she let go of Hugo's hand.

"We've found her," she said. "Klara called Rabbi Benisch early this morning. She's alive. Klara's alive and living in Texas just as we suspected. She's calling him again at two o'clock. We both have to be there."

Giselle flung her arms around her and let out a high-pitched squeal that would normally have hurt her ears. But today was different. Today, nothing could upset her.

At 1:50 p.m. in Rabbi Benisch's house, both sisters and both young Hugos sat silently and expectantly next to the phone.

"She'll be exactly on time," Alicia said.

"You don't know that," Giselle said with a shrug of her shoulders. "She might have changed."

"Changed?"

"People do, you know."

"Oh, I can't believe Klara's changed that much. She'll be—"

The phone rang. Alicia jumped.

Giselle's hand reached out but she pulled it away. "You're the oldest," she said. "You answer it."

Alicia did. "Hello?"

"This is Klara. I'm sorry I'm early but I just couldn't wait."

Alicia had to pause to gather her thoughts. The voice coming from this contraption was quiet, distorted, and sprinkled with hisses and crackles, but it was Klara, it was unmistakably Klara. And she spoke again while Alicia was waiting, while Giselle was nudging her elbow and asking what was happening.

"Hello? Is that Rabbi Benisch?"

"No, Klara. It's Alicia. *It's Alicia.* I'm sorry, but I don't know what to say. It's hard to believe it's really you after all these years."

Then Alicia heard a few sharp breaths followed by a whimpering sound.

"Klara? Are you all right?"

More staccato gasps followed, the sort she'd heard from Hugo in his more tearful moments. Then there was, "I'm fine, I'm just . . . a little overwhelmed. Oh, Alicia, you don't know how many times I've dreamed of this moment. I read so many reports of what was happening in Vienna – of what happened to those who were taken away. There were so many times when I thought you'd both died."

"I have so much to tell you, Klara. It's been the hardest of times. Are you sitting down?"

"No, why?"

"It's not easy for me to tell you . . . and I don't want to tell you, but you need to know."

"About Mama and Papa? Rabbi Benisch told me it wasn't good. Are they both . . .?"

"They didn't survive, Klara. They tried, but conditions were terrible. Our dear brother, my darling Ludwig too, even my little girl."

"Ludwig and Sarah too?" A whimper of sorrow came over the line.

But Alicia was barely listening, her own words had put her back in Riga. For a few moments she was stunned, unable to speak, as she felt the cold presence of her departed family. She heard them all talking to her, sensed Ludwig's arm round her, felt her darling Sarah tugging at her coat.

It took a few moments for her to realize Giselle was saying her name, shaking her elbow, pointing at the phone. That shook her mind back to the present. "We have so much to talk about, Klara, but now Giselle wants to speak to you. When she's finished, we'll arrange the next call, yes?"

"Of course. I've lost you once, Alicia, but never again. I promise I'll call regularly, and we can write as often as we want to."

"I've missed you, Klara." And somehow, from the pit of her stomach, Alicia summoned up a laugh. "Giselle's pulling my arm off, so I'll pass you over to her. I've missed you so much, Klara. You . . . you did the right thing when you went to America. Mama and Papa always said they were relieved that you escaped."

"I never stopped thinking of them, Alicia. I never stopped thinking of you all. We'll speak again soon, I promise."

"We will. Of course."

There was a pause, but no goodbye; Alicia couldn't bring herself to utter the word, and knew Klara felt the same. All she said was, "We'll speak again soon. Here's Giselle."

Giselle pretty much snatched the phone away, but it was good humored, and Alicia understood her frustration perfectly. She knew what was happening. In the hidden corners of their minds – for all three of them, she was certain – there was still a little of that childhood spirit: bickering and an unguarded selfishness jostling for position with genuine love and concern, and all of those things mingling to form an emotional bond that only sisters could understand.

Alicia listened to the final few words Giselle spoke – of how much she regretted losing contact with the family in Leopoldstadt when she moved away with Kurt first to the other side of Vienna and then to Linz.

After that, Alicia had to sit down and think.

It had only been a phone call, but in her heart life had changed forever. First she'd found Giselle, now Klara. Yes, Klara was thousands of miles away, but today that didn't matter. In time they would work out how to stay in touch, but today was a day for simply rejoicing. Klara was alive, and Alicia would hear her voice again, and that voice would tell her she was happy living in America, and Alicia would also say she was happy, and Giselle was happy too, and they would catch up with each other's lives and become good friends all over again, so that all three of them would go back to the way they'd been before the war. That would have made Mama and Papa proud. No, it *would make them proud*, because they were up there right now, looking down upon their three beloved daughters, themselves rejoicing at this discovery.

Over the next few months, the three sisters did indeed catch up. Alicia's obsessive behavior was not merely curtailed but completely forgotten in a haze of regular visits to Rabbi Benisch to talk on the phone and many hours spent writing long letters to Klara and reading her replies.

By 1949 Alicia had her dream. She felt like the three sisters were closer than they ever had been, that they knew how one another would reply to any question. They talked of memories of the rest of the family – the Bar Mitzvahs and Hanukkah celebrations they remembered so dearly. They talked of their plans and hopes for the future. And they talked of their sons – all named Hugo, which was yet one more thing that bound them together.

It was only in the spring of 1949, and completely out of the blue, that Klara made the suggestion.

They'd often talked of seeing each other sometime – of Klara taking the ship to Europe or of Alicia and Giselle similarly visiting America, but it had always been a casual "one day we'll have to" mention in passing. This time was different. Klara told Alicia to share the phone with Giselle, because she had something important to say to both of them and didn't want one to hear it before the other.

"I've been thinking a lot," she said, her voice straining. "As you know, I run a shoe and boot factory here and it's very difficult for me to get away. I've decided that I couldn't possibly ever leave for three weeks or more, so I . . . I won't be able to come over any time soon."

"We'll visit each other someday," Giselle told her, the phone now sandwiched between her and Alicia's faces.

"But don't you see?" Klara said. "We won't. I don't have the time and you . . . well, I guess you both have your lives there and I . . . I understand it's difficult for you."

"Giselle's right," Alicia said. "We'll definitely meet one day. I promise we will. And if we all promise that, then—"

"No, no," Klara said. "I've been doing more than just thinking about it. I don't have time to visit you because my business is doing so well. But that also means I can afford to rent a house – one big enough for all of us, and . . . and I can afford to pay for all four of you to come over here."

"To visit?" Alicia asked.

As soon as the words left her lips, she could almost hear the seventeen-year-old Giselle laughing at her and telling her not to be so slow-witted. The new Giselle said nothing.

"No," Klara said. "To come here to live."

Alicia and Giselle glanced at each other, neither daring to speak at first.

"I don't know," Alicia eventually said. "That's such a big change in our lives."

"You don't need to tell me that. But think about it. What does Leopoldstadt or Vienna have to offer you for your future? Do either of you need to stay there?"

"It's my home," Alicia said. "They took me away once and I came back. It would be hard to—"

"Alicia, think bigger. You too, Giselle. Come to San Antonio. Think of the rest of your lives. Many years ago, I felt the same way as you do right now. I was frightened of being here. But in time I settled. Within six months I could speak passable English. There are opportunities here that Vienna can't give you – and opportunities for your boys, too, when they grow up. Think of them, if not yourselves."

"It would be hard, but . . ." A sigh finished Giselle's sentence.

But what? Alicia wanted to ask her. It was different for Giselle; she'd left Vienna by choice; she hadn't been forced out at gunpoint like some. Alicia couldn't bring herself to express such thoughts, though. All she said was, "I'm not sure. We need to think about it."

"Of course," Klara said. "But if I can make a success of my life on my own, just think what we could do between the three of us. I want a happy ending for the Rosenthal sisters, and I know I can make that happen. You can both work in my factory, and outside of work it would be just like the old days – us three sisters making silly promises to one another. Please, Alicia. Please, Giselle. Let's all make one more promise now – that we'll picture a better and happier life for all three of us living here in San Antonio."

"We'll think about it, and seriously," Alicia said. "I can promise you that much."

"You should. You can learn to speak English, learn to drive, and making friends is so easy. I've done all of that so I can help both of you do it too. And you'll be well paid. Listen to me, I don't want to hear any more about this. You've promised me you'll think about it. And we Rosenthal sisters don't break promises made between us, do we?"

Alicia and Giselle laughed at that, and they arranged the next call for two weeks later.

Alicia did, indeed, think a lot about Klara's offer. But even though she saw Giselle most days, it was over a week before they got around to discussing it.

"It was such a shock," Giselle said. "But do you know what? The more I think about Klara's offer, the more it makes sense to me. I think we should go."

"Really?" Alicia said. "You won't miss Vienna?"

"Oh, Vienna will always be my home, but only a tiny number of people I knew from before the war have returned. In some ways I'm a stranger in my own city.

"You always were more adventurous than me," Alicia told her.

Giselle shrugged. "I've thought it through, and I want to go, but I'm not going alone. I'm not prepared to leave you on your own here. I abandoned you once; I'm not doing it again."

The words went straight to Alicia's heart. "Giselle, you can't put my desires before your own. We're different, you always were more impulsive than me. You have to do what you think is best for you and your son."

"Impulsive?" Giselle laughed. "Hardly. I haven't stopped thinking about it ever since we spoke to Klara. Yesterday I even wrote down the good and bad things about leaving and staying, just to be sure."

Alicia nodded, trying hard to concentrate but failing. She changed the subject, but by the next day had made up her mind. Giselle was right, and Klara was also right. More importantly, if Giselle cared enough about her to put her own wishes to one side – if Giselle was refusing to leave her alone in Vienna – would it be right for her to hold Giselle back?

There followed enquiries with various authorities – both Austrian and American – and weeks of planning the details of the long and complicated journey to San Antonio. Throughout all of that form filling and planning, Alicia told herself she was doing the right thing, that Vienna had no hold on her, that if she made herself stay here just to prove a point, then "they" would have won just as much as if she'd never returned.

But now, sitting in her apartment, watching little Hugo Ludwig pull his train around the four suitcases, she felt like crying, and was worried she might fall to pieces as soon as she heard that knock on the door she was waiting so patiently for.

She'd said her goodbyes to the few friends she'd made since returning to Vienna, and told Hugo Ludwig to do the same to his school friends; she'd signed all the paperwork; the tickets had been paid for and collected, so now there was no turning back, and nothing else to do except get on that train carriage that would be the first leg of her long and life-changing journey.

No. She was wrong. There were a few things to settle.

She stepped around Hugo and over to the kitchen. She turned one chair one way, nudged the other with her hip, then, after a moment's thought, she knocked it so it fell over, it's wooden back clattering on the floor. She turned her attentions to the saucepans resting on the cabinet by the sink, all three nested together with their handles aligned. She separated them and arranged them randomly. *What else?* She opened a drawer and pulled out a sharp pointed knife. Seconds later she'd removed a shoe and was using the knife to scraped dirt from the sole, letting it fall to the floor. She put her shoe back on and in her mind was already washing the knife up. But she resisted, simply tossing it onto the table. Then she stared at it. Then she picked it up and threw it onto the floor.

Out of the corner of her eye she realized she was being observed. She looked across to see her son, motionless, staring back at her. His eyes broke off to look at the dirt and the knife on the floor, and at the upturned chair and the saucepans.

"Why did you do all that, Mama?" he asked.

It made Alicia look at what she'd done. And once she'd looked, she was tempted to straighten the chairs, rearrange the saucepans, pick up the knife, wipe the floor, clean the knife, and probably much more. She shrugged and opened her mouth to reply to her son, but three knocks came from the door and she jolted in surprise.

"Giselle?" she said.

"Hugo Albert," was the reply.

"Where's your mama?" she said, aware of the unwanted alarm in her voice.

"She's on the sidewalk with the suitcases. Are you and Hugo Ludwig ready?"

Alicia took a deep breath, exhaled slowly, and opened the door.

"Yes," she said. "We're ready."

And she was – ready for a new life, one in which she didn't obsess about order and cleanliness. She was now more certain than ever that she would change and enjoy the happy ending Klara had talked of.

§

Giselle stood on the sidewalk outside Alicia's apartment block, suitcases her only company, while Hugo Albert was inside fetching Alicia and Hugo Ludwig.

What with the organization, the packing, and the explaining of everything to her Hugo, she'd hardly had any time to herself just lately. And when she had found a moment or two to try to relax, she'd been so excited at the prospect of going to America that she hadn't given any thought to what she might possibly miss about Vienna. Only now, with the imposing streets of her home city stretching out in front of her, did she dwell upon what she was leaving behind and what she might miss.

She told herself some sadness was inevitable. Over the past few years, she'd experienced a settled existence. She loved being with Alicia – although sometimes she'd hated it too – and had struggled with her dreams of meeting new people and visiting new places, of perhaps finding herself a new husband. During those times she'd craved nothing but solitude, and had locked those dreams away – forever, so she'd assumed – for the sake of her sister and the memory of the family she'd betrayed.

But the part of her that craved excitement and the thrill of new experiences had refused to die, and she no longer needed to struggle with her feelings. Lady luck had smiled upon her and would allow her to satisfy both sides of her desires: she would be with her sisters, but also could look forward to starting a new and exciting life in America.

One thing she definitely wouldn't miss about Austria was the constant reminder of her time on the other side of Vienna where her betrayal had started – where Kurt had contrived to stop her seeing her family, where she'd been guilty of accepting his behavior and not arguing her case forcefully enough.

A small part of her would forever love Kurt despite his many faults, but she definitely wouldn't look back with any fondness on her time in Linz with Kurt's family. Well, she might miss his mother just a little, but not his barbaric father or poisonous sister.

Would she remember the man who had given her and Hugo Albert food and a roof over their heads on that rainy night when she'd learned that the war was over? Yes, he was kind, but how kind would he have been had he known the truth about her? And how many more people just like him were there in this country?

But there was one crucial question she asked herself over and over again: would she still be going to America if Alicia had dug her heels in and insisted on staying in Vienna? She wasn't sure. Yes, she'd *told* Alicia she would stay with her in Vienna if need be. But if Alicia had decided to stay it would have been a selfish decision, perhaps betraying a desire to keep one sister all to herself, so whether Giselle really would have stayed with her was quite another matter and in a few hours would be academic.

And then, when a flushed and nervous looking Alicia appeared on the sidewalk with her luggage and son in tow, Giselle felt awful to have even *thought* those things about her. *Of course she would have stayed with her.*

Sometimes Giselle hated herself. Why couldn't she be someone who truly loved and cared for her sisters? Why couldn't she accept she should have loved her Mama and Papa more and should make up for that by being kind and generous where her sisters were concerned? And what was her real motivation for going to America – to be with Alicia and Klara or for the excitement and new opportunities a life over there would bring?

"Did you check you have the train tickets?" Alicia said.

Giselle had to quickly shake thoughts of self-doubt from her head. "Of course I have," she said a little more tersely than she intended. "Come on, we don't have much time."

They walked in silence to the railroad station, both women more concerned with holding onto their suitcases and keeping their sons in check than conversation.

"Are you nervous?" Alicia said to her as they stood on the platform thirty minutes later.

"Not at all," she said with a shake of her head. "I won't miss this place one bit."

But she was lying. Then again, perhaps that was Alicia's fault for asking her such a stupid question. Of course she was nervous; she was as scared as she'd ever been – except, perhaps, when she'd witnessed Kurt's father commit his crimes just a few yards away from her thumping heart. And this was a deeper fear; her heart wasn't thumping, but she felt weak and could sense prickly heat on her back.

Something in her mind urged her on to support the lie. "No," she added, thinking only word by word. "Good riddance to Vienna and all the trouble it's caused us."

She could see Alicia frown and shape her mouth to speak – probably to ask a question. And she didn't want that. Any tactic would do. She had to say something – anything.

"Why do you ask?" she said. "You aren't nervous, are you?" She was about to support the question with a laugh – perhaps in a mocking tone, but at that moment Alicia shut her eyes and a hand darted up to cover the top half of her face. Giselle could see and hear sadness, so pulled a handkerchief from her purse and gave it to her sister.

Once Alicia's tears had gone, Giselle grabbed her hand, squeezing it, holding it for a few seconds in both of hers. "We'll be fine," she said. "You and I and Klara will be reunited. Vienna has been our home and, in a way, that will never change; it will always be where we came from. But this is a new chapter in our lives, Alicia, an opportunity to start again. We'll do as Klara says: we'll learn English, we'll get jobs, we'll learn to drive and have a car each and in time we'll have a luxurious apartment or even a house each."

"We will. We'll do all those things and so much more. And we'll be together, the three Rosenthal sisters. You're a good sister, Giselle. Thank you."

Giselle smiled sweetly.

A good sister?

Hardly.

A good sister would not have even *thought* of poking fun at her when she was clearly suffering. A good sister would have been more honest about her reasons for wanting to go to America. But above all, a good sister wouldn't have disowned her family and her faith for the sake of a rotten man like Kurt. And yes, he *was* rotten. He'd changed for the better once he'd become a father, but he would have reverted to his former self in time. Definitely. Only a bad person would still have feelings of love for such a man.

That meant she wasn't even a good *person*, let alone a good sister. Still, perhaps in a different environment she would change. Perhaps in America she could become the woman she wanted to be: kind, generous, thoughtful, and hardworking.

Perhaps.

"Hugo Albert!" she shouted as her son stepped toward the platform edge. "Come here and stay here!"

§

Klara had spent many months getting to know Alicia and Giselle again, culminating in her inviting them to come live in San Antonio.

She had to do that as she figured it was the only way she was ever going to see them again. Ma and Pa – both her sisters laughed at those names when they'd first heard them – agreed to put them up at the ranch on a temporary basis, although Klara could almost afford to rent somewhere herself. And that was because the small shoe and boot manufacturing company she'd called Rosenthal Shoes in memory of her Papa wasn't quite so small anymore. Thanks to Ma agreeing to look after Hugo Felix whenever necessary, she'd been putting in sixteen-hour days, and with eighteen women on the production lines had just moved the business to larger premises – large enough to employ five times that figure if – no, *when* – that was required.

That meant she could afford the time and money to take Alicia and Giselle on as trainees and give them the secure footing they needed to feel welcome and to settle in a foreign land.

Another item on her checklist was schooling for her two nephews. It was clearly going to be tough for them because they would have to learn basic English before they could learn anything in the classroom, so Klara sorted that out too. She contacted the Jewish professor from Berlin who'd taught Felix many years before, who was now retired, and under the circumstances was only too happy to teach the two Hugos for free. As for general schooling, they'd been provisionally enrolled since the day after their mothers had agreed to come over.

She was so organized that Pa hit the nail on the head when he said the biggest problem they were likely to have was how to distinguish between the three Hugos.

"I might ask what in the name of all that's holy made you all give your sons the same name," he said with a wide smile, "but Ma told me about the promise you all made when you were little girls."

"When my Hugo was born, I didn't know either of my sisters even *had* sons," Klara replied, "let alone what they named them."

"Of course. And I do think it's very sweet. Hellish confusing, but sweet nonetheless. Let's just be grateful that by chance you managed to give them all different middle names."

The meeting at the railroad station was everything Klara had hoped it would be. Although Alicia and Giselle were exhausted after their long journey, there were enough tears, embraces, and kisses to last the rest of the year.

And Klara could see the wonderment in their eyes despite the tiredness; it was a feeling she remembered from when she'd come to America all those years ago. All the streets were straight and square, the buildings were more modern and more spread out than in Vienna, and many of the men wore distinctive wide-brimmed hats; some of them even rode horses around the streets.

But Hugo Albert and Hugo Ludwig were jaded, hardly able to keep their eyes open, only the bewilderment of this new world keeping them from falling asleep. Klara knew that in time they too would share their mothers' excitement and enthusiasm for life's new adventure once they'd had time to rest up.

Klara had traveled no more than ten miles to meet them, but had hardly slept the previous night and had been on edge all morning. For her, too, this seemed like the end of a lengthy and twisting journey – one that had been worth all the money in the world.

She imagined the best of times blossoming ahead of her.

And a part of her even dared hope that a happy ending was in sight for all three Rosenthal sisters.

Chapter Twenty-Five
San Antonio, Texas, USA. June 2012

"Lud was lying, wasn't he?" Eleanor said as she and Hugo sat down in a diner halfway to Houston.

Hugo tried to ignore her, just looked around and bit on a fingernail. He didn't need that conversation right now. But Eleanor elaborated.

"When he said he knew nothing about your mother, he was lying, yeah?"

Hugo looked left at the counter, the griddle behind it sizzling and smoking, and wondered what was being cooked to within an inch of its life. Then he hooked his gaze to the right, at the passing traffic, wondering where all those trucks were headed and why.

"Hugo?"

"Sorry, what did you say?"

"Are you all right? You've been awful quiet since seeing Lud."

"No, I haven't. Not really."

"Now *you're* lying too."

Hugo pulled his gaze toward her, drew breath to speak, but instead picked up a menu and started running his little finger up and down it. Eleanor tutted and picked up a menu too.

A waitress came over and welcomed them.

"Thank you," Hugo said. "Can I get, uh . . ."

The waitress stood, pen nib poised on pad, staring at him. After twenty seconds she flicked her eyes to Eleanor, who summoned up a smile.

"Mmm," Hugo said. "I'll have . . . I think I'll have, uh . . ." He let out a sigh.

"Aren't you hungry?" Eleanor asked.

He put the menu back and leaned over the table, whispering to Eleanor, "Could you order for me please? Would you mind?"

"Sure I can. Let's see. You want sweet pancakes with syrup and chocolate sauce?"

"Too much sugar."

"Could you go a cheese, pepper and onion omelet?"

"Tends to give me heartburn."

"What about good old burger and fries?"

"That's just starch and meat." He looked up at the waitress. "You got bagels? I didn't see bagels on the menu."

They ordered bagels with cream cheese and sliced ham.

"What's wrong?" Eleanor asked when the waitress had left. And it was accompanied by her *don't mess with me* face as opposed to her *I'll understand* face.

Perhaps it was time for Hugo to try to put the sick feeling he was experiencing into words. He held a finger up to her and said, "Just give me a minute."

Two minutes later she said, "And so?"

His breathing was shallow and not pleasant to experience. Now he knew what to say, but also knew that when he said it – once the thought was outside of his head – there would be no backtracking.

"I mean, have you remembered something your mother said? Did you notice something else on the sheet the attorney gave you? I'd say—"

"I recognize the guy."

"What?"

Hugo closed his eyes and exhaled loudly. "I don't know where from, I don't know how long ago. At first I thought he reminded me of an actor or some other famous guy, but that's not it. I've met him before. The very faint accent, the very slight whistle or lisp or whatever you call it. That and the teeth."

"You recognize the guy's teeth? Seriously?"

Hugo rubbed his chin, deep in mental pain as much as thought. "I don't know if it's that or something else about him. I'm clutching at straws as much as anything. I know I've met him before. I'm trying to process the how and the where. I just can't . . ." He shook his head.

"Come here." Eleanor reached across the table and held his hand. "It's no big deal, Hugo, not if we consider the will and his behavior. From where I stand, I'd be more surprised if you *haven't* met him."

"I'm gonna go back, have it out with the guy. He knows something and he's not letting on."

"No, Hugo." Her hand tightened around his. "It's not the way. Let's just leave it for now, huh?"

Hugo glanced down at their gracefully entwined hands, then around the diner, and pulled his hand away. "What are we, sixteen?"

"You get my point, though?"

"Oh, god," he drawled out. "I know you're right. You're always right, dammit. I just wish my mother had been a little . . ."

"A little less stubborn?"

"A little less secretive – no, a *lot* less secretive. I mean, if she kept in contact with these people, she must have done it all behind my back."

"Don't forget, she could have been calling and writing these two Hugo guys while she was at work or while you were at school or college, not to mention after you'd moved to Dallas."

"I know that. But why? I can't think of a good reason why she didn't tell me. Are these guys distant relatives of hers? Did they help her when she came to Texas? Are they friends of hers?

Children of friends? Whoever these people are, why don't I know about them?"

"Perhaps she was protecting you."

"What does that even mean? Protecting me *from what*, exactly?"

"Hugo, listen to me. Whatever your mother did, however she brought you up, you didn't turn out so bad; I can vouch for that. And I reckon your confusion is down to the difference between a mother and a father."

"What the hell are you talking about?"

"Trust me. I know. A father tends to want to widen his child's experiences – within reason, of course. But a mother's instinct is always – *absolutely always* – to protect. And Klara was a damned fine mother, we both know that. So whatever she did – whatever it was that she kept secret from you – she did it with your best interests at heart."

"I guess. But whatever this big secret is, why didn't she tell me when I was thirty or forty or fifty."

"Perhaps she didn't want to upend the boat while we were bringing up the girls."

"So why not tell me just before she died?"

Eleanor shrugged. "Perhaps she's telling you now – in a roundabout way."

The waitress brought the food and Hugo poured two glasses of iced water from the pitcher on the table.

"You think I'm being a little harsh on her?"

"On her and on yourself. Relax a little. We'll get to the truth one way or another if it was meant to be."

They both picked up napkins. Hugo reached for a bagel but noticed Eleanor was dabbing her napkin under her eyes.

"Hey, I'm sorry, Eleanor. I don't mean to be all grouchy. You know that."

She nodded and sniffed a few tears back. "Seeing you like this is hard. You're not yourself. And goddammit, *I like yourself*."

"You know, if this is upsetting you, we can just turn around and head back home."

Eleanor huffed. "The hell we will. No way. Not now we've started."

"Thank you. I appreciate what you're doing here for me."

"*For you?* Ha! Don't kid yourself, buster. This is more intriguing than any movie I ever saw."

"Well, I'm glad I'm still of some use to you."

"You have your moments."

"Come on. Let's eat."

Each of them pasted cream cheese on bagels, took clean, deliberate bites, and started chewing, Hugo glancing around and watching the world go by, Eleanor flicking her eyes to the side now and then but mostly keeping her eyes on Hugo. He noticed and gave her an exaggerated smile.

"And you're absolutely correct, by the way," he said after forcing down his first mouthful.

"About what?"

"About that Lud guy lying. Even when the air was green with the scent of free cash and any sane person would have agreed to everything, that guy still denied what was written all over his face."

"So we're still headed to Houston?"

"Yeah. Oh, yeah."

Chapter Twenty-Six
1950

Alicia can hear her mama but not see her.

"I'm so hungry my stomach hurts. Please, Alicia, could you find me some food from somewhere? Everything I had has been taken. I don't have the energy to stay awake and when I fall asleep someone steals my bread."

Alicia wants to speak – to tell her mama that the person stealing from her is her own daughter – but a force around her throat holds onto the words. Her neck muscles tighten, battling against the force. She struggles. She succeeds. She coughs and knows she can now speak. She opens her mouth but another voice fills the void. It's her papa.

"Did Kurt give you some cake, Alicia? Did you lose it? Did someone steal it from you? I know you would have given some to your mama and papa if you could have, but there are many thieves around us – people who would let their own parents starve if it kept them alive."

I shared it with Sarah and Hugo, Alicia thinks. *I thought they needed it more than anyone. Isn't that what a good mama does?*

"I thought *I* was a good mama," Alicia hears. "Didn't I deserve some cake?"

There wasn't enough to go around, Alicia wants to say – to scream out. *There wasn't enough and I was trying to do the best thing for my children.*

But the words are stolen from her mouth like candy from a baby – or like rotten bread from a desperately sick mama. She tries to speak once more, forcing air up through her throat and out of her mouth, but it only forms baby talk.

And that makes someone laugh.

It's her brother. His face is more contorted than she remembers. He lifts his hand. A twisted finger points at her.

She tries to speak again, straining to spit out even one coherent word. She wants to tell them all so much how sorry she is, but is unable to utter anything, and in frustration lets out a long scream.

Alicia felt her body being shaken. She heard her son before she saw him. "Mama! Mama! Are you all right? I heard a scream. Wake up! Wake up!"

Alicia gasped in shock as she roused herself, sitting up and wiping the moisture from her brow. "I'm sorry, my dear. I was having . . ." She broke off as she lifted her nightdress, sodden with sweat, away from her clammy skin.

"Was it another nightmare?" Hugo Ludwig asked.

She held him and pulled him to her, hugging him, kissing him on the temple. "No, my darling. It was a dream. It was only a dream." She squeezed him once more, then gently pushed him away. "Go back to bed and I'll see you in the morning, and we'll have pancakes for breakfast."

"You aren't going to talk to yourself again, are you, Mama?"

"Don't be silly, darling. I don't do that. Now go back to your bedroom and go to sleep."

She lay still until she heard the creak that told her he was in bed, then pulled the covers off and stepped out onto the wooden floor.

She was pleased. It had taken him less than a year to learn good English. For her it would take longer to become fluent – she knew that – but hers was still passable. She'd worked hard both on her English lessons and at the shoe factory, and Klara had rewarded her with promotions that had taken her off the production line and onto more responsible – and better paid – duties. She was now earning enough to rent a small two-bedroomed cabin on the other side of town, while Giselle, also earning well, had chosen to save her money and stay with Klara at the ranch house.

And perhaps more changes were to come, because Klara was holding a meeting tomorrow – well, by now that meant later this morning – and had told Alicia that she had to attend. Alicia was guessing she was probably going to unveil some plan for another expansion of the company.

Alicia had other, better plans, and was anxious as to how she would break the news to her two sisters: Eugene had asked her to marry him.

Alicia silently switched the light on and knelt down in front of the chest of drawers. She inched the bottom drawer out to avoid any squealing sounds and tipped the contents – socks and stockings – onto the floor. After jumbling the socks up with her outstretched hands, she started sorting them back into matching pairs, and into groups by color. She thought she'd sorted them last night, but clearly hadn't. After all, if she had, why would she be repeating the chore?

Whatever she'd done before, within ten minutes the socks and stockings were now all neatly sorted. She shut the drawer, then felt ashamed that she'd wasted time she should have spent sleeping. *Of course* they'd already been sorted. She cursed her stupidity, then opened the drawer again, thrust a hand in, and mixed them all up. That would help. If nothing else, it would give her something to do if she had some more spare time – if she couldn't sleep.

The episode reminded her of that frightening time when she'd still been living with her sisters at the ranch.

They were having a game of cards, and Alicia had excused herself and gone to the bathroom. While in there, it had suddenly struck her how disheveled everything was: the soap, brushes, cloths and shaving razors were not only dirty and covered in small hairs, but were also arranged randomly. Worse still, the medicines in the cabinet were dusty and not arranged in any order. So she locked the door, cleaned the dust off the medicines and arranged them in alphabetical order, then washed the soap, brushes, cloths and razors so they were almost as new and arranged them all at the same angle.

Then she realized that her sisters wouldn't have understood, so she swapped a few of the medicines around, and then smeared the other objects with some dirt she'd managed to scrape off the floorboards and arranged them as far as she could tell exactly as they had been before. Klara gave her a strange look when she emerged, and Giselle asked what had taken her so long, and whether she was ill. No, they wouldn't have understood, so she simply said she didn't know what Giselle was talking about, and quickly continued with the card game.

The experience forced her to move out and into her own place. She wasn't going to let them – or anyone – find out about her habits. It wasn't that she thought her behavior was abnormal. It probably was, but doing those things made her feel better, helped her relax. And she was content to be like that so long as in the company of others – at work, for instance – she gave the appearance of being a fine, reasonable, and regular woman who nobody would suspect of once scrubbing her son's back until it bled.

She deeply regretted that incident in particular, the image of him crying as she scrubbed was etched on her mind, so she knew there was a problem. But the bigger problem was keeping a lid on it – *keeping control*. Hence the cabin on the other side of town – far enough away from her sisters so that they wouldn't drop by without calling first, giving her time to make just a little mess around to put them off the scent. The cabin was also small enough to be easy to keep clean – a key factor when she'd been looking for a place.

It was also how she'd met Eugene – at the cleaning products section of the local store where he worked. Eugene was a kind and gentle man. Hugo Ludwig liked him, and Alicia was sure that in time the happiness Eugene would bring her would start a new chapter in her life, and would silence those voices so that Giselle and Klara would never need to know about them.

She shut the sock drawer once more, closed her eyes, and waited for the voices. They soon came, along with the stench of dampness, of mold, and of human waste in every sense of the phrase.

"Alicia, my dear," Mama says, "could you turn the light out and come back to bed please?"

"Are you cold?" Alicia replies without turning around.

"Cold and hungry too. Do you have any food?"

"No, Mama. I've given all mine to the children."

"Because someone's stolen mine. I'm certain I had bread under my sleeve."

"This place is full of thieves, Mama. I only hope they can live with their shame."

"Come to bed," Papa says. "I'm hungry too. And I'm so cold. I think someone stole my blanket."

Alicia turned and fell onto the bed. She grabbed a pillow and started thumping it against the mattress. "Leave me alone!" she shouted. "Ludwig has gone away, why can't you? I don't want you here!"

She thumped her head against the pillow. She had to sleep. There was that meeting to get up for in the morning – the one she absolutely *had to* attend. She told herself to imagine what it might be about – if only to take her mind off those unwanted visitors.

§

Unlike Alicia, Giselle hadn't yet moved herself and her son out of the ranch house. Neither had she learned to drive, relying on Klara to take her to the factory.

She thought it odd that Alicia had felt the need to spend her wages on a car and renting a cabin, whereas she preferred to let the money pile up in the bank instead. Not that having a car and her own place was unusual, but it was *Giselle* who had always been the sister to act on impulse and let flights of fancy carry her away. It was *she* who should have been splashing her money, and *Alicia* who should have been carefully putting hers away.

Nobody had asked Giselle what she was going to do with the money she was saving, but she knew they were all itching to find out. This was supposed to be the country where any dream could come true, and Giselle had come here with a dream of experiencing excitement and thrills – of a world the old Giselle would have thrown herself into and reveled in until the sun came up. But it soon became apparent to her that some kind of mysterious internal compass had other ideas. The truth was that a grand house or a car or a heady lifestyle didn't attract Giselle in any way; in fact, the very thought turned her stomach. Sanctuary would make her happy – like the sanctuary she'd had back in Vienna. In fact, she craved something much better than she'd had in Vienna. She didn't yet know what "much better" meant in that context, but she had time to find out.

Yes, a home of her own would provide more privacy and so would be a sanctuary of sorts, but during the day she would still have to mix with the people at the factory, and she hated that prospect. She hated it so much that she'd made sure she was promoted off the shop floor even before Alicia had, which turned the tables on her. Oh, they were perfectly pleasant people – hardworking, welcoming, cheerful – but she felt she simply didn't *belong*.

As the person in charge of marketing and advertising she still had to meet people, but those meetings could be shortened to a minimum.

So no, even a home of her own wouldn't bring the level of privacy she craved.

She wasn't exactly sure how her preferred level of privacy could be achieved – and, crucially, how her son would be catered for in such a scenario – but over the months a vague notion – a fantasy, so it felt – had gradually started to crystallize in her mind. She didn't dare tell a soul that there even *was* a plan, let alone its detail, because Klara or Alicia would doubtless have found out and tried to talk her out of it.

So she took breakfast at the same table as Klara and the two boys, said hi to the two people she'd gotten used to calling Ma and Pa, and held polite conversation with everyone because today was just another normal day.

Well, almost.

Today looked like being subtly different. Across the breakfast table, Klara reminded her they both had to be on time today as she had an important meeting to chair first thing, and Giselle's presence was not optional.

And that was just like Klara – to state her requirement in such an official way even though they were all sharing coffee and bagels. Why couldn't she have simply said there was a meeting she wanted Giselle to be at? Why couldn't that stuck-up sister of hers . . .

And there Giselle stopped her train of thought. She was traveling along that dark, destructive road again of having inconsiderate feelings toward Klara – the sister who had contacted her, paid for her to travel to America, arranged a roof over her head, and given her a pretty good job.

Klara had been so good to her, had effectively given her a new life, whereas she had hardly ever been good to Klara. So why was there this inexplicable dislike of her? What had Klara done that was so awful? The answer was a big, fat nothing.

There was nothing wrong with Klara.

There was everything wrong with Giselle.

The urge to say something unpleasant to Klara – to snap at her – had been there so many times over the last few months, but Giselle had always successfully resisted it. Could she suppress those feelings forever? It was unlikely. Just as unlikely as her suppressing nasty criticism of the *oh so perfect* Alicia.

And if she was being honest with herself, it wasn't as if she had singled out Klara and Alicia as people she disliked. She disliked many people – no, *most* people. It was just that in the case of her sisters, she hated herself for feeling that way about them.

Whenever she thought back, she realized she'd been twisted in that way ever since those years spent in Linz, where she'd lived a double life: one persona to show to those around her, another in her own mind. Had that experience warped her personality? Was that the reason she was so two-faced? Or had she always been like that? All she knew was that she didn't feel comfortable showing anyone her true colors. Instead, she kept those feelings under lock and key, festering and multiplying in secret like some particularly malignant germ or virus that was always threatening to unleash its malevolence.

Over the years, she'd tried to work out why she was such a horrible person – betraying here and deceiving there. Even giving evidence against Kurt's father – on the face of it a brave and morally commendable act – made her hate herself. She hadn't done it because it was *the right thing to do*; for a while she'd thought she had, but that was just wishful thinking, a cover of sorts. She'd done it out of hatred of Kurt's father, which was in reality hatred of herself for betraying her own family. Yes, the years with Kurt and his family had certainly changed her for the worse, but that was all in the past; she could no longer blame them. The blame lay within herself.

And then there was her own son. She'd started snapping at him for every minor error, immediately overcome with regret and apologizing, only to scold him again soon afterward.

In time she realized the fault in him: he was starting to look like Kurt. Oh, of course she knew that wasn't his fault, but with every passing year his face reminded her more and more of Kurt. And of Kurt's parents. And of Kurt's sister.

She'd agonized in silence over what to do with him because the issue was hardly likely to get better: he was only going to look more and more like Kurt as he got older. In her more lucid periods, she'd told herself off for even having the faintest notion that little Hugo Albert might be to blame for anything; it was hardly his fault who he looked like, and in every tangible respect she loved him every bit as much as any mother loved her child. But in her most secretive, dark thoughts she wondered what she might do with him in years to come.

The vision of him turning into Kurt – or even Kurt's father – was a living nightmare with no escape; well, perhaps there was one way to escape.

Due to all these unpleasant thoughts caged inside her head, that vague notion of an escape plan both festered and developed in the back of her mind. Instead of making Klara's and Alicia's lives difficult, she would go somewhere else. Exactly where didn't matter, but someday she would leave.

It gradually became apparent to her that that was why she'd been so protective of the money she was earning – it was her security blanket, not so much a *get out of jail* card as a *build yourself a jail* card.

But just for today she would put that idea back in its armored box, put on that prodigal sister face, be pleasant to Klara, hitch a ride into work with her as usual, and go to that damned meeting, where she would force herself to be pleasant to Alicia, and simply nod and agree to everything Klara suggested. This was Klara's business after all, and despite the fact that Klara had involved her two sisters in the running of the business more and more over the last year, those sisters were only there to give Klara encouragement, to make the occasional suggestion, and to rubber stamp her decisions.

How much longer could Giselle keep up the charade?

She had absolutely no idea.

§

By the time Klara, with Giselle in tow, entered the bare but perfectly functional meeting room, Alicia was already waiting for them.

It made Klara smile inside. She could always rely on her eldest sister. She'd always been confident that Alicia would work hard and progress through the business, and she hadn't been let down on that score; from machinist to supervisor to head of manufacturing, Alicia had repaid her faith with interest.

They now employed almost sixty people in total, so they were doing *something* right. Perhaps that something was Alicia, but it also might have been Giselle.

Giselle had been something of a wildcard; Klara hadn't ever planned her progress within the business, but in discussions Giselle had put forward some imaginative ideas. Subsequently, once she'd been given the opportunity with advertising, she'd shown a genuine flair for creating eye-catching posters and radio advertisements.

Both Alicia's and Giselle's current appointments had been made within a year of them starting, and nobody really believed it was *all* due to merit. And that was a fair point. Would they have progressed so rapidly in a company not owned by their sister?

Probably not, but merit was a complex principle and the fine health of Rosenthal Shoes appeared to vindicate Klara's decisions. She'd taken a gamble – one with its roots more in personal trust than corporate customs, but that gamble had paid off. And now, at this meeting, she was about to reveal why she'd made that gamble in the first place.

After the usual greetings, Klara shut the door and sat at the table between Alicia and Giselle, causing them to exchange puzzled glances.

"Aren't we having a meeting now?" Alicia said.

"We are," Klara replied. "Just the three of us."

"We're talking about a business meeting, yes?" Giselle asked.

At that point Klara switched to talking in German. "This is more than a business meeting," she said. "It's about the future of Rosenthal Shoes. Not how it's run, but who owns it."

"But *you* own it," Alicia said. "Yes," Giselle added, both now also speaking in German.

Klara lifted her leather satchel onto the table and opened it. "I've had some draft documents written up, which I want you to take away and read thoroughly." She handed each of them a few sheets of paper, which they started to scan through.

Alicia was the first to react. "But . . . this transfers one third of the company to me," she said, switching her gaze between Klara and Giselle, the latter still poring over the document.

Klara nodded. "I want to share the company. We are the three Rosenthal sisters. None of us are now Rosenthals, and yet we are all still Rosenthals in our hearts. I'm doing this in memory of Mama and Papa, our brother too."

"I . . . I don't know what to say," Alicia replied.

"You could say you're pleased. I mean, I don't expect thanks; I'm simply doing what's right, but you could smile."

"I can't accept this," Giselle said quietly, only now looking up.

"Why not?" Klara replied. "You won't be losing anything. I can assure you it's legally binding, but you can consult your own lawyer if—"

"No, no, Klara. I trust you. You're my sister. I trust you with my life."

"In that case, all you need do is sign the document after you've read it properly, then you'll own one third of Rosenthal Shoes."

Giselle gave her a look of . . . *was that pity?*

"Don't you see?" Klara told both of them. "We can think of this as Papa's business being passed down to his three surviving children."

"I have to be honest," Giselle said. "This isn't fair."

"Not fair?"

"I don't deserve it."

"What do you mean?"

Giselle's face was a muddle of twitches for a few seconds, and she needed a couple of long, calming breaths before replying. "I've done so many things that I'm . . . well, yes, *ashamed of,*" she said, her eyes starting to water. "I betrayed my family. I betrayed my faith, my people. You know that's true."

Klara was about to reply – to tell her that was all in the past and forgiven – when Alicia spoke up.

"I'm afraid I can't accept this either," she said. "I'm so sorry, Klara. It's not that I'm ungrateful, but I . . . I too betrayed Mama and Papa."

"What are you talking about?"

"I was . . . negligent. They were in my care and they didn't survive while I did. I put my own safety before theirs. And I won't ever be able to forgive myself."

Klara couldn't understand. She knew Alicia's history; she knew what had happened.

Or did she?

"Alicia," she said, now staring at her sister. "You can't blame yourself for what happened. It wasn't your fault they died."

"Well . . ."

Klara looked to Giselle for support.

"Alicia?" Giselle said, her words slow and deliberate. "Is there something you haven't told us about Mama and Papa?"

Alicia's jaw hovered for a few seconds.

"Surely . . . you didn't have anything to do with their deaths?"

Just as Klara was fearing the worst, Alicia said, "How could you think such a thing? I just feel that I could have done so much more to help them, that's all."

"I understand," Klara said. "We both do. But we know you did all you could to help them. You have absolutely nothing to be ashamed of."

"If any of us should feel shame, it's me," Giselle said.

Alicia shook her head. "I can't help how I feel."

Giselle turned to Klara. "I think you should keep the company to yourself. I understand what Alicia is saying. Whatever happened, she feels shame, and so do I. I don't deserve what you're offering. It wouldn't be right."

"But . . . but . . ." Klara spent a while searching for the right words. "You aren't the only ones to have done something you feel ashamed of," she eventually blurted out.

"Really?" Giselle said. "What have you possibly done that you could be ashamed of?"

An image of Larry on a dark, traitorous night so soon after Felix had died flashed in and out of her mind. The more she tried not to think of her son, the more his face – its features resembling Larry's as much as Felix's – reminded her of the night she'd tried so hard to forget.

Could she tell them the truth? After all, they might have thought they betrayed their family and their people. But Klara had betrayed the man who mattered most in her life.

As sisters they were supposed to be close, able to confide in one another. For a fraction of a second the first words of a confession of sorts formed on her tongue. Then she drew her thoughts back to sanity.

No, it didn't happen. *That didn't happen.* The truth was that she slept with Felix just before he left for what turned out to be his final tour of duty, and little Hugo was the result. That was the truth. It was the truth *and always would be.*

She let out a long sigh. "What am I ashamed of? Well, I guess I deserted my family, jumped in the first lifeboat I could find and left them on a sinking ship."

"But Mama and Papa wanted you to get into that lifeboat," Alicia said. "They always told me they were relieved you escaped before it was too late."

"Look," Klara said. "Let's leave aside who is and isn't ashamed. What I'm saying is that it could so easily have been one of you two who escaped to America or elsewhere and I who ended up hiding out somewhere or being taken to one of those disgusting camps. I'm saying that fortune played a big part in our lives, that I was lucky, and that I want to make amends. I want each of you to have a third of the company."

"Well, I've given my answer," Giselle said. "I don't want to spend the rest of my life thinking that I owe you something."

"It would be a gift. You wouldn't owe me anything."

"Nevertheless, you talk about making amends, but there's no need for that; it's *you* who has built this company up."

"And I feel the same way," Alicia added.

"Don't you think this is ridiculous?" Klara said. "At the moment you have good jobs and good incomes. This will cement those benefits; you'll share in the profits of the business."

Alicia and Giselle simply stared at her. She felt forced to continue.

"Apart from anything else it's as if we're . . . we're standing up to Hitler and his followers, showing them that they haven't won, that they haven't destroyed our family."

Now her sisters looked down, both appearing pensive.

"Well?" she asked them.

"Sometimes it's hard to be sure who's really won," Giselle eventually said.

"I don't know what you mean by that."

"I know exactly what she means," Alicia said.

"Well, tell me, please. We're sisters, aren't we? I know you've both had a terrible time but surely we can share our problems."

A long silence was eventually broken by Giselle.

"Oh, Klara," she said. "I know you always wanted that happy ending, but sometimes . . . well, sometimes the damage is simply too great to repair."

"So talk to me," Klara said. "Both of you. Tell me what damage you're talking about."

"It's hard to put into words," Alicia said. "I guess however much support and help you get, however hard you try, sometimes the past can . . . I'm sorry, but I can't say anymore. And thank you for your offer, but I can't accept."

Klara's eyes lingered on Alicia for a while before turning to her other sister.

"What about you, Giselle? Surely you can tell me if you're having problems."

Giselle shook her head. "It's better for us all that I don't talk about it. I'm sorry. But I can't accept your offer either."

"And that's your final word?"

"It is," Giselle said.

"And you, Alicia?"

"I'm afraid so."

Klara pursed her lips and started nodding. "Okay," she said with an air of finality.

She should have been happy. She had a successful business and had been reunited with her sisters. This arrangement should have been the cherry on top of the cupcake. They didn't want to take her up on the offer right now, but perhaps sometime down the line they would.

"Alicia," she said. "Where do you see yourself in . . . let's say . . . five years' time?"

Alicia concentrated on her fidgeting hands for a few seconds, then looked up and opened her mouth to speak. She stalled and stared down again, then spoke without looking at her sisters. "Could I be honest with you? With both of you?"

"Yes," Klara said.

"Of course," Giselle said. "What's wrong?"

There was a long pause before Alicia said, "I have some news. I'm . . . going to marry Eugene."

"Oh, that's wonderful," Giselle said.

"Of course," Klara said. "We're both happy for you. But why does that affect the business?"

"Because I'm not sure how long I'll be staying here."

Klara laughed as she spoke. "The world's changing, Alicia. You can be married and still work."

Alicia looked down, a tic jerking one side of her face.

"Is there something else?" Giselle said.

"You can tell us," Klara added.

"It's complicated. Sometimes I don't feel well. I don't want to go into details, but Eugene will be a big help to me." Now her eyes flicked up, her gaze hopping between her sisters. "I'll be better in a year. But the next few months, I'm not so sure about."

"Well, okay." Klara glanced at Giselle. "We understand. If we can help in any way—"

"You can't. Please. Just forget I said anything. I can't thank you enough for the job, Klara, it takes my mind off my problems for a while, but I can't cope with any extra responsibility."

"If that's what you want."

"I do."

Klara turned to her other sister. "What about you, Giselle? What do you want to be doing in a few years' time?"

"Well . . . as Alicia has been honest, I feel I should be, too."

"Are you also not very well?"

Giselle shook her head. "I don't have health problems. I just . . . I feel there's something I should tell you – both of you. It's not fair on you otherwise. And please don't ask me more or bring this up again. You've been good to me, Klara, better than I deserve. I'll do my job as well as I can, but I don't want to own any of the company. You shouldn't involve me to that level, because I have . . . plans."

"Plans? What do you mean?"

"I mean . . . plans to move away from here."

"What?" Klara said. "Move away to where?"

"It doesn't matter where. Hugo Albert is my primary concern. I need to be certain he'll be properly looked after."

"I don't think I understand."

"I can't say I understand either, but I . . . I feel I need to escape."

"Escape?"

"Please, Klara, Alicia. I hope I can trust you both, but don't ask any more questions and don't tell anyone."

Klara held tightly onto the hundred questions that danced on her tongue. "Well . . . as you wish, if you're sure."

Giselle nodded silently.

"Is that the end of the meeting?" Alicia asked.

"I guess it has to be," Klara said.

Alicia and Giselle prepared to stand, but Klara held their hands and asked them to sit. "I just want to say one more thing," she said. "Then we can all leave."

They sat in silence for a few moments, then Klara spoke.

"I remember starting this business three years ago. I was in a new country, widowed and with a baby to consider, I still had one or two problems understanding the language. But I managed to make a small success of it, mainly through working eighty hours a week or more. And I'm not making myself out to be a martyr. I was lucky. I was lucky to meet Felix, and I was lucky to escape Vienna when I did. But I worked hard. And do you know what my motivation was, what has kept my shoulder to the wheel these past few years? It wasn't money. No, no. I thought of you, Alicia, and you, Giselle, as well as Mama and Papa and poor Hugo. That's why I chose the name 'Rosenthal' – it hasn't been my name for a long time now. I do what I do for my family, for its memory, and for the future of the three of us. Have things your way; keep your pride if you wish, but one way or another I promise I will give one third of what I own of this company to you, Alicia and one third to you, Giselle. It's what Mama and Papa would have wanted. It's for them and our brother Hugo as much as it is for you. It's our history that spurs me on."

Alicia and Giselle looked at each other.

"Now, let's get back to work," Klara said. "We have a company to run. Just remember that I keep my promises, and I have a good memory."

"And you always were stubborn," Alicia said, smiling.

"Thank you," Klara replied.

Chapter Twenty-Seven
San Antonio, Texas, USA. June 2012

Eleanor, Hugo, and their full stomachs were back on the freeway headed for Houston and for the house of their second secret Hugo: Hugo Albert.

"I know you said to leave Lud alone," Hugo said from the passenger seat, "but I need to try again."

"You mean, to *visit* him again?"

"Perhaps one more time. Someday. Point is, quite apart from this little mystery, I'm duty bound to make sure he gets what's legally his."

"We'll see. I figure he might change his mind when he's had time to think."

"But if he still doesn't want to play ball, I guess I just have to mail him a check and . . ."

"And what?"

"And . . . forget about him."

"Hey, let's not give up on the guy just yet, Hugo. In the meantime, we should try to come up with scenarios that might explain why he's lying."

"My best guess is there's something that Lud is ashamed of or even *scared* of, because we sure hit a couple of nerves back there. But we have to accept that we might never find out what the hell is happening in the guy's head. We have to let it go and hope that our second secret Hugo won't be as difficult."

"Whether he is or not, you're doing the right thing."

"What do you mean?"

"Some people would be put off visiting our secret Hugo number two after what happened back there with number one."

"Oh, I haven't decided whether I'm going to ask this one any questions. I might just tell him he has an inheritance due and leave it at that."

"Really? You don't want to know what he was to your mother?"

"Hey, you know I do. But . . . well, I found that awkward back there, like I was torturing the guy. I don't want it to happen again."

"You want me to do the talking this time? I could even go on my own if you want, leave you in the car or someplace else."

Hugo let his silence answer that one. They both knew there was no way he would be able to hold his tongue. He took out the sheet of paper, stared at the address, and started silently rehearsing different – more subtle – ways of asking questions.

He'd made no progress whatsoever by the time they pulled up outside a neat and tidy bungalow with a modest roof terrace, which was on a street of equally neat and tidy properties.

Hugo looked at the piece of paper again to check the number while Eleanor waited.

"You think I should just do the same as last time?" he asked. "Just knock on the guy's door?"

"Well, I reckon you could wait until there's a glorious sunset, then serenade the guy while he's standing on the balcony, gazing wistfully over the—"

"Hey, quit that. You know this isn't easy for me."

"I do. And I'm sorry." She looked down, her face showing no emotion. "Force of habit. I know it's hard and I know this is important for you. But I guess, uh . . ."

"What?"

"You sure you don't want me to do the talking?"

"Would you mind starting off, then I'll take over?"

"Complicated, but okay."

A minute later, they were standing at the door. He nodded. She knocked. The door opened almost immediately.

"Hi, there. Can I help you?"

The woman was hard to judge. Somewhere between fifty and seventy, Hugo figured. She had frizzy black hair, dyed by the look of the roots, oversize glasses that perhaps hid crow's feet, and a mouth full of yellowed teeth and space. She had a soothing, welcoming voice, reminiscent of a well-played violin.

"We're looking for a Mr. Hugo Albert Hinkler," Eleanor said.

"You got the right place. He's my husband." She spoke with a warm smile, but Hugo knew those didn't always last, so told himself his best manners might help this time.

"My name's Hugo too – Hugo Goldberg, and this is my wife, Eleanor. If it's possible, we'd like to talk to him about my mother, Klara."

Her brow furrowed. For a moment Hugo thought she was going to cry. "Oh my God," she said, gasping heavily. "You're Klara's son?"

"Yes, you see—"

"Hey, come on inside. Come, come. Albie's next door; he helps the old guy with his gardening. My name's Judy, by the way."

"'*Albie*?" Eleanor said as they all walked through the hallway. "You know him by his middle name?"

"Silly, I know. He's just always preferred being called that."

They entered a cozy living room with two sofas angled to look directly at a large TV, which immediately got switched off.

"Make yourselves comfortable. Can I get you some coffee?"

"Thank you very much," Hugo said, "but we had a large lunch not too long ago."

"No matter. I'll tell Albie you're here, but I know he'll be fifteen minutes or more, and I'm busy planting out back and if I don't get them in soon they'll die, so I'm afraid I'll have to leave you two alone."

Eleanor and Hugo said that was fine, and Judy left.

"She's very trusting," Hugo said.

"Because you mentioned your mother's name. She clearly knows something."

"Hope so. It's been a long detour on the way home otherwise." Hugo perused the ornaments of cats and dogs on shelves that covered two walls of the room. They both spent five wordless minutes doing the same, occasionally checking through the gap in the door, through which Judy could be seen kneeling and digging in the back yard. Then Hugo decided that if another five minutes passed by, he would approach Judy and ask if they could simply go find Albie themselves.

Those five minutes came and went. Hugo opened his mouth to tell Eleanor what he was about to do, but he'd only managed to get her name out when her cell phone rang. She picked it up immediately.

"Hello . . . yes . . . oh . . . oh, well, thank you. Thank you so much."

"Who is it?" Hugo hissed.

She pointed to the phone with her spare hand. "It's him," she mouthed. Then she talked into the phone again. "Lud, my husband's here. I'm putting you on speakerphone now, okay?"

Hugo quickly glanced out back, where Judy was still elbow deep in soil, which meant they had some privacy.

"Can you hear me, Hugo?" the voice said a couple of seconds later.

"I can."

"It's Lud here – or Hugo Ludwig Tannenbaum to anyone who knows my history."

"Hello, Lud. I'm so pleased you called back."

"Listen, I'm sorry I was a little rude to you earlier. I, uh . . . I find it hard to talk about certain things in person – things about my mother. It's easier over the phone – still hard, but not impossible, if you get my drift."

"That's just fine," Hugo said.

"Thank you so much for talking to us," Eleanor added. "Just try to relax and say as much as you want, huh?"

"I'll give it a go. Y'see, there's been a lot of stuff running around in my head since you happened by, and in the end I figured it would be for the best if I told you about my mother, Alicia – Alicia Rosenthal as she was before she married my father."

Hugo's throat turned hot and dry at the mention of his own mother's maiden name – the name she'd used for her business. He took a nervous gulp, leaned in toward the phone, and said, "I'd really love to hear what you have to say, Lud. Just relax and take your time."

Chapter Twenty-Eight
1951

Alicia had now been married almost a year, and marriage second time around genuinely did dull the pain of losing her first husband. Ludwig had been the love of her life, and nothing would change that, but she did love Eugene and he definitely cared for her.

After a modest wedding, she, Hugo Ludwig, and Eugene had moved to a larger house on the outskirts of San Antonio. Alicia had insisted on buying a new house as everything inside it would be unused and easier to keep clean, and Eugene had happily gone along with that.

So life was wonderful. The voices hadn't exactly gone away, but with Eugene's help she'd come to terms with them, and they didn't upset her the way they had done before.

And Hugo Ludwig was content with his new life too. Weekends, he and Eugene would go away to see a sports game or for a long hike, leaving Alicia to take care of the housework. As she'd hinted to her sisters, marriage to Eugene signaled the end of her relationship with Rosenthal Shoes, but she still kept in contact with them. She did that via Eugene, because she didn't like talking on the telephone to them; it was such an unhygienic thing.

Today was the first Wednesday of the school holidays. And while her husband and son had gone to a junior baseball game, she'd been left alone to give the house its usual Spring clean.

It wasn't Spring, but anytime was good enough to give the whole house a "darned good scrub top to bottom, side to side, end to end" as she put it. And also, she wasn't quite alone.

She was *never* alone. But by now she'd come to accept that.

When she heard the car pull up outside, she had to check the clock to believe the time. She must have been cleaning for five or six hours with no break and was exhausted. But it wasn't as if anybody else was going to do the housework.

When Eugene stepped inside, she tutted and told him to shut the door to keep the dirt out. Only then, as she looked up, did she notice that he was on his own. And he looked upset, his cheekbones noticeably ruddy.

"Where's Hugo Ludwig?" she said, glancing behind Eugene, but still not getting up from the wooden hallway floor, her hands not ceasing their circular motion.

"I, uh . . . I've left him with my ma and pa."

Alicia laughed. "That's one less pair of shoes to dirty the floor. Talking of which . . ." She nodded toward his feet.

He obliged, taking his shoes off.

Then taking his socks off.

Alicia scrubbed some more, grunting as she spoke. "I need to get on with this if you don't mind."

"Of course." Eugene approached her, then bent down and kissed her forehead. "You know I love you," he said, his voice weak, his smile faltering.

"And I love you too, Eugene. But I have work to get on with."

He padded upstairs while she continued scrubbing.

When he came back down, she'd just finished the hallway and was still on her knees, admiring the results of her work. It was as good as new. Then she noticed Eugene was carrying a suitcase, which he let down next to the front door.

"Put some shoes and socks on," he said.

"But I need to start on the kitchen floor; I haven't washed it today."

He stepped over to her, held her by the arm, and slowly brought her to her feet. "Shoes and socks, Alicia. Please?"

"Well, okay."

She did as he asked, while he put his shoes and socks back on too. Then she felt his arms around her, squeezing her. A kiss warmed her cheek. That was nice. Eugene was a good husband. He'd been more than understanding. He held onto her for almost a minute before letting her go and picking up her coat, holding it up for her to put on.

"It's not clean."

"It's clean enough."

She put it on while he picked up the suitcase and opened the front door.

She noticed that the suitcase was pink.

"Come on," he said.

"I can't go on a train," she said, her heart thumping, fully aware that her nerves were coming through in her voice.

"It's not a train. It's my car. And it's fine, Alicia. Everything's fine."

"Did you clean the seats?"

"Yes, I cleaned the seats."

"Where are we going?"

"We're going someplace real nice, someplace you'll be happy."

"Somewhere clean?"

"Very."

"Well, okay."

They walked to the car, Eugene with his arm around her shoulders, guiding her. As usual, he opened the car door for her because the handle might have had some dirt or germs on it, then he put the suitcase in the trunk and they set off.

"You do trust me, Alicia, don't you?"

"Of course I do. You're my husband, and I love you. You're everything I want."

"I love you too. I always will. So I'll always try my best to . . . to make you happy, and . . ."

Alicia looked across. Eugene's face was twitching, his eyes were blinking rapidly. He looked upset again, but Alicia had no idea why.

"Did I do something wrong, Eugene? You would tell me if I did something wrong, wouldn't you?"

"It's fine," he whispered. "You've done nothing wrong; you're going to be just fine."

§

Giselle entered the offices of Rosenthal Shoes and was disoriented for a moment. After a brief exchange with the woman on reception she headed for Klara's office.

She stopped at the door, uncertain. Klara was there, but she was with three men, all of them sifting through samples of leather and discussing their relative merits. When Klara saw Giselle, she asked the men to leave.

"This place is bigger," Giselle said. "You have new offices."

"We're expanding again," Klara said as she shut the door behind them and gestured for Giselle to sit down on what looked to be quite expensive chairs.

"I'm happy for you. You deserve it."

Klara shrugged. "Some luck. Lots of hard work. And plenty more hard work still to do. There are still many opportunities, you know."

"I haven't come here for my job back."

"That's a shame. We've missed you these past six months."

"You've done fine without me."

"Would anything make you come back?"

Giselle took a moment to think – or rather, to make it look as if she were thinking. "That's very kind of you, but no. I've come here because I have some news, something I wanted to tell you in person."

"Oh? Is it about your work at the homeless charity?"

"I don't work there either, not anymore."

Klara simply nodded. Her face betrayed no sign of being surprised. That was typical Klara, being understanding. Well, *trying* to be understanding. She didn't actually understand. Nobody did. Giselle had gotten bored of the staff at Rosenthal Shoes toward the end of last year, and had started to find them irritating. That probably explained why she'd been rude to one or two of them. A normal employer would have fired her, or at the very least reprimanded her, but not her sister.

So she'd walked out in the middle of a meeting, and even felt bad about that, so figured that charity work might salve her conscience, might help her put all those pet hates into perspective. It didn't. She got tired of working with those people too. She did, however, meet Thomas there.

"I'm moving away from San Antonio," she said to Klara.

Now Klara reacted, her face tinged with discomfort just for a moment, until her poker face returned. Again, typical Klara. "Where to?" she said.

"I'm going with Thomas to live in Houston."

Klara couldn't stay calm at that. She blushed, a grave expression casting itself over her face. "But why? Why leave? And . . . and what about Alicia? She needs our support."

"I feel bad about leaving Alicia. Just as I feel bad about leaving you, leaving this place, leaving the charity. I feel bad about everything. That's the problem I have. And that's why I'm going. I just . . . I just don't get along so well with people around here. I don't know why, but it's as if I need a change, or to go look for something else."

"Have you told Hugo Albert about the move?"

"Oh, he's raring to go. He loves his Uncle Thomas. In fact, he loves his Uncle Thomas more than he loves me. Which is understandable. I haven't been the best mother to him."

"Don't say that, Giselle."

"It's true. I want my son to be happy, to have a childhood full of good times. And Thomas does that, he makes him happy. Isn't your son's happiness the most important thing in your life?"

"Of course it is."

Giselle nodded. "Well, it's the same with me. I don't think Hugo Albert would be happy living alone with me. I'm not . . . good for him."

"You will keep in touch, won't you?"

"Oh, yes. Well, I need some time first, some space to myself, as they say. I need the freedom I don't have in San Antonio."

"But you'll write after that, yes? And you can write Alicia too."

"We'll see." Giselle stood. "You deserve better for a sister than me, Klara."

Klara stood and approached her. There was an awkward, mechanical embrace.

"I'm sure you've made up your mind," Klara said.

"I have."

"I'll miss Hugo Albert."

"Of course."

"And you too, obviously."

"Yes."

"So, is this it? Is this goodbye?"

"We leave in the morning."

"Oh, I see. And if somehow you can't stay in touch, could you ask Thomas to drop me a line now and then?"

"I'm sure he'll do that."

"Good luck in Houston. I hope it makes you happy."

"So do I."

Giselle left the office and heard Klara calling the men back in to restart their business meeting. She heard Klara use the words urgent, crucial, critical, and costs. Klara was going to be all right. The business was going to be fine. Klara wouldn't need her, and neither would Alicia; Giselle could do absolutely nothing to help Alicia.

As she walked away from the building, she resisted the temptation to turn and take a final look at the Rosenthal Shoes premises. Something told her she would never see it again. But that was fine.

§

It was almost ten o'clock in the evening when Klara's phone went off.

She'd put Hugo Felix to bed, eaten supper alone, washed up, and was sitting at the dining table going through some marketing campaign plans at the time, and the house was silent so the bell made her jump. Not wanting to disturb Hugo's sleep, she rushed over to it.

"Klara?" the tired voice said before she could speak.

"Eugene? What's happened?"

"I'm sorry to call so late, but it's your sister again. She's . . . well, today I took her in, just as I told you I would. I stayed with her as long as possible, but I had to get back to pick up Hugo Ludwig from my folks."

"Of course," Klara said. "I understand."

Klara took a seat. She and Eugene had discussed Alicia's condition many times over the phone. She'd hoped that it wouldn't come to this, and her heart ached at what had become of her sister. She'd had suspicions for well over a year, but had dismissed them as quirks caused by the stress of the various ordeals she'd gone through years ago.

"How long?" she said.

"Only a few months, I hope. We'll see."

"I hope so too."

"I tried my best, Klara. I thought I could make her better."

Klara could hear Eugene weeping over the phone. She neared that edge herself but pulled back, telling herself it wouldn't help, taking some deep breaths and looking over at the business documents she'd left on the table to focus her mind on the practicalities of life.

"Listen to me, Eugene. Nobody is going to hold this against you. Everybody knows how much you care for her."

"But . . . I thought I could help her."

"And you *can* help her, Eugene. You *can*. What you can do is look after her son, give him a stable upbringing. Keep him well and look after him until she . . . well, you know."

"But . . . should I tell him?"

Klara paused and thought for a few seconds. Or, at least, made it sound as if she was thinking. The fact was that she already knew the answer to his question. She'd already made her mind up that her own son would be protected from what was happening, and now knew Alicia's son should be too.

"I don't think so," she said finally. "He's twelve now, isn't he?"

"Almost thirteen. But he's a sensitive little guy. Perhaps even fragile."

"Well, that's your answer. I think you should tell him his mother has gone away for a while, and whenever he asks where she is, tell him it doesn't matter. If he asks when she'll be coming back, tell him you don't know. Trust me, in time he'll stop asking and get on with his life. And when she eventually returns it'll be a huge surprise for him."

"Could you help?"

"With Hugo Ludwig?"

"Yes. You're his aunt. Are you able to look after him?"

375

Klara went to speak, the words forming on her tongue. *She was too busy running her business, and didn't want the association to hamper her own son's upbringing.* Other words came to her rescue.

"I haven't even seen him for almost a year, Eugene. You've become much closer to him than I ever was. And you would take care of him, wouldn't you?"

"You kidding me? He's like my own son. I'm just thinking that he needs a mother, is all."

"You know, I think Alicia would agree with that. Perhaps it's something for you to think about. But for now, I think you should wait and see what happens."

"You'll stay in touch, won't you, Klara?"

"Of course I will. And I'll visit Alicia. Remember that I love her as much as you do."

"You don't need to say that, but thank you."

"Well, dry your eyes, try to be positive. You might even find that life will be easier from now on."

Klara, realizing that was a horrible thing to say, closed her eyes and gritted her teeth.

"But I'm still in love with her," Eugene said.

"I know you are. Alicia chose a good husband. But it's late. I have to go."

"Can I call you?"

Klara drew breath, keen to phrase her thoughts so as not to offend. "I'm always here, Eugene, but I'd prefer that you write unless it's urgent."

"Of course."

They said goodbye. Klara sighed and gave her head a disconsolate shake.

Then she returned to the dining table.

"Where was I?" she muttered to herself in German. "Yes. The winter boots marketing campaign."

But she was unable to read. She wiped the tears away. Nothing in her life had worked out as she'd planned. She had a successful business and was financially secure, but that wasn't everything. Not at all. She was the one who wanted the three sisters to remain close and live happy, fulfilling lives in memory of their parents. Nothing had worked out how she'd hoped when she'd spent those lonely days longing to be reunited with her sisters. What had happened to Alicia wasn't her fault, and possibly the same applied to Giselle because she clearly had some personal issues that nobody could help her with.

A shrill voice from the doorway broke her train of thought.

"Mama?"

She sniffed, wiped her eyes on her sleeve, and summoned up a warm smile. "What's wrong, Hugo?"

"I can't get to sleep."

Klara beckoned him over, knelt down and held him close enough so that he couldn't see the tears rolling down her cheeks.

This cheerful boy enveloped in her arms was now all she had. He was only five, and at that age had the opportunity to forget what was best forgotten – an opportunity that wouldn't be around for much longer.

She held him tightly and promised herself that from now on *he* – not Alicia, not Giselle – had to be her priority.

"I'll get you some warm milk," she whispered. "Would you like that?"

"Yes please, Mama."

"Go back to bed and I'll bring it to you."

As she watched him scamper away, her thoughts were with him. She wouldn't change her mind. She'd decided a long time ago that he would never find out the identity of his real father. That decision might have originally been taken for selfish reasons, but it turned out to be good for Hugo; anything else would have confused the poor boy.

But she wanted more for him. And she would hold firm on that. There would be no misery in his life; he would be a carefree boy, and would enjoy a life full of humor and love and hope, a million miles away from the horror, the misery, and the heartache of the life her family had endured.

So now she promised herself that she would shield him from *all* harm, do everything in her power to turn him into a healthy, contented, well-educated, and balanced individual. She would do that even if it meant hiding the more harmful aspects of her family history from him until he was old enough to understand.

And Klara didn't break promises.

Of course, she had also promised that one way or another her sisters would each get one third of Rosenthal Shoes to pass onto their sons.

But she had a lifetime to work out how she was going to achieve that.

Chapter Twenty-Nine
Houston, Texas, USA. June 2012

In the cozy living room of Albie and Judy Hinkler, Hugo tried his best to still his heartbeat. The voice coming out of Eleanor's cell phone was distorted, and with his failing hearing, every little helped. In the distance he could still see Judy. He and Eleanor were alone.

"I'm afraid I lied to you when I said I didn't know anyone named Klara," Lud said. "I'm sure you guessed that, and I hope you forgive me. Guess I was confused. I panicked and said the first thing that came into my head."

"We understand," Eleanor said. "Forget about it."

Hugo silently told her to be quiet, and Lud continued.

"And I remember you too, Hugo."

"Really?" Hugo said. He mouthed, "Told you so," to Eleanor.

"Oh, yeah. Little Hugo. We called you Hugo Felix back then. You must have been four or five the last time I saw you, but I definitely remember you. I was around eleven, I guess."

"So, what's the story with you and my mother?"

"The story? Oh, where do I begin?"

"How about when you were around eleven?"

There was more nervous breathing while Lud collected his thoughts.

"Well, I had a difficult childhood, and my mother – that's Alicia – she knew that. There had only been the two of us for many, many years, and we'd been through a lot together. My memories of her at that time were . . . strange, to say the least; the details aren't important. Anyhow, it must have been around that time, when I was eleven, perhaps twelve, that she got together with a guy, name of Eugene, encouraged me to call him Pa, which I did. They quickly got married. And he was a good guy.

"Life was stable for a while – perhaps a year, perhaps half that, I'm not sure, but there were no surprises or dramas. And then one day I got home and my mother wasn't there. Pa told me she'd had to leave in a hurry, and that she'd asked him to take care of me. That was hard for me because I hadn't known him too long. But he stood by me, looked after me. I didn't know at the time that I wouldn't see my mother for five long years. In that time, I screwed up everything in school, and he must have divorced her and got married again. He told me to call this new woman Ma, which I did. My real mother was brushed under the carpet – never mentioned. Was only when I turned eighteen that Ma and Pa sat me down and told me what had happened, that they had to look after me because my real mother wasn't very well, that she was in hospital. I asked when she might be coming out. Pa said she'd been undergoing treatment for years and wasn't likely to come out anytime soon. He also said he cared a lot for her and was looking after her."

Long, exhausted breaths came over the phone. Eleanor opened her mouth to speak but Hugo shook his head, and they just listened on.

"You see, my mother had severe mental problems and was unlikely to get better. She needed help, and, uh . . . well, the hospital was more of an institution. And to my eighteen-year-old self it all seemed to fit. I'd always known she was a little odd when I was a kid, but when I heard she was in an institution, well, the memories came back to me quite strongly – of her forever wiping tables or scrubbing floors or arranging something meticulously just so, or how she was particular about right and left turns, or when she talked in her sleep or scrubbed my skin too hard when bathing me. When I got told about her, those memories made some sort of sense. They say kids take whatever treatment they're given and think of that as normal, but even as a kid I knew something wasn't right with her. Ma and Pa said they'd tried to keep her out of my life with the best of intentions, but they knew it hadn't quite worked out and they regretted it. They asked me if I wanted to go see her. And soon afterward, Pa took me over there."

Neither Eleanor or Hugo moved a muscle, both staring at the cell phone as if they were about to make sense of it all.

"They warned me before the visit that she was deranged – and that was the word they used because they didn't talk of 'mental health problems' back in the day – but I told them she was my mother and I still wanted to see her. And that was true; I wanted so much to see her that it made me weep. But when I set eyes on her there was nothing in my heart, not at first, and that upset me even more. I hardly recognized her. Her hair was cut short – almost skinhead. Ma and Pa complained to the staff but were told she wanted it that way. Her skin was red with eczema, her frame bony and almost in a permanent crouching position. But when she spoke, I knew her. *I just knew her.* It hurt me inside, and that hurt hasn't gone away in half a century or more. It was the tone, the song of her voice, but mostly that foreign accent. She was definitely the mother I loved, but it wasn't the pleasant experience I'd been dreaming of.

"On the way back home, Pa told me she'd been born in Vienna and had come over just after the war, and that I had too, and that my real father had died during those years. I told him I knew all that, I just hadn't ever talked about it. He said that for my own good he hadn't brought the subject up. And I guess I'd been too concerned with being a teenager to worry too much about that sort of thing.

"I visited her a lot over the next few years. It wasn't hard to understand why she was in that place. It was a control thing. She said she heard voices – voices that she couldn't control and that scared her. They gave her pills to calm her nerves, but she needed ever larger doses, and all they ever did was zombie her out.

"Wind the clock forward a few years, I got a good job, married Lizzie – who you've met, and we got our own house. I kept up the visits, of course. She was my mother, after all. I felt terrible every time I left, so some weeks she stayed with us. She got a little better at first – I reckon just because of the company, and they lowered the doses of drugs. But the voices kept coming back and her behavior became erratic. When Lizzie and I had our first child it just wasn't safe – not that my mother would intentionally harm a baby, just that her demons could make her do dangerous stuff. So she had to go back to that place. I'm real sad to say she never came out.

"But I carried on visiting. On most days she was pretty normal – asking mundane stuff about how my job was and how the kids were doing. But she cried a lot too, said she could hear people calling out to her from what she called 'those horrible places.' By then Pa had told me what she meant by that: a hell-town called Riga and then the Auschwitz concentration camp. Only once did I ask her to tell me more about her experiences – I had some dumb idea that talking about it might help her. It didn't. Just the opposite, as it goes. She put her hands over her ears, went wild-eyed, and told everyone to shut up. Then there were the times she kept saying she had to go back there, and I asked her why, and she said she promised them all that one day she'd visit their graves. I did more research, and I had a good idea what had happened to her there, which I found real upsetting, so I never mentioned the subject again for both our sakes."

There were now gasps coming from the cell phone, as though Lud was trying to calm himself down, and during a long pause Hugo tentatively chipped in.

"Must have been real hard for you, Lud. How long did you keep up those visits?"

The reply was a while in coming.

"Oh, till the end. You got to when it's your mother, you just got to. But you're right; it was hard. Screwed me up just a little bit more every time I met her, I reckon. But I didn't care. It was about 1970 when they diagnosed her with liver problems – probably from all the drugs she'd been pumped with. Then something strange happened – something that'll always stay with me. She seemed to get better – mentally, leastways. She looked and sounded happier. She said she didn't need to block out the voices anymore, that she'd made her peace with them, that they were her friends. She started talking about her two sisters – Klara and Giselle – reminiscing about them all growing up together in Vienna, saying how they lived in America too. Then I remembered, because I'd met them and each of their sons when I was a kid, but I'd shut out those memories. It was only today, when you called, that I realized Pa must have kept in contact with your mother – my aunt Klara. He must have told her my address."

"Did you ever consider trying to find Klara and Giselle?" Eleanor asked.

"I have to say, Ma'am, that the idea often crossed my mind. There was a time when I promised my mother I'd track her sisters down and reunite them all. I was humoring her. It hurts me to say it, but I wouldn't have had the first clue how to go about finding them, or perhaps I was too lazy, and she was very ill by then, not in a fit state for anything traumatic. She wasn't even sixty when she died."

"Oh, Lud, I'm so sorry."

"That's okay, Ma'am. Was a heck of a long time ago now. I've long since had the best years of my life. Got eight beautiful grandchildren and still counting, besides which . . . well . . ."

"What is it?" Hugo said.

"I'll never forget those final few weeks with my mother. I took unpaid leave to be with her. That time with her meant everything to me. She was content. Hard to believe, I know, but she said she hadn't been so happy since she was a little girl growing up in Vienna, playing with her friends in the streets, running around the local park, going to parties and suchlike with her family. I got the feeling she'd found her own kind of peace with those voices. It made me much more content with my own lot in life, made me appreciate how lucky I was. And yes, I was even lucky I had her as a mother. I know that doesn't sound right considering what happened, but I'm absolutely certain she did what was best for me, which is everything you want in a mother."

"I'm pleased for you both," Hugo said. "And I have to thank you. I never knew in all these years my mother had two sisters."

"A brother too, so she told me."

"Really?"

"Yes, sir. Name of Hugo, apparently. He didn't survive the war, but the thing about all three sisters calling their boys Hugo – well, that was in his honor, see."

"You're kidding me."

"No, sir. They all made a promise as little girls that's what they'd do."

"Wow."

"Perhaps now you can understand how my nerves got the better of me when you visited."

"Of course we can," Eleanor said. "Thank you once again."

"Lud?" Hugo said. "I'd really like to talk more with you. Would you be interested in meeting up again someday?"

"Well . . ." There was a tired groan.

"We are cousins, after all."

"I guess we are, Hugo. But ... well, my mother and your mother ... it was a whole other generation. I guess I'm scared. Don't ask me what about, but I'm scared." There was another long pause. "I don't think so, Hugo. What's done is done. But I've got your wife's cell number if I change my mind. All I can ask is that you don't contact me."

"We won't," Eleanor said. "Not if you don't want us to. We can promise you that."

"Thank you. And I'm sorry for your loss. I hope what I've told you has helped in some way."

"It has," Hugo said. "It has a lot."

"Well, goodbye."

Hugo and Eleanor said goodbye and Lud hung up.

Eleanor stared at Hugo, but Hugo's gaze was a million miles away.

"You okay?" she said after a long pause.

He snapped himself out of his trance. "Think so. Kinda hard to tell."

"You got your answer."

"Yeah. Mother had two sisters and a brother. Just throws up more questions, though."

"I think we both know why she didn't want to tell you about Alicia – stuck in an institution like that. Back in the day there wasn't so much sympathy for that sort of thing, it was just a shameful secret that had to be swept under the carpet."

He nodded. "When you put it like that, yeah. But she could have told me later – ten or twenty years ago."

"You know, I think I get her reasons for doing that too. Why upset an applecart that had been rolling along just nicely for so long? What would be the point?"

Hugo thought about the few occasions he'd asked his mother about relatives – like when the kids at school had talked about their brothers, sisters, aunts, uncles, and cousins, and he'd come home and asked whether Grandma, Grandpa, Uncle Larry, and Aunt Deborah were all the relatives he had or whether there were more. The answer had always been pretty much the same: "Not really," or, "Not worth worrying about," or, "Not that we're close to," or the one that really settled the matter: "Aren't those four enough?"

And to give his mother her due, they *were* enough – particularly Uncle Larry, who was always generous with both his time and his money.

Hugo was kicked out of his comforting reverie by the appearance of a shadow just outside the doorway. A man with thinning grey hair matted with sweat appeared and said, "Are you Klara's folks?"

They stood up and Hugo offered his hand. The man had a firm, confident shake.

"I think Judy already told you my real name's Hugo, but everyone calls me Albie."

"And my name's Hugo too – Hugo Felix Goldberg. This is my wife, Eleanor."

"Hello, Ma'am." He nodded to Eleanor and turned back to Hugo. "Judy tells me you want to know about your mother and my mother?"

"Any information you have would be good."

"I'm pooped. Need a glass of cold milk. Can I interest you?"

"Could do with something stronger," Hugo muttered.

"Say again?"

"We'll have milk," Eleanor said. "Thank you very much."

A few minutes later all three of them were seated around three glasses of chilled milk. Hugo explained the finer details of his mother's will. Albie didn't appear excited, more like sad or regretful. Then he drew breath.

"I have to say I've thought about you and your mother quite a bit over the years."

"So you knew about us?"

"Oh, I remember you from way back – *way, way back*. There were three of us Hugo cousins, you were the youngest. I often wondered what had become of the other two and their mothers." He stared into space for a few moments. "You want me to start by telling you about *my* mother?"

They just nodded.

"Well, her name was Giselle, and she was a ... a strange woman by most accounts, I reckon you'd say. She went her own way, made her own decisions. After turning eleven, I spent most of my childhood with my step-father."

"Do you know what happened to your real father?" Hugo asked.

"That would have been my mother's first husband. She never talked about him, and I was too young to remember him. When she got married again, she told me her new husband was my father, which doesn't make sense now, but as a little kid I accepted it and so I got used to calling him Pa. Just as well I did, because the marriage didn't last and she insisted I stay with him while she moved out."

"Did that make you feel rejected?" Eleanor asked.

Albie shook his head. "Should have done. But my stepfather was a great man. I had a good time with him."

"Where did your mother go?" Hugo asked.

"Mmm ..." He rubbed his chin thoughtfully. "Well, I didn't find that out for a long time. I was too young to think about that sort of thing. At first, she visited me every few weeks. And I remember those visits well. She would hug me so tight my little bones nearly popped, and she kept asking me whether I was happy, whether I ever went hungry, whether I liked living with my new father. All of that felt peculiar at the time – the fact that she doted on me so much and showed genuine concern but then she would leave, and I wouldn't see her again for a couple of weeks. And then, after six months or so, the visits completely stopped."

Thoughts of soulless, gray institutions flashed up inside Hugo's mind, and by the knowing glance from Eleanor she was thinking along the same lines.

"And after those visits stopped, you didn't even see your mother, like, at weekends?"

Albie shook his head. "Apparently, she didn't want that, just wanted to be alone. Of course, for a while I missed her something terrible – I *do* remember that, but I had a good childhood. And she knew that. She would have taken me away if I was unhappy, I'm certain she would."

"Still," Eleanor said, "It must have been very hard for you to accept your own mother treating you like that."

Albie gave an upturned smile. "I know it sounds that way, but no, not really. I had good friends at school, my father remarried a woman who already had two children, and we all got along just fine. I guess I thought it was all normal, so I got on with my life and I was well cared for by a ma who wasn't my real mother and a pa who wasn't my real father. I did miss my real mother, I definitely missed her, but the bottom line is I was too busy enjoying life to let it get to me. I reckon Pa deliberately kept me busy with hobbies and interests so as I didn't have too much time to think, and I also reckon that must have worked because I had a great childhood as I remember. If Giselle wanted the best for me, then she made a good choice. That sounds a strange thing to say, but later I found out it wasn't strange at all. She as good as planned it that way, she wanted me to have that good life, thought it would be a better life than the one she could give me."

"But how do you know all that?" Hugo asked.

"I'm guessing Albie hasn't finished," Eleanor interjected. "Is that right?"

Albie held a finger up. "You see, I grew up accepting that my birth mother didn't want to see me, and it didn't bother me at first – perhaps I hid the hurt, I'm not sure. I went off the rails a little as a teenager – although nothing too serious: just drinking too much, a few fights – but as time rolled by, I recovered and, well, I guess I just grew up. And I grew up pretty good, though I say it myself. I met Judy and we started a family, got this place. The people I'd gotten used to calling Ma and Pa got old, then Ma sadly died in the early nineties. And that really hurt, even though she wasn't my birth mother. Anyhow, soon after that – in '96 I reckon – when my father was ill with prostate cancer in his eighties, he told me about the deliveries."

"The *what?*" Hugo said. "Deliveries?"

"Yes. Exactly. We were skeptical at first – me and Judy. And when the physician told us the cancer could be making him a little confused, we just dismissed it. But my father kept saying we had to carry on paying for the deliveries. He gave us details of a local firm who gave us the list of items – all basic foodstuffs – and confirmed the address. We asked him what it was all about, and he broke down, told us it was my real mother, Giselle. She was living in the wilds and still relied on him to support her. I think he still loved her despite marrying again. I asked him why she was living like that, and he didn't know exactly, said he had an idea she felt bad about something she'd done during the war, but she wouldn't talk about it – not even to him. We told him not to worry, that we'd sort it all out, and we did.

"The deliveries continued, and I assured him they always would. In my mind I put the whole thing to one side because he was near the end and we had to give him as much of our time as we could. It was only a couple of weeks after his funeral that Judy and I plucked up the courage to drive out to this place, to the back of beyond. It was something I just had to do, whether my real mother wanted me to or not, and I had absolutely no idea whether she might welcome me or get upset about it.

"Anyways, it took a while to find – had to be twenty miles or so from the nearest town and it was little more than a log cabin. We knocked on the door and this old woman answered. She had a lean frame and straggles of grey hair almost covering her face. She obviously hadn't washed in a while. I was shocked, but I could see my own face in hers, if you get my meaning. And she knew who I was too, burst into tears on seeing me. Inside the place, it was very basic but clean and tidy, with a few books and ornaments, and what must have been hundreds of photos of me on the walls. I'm not kidding – hundreds, as a boy and as a man, and also some with Judy and our kids. She also had lots of letters detailing my progress in school and beyond. It was all very surreal and hard to take in at first."

"I can imagine," Eleanor said. "Sounds so strange."

"Sounds positively spooky, but it didn't feel like it at the time, not after a few minutes, leastways. It was my mother, after all, and this was proof she cared a lot about me. She grew fruit and vegetables out back, had a well nearby, and with the provisions my father had been sending her she seemed to be surviving just nicely. The only difficulty she had was talking, she could only manage a few words at a time. I guess living alone for so long had taken its toll. But she had a battery radio, so wasn't completely cut off from what was happening in the world.

"She told me that after the war she tried so hard to fit into society but simply couldn't cope with life – couldn't deal with meeting other people and living in a town and working and going into stores. So she made the decision to get away and live on her own, but she didn't want to bring me up in that sort of environment so she did the best thing for my future: she found a man who would care for me like a father should. She said it was the hardest decision she'd ever made in her life. And years later, I found out she'd made quite a few hard decisions in her time. Anyhow, she said she knew Pa was a good, kind man, and that her biggest worry had been how I would cope with my new mother. She was so pleased when I told her how well life had worked out for me, said it was a huge weight off of her mind.

"Over the next year we visited her quite a few times. She said she had a couple of sisters who had come to America at the same time she had, but that she didn't want to see them and they definitely wouldn't want to see her. We asked why, but she shook her head and told us not to ask again. Eventually we managed to persuade her to move back here and stay with us. And she was happy here, started talking to people, even visited our synagogue once or twice. She stayed with us for two years, and it was lovely to have her around. While she was here, she started talking more about her past, and I plucked up the courage to ask her about her sisters, and to my surprise she told me all about them, even said she might contact them. But soon after that, early '99, she died in her sleep. Doctor said her heart gave in."

"My God," Hugo said quietly. "That was my Aunt Giselle?"

"It was. That was my mother."

"And what did she tell you about my mother?"

"Klara? Apparently, she was the youngest child, the brains of the family, and was the first to come over from Austria. She started up a business here and later on persuaded my mother and Alicia to come here too. My mother said Klara had big plans, thought they'd be the three sisters again and it'd be all like some big 'happy families' ending to their story, but it didn't work out like that, that they became kind of uh . . . *estranged*, as you might say. In time, my mother also said something about perhaps after all these years they might have forgiven her. She didn't say what for, and she never got the time to find out whether they had."

"And she never told you where they lived?"

"We could never get that out of her. All she said was that Klara ran a shoe outfit someplace in Texas. I thought she meant some little store; it was only much later, when I heard some news article about Rosenthal Shoes, and knowing my mother's maiden name, that I put two and two together. I had no idea your mother was so successful and it was such a well-known brand. I'm sorry now that I didn't try harder to contact your mother. I reckon part of me was afraid of what I might find, because I didn't know what they'd fallen out over."

"Guess we'll never know that," Hugo said.

"Perhaps that's not such a bad thing," Eleanor added.

Albie nodded. "True, true. But there is one mystery you've solved for me."

"What's that?"

"Something my father said just before he died – again we put it down to his confused mental state. He asked us if we were thinking of moving house anytime soon. We asked why he wanted to know that. He said if we ever moved, we should be sure to leave our address with the new owners of this place for mail forwarding. Was most insistent about it. Didn't make sense at the time. Does now."

Hugo thought for a second, then laughed. "Because he wanted to make sure my mother would always be able to find you."

"Exactly."

"My mother must have made him promise to keep her informed. She could be pretty determined about that sort of thing. Jeez. It was like she planned all along for the three of us to meet up. Sly old thing."

As they all sat thinking about what they'd learned, Judy came in from the back yard, poured herself some milk, and sat down. Albie filled her in, and the four of them drunk, chatted about Houston and Dallas, and told each other a little about what they'd done with their lives, until Hugo suggested he and Eleanor leave them in peace and get back home.

"Albie?" Eleanor said as they all stood. "Are you interested in staying in touch with us?"

"Hell, yeah!" A hoarse guffaw filled the room. "I found a long-lost cousin. I got another blood relative. Do you know what that means to me?"

"I think I do," Hugo said, starting to grin. "And you know that our other cousin – the third Hugo – is still alive too."

"You're kidding?"

"Still lives within spitting distance of San Antonio."

"Jeez!" Albie exhaled loudly and hung his head low. "It's a lot to take in."

"I know what you mean. And I think we all need some breathing space."

"But you'll leave me your address and contact number?"

Hugo nodded. "Email address, too."

Fifteen minutes later, Hugo and Eleanor were on Interstate 45 North headed back to Dallas.

"Do you really think you'll all keep in touch?" Eleanor said. "I mean, good intentions are nothing more than that."

"I'll certainly do my best. And I hope Lud gets back to us again. It's clearly what Mother would have wanted. After all she went through, I think she deserves that much."

"I've been thinking about that."

"About what?"

"About why she didn't simply tell you about your cousins before she died."

Hugo thought about that for a moment. "Stubbornness?" he ventured. "She had that in spades, which I don't need to tell you."

"Could be. Or . . . it could be that . . ."

"That what?"

"Well, it's obvious from her will that your mother wanted the three of you to find one another, but if she'd told you while she was still here, and it turned out your cousins didn't want anything to do with you or your mother, well, what would that have done to her?"

"She couldn't have coped with that. And I guess, bearing in mind what we now know, she probably didn't have much faith in happy endings."

"But I do, Hugo. *I do.* And I reckon we'll hear from Lud again."

Epilogue
Texas, USA, September 2014

"Cheers, gentlemen," Hugo said.

He almost had to shout to be heard above the music. Claude's Jazz Bar wasn't the best place for conversation, but Albie had assured him the music was the finest on the East side of Houston.

Beer glasses clinked.

And that clink took Hugo back to their first meeting in a Dallas bar two years ago. It had happened three months after his and Eleanor's journey across Texas to find the two mysterious Hugos who turned out to be his cousins. That was the very first time all three Hugos had met up. Of course, that wasn't strictly true; it was the first time they'd all met up *as adults.*

They'd met up on that first occasion for Hugo's birthday, with no thoughts that it might be anything other than a one-off event. At first, they were all nervous, and so conversation was limited to the niceties of their journeys and ordering drinks.

But Albie was the least nervous.

"I think it's great for us all to finally meet up," he said after the drinks had been brought to the table. "We got a lot in common."

Lud grunted.

"You don't think so?" Hugo asked as he brought the glass of beer to his lips.

"I'm sorry. That sounds ungrateful. I want you to both know I'm happy to meet you, but I'm not sure what we have in common."

"What about our shared history?" Hugo asked. "Call it *heritage* if you prefer."

"Well, perhaps."

"Yeah," Albie said. "What about all the crap our mothers went through in Vienna? How about that for starters?" He glanced at both of them. "I take it both of you know about that?"

Hugo was about to answer, but he wasn't completely sure what to say, so let Lud speak first.

"I, uh . . . my mother, she told me a lot – most of it pretty horrific. I never quite knew whether to believe it or not. You know, what with her mental state and all that."

Albie was nodding. "I'm guessing she told you the truth, Lud. My mother was strange, but there was nothing wrong with her memory. She told me tales that made my hairs stand on end even when I was a grown man and had been through quite a bit myself. How about you, Hugo? Did your mother ever tell you about Vienna?"

"Not really. I don't think she wanted to scare me. But I read up on it."

"You mean, history books?" Albie gave his head a disdainful shake. "We ain't talking about the politics what's in history books. We're talking about what happened to our mothers day-to-day in Vienna."

"My mother never told me much about that, not much at all."

"Probably trying to protect you."

"Makes sense."

"Means you got a lot of catching up to do on your past."

And that first meeting was all about exactly that – Hugo learning more details of what had happened to his mother, his aunts, and all the Rosenthals in Vienna. And after that first meeting, those disturbing events were pretty much left to one side, never to be forgotten, but also never to be allowed to dominate the here and now. That first talk had done the trick; it had created a bond between them, and they agreed that it wouldn't be their last meetup.

That explained why today, two years on, they were in Claude's Jazz bar, Albie doing the lion's share of the talking, Lud chipping in with occasional dark-humored wisecracks, and Hugo mostly holding his own.

And now, while the musicians took a short break, Hugo felt it was time for him to step up to the plate. After a gulp of beer, he cleared his throat to attract the attention of Lud and Albie.

"Guys," he said, "I have a special announcement to make. It's something Eleanor asked me to forewarn you about in good time."

Asked wasn't quite the right word. *Instructed* would have been more accurate. And *reminded of about half a dozen times* was fully correct. Back home the previous day, he'd been looking at himself in the mirror, checking the cut of the new jacket he'd bought especially for his trip to Houston, when she'd told him.

"Do I look okay?" he'd said, standing tall while Eleanor pressed his shirt.

"You look just fine," she replied. "Not that it matters. I don't think they'll care about what you're wearing. They never do."

"You're probably right. Guess I just want to look good for Mother's sake."

"And for your Aunt Alicia and Aunt Giselle."

"Yeah. Them too. But it's kinda like I'm representing Mother." He frowned and cut his eyes to slits. "Say, you got to know Mother pretty well over the past forty years. All this would have made her real happy, wouldn't it?"

Eleanor thought for a moment. "You keep in touch on the phone every week or so. You meet up three times a year – on each other's birthdays, and I know you'll carry on doing that. What's for her not to like?"

"It's funny, the longer she's gone, the more I think about all that stuff that went on in Austria, and the more I think . . ."

"Go on, what?"

"Oh, nothing."

"Go on, tell me what's going on in that cluttered old mind of yours."

"Uh, well . . . I, uh . . . I just miss her, that's all. I miss her and I can't forget her."

"That's the general idea. You shouldn't." She pulled the lapel of his jacket. "Come on, take this off. Don't get it dirty before you've even worn it."

He slipped out of the jacket.

"And something else you shouldn't do is forget to tell them about next year."

"I won't."

"Good. Don't."

Except that Hugo had been lying to her when he'd talked about missing his mother. Oh, he did miss her, of course *he missed her* – much like he would miss his thumbs if he woke up one morning and they were gone. But that wasn't what had really been going on in his "cluttered old mind." He hadn't been able to tell her what he'd really been thinking – perhaps because he couldn't quite work out the way to phrase it, or perhaps because his thoughts weren't quite appropriate.

But now, in Claude's Jazz Bar, after a glass of beer, his inhibitions had slackened, and he felt able to vent his true feelings.

"Before I tell you the announcement," he said, "I wanted to share something else with you."

"Get on with it," Albie said.

"Well, it's about my dear mother – about all the Rosenthals, in fact."

"What about them?" Lud asked.

"I think you guys will understand this, but it's funny, the longer my mother's gone, and the more I think about all that stuff that went on in Austria and Germany, the more I feel so proud that, well, how can I put this . . ."

He sighed, struggling.

"Let me guess," Lud said. "You're thinking about how those bastards didn't win — that they tried their damnedest to eradicate us, but they failed?"

"That they didn't split us up?" Albie suggested. "That we're all still here, still celebrating our lives, still proud of our families?"

"Of our *family*," Lud said. "The Rosenthals."

Hugo laughed inside; a little of it leaked out. "Yeah. Say, you guys can read my mind."

"Hey, we're cousins." Albie lifted his glass up. "To the Rosenthals," he said.

Another clink. Three more gulps.

"We should be particularly proud of our Uncle Hugo," Lud said.

"To Uncle Hugo," Hugo said, raising his glass again. "He must have been one hell of a guy for us all to be named after him."

Another clink. Three more gulps.

And a moment's thought for Hugo. These two guys were actually more than cousins; by now they were firm buddies. Hugo knew this was going to be a long night. Then again, they had the three days together — tonight was the warm-up, tomorrow was a jazz festival, the next day would involve a quiet meal out before he headed home.

Until the next birthday.

Because that was now the law. Kind of. They were all retired. They had time to spare. And thanks to Hugo's mother, they all had a little money. Three birthdays, three long get-togethers. Lud usually chose a Gulf Coast fishing trip out of Mustang Island, Albie would drag them all to a jazz festival, and as for Hugo, well, he would show them the sights of Dallas, including museums and the Cowboys if there was a game on and if he could get tickets, finishing with a meal out. However . . .

"Anyhow," Hugo said. "My announcement."

"Is it about next year?" Lud asked.

"Hey, how did you know?"

Lud shrugged and patted Albie's shoulder. "Like you said, we're cousins, we can read your mind."

"Exactly," Albie said. "And we know next year you'll be seventy."

"So tell me, smartass, what's happening for my seventieth?"

"Museums?" Albie said with a crooked smirk.

"Football game?" Lud suggested, snickering.

"You're funny guys. But no, you're both wrong. To celebrate me reaching my allotted three score and ten years—"

"If you make it that far," Albie interjected.

"Okay, okay. If I survive tonight and tomorrow and live to see that birthday, you two gentlemen and your good wives are all cordially invited to a three-day extravaganza in Vegas."

"Really?" Albie said. "You're not kidding?"

"I wouldn't kid you guys."

"I'll drink to that," Lud said, raising his glass.

Glasses clinked. Beer was gulped.

"Say, Lud," Albie said. "You thought about our next fishing trip?"

Lud nodded. "I was thinking river this time, just for a change."

Hugo had started to enjoy fishing again – it reminded him of the trips his Uncle Larry used to take him on as a kid. So he just sat back, bathed in the background music, and let his two cousins gab away. Whatever these two guys wanted to do was fine by him.

And somehow, he was sure it would be fine by his mother too.

It had taken a long, long time, but now she finally had that happy ending she'd always wanted.

ABOUT THE AUTHOR

Ray Kingfisher was born and bred in the Black Country in the UK, and now lives in Hampshire. He writes fiction in a variety of genres under different pen names, most notably Ray Backley. For more information please visit www.raykingfisher.com or feel free to email Ray at raykingfisher@gmail.com.

By the Same Author

If you enjoyed this story please leave a review on Amazon and Goodreads, and feel free to check out Ray Kingfisher's other titles:

§

Under Darkening Skies

§

Beyond the Shadow of Night

§

Rosa's Gold

§

The Sugar Men

§

Matchbox Memories

§

Tales of Loss and Guilt

§

Writing as Rachel Quinn:
An Ocean Between Us

§

Writing as Ray Backley:
Never Be Safe
Bad and Badder
Slow Burning Lies

§

Writing as Ray Fripp:
I, Smith (with Harry Dewulf)
E.T the Extra Tortilla
Easy Money

Printed in Great Britain
by Amazon

81158310R00233